On the Dotted Line

Kim Carmichael

ALSO BY KIM CARMICHAEL

Novels:
The Indelibly Marked Series:
Permanent
Temporary

The Hollywood Stardust Series
Typecast
Limelight
Idolized
Supporting Roles: A Hollywood Stardust Short

Draw the Line

Trifecta

Novellas:
Closure
Predictions

Shorts:
Interchangeable
The Promise
Made for Two (Three Times Lucky Box Set)

Children's Book:
My Daddy Wears His Art

Published by Rebel Romance,
An imprint of Irksome Rebel Press
Los Angeles, California

Kim Carmichael

On the Dotted Line

A NOVEL

Copyright © 2014 Kim Carmichael

http://www.irksomerebelpress.com/

Book Design by Tamara Eaton

Cover Model Scott Nova

Cover Design Julia Clare

ISBN-13:978-0692360316

Dedication

To everyone who was ever told they couldn't
and then went ahead and did it anyway.

Acknowledgements

My husband – You always tell me I can.

My two sons – You always support me.

B,C,B – My fluff balls who make me smile.

Tamara Eaton – My rock, my editor, my friend – you are my support system through it all.

Julia Clare – My amazing PA and incredible designer.

Teresa Neely Martin – The comma whisperer, proofreader extraordinaire and my friend – you have an amazing eye.

Scott Nova – For giving Randolph a face.

Solera Winters – For every late night you read.

JR – If it wasn't for you I couldn't do any of this.

Michelle, Eva & Alexis – My real life rocks.

Tom Brookhouzen – Because you always protect me. I'm glad you're on my side.

Scott Evans – Thank you for understanding my vision.

On the Dotted Line

Chapter One

"DON'T GET MARRIED FOR LOVE." Randolph Van Ayers III pressed two fingers to his left temple. The throbbing in his head reverberated throughout his body. Though he wanted to go home and lie down, if he came home with anything his mother considered an ailment, he would end up quarantined in one wing of the house no matter how many times he told the woman headaches weren't contagious. The Mitchell Art Gallery presented him with a definite upgrade to being a medical pariah.

"Maybe you should look inside yourself for love." The owner of the gallery, Slate Mitchell, stopped in front of a photograph of the back of a man's head staring out into space. "However, I am still reeling that I didn't get an invitation to your wedding, love or not."

"Don't spew your rhetoric at me." It took all his effort to shake his head at the oversized, overdone image. The print wouldn't be worth anything in his lifetime. "I didn't even want to attend, not that it matters since I didn't get married today for love or otherwise. However, I do thank you for the party in my honor."

"Nothing like an impromptu birthday party to blunt being left on the courthouse steps with no bride." Slate patted him on the back.

"I appreciate how you've kept this low key as I asked." His life had been reduced to a frat party in an art gallery. Earlier a keg was delivered.

"It's only small if the police don't get called. I have some better ones over here." Slate guided him through the wide-open space designed to be a showcase of the latest local artists. Anyone in the city with seven figures behind their name wanted to be the next person to discover the artist of the second, and the gallery was in the perfect spot in LA to make waves without the cost per square foot of more trendy or upscale areas.

They stopped in front of another wall of photographs. "These would go with the sculpture of the birds you bought last month. Different artist, but similar feel. I can get you a discount for your special day."

He assessed the black and white photograph of a little bit of nature left in the Greater Los Angeles area. Mountains, clouds and birds in perfect juxtaposition of smog and the city. "A discount. Happy birthday to me."

"Well, it's the least I can do for the man whose bank made it possible for me to become the new go-to gallery for poor little rich boys such as yourself." Slate motioned toward the next photograph.

"Remember until you pay off your mortgage, my bank owns you." Randolph took a breath in an attempt to focus on the potential of the picture. "Maybe you should default on the loan, after midnight tonight it will no longer be my bank and I will no longer be rich." While he considered Slate one of his better friends, he knew once the money ran out the friendship would follow.

"Come on, that story you tell is just a pick up line. You can stop now." Slate stopped and motioned toward the next piece of art, namely his girlfriend, Jade. "And here is a masterpiece."

"The story is totally true. Randolph told me the story when we were dating, it's incredible, and true." Dressed in a nude body suit with a hat made up of flowers Jade uncoiled her body, stretching her arms out and taking her time standing up. She came over, kissed them both on the cheek and hooked her arm in Slate's. "I'm blooming."

"Baby, it's a story designed to make girls have the expression on their face you have right now. You didn't really date him, you only went as his plus one to that finance event when he was desperate." Slate chuckled and kissed the top of her head. "You make a beautiful flower."

Randolph met the little piece of living art a few years ago at a financial conference when she donned her other persona as a property manager. Her parents owned some select buildings throughout Los Angeles and she took care of them when they retired. He invited her to accompany him to an event, but rather than a kiss goodnight he ended up with a friendship instead.

However, the slight blush and smile on her face spoke volumes. Women loved his pathetic all too true story.

If only it were a story.

"Unless he got married by his thirty-third birthday and stayed married for a year, he would lose his inheritance." Jade pressed her hands to her chest. "He signed a contract and everything."

Both he and Slate groaned.

Jade let go of her boyfriend and flung her arms around him. "I'm so sorry. I would help you if I could."

"Can I borrow you for twelve months?" A plus one was better than nothing. He needed to face the fact he was never going to have a relationship for anything other than money. Hell, he probably got left at the courthouse for a man with a larger trust fund.

"No, you may not. She is not on loan." Slate pulled her away. "Plus, he doesn't want to get married for love.'"

"Well, he may not want to get married for love, but getting married for money isn't working for him either." Jade returned to Slate and wrinkled her nose.

"It doesn't matter. It's over unless a bride drops into my lap in the next five minutes." Since he created the situation, he would live with the repercussions. In the end, his father's entire scheme had been built around his failure. At least for once he would prove the man right.

"Can we study the art?" Slate walked backward, corralling them to the next piece.

"I need to finish getting ready for the party and Willow's here. She said she wanted to talk to me so I invited her." She waved her arm. "Come here and say happy birthday to Randolph."

An ethereal cloud of yellow and white swirls materialized out of the corner of his eye.

He tightened his jaw and finally did Slate the favor of staring at the next work. Maybe Willow Day would vanish if he didn't look directly at her. Everyone knew ignoring the problem made it go away.

"It's Randolph's birthday?" she asked.

Her voice brushed over him, as soft and supple as her name. If only the rest of her matched. A new tenant in one of Jade's buildings down the street from the gallery, he crossed paths with her a few times in the last couple of months, but the encounters were always the same. No, pretending a problem didn't exist never made it go away. He squeezed his hand into a fist.

"We're having a party for him." Jade dragged her over.

With the woman standing directly in his line of sight, he needed to look. The way she gazed at him always made him think she was intrigued or interested. Again, her appearance didn't match her attitude. Long, straight blonde hair literally floated around her as if she managed to get someone with a fan to follow her around. Unlike most women in Los Angeles, she wore little makeup, only enough to enhance her light blue eyes, petite features and glowing skin. He suspected she had a nice little body under all the flowing layers of clothes. She didn't stuff herself into her wardrobe leaving little to the imagination. Someone would have to really search and discover. No, nothing on her was man made or artificial, everything natural. A rare find.

"Well, Happy Birthday." She graced him with a smile.

The same smile sucked him in the first time he met her. Though it lit up her face, he sensed something beneath her upturned lips, something he wanted to get to know until he actually spoke more than two sentences to her. "Thank you."

"Scorpio." She tilted her head. "I should have guessed."

Case in point. He swallowed. "I hardly think a bizarre alignment of planets and stars millions of light years away from me on the day of my birth have anything to do with my personality. Wouldn't that mean anyone born on my birthday should be exactly like me?"

"Let's hope not." While her voice came out soft and sweet, her words were hard and cutting. She gave Jade one of her multi-layered smiles. "Sorry I'm late."

"It's fine. I'll meet you back in Slate's office." Jade pointed.

Without any more well wishes, Willow walked through the gallery.

Jade glared at him. "I'll be back for your party." She spun on the ball of her bare foot and left.

"What's your poison?" Slate motioned toward the photo.

"I want something different, something with some bite." Everything presented to him seemed trite, done before. He longed for something unexpected.

"I think you have enough bite for everyone." Slate shook his head. "Especially Willow."

He exhaled. "She called me a Scorpio."

"How dare she call you your own astrological sign?" Slate tucked his notepad back into his pocket. "She's such a meanie."

"It was the way she said it." He stopped in front of the next photo. The artist quite literally took a picture of nothing. A big black square hung on the wall, creating a hole in the middle of the show. With a bit of metallic paint it might have potential, as long as the artist had the vision.

"Aw, did Randy get his feelings hurt?" Slate raised his voice as if he were talking to a baby. "She's having a hard time."

"What's wrong with her?" He stared into the nothing. Maybe the artist was trying to depict potential rather than emptiness.

"Everyone goes through ups and downs, some downs are just lower than others."

Damn it. He glanced at his friend. The few times he met her, their encounters were always the same. She would materialize, he would try to speak, something strange would come out of her mouth, leaving him no choice but to comment and she would walk away. "She's back in your office, meeting with Jade." In his distraction with his own situation, he neglected to pick up on the significance of the Jade meeting, especially if Jade was interrupting one of her art performances.

"Yeah, Jade, her landlord. Go grovel, it will do you some good."

Money woes, one of the world's great equalizers. "I'll take this one. It speaks to me." He strode through the gallery, stopping short outside Slate's office at the sound of her voice.

"I don't have any money left, and you can't keep extending my rent payment," Willow whispered. "It's not right, everything is off balance."

He put his back to the wall to listen.

"Don't worry about the rent, it's fine." Jade's tone was one of compassion and authority. "Right now we are working on the barter system. Just keep me in products and tea and we are fine."

"I can't do that. I just need to sell a little more at the shop." Her voice was broken but not destroyed. "I did a little research."

At the rustling of papers he inched toward the doorjamb trying to spy what she would produce.

"What's this?" Jade raised one of the documents.

"There are companies who will give loans to people in need."

She let out a nervous chuckle. "Funny the people who need the loans the most are the ones who can't get them."

"Willow, these are loans designed so that no one ever pays them off." Jade shook her head.

A shudder ran though him at the thought of the interest rates alone. Those loans were no joke and lured in desperate people who needed money fast and under the most dire circumstances.

At his realization, he glanced at the time and resumed his eavesdropping.

"Hey, I didn't mean for you to spy. What are you some kind of creep?" Slate came from the other direction and pushed him into the office. "Look at what I found lurking about."

He stumbled into the room and his head spun. Once he regained his footing, he gave Jade a half-hearted wave and glanced at Willow. If possible, her light complexion was even paler, almost translucent. He recognized her pallor. It was the same look he saw whenever someone honestly needed funds. Somehow he needed to tell her he had her stay of execution, and it would only require one year of her life.

Jade narrowed her eyes at them.

"I wanted to grab something to show our peeping Randolph." Slate went to his desk and picked up his tablet computer.

Both Jade and Willow focused on Randolph.

"I don't believe Willow should take out one of those high interest loans." With all the attention on him, he did the only reasonable thing and brought sanity to an insane situation. The vice around his head seemed to tighten and he rubbed the back of his neck. "She needs to create as much inventory as possible for her shop because that is the only sure way she will have money coming in."

"I need the loan to buy the materials to make my inventory." Willow lifted her chin.

"Not if Jade is letting you take a break on the rent." He returned his hand to his temple swearing he felt the pulse of pain through his fingertips.

She hugged her papers to her chest. "My supplies are very expensive."

"Willow's morning tea actually works. I feel great." Slate looked up to the ceiling. "What's it called?"

"Activi-tea." Jade went to Slate and hooked her arm in his.

"We also loved the one you call Boo-tea."

The vision was a bit too nauseating and he returned to the matter at hand. "There are many grades of materials, just change some of it up to save money. It's done all the time. I think the issue lies in not knowing your true profitability and not having a focus on your product offering."

"Some say when you are out of quality you are out of business." Willow's eyes widened.

"There are others that say the same about money," he countered.

Silence encompassed the room.

"Slate," Jade whispered.

"Hey, I really did want to show you something, and wanted to talk to you about the artistic co-op. Look at this." Slate basically shoved the tablet in his face. "Remember that artist who creates those murals in the middle of the night in little hidden spots? They call him the Mural Man."

He nodded and restrained any reaction to the article and the picture. Instead, he kept his focus on Willow.

"Whoever it is struck again last night and painted over some graffiti." Slate stood next to him and enlarged the picture. "Wonder what this art would be worth. It's different. I definitely need to get someone like him involved in the project."

"I may have another way to help you." Without acknowledging Slate, he lifted his chin toward her. "A different kind of proposal."

"Honestly, Mr. Van Ayers, I'm not interested in anything you have to offer." She reached into her bag, pulled out a little jar and held it out to him. "I do believe you need this though. Rub it on your temples for your headache, and later you can tell me if I skimped on my ingredients."

He took the jar. How did she know he had a headache? "Maybe we should talk in private."

"Or not at all." She spun back around to face the desk.

"Come on Birthday Boy, let's go get your party started." Slate corralled him out of the office.

"I'll be right there." He watched Slate stroll down the hall and resumed his position with his back pressed against the wall, once more glancing at Willow and at his watch. They needed each other and he had only a little more time before his life had insufficient funds.

* * * *

"Let me run some numbers and some options." Jade straightened the pile of papers on her desk. "Why don't I see if I can find you a less expensive apartment in one of my other buildings? If not, I can ask around."

Since Willow's move to Los Angeles and opening up a small shop for holistic healing, Jade and her boyfriend, Slate, had been nothing but kind to her. Somehow the universe took care of her by allowing her to meet Jade at a metaphysical faire during one of her friend's performances. Afterward, they got to talking, and she helped her get into the building only a few doors down from Slate's gallery.

Jade and Slate understood her vision and always referred customers, but it wasn't enough. Though everyone loved her teas and wellness elixirs, she couldn't sell enough to catch up. Whenever she started to make any money, she needed to buy more materials and could never quite get things to even out. As a last resort, she even took something from the one person who had given her the most without telling her. "Jade." She chewed her lip trying to figure out exactly how to say what she wanted.

Jade continued to read the papers. "Yes?"

"Nan and I moved into the upstairs of the store a few weeks ago." She dug her nails into her palm, but she promised Nan, the woman who raised her, she would tell Jade the truth. With the words out, the weight on her chest lightened a bit.

Jade looked up from the documents.

"I'm sorry, I should have said something." Her mouth dried out. "If we can just stay a little longer."

"Is Nan okay going up and down the stairs?" Jade winced.

Leave it to Jade to be concerned with Nan and not call attention to the fact they didn't have a real home. "Yeah, it takes her a minute, but she needs the exercise."

"Please be careful, and if there's anything you need--"

"I'll figure it out." Not wanting to take one more thing from her friend, Willow cut her off. "The universe will make its decision, and if we can't get caught up we will leave."

"I'm fine, seriously." Jade gave her a smile and held her arms up. "I am a work in progress and I'm blooming. Just work on it okay?"

"I have something for you." She smiled at Jade's costume wishing she had the ability to bloom as well. While she may have received a reprieve, she didn't get the pardon. Her friend and landlord gave her an incredible deal on the rent. She looked inside her oversized bag in search of her meager offering. Not that she wanted or expected one. "Hold on." One day she would remember to carry a flashlight, but she would put it in her purse and it would end up at the bottom. She turned her bag over onto her lap. Her wallet, crochet project, various stones she picked up along the way, pictures and more paperwork tumbled out.

"Wow," Jade gasped. "Amazing what that bag holds."

She rifled through the assortment and held a piece of jade she made into a necklace out to her. "It seemed fitting."

"You don't have to."

She gave her the gift. "Jade is green, the color of healing and hope. It is also for luck, though I already think you are pretty lucky." Karma, the universe, or the gods blessed Jade with a great career and parents and a wonderful boyfriend. The woman fit her name. Maybe one day her own energy would change. Nan kept telling her to be patient, she was paying her dues. The only problem was she already had too much debt and needed a windfall. All her troubles came from the material world or the fact she had no material.

"I think I should change into something more befitting Randolph's birthday." Jade took off her hat of flowers, stood and put the necklace on as she headed for the door. "Thank you."

"Thank you." She scooped everything back into her purse and joined Jade.

"Absolutely." Jade nodded. "You're going to stay for the party, right?"

With nowhere else to go, and reluctant to face Nan yet, she shrugged.

"At least go have a drink or something, and give Randolph something to look at." Her friend winked.

She tensed. "Maybe I'll sneak away and let him have his day."

Jade headed toward the door. "I think he likes to tease you so he can get your attention."

Her cheeks heated.

"Someone's blushing." Jade raised her eyebrows. "I'll see you out there."

She stood in the small hallway by herself. Music and laughter echoed through the building and all around her. Not in the mood for a party, she decided maybe the best course of action would be to take a walk and clear her head before returning back to her makeshift home.

Wanting to make a clean getaway, she tiptoed toward the exit. The noise indicated the party was in full force with food, drinks and a ton of people.

In a self-indulgent moment she stopped and glanced around, instantly spotting Randolph. The man stood out in his tailored suit giving him an air of power, but his blond curls and mischievous green eyes gave him a playful air and were equally as fun to look at, the same way she would stare at teen idols when she was younger.

All she knew about him was his family owned a bank, actually banks and he was exceptionally, incredibly irritating. Irritating in the same way a clothing tag would scratch at someone's skin but it couldn't be ripped out. The few times she talked to him only ended with him being condescending, and her saying something to try to match it. The man was in no way good for the psyche. Yes, he was irritating and he also was coming her way.

She turned away, wondering how bad it would appear to go running. With fleeing from the scene not an option, she straightened up.

"May I get you a drink?" He flashed her a smile of perfect pearly whites fit for any pre-pubescent girl's wall.

Okay, if he was going to be nice, she would return the gesture. Maybe it would even out all the bad energy. "Thank you. I think I'm just going to go, but I do wish you a happy birthday."

"I wanted to talk to you. I think I can help you." The smile didn't waiver one bit.

"I'll be fine. I would rather not have any more business advice." She took a step backward.

"It wasn't business advice, but rather a dose of reality." Still the smile, but he glanced at his watch.

"Reality?" Why couldn't he leave them be at a happy birthday and a disobedient curl falling on his forehead?

"Yes. I know you live in an alternate universe, but I wanted to bring you back down to earth." He put his arm out as if to guide her to do what he wanted.

Her heart seized and she broke out into a sweat. She longed to slap him across the face, but held back. "One day I hope you regret the fact you never visited an alternative universe, but I'm sure by then it will be too late for you. Enjoy earth." She swallowed back the burning bile in her throat and rushed out of the gallery into the alley.

Nan always said all she needed was fresh air and a night sky to be happy, her way of explaining how material things didn't matter. However, when rain started or the temperatures soared or sank, it was pretty nice to have a roof over her head. After everything the woman had done for her, she needed to figure out some solution before they ended up on the street.

"You left before cake." Randolph's voice seemed to fill the alleyway.

She wrapped her arms around her shoulders and stared up at the stars wondering if up there somewhere a female on another planet gazed in her direction with some jerk banker bugging her from behind as she tried to figure out how to fix her life and her credit score. Did they even have FICO in other galaxies? "I think I've watched you blow enough hot air for the duration. I can picture it just like I was there."

"I didn't know you were clairvoyant as well." He chuckled.

Shivers overtook her with each inch he came closer. "I'm not, but I still see you leaving me alone."

"I deserved that, and I do want to apologize for my comments earlier." He stood beside her and glanced at his watch. "Also, as I said before I wanted to talk to you."

"Is this a timed conversation? Can it be less than ten seconds?" His aura clashed with hers making it impossible for her to concentrate and causing ugly words to leave her mouth.

"I may need a little more than ten seconds." Once more he looked at his watch.

"But not much more." She turned to him.

"Now that hurt." He lowered his arm, then, as if he couldn't control himself, he lifted his wrist to his face again.

"What could you possibly need to talk to me about when you have something so pressing going on with your watch?" The acid of negativity Nan spoke of built up in her blood, singeing her skin.

"I'm sure my paltry little problems aren't enough for you to miss an appointment or party over."

"First, your problems are huge. Let's make no mistake about that." He shoved his hands in his pockets and leaned back on his heels. "Second, you're not the only person in this alley with huge problems."

She studied him. All her life she had been reminded not to judge on outward appearances and material possessions, but the man's shoes cost a small fortune, his cufflinks a large one. What did this man even know of problems? Also, who wore cufflinks anymore?

"May I tell you?" He glanced at her.

"Fine." She swallowed, preventing herself from letting loose another insult.

"What if I told you I was supposed to get married today?"

Only because his voice lowered as if it wanted to fall on the gravel and be run over did she manage to forgo the comment about a ten-second honeymoon. "I would say check your watch again, you only have a few hours left."

He paced in a circle ending up back in front of her. "She cancelled on me at two o'clock, right before I was supposed to meet her at the courthouse."

Though nothing appeared funny, she sucked in her cheeks and waited for the punch line. She refused to succumb and ask what happened only to have him make a snide comment about numerology or something. "Well, look at the bright side, you got to buy some art instead. Something much quieter with lower maintenance." She slighted a woman she didn't even know as if his situation were personal. It wasn't like she was planning on marrying the man. Somehow he brought her to new lows.

"All my life I had these goals I had to meet. My father actually has a checklist and every time I meet one of the milestones his personal assistant notarizes the list." He seemed to be speaking more to himself than her.

"What kind of goals?" She balled her hand in a fist not wanting to become engaged in his tale.

"Valedictorian in high school, charity work." He counted the items off on his fingers. "Summa cum laude graduate in college. I had a 4.0 average."

"Ask a banker a question and he gives you his numbers." She

bit her own tongue to stop the laughter.

"I had one more item on my list, something my father added and then I was done." He straightened up. "One more and my trust fund, the business, everything would be mine. My life would be mine."

"One more thing?" She crossed her arms. His gaze intense, those green eyes darkened turning almost black as if they wanted to absorb everything and give nothing in return.

"I had to get married by my thirty-third birthday. Stay married for at least a year, and on my thirty-fourth birthday I would be free." He turned to the ground.

For a moment they didn't speak, only the music from inside the art gallery interrupted their silence.

"Now who is living in the alternate universe?"

"I wish it were me." He repeated his action of walking around in a circle.

"You're not kidding about this list are you?" She stepped toward him.

He shook his head. "I'm completely serious."

"So what happens if you don't make it?" Fairytale or not, she wanted to know the end. At least the story was an amazing distraction from her issues.

He rubbed his hand over his face. "I don't lose. I can't lose. I won't lose."

"Do you have a bride in your pocket and a Justice of the Peace around the corner?"

"I have a charter plane at my beck and call." He lifted his head. "And I have you."

Everyone had their certain moments in life they would always remember. Some of these moments were shared with the world such as man landing on the moon. Other moments like special birthdays or life changing events one was supposed to keep forever. Then there were the moments, little flashes that stuck with someone for the rest of their lives but would be meaningless to anyone else.

Randolph mentioning her, marriage, and a charter plane together qualified as one of those moments in her life.

She forced herself to take a breath, move, react in any sort of way to his idiocy. "I think the fever is getting to you. Maybe you need to go home."

"Actually, I feel surprisingly better. I think what you gave me worked." He tilted his head, his curls tumbling off to one side with the motion.

"So says the naysayer." No one was ever surprised when a prescription worked, but everyone was amazed when what nature doled out did the job. Actually, she was amazed he gave her remedy a shot.

"Maybe you're on to something." He pointed at her. "At last my head isn't pounding. You did that."

"Then I need to go home. I think I'm going to be sick." She needed to go anywhere deemed a Randolph-free zone. She walked down the alley toward her store, the gravel digging into the bottom of her sandals.

"Lest you forget you don't have a home." He called after her.

"Don't let him get to you," she mumbled and forced herself forward. He must have continued to eavesdrop on her and Jade.

"How much longer are you going to be able to put off not paying your landlord?"

His words hit her, and nearly knocked her over.

"You know you may have something I need, but the street goes both ways." He followed her down the alley.

Not wanting to hear whatever argument he spewed, she continued her trek.

"What is it you want Willow? What if I told you I could make it happen?"

"I just want to be happy." Her steps slowed.

"You know, if you married me I would get the rent current within three seconds of saying yes and you would never fall behind again." The man continued. "I could also make sure you never had to buy anything but the best ingredients for your store. If your headache remedy is any indication, they work."

Her mind yelled for her to keep walking. At the end of the alley she would be at her shop, go up the flight of stairs, make a cup of tea and get rid of his bad vibes.

"I can make you happy. I have the money and the connections. You would be set, all for only three hundred and sixty-five days of your life."

Some force beyond her control made her turn to him.

"You know, I'm thinking that living in mansion may be a better alternative to your cramped quarters above your store." He inched toward her. "Think about it, all your expenses paid, time to concentrate on anything you like, luxury living, and at the end..."

Once again she found herself face to face with him.

"This time next year, your own business is perfectly set up and you'll have seven figures to do with what you please."

Seven figures? Images of stacks of money, stacks and stacks of money like a cartoon appeared in her mind. She barely ever had three figures to her name let alone seven. Still, she opened her mouth, inhaling to get the power to tell him exactly what she thought of his offer, how she couldn't be bought and sold.

"Don't give me the line about money not buying happiness." He leaned forward. "It may not buy happiness, but it buys security, wellbeing and potential."

Maybe the man should have been an attorney instead. She almost believed him. Almost. "I am sure if you have all that money you could find a different girl much better suited for your needs." She pointed toward the street. "Hollywood and Vine may have what you're looking for."

He held his hands out as if tossing the ball into her court.

Curiosity alone made her ask the next question. At least she told herself it was curiosity and not consideration. "What would this marriage entail?"

"Funny you should ask. I happen to have a prenuptial agreement I can tweak rather easily." He reached into his suit jacket pocket and pulled out a folded paper. "For the duration of the year we would need to live at my family's mansion. We would have our own wing."

"Of course, and I'm assuming a chef, maid and butler as well." The minute she returned home she needed one heck of a cleansing to make everything she heard go away.

"Five maids, maybe six, one butler, several various assistants, a chef, and a chauffeur." He flicked the paper. "We need to be in the same bed every night. We must be together by midnight."

"What happens if we're not? Will you turn into a monster?" She tapped her foot. "Actually, I think you're already a monster, so maybe we'll all turn into pumpkins."

"I never want us to appear anything other than happily married." He went on without a hitch. "We spend the holidays up with my grandparents in Vermont."

"You have grandparents?"

"We all have our shortcomings." He shrugged. "I am not to compensate you for your year of service."

"But..." She swore before this conversation finished she would slap him or herself for thinking about the monetary gain and she forced the visions of those perfect piles of money out of her consciousness.

"However, there's a loophole even my father didn't consider." He raised one finger. "I am allowed to be involved in your line of work, and every decent husband gives his wife a monthly allowance. How else can you do all the things that make you a good wife?"

"I don't think anyone could make you a good wife, least of all me." She curtseyed. A long forgotten tingle in the back of her nose indicated tears might be on the way. "I bid you goodnight Mr. Van Ayers, and thank you for my bedtime story."

"You know, until I saw you tonight I gave up. I never give up."

A nuance in his voice, a small shake, a fault in the perfect timbre made her pause. Nan always told her to look for the subtle signs. The truth and the beauty would be found in what most people overlooked. She lifted her head. Any semblance of amusement or a smile vanished from his face. "Why me? Just because I don't wear a suit doesn't make me your fool."

"I don't think you're a fool." He held his hand out as if to stop her. "I thought above anyone else on the planet you would be open-minded to helping us both out."

A breeze whispered through the alley. Chills ran through her and she hugged herself since no one would be around to do it for her. "You're serious."

He remained silent.

"The story, the list, the marriage, the money, you're not joking." She stomped her foot. "Swear to me you're not joking."

He put his hand over his heart. "I would take an oath if I could. You can notarize my words."

She closed her eyes needing to block out everything and think. The answers to her problems couldn't be as easy as a year penance with some snarky, albeit gorgeous, banker.

"Starting the second after you sign the marriage license you will never have to worry again about any of your so-called material things again. You will be set for life." Randolph's words vibrated through her. "So will your Nan."

At the mention of her only family, she opened her eyes. A life where Nan could relax, do her work, teach her and never have to scrimp for the little she needed. An opportunity to give back a small bit what Nan gave to her. Their future would be assured, and they could buy a house, a real house. "I'm not sleeping with you." What was she saying?

He cleared his throat. "You must sleep with me, but you don't have to *sleep* with me. I will have you know there will be a fidelity clause in the contract."

She decided not to mention there was no need for such a thing. Her life was a fidelity clause.

"If you agree, I will draw up your official contract on the plane. We will spend the night in Las Vegas and tomorrow you will need to move." He returned the paper back to the secret pocket in his jacket.

"Nan needs to come with me." Was she saying yes? Her heart stopped, skidded to a halt. "She gets full use of the kitchen."

He narrowed his eyes and stared off as if thinking.

"Nan comes or you are out your business, your trust fund and your sleeping only partner." Though she knew she should walk away and forget this whole deal, she stood her ground, unsure if she wanted the deal or only wanted to win. Randolph the third brought out Willow the terrible.

"You're a tough negotiator." He put his hand out for a shake. "If Miss Nan moves in and creates havoc in Chef's kitchen, do we leave now to get married?"

She stared at his offering, a large hand with long fingers and perfectly manicured nails. Karma and prayer wouldn't provide for her or Nan, they were days away from not being able to afford food. They needed a miracle, and as Nan would say, sometimes miracles happened in the most unexpected places. One year for the rest of her life.

She glanced up at the stars, took a breath and put her hand in his.

Chapter Two

"I ADDED THE NANETTE RIVERA conditions to the contract, do you have the papers?" Randolph held his hand to Peter Ward, his personal assistant.

Out of the corner of her eye she watched the men while she continued to crochet the squares for her latest quilt, thankful she always kept something in her bag to work on.

"Take it down a notch, Randy." Peter leaned over and pulled the pages off the printer.

Yes, a printer in the limousine. For some reason, out of everything that small detail caught her attention. Of course, in the last two hours she had been whisked away to a charter airport in the valley and flown to Las Vegas in a private plane that was more like an airborne decadent living room, but the printer stood out. Her world seemed off center and strange.

"This looks all in order." Randolph swiped the sheets away from him. "Get your notary book out."

"Did you forget the word please?" Peter reached into his briefcase, pulling out a book, a stamp pad and a few other accessories setting them up on the desk with the printer...in the limousine.

Other than watching the ostentatious display of lights of the most over-the-top city in the world, the most entertaining part of this journey had to be the banter between the two men. Randolph may be the boss, but Peter threw his attitude right back to him.

"Please." Randolph pulled a pen out of his suit jacket pocket, signed and slid the papers across to her. "Here you are future Mrs. Van Ayers."

She set her crochet down and put her palm over the

document. "This is very formal." Something about putting what should be a sacred agreement between two hearts all in writing seemed against the natural order of things.

"A well written contract is formal and a necessity." He held the pen out to her. "Documents and signatures are what make the world go around, and they are usually considered sacred. Let's get this initialed and signed. It's after ten already, we have to get the license and get married in less than two hours."

"I should read this." Not that she ever read any other contract. Her heart didn't as much pound as it fired off in rapid succession. She lifted the paper and squinted trying to make out the tiny print.

"It's everything we already reviewed." He shoved the pen in her hand.

Not liking his attitude, and needing to take a few cleansing breaths before moving forward, she put the document down. "I get sick when I read and drive."

"You are knitting and driving."

"Crochet. I am crocheting and driving." She resumed her craft.

He strummed his fingers on the desk. "Willow, all you need to do is sign."

"Dolph, calm it down." Peter shook his head.

"What? She has all year to read the paper." Once more he held the pen out to her. "For the rest of the year she only has to do three things. Sign the contract, sign the marriage license and say 'I do.'"

For the last two hours she had been tossed around with Randolph, allowing him to take control, but she wouldn't be talked about like she wasn't here. "Randolph, I am not sure how you spoke to the woman who cancelled on you today, but I am quite sure your condescending tone may be part of her leaving you right before the altar." She sat back, sinking into the leather seat.

"For your information, I added more to the monthly allowance, in fact much more than I was offering the first woman. Call it a short notice bonus." Though his tone was restrained, she picked up on his negative vibes.

"I will sign the paper when I feel it is the right time. You just said signatures were sacred." She crossed her arms and decided to forgo any comment about the other woman. What he did and whom he wanted to marry before wasn't her concern. Their arrangement was business, nothing more.

The limo turned, jostling them as they made their way into a driveway.

"We're finally here." Peter tossed his items back into his bag. "Willow can read it in the office and get all her signing done at once."

Randolph glanced down at his watch. "We are cutting this close, we have no time for formal document reading, but I suppose I must compromise."

The limo stopped and without waiting for the chauffeur or Peter or Randolph, she opened the door and exited.

"Willow!" Randolph scrambled out of the vehicle after her. "Where are you going?"

She stopped short and he collided with her.

Before she fell, he wrapped his arm around her waist and righted them both. "I can't have you hurting yourself." He kept hold of her.

She pushed him back. "At least not until the year is up."

"Willow, we are just on a time constraint." His tone sounded as if he were talking to a child.

"I didn't cause it." She walked toward the building.

"We could have sped things up in the alley." He rushed ahead and opened the door for her.

"Maybe you shouldn't make such proposals in an alley." She walked inside.

Peter came over and guided her into an elevator.

Randolph slipped in with them. "What? Are you upset because I didn't propose properly?"

"Seriously." She snapped.

"Here, let me remedy the situation." In the middle of the elevator he got down on one knee.

She tightened her jaw refusing to be part of this mockery of something most people took as more significant than an ATM transaction.

He pressed his hands together as if he were praying. "I am begging you with my mind, body and soul to be my bride, will you marry me?"

The elevator doors opened. Several people waiting to get on clapped.

"We get out here," Peter mumbled.

"I think I preferred you in the alley." She stepped around him and headed straight ahead causing their audience to part for her arrival.

Unwilling to be guided anywhere or to be told what to do one more time, she stomped over to the line indicating marriage licenses, surprised at the many people already ahead of her. She took in the couples. Some brides were already in their wedding dresses, others in jeans and a t-shirt. One duo definitely needed to make a stop at the maternity ward after their ceremony. She was quite sure none were there for her reason.

"Peter, I don't want to wait in line." Randolph joined her and handed Peter a wad of what appeared to be one hundred dollar bills. "Willow, please take this very fast moment for some light reading material." He handed her the contract.

She took the document, crumpling it in her hands as she watched Peter quite literally pay their way to the front of the line. The waste made her turn away. She only hoped a few of these people needed the money and would put it to good use.

The man literally had no respect for anyone but himself and his needs. What she really wanted was to tear the contract up, throw the pieces in Mr. Van Ayers the Third's face and hitch a ride back to Hollywood. She took a breath and read the pages, pressing her hand to her chest at the sum he put in her monthly allowance. Most people she knew didn't make that much in a year, maybe two, or three. "Randolph."

"Is anything incorrect?" He put his hand on the small of her back and leaned in, the scent of his cologne swirled around her, decadence and expense mixed with something earthy. Maybe something grounded him.

"This is too high." She pointed to the figure.

"No, it's exactly right." He flicked the page. "I added some for Nan as well."

She stopped and studied him. Nan? In the middle of their whirlwind he added some for Nan? The earthy part of his cologne definitely took over.

"She will need things I'm sure." He furrowed his brow.

"I can't sign this." She handed the contract back to him.

"Randolph!" Peter called to them from one of the clerk's stations. "We're ready."

Instead of waiting for his answer, she joined Peter. He already had his notary seal and book out ready to go.

"I was told you need a marriage license?" The woman behind the counter smiled at her.

"Yes." She returned the gesture.

"You need to sign the contract." Randolph leaned over.

"I'm not signing that." She gave the lady her identification and filled out her portion of the form, including adding her signature. "It's too much."

"You'll sign the license, but not the contract that protects you?" Randolph completed his section as well. "I will determine what is too much."

"Here you go. Everything is in order." The woman handed them the papers and winked at her. "I included a list of chapels. One is right around the corner. Get him now while he wants to give you too much. It won't last."

"Willow." Peter motioned her over to a clear spot on the long counter. "This will be fast."

She joined Peter. "I'm not signing the contract."

Randolph came over, took her shoulders and turned her. "Willow, I have the money and I want you to have it. I am asking you to sign it now. Yes, I'm in a rush, and yes we could do it after the fact, but I want you to sign before we get married. That's the right thing to do. I will not reduce the amount. " He slapped the papers on the counter and whipped out his pen. "Right here on the dotted line."

He remembered Nan.

She swiped the pen away and without reading anything, but noting the line was indeed dotted, she signed the contract and the notary book. Her utter disregard for something someone held sacred chilled her body.

Peter quickly took her thumbprint and shuffled everything away.

Randolph wiped the ink off her thumb as they left. "Also, let me tell you never to show your winning hand in any business deal. If someone pays you too much never say a word and collect your winnings."

At his words, her throat constricted, but she managed to get the next statement out anyway. "What if someone pays you too much on purpose?"

"Everyone has their own motivation Willow, remember that." He held the door of the elevator for her.

Yes, everyone had their own motivation, and somehow she let him outsmart her on day one. She needed to keep her eyes open for the rest of the year.

* * * *

"Would you like to pick the package?" In an attempt not to be a lunatic, Randolph held out the brochure from the small chapel around the corner from the courthouse.

Decorated with copious amounts of draped white silk, plastic flowers and fake doves, their location perfectly fit his image of what a quickie wedding chapel in Vegas should look like.

Willow shook her head. "I'm good with the 'I do' special."

Without lifting his wrist he glanced at his watch. Thirty minutes.

Time didn't matter in her world, but in his universe, no matter how he wanted to change it or fight it, time was everything. Payments, interest, literally every deal he ever made narrowed down to seconds.

"Let's just do this, I'm exhausted." She sighed.

The woman behind the counter watched them, her jaw jutted out and she narrowed her eyes, taking them in.

They should have entered breathless, not from arguing, but rushing because they couldn't wait to be together.

"I know we have a half hour, but may I have three minutes to collect myself?" Willow asked the question to the woman not him.

"You can take ten." The woman patted her hand. "We have a bride's dressing room. It's nice and private." With a glare in his direction, she guided Willow away.

He held his hand up. Willow could have all the time in the world in thirty minutes.

Peter hit his shoulder. "She signed the contract, she signed the license, we made it here and by 11:59 you will have a wife. You need to chill."

"She knows the importance of this." He squeezed the bridge of his nose.

"It's not her fault you decided to prove a point and wait until the last day."

"Don't judge me. You knew what you signed up for when you came asking me for a job." He wouldn't call Peter a friend as much as he would call him a confidante in almost everything. Almost.

"You offered it." Peter stared him right in the eye.

At least the two of them tolerated each other. He could make a single-spaced list pages long of assistants who didn't work out for him. Another man of privilege, but without the contacts or the drive, Peter understood him. Their mothers worked for some of the same charities and their demons played nicely in the same sandbox together. "That I did, and I don't regret it for a second."

Peter gave him a slight nod and that was all they needed to move on.

"Can you get something simple, not embarrassing for her, but maybe smack of something other than what this is?" He took a breath and picked up the brochure. "Let me talk to her for a second."

"You have two seconds." Peter plucked the brochure away.

The moment the lady returned, he walked to the back without asking permission and found his bride-to-be sitting on a crushed red velvet bench. He sat next to her. "I promise that once this is over the accommodations will be five-star." The operative word being getting the ceremony over, every minute seemed to inch by when he wanted to sprint.

"What was she like?" She stared into the mirror across from them.

He studied her refection, noticing her absolutely perfect and petite features. When silent, she was the personification of sweet and serene. "What?"

"The woman you originally lined up for the job." She crossed her leg, the slit in her skirt now showing off a bit of skin.

For the first time tonight he paused before answering, taking time to consider his words. "No one really. Someone I knew for a while."

"You never fell in love?"

For the woman who didn't speak for most of the flight here, when they needed to hurry the most he suddenly had a chatterbox and was at her mercy. Rather than fight, he answered. "No. I tried, but no. Maybe I've been too fixated on the end so I never allowed it." He shook his head wondering where those words came from and wrung his hands together.

"Everything in this place is artificial." She shook her head and stood. "I'll be there in a minute."

Though he wanted to protest at her delay, drag her back in front of whatever official would perform the lightning ceremony, he bowed his head and slunk back out to the front.

"I got everything taken care of." Peter gave him a thumbs-up.

"If we're ready we can meet her in the chapel." The woman plastered a plastic flower smile on her face.

"Yes." Not caring if he rushed her, he pointed forward.

"You didn't need to pay for another witness." Peter elbowed him as they entered the chapel. "You got me."

They both stopped at the end of the aisle.

"This is the Chapel 'de Amour." The woman wiped her hand around the small space chock full of a lot of...a lot, and all artificial.

The theme from the front room carried on to the chapel, but in grander proportions with bright pinks and reds. Hearts and cupids ruled every available space.

"You'll never forget this. I made sure to order pictures." Peter laughed.

"Thank you, and until now I thought it would only live on in my nightmares."

The official entered from the back and motioned them forward.

They joined him.

"I'm Reverend Calloway." The older man in a white robe gave them both a smile and lifted a paper. "Your associate indicated you wanted a basic ceremony."

"Fine." He searched each entrance to the gilded wonderland waiting for his wayward Willow.

"He also ordered the commemorative license holder, the champagne glasses and bottle of champagne."

"Where is she?" He looked at his watch and then Peter's. "We have fifteen minutes."

"Anxious are we?" The minister chuckled. "Mimi is probably just giving her a little sparkle. They may be a bit."

They were nearing single digit minutes. His throat dried out, but he found the strength to inhale. Apparently these people didn't understand the urgency. Even Peter raised his hand.

Before he let loose, bizarre recorded organ music filled the room and he turned toward the entrance of the chapel.

The doors opened and Willow entered.

Well, Willow and a ton of artificial glitter entered. Reverend Calloway wasn't kidding, the front woman donned his short-term fiancé with a veil and tiara and a bouquet of flowers, but everything from her head to her toes seemed dusted with glitter.

"I got the veil option." Peter winked.

"And the bejeweled option." At last calmness claimed him, the same kind as when sleep finally found him, or the aspirin started to work on a headache. He smoothed down his jacket.

Even in the saccharine setting, the ethereal quality Willow possessed shined through brighter than the sparkles. If they had time for a white dress and clean up, she would have been a magnificent bride, one he couldn't help but paint on the beach at sunset or in a forest with flowers in her hair. Watercolors would suit her best. Maybe one day when her dreams became a reality, and her Nan was settled, she could smile about their brief time together.

He held out his hand when she joined him. Playing her part to a T, she handed her bouquet to Peter and laid her hand in his.

"Dearly Beloved..."

No sooner did the man get the second word out than Willow raised her hand. "Stop."

"Keep going." He grabbed her hand back. His heart threatened to burst out of his chest and he broke out into a sweat.

"No." She resisted.

"We're getting married." He widened his eyes. How dare she leave him with less than ten minutes to spare? Where would he find another girl, the only option now was that woman at the front.

"I won't say these vows." She lifted her chin.

"Would you rather recite your own vows?" Reverend Calloway

asked.

"Yes." They both said in unison. Right now he would hire a screenwriter. One thing about Willow, at least she was genuine and wouldn't say words she didn't mean. An admirable quality for anyone, but especially a wife.

"Very well." The man glanced down at the paper. "Willow, why don't you tell Randolph how you feel?"

He restrained himself from telling her to get on with it, and they faced each other.

Her hand trembled only slightly, and she inhaled twice. "Randolph, when I woke up this morning I never anticipated the turn my life would take tonight. After today a piece of us will always be intertwined. I hope you get everything you want out of our union." She stared up into his eyes. "I promise to do my best."

"Randolph, do you have anything to say to Willow?" The minister nodded at him.

The urge to pull her closer overtook him, but he resisted and chose to lace his fingers in hers. Her words were elegant and telling to the kind of person who somehow saved him. Maybe the energy she spoke about was upon him tonight in the alley.

He stepped toward her and gazed into those eyes. The light blue was more of a tint rather than a pure color, completely unique, exactly like her. "Willow, you came into my life when I needed you most. I promise to make sure I deliver what you need to make your dreams come true. You are genuine, the real article and utterly stunning."

A blush stained her cheeks. She licked her lips and blinked several times, taking one step closer to him before turning back to the official.

"Wonderful." The minister gave them a broad smile. "Though we are keeping with our own special ceremony I still must ask if you, Willow Day and Randolph Emerson Van Ayers the Third take one another as their lawfully wedded spouse?"

He held his breath. The next four words had him sliding into home.

Willow faced him. "I do."

Without waiting for the go ahead, he answered. "I do."

The minister put the bible down. "Are we exchanging rings?"

"Oh." Willow's blush instantly vanished.

No matter what galaxy they lived in, every woman wanted the ring. Apparently someone didn't read the contract too close, the mention of the rings was in section three point nine. "I have the rings." He let go of her only to retrieve the box out of his suit jacket pocket.

The second he opened the red leather box with the two rings, she gasped and put her hand to her chest. "Randolph, I can't take that."

"This was my great grandmother's ring." He lifted the six-karat marquis yellow diamond out of the box. "For as long as we are married I would be honored if you wore it."

Her focus shifted between him and the ring. She nodded her understanding and with a bit of color returning to her face, held her hand out.

He slipped the ring on her finger. "Perfect fit." The way she basically told him she didn't expect the ring permanently renewed a bit of his faith in the world, as did the way she wouldn't sign their contract right away because she thought her allowance was too much. In his whole life no one ever complained of extravagance. Maybe they were destined to take this journey together.

"My turn." She plucked his great grandfather's platinum band out of the box, closing her hand around the jewelry. "It has good history."

"I hope so."

She put the ring on his finger, the visible proof he'd succeeded, and they stared at each other. In anticipation of the last sentence, he squeezed her hand.

"By the power vested in me by the state of Nevada, I now pronounce you man and wife." Reverend Calloway said the magic words.

Peter lifted his watch and nodded.

Five minutes to spare.

"You may now kiss your bride."

At the acknowledgement he won, he took the woman who made his life possible into his arms. "I will never forget what you did for me," he whispered the words across her lips and their mouths connected.

He planned on giving her a chaste, sweet kiss. A simple kiss of gratitude, one to seal the deal, something to create a basic bond.

Instead, she instantly reacted. Rich, plump lips molded to his, filling his mouth with such as sweetness that he had no choice but to part his lips to take a better taste.

A small moan escaped her throat and she wrapped her arms around his neck. With an unexpected need stirring inside him, he held her tight against him, her breasts pressing against his chest, and bent her back as their tongues dared a small touch. Call it relief, need or something completely different, every nerve ending fired off, shooting stars through his whole being.

"Talk about a whirlwind marriage." Peter's voice interrupted them.

Willow's gasp broke their kiss. He stood up, blinking to bring their gaudy surroundings into focus, but he only saw his new bride with her fingers pressed to her lips.

"Well, may I present to you for the first time ..." The minister took a breath and peeked down at his notes. "Mr. and Mrs. Randolph Emerson Van Ayers the Third."

Peter clapped.

"I wish you the best of luck." The minister nodded.

With a lifetime spent planning every move, reading every line, watching everything with laser-like precision, the kiss threw him off. He stared at Willow.

Chapter Three

"Mrs. Van Ayers, would you like another glass of champagne?" As they walked down the hallway top floor of the luxury hotel on the Las Vegas strip, Randolph held the bottle up. "We have to finish it, it's part of our wedding package."

"That's not the champagne that came with our wedding package." She held her glass out for more of the incredible treat. After the wedding Randolph took one glance at the bottle the chapel gave them, dubbed it unacceptable and by the time they returned to the limo, Peter procured something more to Randolph's liking. Though she would never admit it, the drink was amazing. Bubbles of expense tingled across her tongue. Though it caused a lot of bitterness, sometimes money tasted sweet.

They continued toward their room and Randolph filled their glasses once more, finishing off their second bottle. "Mrs. Van Ayers, I propose a toast to you. You saved me from myself." He tapped his glass against hers. "My long search is over."

A bad case of the giggles found her as an image of him in his suit and tie searching for buried treasure flashed in her mind. She stopped and bent over, the laughter paralyzing her.

"What is it?" Randolph put his hand on her back.

She caught her breath enough to get her words out, but the pressure built. "I have a feeling you've never searched for anything in your life." She straightened up and leaned her head back to capture the last few drops of the amazing liquid, tripping on her own sandal. The floor didn't want to cooperate with her feet. "Oops."

In one graceful move, Randolph caught her, lifting her as if she didn't weigh a thing. "You're wrong. I searched for you." His green eyes darkened.

Her world spun at the sudden movement, but her body tingled at the way he stared her down. "Well, you had to search for your current wife in an alley."

"I couldn't have found a better one on Rodeo Drive." He brushed one fingertip across her cheek. "Trust me."

The man changed once they made it official. His soft touches and sweet words coupled with the champagne riled her up. "Oh."

"I think we should go to our suite now." He carried her down the hall. "Unfortunately, we drank our dinner and I need to learn to take care of my wife better."

She licked her lips at the way he glanced at her with an alcohol induced twinkle in his eye, but willed the little flutter in her stomach away at how he kept calling her his wife. Though technically true, it wasn't spiritually true. "You just don't want me dropping dead before the year is out." She needed to say something to make him stop.

"Honestly I don't want you dropping dead at all." He tilted his head and one of his curls sprang down on his forehead. "Never. You will forever be a part of me."

With no response to those amazing words, she went with her gut and curled one arm around his neck, pulled him down and kissed him.

Suddenly a set of soft lips were upon hers. The same lips she discovered at her wedding. In need of another sampling, she opened her mouth to try out that tongue once more.

"Should we get you to your room?" A male voice interrupted them.

"Peter's still here." She tapped her husband. Her husband? "Oh my God."

"What's wrong?" Randolph looked around.

She motioned for him to bend down and cupped her hand over her mouth.

Randolph offered her his ear.

"You're my husband." She hoped he realized the enormity of it all, because she didn't know if she realized it.

"And you are my wife, Mrs. Van Ayers."

"Mrs. Van Ayers." She needed to hear herself say her name aloud. What had she done? Lost in her thought she used her nail to trace the outline of his ear. "You have a very nice ear."

"Where is this room already?" Randolph lifted his head.

"Right here." Peter stopped in front of a set of double doors and held up a card. "I have your keys right here."

"Don't you think keys were better when they were keys and not just some plain nothing?" She scowled at the white plastic credit card looking thing with the hotel logo on it. "Totally not sexy at all."

"What is sexy?" Randolph carried her the last few feet.

Her mind didn't want to focus, and she couldn't remember what she wanted to think about. Something about ears or maybe her name. "Real keys, real kisses." She narrowed her eyes, studying his ear some more. It had to be ears. "Someone sucking on your earlobe? I think it's a forgotten erogenous zone."

He stepped backward over the threshold and snapped the unsexy keys out of Peter's hand. "Say goodnight to Peter." He opened the door.

"Goodnight, Peter." She waved at him as Randolph took them inside. She held on to her husband. The world moved with them and she quickly made out a huge room with ultra-modern furniture overlooking the Las Vegas Strip. All the lights sparkled outside the darkened room.

"I think we should get you to the bed." He didn't take his eyes off her.

At last she remembered what she wanted to think about, her name. "You didn't say it." She stuck her lower lip out to let him know she didn't approve.

"What didn't I say?" He put her purse and shawl aside.

"For a man with very good manners and my husband, I can't believe you don't know." She reached up and flicked his earlobe with one finger. Her mouth watered. Wait, maybe her thoughts were of ears after all.

"Forgive me for my *faux pas*." He laid her down on the bed and joined her, putting his hands on either side of her and lowering his head to the crook of her neck. "What if I make it up to you, Mrs. Van Ayers?"

She squirmed at how his voice vibrated through her whole body. "I suppose you can."

He trailed his lips up her neck to her ear.

She held her breath.

He ran his tongue around her ear creating a slow circle of shivers. "Better?"

All he succeeded in doing is making her want more. "Not yet."

"Let me try harder." He blew into her ear.

Unable to get comfortable, she continued to writhe. "Getting there."

"How about this." He took her lobe between those lips and sucked.

"Oh, God." Her body turned into nothing but a bundle of sensation, and going with what her body told her to do, she slid her hands underneath his suit jacket.

"Hold on, I think I'm missing something, Mrs. Van Ayers." He leaned up, removed his jacket and tended to her other ear, repeating his series of licks, kisses and sucks on her opposite side.

"Now I'm balanced." She gave in and raked her hand through his curls admiring how they shined with the glitter they doused her with. Perhaps she only wanted to think about his hair.

"I will strive to keep you perfectly even." He glanced at her. "May I kiss the bride?"

"You already did that back in chapel and in the hall." Though she could go for some more anytime.

"Correction, you kissed me. I think it's my turn now." He lowered his lips to hers.

All her random thoughts dissipated at his kiss. Thoughtful yet passionate, he took his time to taste each of her lips before deepening the kiss and finding her tongue with his own.

He wrapped his arms around her, holding her tight.

Any last bit of control she possessed was lost the moment he moaned. The weight of his body was perfect to keep her from floating away, the bulge in his pants hitting her in exactly the right way to make her want to lose control. She pulled his starched shirt from his pants, sneaking her hands up his back.

Randolph slid his mouth down her jaw to her neck. His light kisses teased each of her nerve endings to life.

"Randolph." Like it or not, he was her husband and he was turning her on. Her inner primal self wanted him.

His hand traveled down her side, grazing her breast, and rested on her waist. "Do you need something?" He spoke into her open mouth before finding her lips once more.

She answered by kissing him harder and raising her knee. Every time she shut her eyes she seemed to spin, and rather than fight the feeling, she let it overtake her, doing how she had been taught her entire life and going with what she wanted, what would make her happy. As if led by some unknown force, she pried her fingers into the knot in his tie and untied it.

He broke their kiss, stared into her eyes and snaked his hand inside the top of her dress. "Willow?"

"Yes." Her breath caught. He cupped her breast in his palm. Without breaking eye contact, she slowly pulled the tie out from his collar.

"No bra?" He grazed his thumb across her nipple.

She bit her lip. Already her entire being was over sensitized. "Never wear them." She managed to release two of the buttons on his shirt, but gave up on the work and yanked it open the rest of the way. Satisfied the way the buttons popped off, she ran her fingertips across his smooth chest.

"What else don't you wear?" He shimmied out of the wrecked shirt, throwing it off the edge of the bed.

She trailed one fingertip up from his belt buckle, over his flat stomach and up to his neck. "I'll give you one guess."

"Yes." He crushed his lips to hers.

Sensation, arousal and desire encompassed her. They kissed and touched, igniting her whole body.

She lost herself in the way he held her and how his muscles rippled beneath her hands.

Finally, he discovered the fact that she didn't wear underwear, and his hand skimmed over her, taunting and teasing, until he treated her to one finger and a second. "So maybe you like me just a little." He chuckled.

She held on to him for support. "You're very handsome."

"You are very beautiful." Once more he kissed her and applied pressure where she needed it most.

She shook her head.

"You are. I watch you enough to know."

"Really?" His naked body pressed against hers. Though she never remembered either of them removing the rest of their clothes, the proof of his arousal rested against her inner thigh, hot, thick and ready for relief.

Off in the distance the telltale crinkle of a condom wrapper told her satisfaction would soon be hers. She reached down, biting her lip when she could barely get her hand all the way around him. "Randolph."

"May I give my beautiful wife a real wedding night?" He sheathed his erection.

"Yes." At the moment she would gladly trade her monthly allowance for an orgasm.

With no resistance, he entered her and sucked in his breath.

At being filled, she gasped and dug her fingernails into his shoulders. Her body opened up for him, welcoming the invasion.

"You're perfect." He put his hand behind her head and gave her a deep, languishing kiss.

All the rushing from earlier vanished, and he took his time with liquid smooth strokes that built her arousal at the perfect rate.

She shut her eyes, focused on the sensations around her. Their scents intermingled with their bodies, his breath quickening, the way they moved together, no longer two separate people but a unified force together.

"Willow." He slid one hand under the small of her back as if he couldn't get close enough to her. "I need you."

In desperate need of more as well, she wrapped her legs around his waist, imbedding him further, allowing him to rub against her in the exact right way. Insatiable heat swirled around her, begging to explode. She couldn't wait. "I'm there."

"Now, Willow." His fluid thrusts became hard and deep right as her body demanded it.

Uncontrollable bliss burst through her. "Oh." The ecstasy intensified and she sucked in her breath and grabbed onto him, not wanting to ever let go of the source of pleasure. "Don't stop."

"I can feel you throbbing." He tensed. As his own end overtook him, he ground into her "God."

Their bodies pulsed in time, spoke their own language in a rhythm only two people could create together in the most intimate of moments.

For the first time she wasn't left wanting or unfulfilled. Spent, her muscles relaxed, giving her a few lingering quivers and finally covering her in a blanket of calm and release. Sex in its most basic state was healing and cleansing.

"Don't move an inch." He brushed her lips against hers and got out of the bed.

Beyond her control, her eyes closed and she called to the man she married. Behind her eyelids she sensed the room darkened. "Randolph?"

"You're not alone, I'm right here." The bed jostled with his return. He gathered her up in his arms and got them under the covers.

Part of her expected him to turn over to his side of the bed, but another part of her loved the way he continued to hold her. She had no choice but to go with it, but not get too close or too used to him. "This bed is comfortable." She never took for granted a clean, soft bed.

"I'm glad you like it." He tilted her face up to his and gave her three soft kisses. "Should we sleep?"

"We made it." She rested her head in the crook of his neck. "What else do we need to do?

"I'm going to take care of everything." He ran his hand through her hair.

Though she longed to drift off, she fought her need for a moment to relish in his words. No one besides Nan ever took care of her.

* * * *

Randolph opened his eyes into a haze of dreamy gold. No buzzing of an alarm clock, ringing vibration of a cell phone, or his own body jolting him out of his sleep awakened him. He simply opened his eyes to a quiet, peaceful room with his brand new spouse in his arms.

Spouse.

Her hair covered his face, her light breathing let him know she still slept, and best of all, her naked body contoured to his, waking up the rest of him. Somehow he found the angel who rescued him from himself. They may have spent most of their casual relationship taking spars at each other, but if last night were any indication, the year would fly by leaving them both satisfied on multiple levels. Hell, for the first time ever he made it through the night with another person in the room with him. Normally he snuck out citing work as an excuse not to stay when his own sleep issues were the true culprit.

With her back turned to him, he ran his hand over the inward curve of her waist. He took in her profile. His wife possessed a beauty rarely found in Los Angeles, natural, sweet, and genuine. He lowered his head to her shoulder and gave her an open mouth kiss.

"Um," she moaned and tilted her head giving him access to her neck.

He took her invitation, trailing kisses and light nips up to her ear. While on his watch her ear would never go unattended and he guided her lobe between his lips.

"Randolph?" Her voice low, sleep filled and breathy.

"Good morning Mrs. Van Ayers." He slid his hand up her perfect skin to her breast, rubbing his palm over her already hard nipple.

"Good Morning." She twisted around to face him.

Her cheeks flush with waking up and her tousled hair only served to enhance every one of her features. No need for breakfast, instead he wanted to feast on the woman in his bed, and get to know the person he would be spending the next year with. He leaned forward and kissed her, something light, a little appetizer, but enough to make him want more. "Come here."

"I'm right here." Still, she turned over.

"That's better." He moved her hair away from her eyes and kissed her again, a little deeper with his tongue tangling with hers. His morning erection throbbed, especially with the way she returned his attentions and lightly scratched her nails down his arm.

"Randolph." She pulled back and pressed her fingertips to his lips.

"Yes." He wrapped his arm around her and swirled his tongue around her finger.

"I didn't expect you to be so..." She turned down to his chest.

At the pink taking over her cheeks, he smiled. "So what?"

"So passionate."

"I didn't know you expected anything with me." He let out a

chuckle. Yes, he caught her staring more than once, but he always thought she wanted to curse him or cast a spell on him. "What else did you expect?"

The pink turned to crimson.

"Well, you know what?" He reached down to her leg and hooked it over his hip.

Through her lashes, she peeked up at him. "What?"

"I did expect you to be as limber as you are." He raised his eyebrows and went to kiss her once more.

A pounding at the door interrupted them.

"Who's that?" She grabbed him.

"I don't know." As if he could see through it, he looked over to the door, but wanting to get back to the matters at hand, faced her once more. "Forget it. It's probably housekeeping."

"Dolph!" Peter yelled through the door and knocked again.

"Has the man ever heard of a cell phone?" He tensed, vowing only to get up if the man knocked again. If Peter was breaking down doors he must need something. After all today was a workday.

As if on cue, Peter knocked again. "I have your cell phone!"

"Damn it. I have to let him in." He glanced at Willow and slipped out of the bed, running his hand through his hair. They made a complete and utter disaster out of the room. "Let me get you a robe and I'll order us breakfast."

"I'll just go take a shower." She wrapped the sheet around her, got out of the bed and without a glance back in his direction, went to the bathroom.

Peter resumed his knocking.

"Hold on!" Instinct made him want to call for someone, anyone to clean up the mess, but with no one there, he gathered up their clothes and other various things, tossed them in the middle of the bed and threw the comforter on top. He frowned at the lumpy bed, but forced himself to walk away, finding one of the robes he spoke of and opening the door. "What?"

"First, you left this with me." Peter held up his cell phone.

"Really?" On a normal day he wouldn't have made it five feet away from his phone. He plucked the device away from Peter. "What else?"

"Second, I spent the morning rearranging your schedule, but

you still have two conference calls, one with the Hartfords on their investments. Slate called you twice." Peter shoved him aside and entered the room.

He followed his assistant and glanced at his phone. Even though the damn thing only held megabytes of data, the millions of the emails inside weighed his hand down.

"What the hell have you done in here?" Peter sat down at the table, took out his computer and looked around the room, a smile taking over his face. "Did someone consummate their union last night?"

He joined Peter and put his head in his hand. "I need coffee and Willow needs food and tea. I don't know if she drinks coffee." In truth he didn't know much, if anything, about her.

"I ordered food." Peter laughed and set up his computer. "I think I know less about her than you do."

"You know we're married." He took a breath and opened his email, the blue bar at the bottom slowly crawling across the screen, the number of messages already in triple digits.

"She doesn't even like you." Peter clicked away on the computer.

"She likes me better now." The corner of his mouth twitched, fighting a smile. "You could have come about fifteen minutes later."

"That's it? Fifteen minutes?" Peter broke into a round of laughter.

His phone vibrated and like a trained dog he hit the button. Another five emails came through. He scanned the messages and squeezed the device. "We need to get back to LA." There was no time for morning after sex and dealing with his wife, he needed to keep with the task at hand and get to work. A rush of anxious adrenaline coursed through him and he stood.

"What's up?"

"I have a hundred calls to make. The more I put them off, the worse this is going to get." His head pounded, a headache would soon be on the horizon and he squeezed the bridge of his nose. "We should have gone home after we finished our business. Staying here was a complete waste of time."

"Then we should get going right away. We wouldn't want to waste any more time."

At the sound of Willow's voice, he lowered his hand.

In a matching robe to his, his new wife entered, fresh from the shower with her hair wet and slicked back and her skin glowing from the heat of the water. If only Peter came fifteen minutes later. Maybe twenty. Fine, an hour. "I'm sorry, we have to hurry. My absence from work was unplanned and I need to get back."

"Boy, the other girl didn't even get an overnight trip." She waved to Peter. "I have work today too."

"Speaking of your work..." Before he finished the question his phone vibrated again. With his jaw clenched he stared down at the screen. "My father emailed me." One day the sight of the man's name wouldn't cause him to break out into a sweat.

"Does he know what happened last night?" Peter asked.

He peeked over at Willow and couldn't help but smile. "No. I think for once I'll blindside him instead of the other way around."

"Your mom is going to pass out. What would have been a surprise elopement is now complete with a mystery bride." Peter shook his head. "Did you tell Willow about your mom?"

"Your mom?" Willow crossed her arms.

"It was in the contract." Though she insisted on reading the document, she didn't pick up on some of the finer points.

"Maybe the night was hectic, but I don't remember any parents being mentioned." She crossed her arms. "Don't blindside me."

The sweet woman who curled up to him in bed all but disappeared. He sauntered over to the bed, threw back the comforter and in the pile of clothes located his jacket, pulling out the folded contract. At least one of the copies. He turned to the third page and held the paper out to her. "To paraphrase, my mother is not aware of the marriage clause my father put in my contract, any mention to her or a member of her circle of friends and family will result in a penalty."

"You would be penalizing someone who has nothing." She lifted her chin.

"Not this time next year." Fine, she may not have read the contract, but she was savvy.

"You could have simply asked. I wouldn't have said anything." She walked around the far side of the bed and rifled through the clothes. "Rather than trying to control everything you should go with the flow more."

Yes, the woman was the type who kept their word, but he learned from the best and put everything in writing. The flow didn't exist in the land of the Van Ayers.

"What did you want to ask me about my business?" She lifted his torn shirt between two fingers.

"I wanted to know the last time you paid rent to Jade and the amount." The image of the back rent made him itch like he wanted to break out into hives. It was the first of many to-dos he had relating to her.

"Do you need that now?" She dropped the shirt and picked up her dress.

"Peter." He pointed at the rags. "We need to be able to walk in public."

"Let me order you guys some stuff just to get to the airport. Food is on the way." Peter picked up the house phone. "Willow, the sooner we have that information the better. We have a little time."

"Okay." She wrinkled her nose at the dress, let go of it and retrieved her purse. "I have my checkbook in here. Just give me a second."

With his phone in his hand he sat down at one of the side chairs. Again, he scrolled through the emails avoiding opening the one from his father.

Out of the corner of his eye he watched her dig through the oversized bag.

"Checkbook." She took her wallet out of the bag and opened it only to have two crumpled dollar bills and several papers fall onto the bed.

"Peter." At the storm of items bursting forth from her bag, he swallowed. "Are we getting coffee soon?"

She dropped the wallet and resumed her digging. "Hmmm."

"You didn't lose your checkbook did you?"

"No, I put it here." Without as much as a warning, she turned the bag over spilling the entire contents of the bag onto the bed with their clothes.

Curiosity, sick curiosity made him look, sort of like a ten car pile-up, or a train wreck, or a big huge mess on the bed with no maid to clean it. "My, that purse certainly holds a lot." His mother's handbags were little gems that cost small fortunes. They held only enough to get her through a lunch or dinner and then were returned to their dust bags and placed in order inside the closet specially built for purses and accessories.

"Well, I never know what I'll need." She rifled through the various things.

From a hairbrush to makeup, to papers, stones, and even a candle, her purse was a scavenger hunter's dream. "Do you need to take this with you?" He leaned over, moved aside two balls of yarn and plucked a long green feather out of the pile. They should have used it last night.

"I found that. It's beautiful." She took her treasure and set it aside. "I didn't have time to put it with the rest."

"Oh." He didn't want to think of what the rest entailed.

"Here we are." She unearthed an old, cracked blue plastic checkbook. "Let me see."

The suspense built as she thumbed through the pages and counted something off on her fingers, and he held his breath.

She tilted her head and bit her lip.

"May I?" Unable to wait another second, he held his hand out.

"You want to see?" She pressed her financial record to her chest.

"Well, we are married."

While he thought he would be met with much more resistance, she surrendered the book.

"I made my last payment here for half." She pointed to an entry.

"Well, you have very neat handwriting." At least she kept a record. He took in the date and completed a quick calculation in his head. Her situation was more dire than he imagined.

Rather than meeting his eyes, she gathered up her belongings.

"Let's get back to LA and when we go pack up you and Nan, maybe Jade will be at the gallery. We'll go get you current." He went to tuck the checkbook in his pocket, but realized he still wore the robe.

"We don't have to do that." Her voice lowered.

Maybe she didn't want to face her landlord after her financial fiasco. "Would you like me to go fix the rent situation myself?" She shook her head.

"Would you like me to give you the check and you can pay?" Then again, maybe she wanted to do it herself.

Once more, she took her head.

"I promised I would get you paid." He leaned down to try to see her face. "In fact, if you like, we can go to the gallery. I'll slip Jade the check and maybe we can take them out for drinks or something. Then we can tell them how we managed to fix each other."

She didn't react, only continued to stare down at the bed.

"Willow, tell me."

"Do you think we can *not* tell Slate or Jade about what we did last night?"

"We're married. I think last night was a given, but I have no reason to make everyone jealous." No matter the circumstance he could charm with the best of them, plus he only stated the facts.

"Not the sex." She pressed her hand to chest. "The marriage."

"So you don't mind if I go on and on about my awesome conquest, but you don't want me to tell them I made a legal woman out of you?" He didn't understand.

She answered by not answering.

"May I ask why?"

At last she lifted her head. "Well, your mother may not know the truth about your nuptials, but our friends do, and I would rather them not think that I am the girl who helped you gain all your material possessions."

"Is it that, or do you not want them to know that I am the guy who helped you gain all your material possessions?" He pointed at her.

Her jaw tightened.

"Don't you think it's going to be hard to hide it?" To prove his point he glanced down at his family's ring on her finger.

"Don't tell me you don't have any secrets?" She crossed her arms, hiding the ring. "Maybe we should keep our work and personal life separate."

"That sounds like something you would say." Peter laughed.

The silence that took over the room was saved by a knock at the door.

"All right Mrs. Van Ayers, we'll do it your way." He bowed his head. Yes, he had his secrets, none of which she would guess. In fact, his secrets needed to take a hiatus while he dealt with his marriage. Afterward, without any bindings on him or his life, he could be himself.

* * * *

Randolph opened his car door, smoothed down his suit jacket, and slipped into the driver's seat. "Would you like to stop somewhere and pick up some new clothes? My treat, of course." While Willow may not want to admit they were married, the matching sweat pants and hotel t-shirts they wore during the trip back to Los Angeles definitely told the world they were together. One thing was certain, the clothes were not at all suitable for bringing home his new bride.

"I have clothes at my place." She held out the oversized bright red shirt and shrugged.

"Okay." He continued his ride down Wilshire. After they landed and made their way back to the city, he finally had to admit there would be no time to finish his work and his homecoming. Instead, they went with Peter to his office where he snuck in, changed into a spare suit, grabbed some files to take home and left his assistant behind to fix the shambles of his schedule.

They neared Rodeo Drive and passed one of the high-end department stores where he knew many of the managers. "I just thought you might want something different."

"Different than what?" Her voice became tight, her words terse.

"Just different." He pointed to the store. "You will be meeting my parents for the first time in just a little bit." His mother would have fainted at the sight of him in the tacky hotel attire, and like it or not he wanted Willow to make a good impression. It would make the impending scene much easier.

"I'm sure I can find something at my place that will be suitable."

"Is it a suit?" Only semi-serious, he forced out a chuckle. Most women would have died to go on an all-expense paid trip to the land of the designers, but not his wife. Intriguing.

"It will be whatever I decide to put on." She crossed her legs and stared out the window.

They didn't say much as they drove the rest of the way to Los Angeles. The moment they turned down what Randolph wanted to dub proposal alley toward her shop, Willow wrapped her arms around her shoulders and fidgeted in her seat.

"What's the matter?" He peeked at her and then down the small passageway. Slate and Jade stood together down the alley. "Did you want to say hello?"

"We need to figure this out." She combed her fingers through her hair. "Can you park by my place? Look at us."

"I really wouldn't worry about that." He clutched the steering wheel. While Slate donned some sort of white fedora and a billowing white shirt, Jade wore a dress of blue ribbons. He doubted they would notice a t-shirt. Willow's plan of hiding their relationship seemed a bit out of character for her. "Remember, I was more than happy to fix your clothing."

"I won't be put in one of your expensive uniforms. I would rather be in this." She exhaled. "And we discussed what we are not discussing already."

"Again, I ask how do you plan on hiding us for 364 more days?" He pulled up next to her store.

"May I go in and talk to Nan first and then I'll get you?" She grabbed the door handle.

"Is she allowed to know we're married, or should we just tell her we're living together in sin?"

"Can you please wait here while I talk to Nan?" She got the words out through clenched teeth.

"I'll sit here like a good husband." He saluted her and put one finger over his lips. "Oops, I said the H word."

She gave him a glare and left.

He watched her go inside her store and sat back taking a moment to stare out the windshield. Jade kissed Slate. Her ribbons blew in the light breeze and Slate took off his hat and bowed to her.

The two were truly in love. A real connection was something that always seemed to elude him to the point where he had to find a woman as desperate as himself and then pay her off.

After another two kisses, Jade turned and entered the gallery. Slate spun on his heel, returned his hat to his head, and charged straight for his car.

He pressed the button to roll down the car window, his ring catching a ray of light and hitting the corner of his eye.

Slate came over and bent down. "Jade wants to know what you're doing with Willow."

To hide the evidence, he lowered his hand and slid his fingers under his leg. "I'm dropping her off at her shop."

"You left your party, she left your party, and you were seen leaving said party together. She wasn't home all night and now you drive up with her almost twenty-four hours later." Slate slapped the top of his car. "You look tired and terrible, so you must have had a great time."

"That is quite an assessment for someone dressed as a bleached pirate." He pulled his lower lip.

"Jade is the sky and I am a cloud, I float around her encompassed in her essence." Slate narrowed his eyes. "Also, even though I am nothing but part of the atmosphere, my essence wanted me to tell you that if you hurt Willow because you're licking some wound at your inheritance or whatever, she will get even with you." Slate narrowed his eyes.

"I never even implied I was licking wounds." Fine, he stooped to the sex card, but Willow didn't want the marriage mentioned.

Slate chuckled and they both nodded speaking the universal language of men. "So, what are you licking?"

He looked up to the ceiling of the car.

"Oh, man." Slate hit him in the arm. "So, exactly how natural is she?"

He motioned for Slate to come closer.

Slate turned his ear in his direction.

"Just like in nature, there are always unexpected surprises."

Slate rubbed his chin. "Interesting."

The door to Willow's shop opened and she appeared in what seemed to be some sort of gypsy costume complete with a long maroon flowing skirt, a huge belt cinching in her waist and a ruffled shirt topped off with a blue velvet vest. While the outfit did wonders to show off her shape, somehow he didn't think she changed to look nice for him. In fact, quite the opposite. He rolled down the passenger side window.

She stopped the second she spotted Slate. "Hi."

"Maybe the four of us will go out soon. Jade would like that." In keeping with his character, Slate bowed to her. "I have to run. We're going to a performance and to check out a new artist. I want to create some buzz for the co-op as well."

Once Slate was out of earshot, Willow opened the car door. "Why does he think we can go out together? I thought we weren't going to say anything."

"I didn't, he only thinks we had sex." He tilted his head. "When you show up with their money you can explain how you earned it so quickly. Then again, maybe I can open up a secondary business."

"I guess I'm bought and paid for anyway."

"You put yourself up for sale, but at your prices you should really be on Rodeo."

Caught in a standoff, they stared at each other. He played the game every day in his work, and didn't flinch. In contrast to his absolute control, she opened her mouth, closed it and bit her lip.

He remained perfectly still.

Like a fine vase in a 5.0 earthquake, she cracked. "Nan wants to meet you. If you avoid calling me a prostitute in front of her, she may not put a hex on you."

"What you call a prostitute, I call my wife."

"I thought we needed to get to your place."

"That we do." He stepped out of the car. "Time to meet the family."

Willow's outfit jingled as she turned. He rushed over and opened the door for her, and stepped inside her store. The soft fluttering of bells rang throughout the space and he was accosted by mass quantities of knick-knacks, fabrics and various other things he barely recognized.

Having never ventured into her shop before, he blinked to bring everything into focus. "If I breathe, I'm still going to be able to drive us home without getting a DUI right?" The scent of herbs, spices and flowers wafted all around him.

"It's incense, try inhaling, it may do you some good." She guided them through a set of deep violet drapes into the main store.

More colors committed assault and battery on his senses. Every wall was painted a different deep hue, purple, green, blue and covered in everything from mirrors and crystals to shelves chock full of her yarn creations. The urge to create overtook him and he wondered if she would eventually allow him to make some alterations. "This is quite impressive."

"Is that your way of telling me you're not impressed?"

Ignoring her comment, he stepped over to an entire wall devoted to jars and bottles of different types. "Willow's Wonders?" He picked up one tall bottle. "Lavender and chamomile salve?"

"Those are the holistic and therapeutic products Nan and I create." She joined him, returned the bottle to its spot and pointed to the front of the shop. "Over there is where I make my teas."

"I've heard people discuss them." He nodded. "You have an awful lot of different things here. Maybe you need to streamline."

"Our process is not made to be efficient, it's made to heal and calm."

At an intruder's voice, he turned.

"Not everyone is the same, so we need to offer many solutions." A short, round older woman in a purple floral muumuu approached.

"It may help to make the store more profitable. Sell deep not wide." He stepped forward, bowed slightly and held out his hand. "Nanette Riviera?"

She grunted, but gave him her hand. Actually, she took his hand. "He's nervous."

"He should be." Willow laughed.

Though he longed to take his hand back, he remained still. "I'm standing right here."

"As you describe it, he just got everything he wanted. Why should he be nervous?" She turned over his hand and gazed down at his palm. "Look here, Chiquita."

Willow joined Nan. "Interesting."

"What does it say?" He shifted his weight from one foot to the other.

"What does what say?" Nan turned his hand over and back again.

"My palm."

Nan put his hand up to her ear. "I don't know. We don't read palms."

Willow bit her lip, but couldn't stifle her smile.

"But you are telling me you're nervous, you want leave and you hate being out of your element." She released him.

He shoved his hand in his pocket. "We do need to get going. If you want to pack a few things now, we can hire some help tomorrow to get everything organized."

"I'm ready." Nan shook her head. "No need for assistance."

"I'll be ready in ten minutes." Willow put her hand on Nan's shoulder and kissed her cheek. "Thank you for doing this."

"Change is life." Nan patted her. "Randolph and I will talk."

Willow disappeared up the small flight of stairs. He pulled at his lower lip, not even wanting to imagine what would take only ten minutes to pack. His sock drawer would take twice as long. Well, sock drawers.

A shudder ran through him, the same one as when someone came up to close behind him. He needed to face the inevitable and put a large Ivy League smile on his face before turning to Nan.

The woman narrowed her eyes.

He swallowed and went to say something endearing. Maybe tell her she looked lovely?

"Remain silent."

He pressed his lips together.

She held one finger up.

He bit the inside of his mouth, examining the olive-skinned woman with her dark hair pulled back in a bun.

She tilted her head left, right and left again.

At last she nodded.

"May I speak now?" He dug his nails into his palm, unwilling to be the butt of another one of her jokes.

"Interesting." She chuckled.

"What is it?"

"For someone who follows directions, you chose a strange time to be bad." The corners of her eyes lifted in what seemed to be amusement.

"Who said I follow directions?" Not wanting to stand in the middle of the tiny room any longer he motioned toward a couple of chairs and a table in the front by some books.

"The list your father made you. You must be very determined or very weak." The woman waddled over.

He pulled out the chair for her. "Which do you think it is?"

She plopped down in the wrought iron chair and looked backward at him. "You convinced my Chiquita to go along with your foolish plan."

"Ah, but she had me agree to take you along with me. In fact, she had me write you into the contract." He took his seat across from her.

"Willow's strength was never in question." She strummed her fingers on the table.

Silence overtook them and the woman's words echoed in his head. "For the record, I have done plenty of bad things."

"You are hiding something." She chose an apple out of the little basket on the table. After examining the fruit, she rooted around in the basket and pulled out a little paring knife. "But you don't know who you really are."

"What do you mean by that?" Could the woman read minds? Who was she to pass judgment on him?

Rather than answer, she peeled the apple, the green peel coming off in one long spiral and falling to the table. She cut a wedge, pierced the section with the tip of her knife and held it out to him.

"I don't care for apples, thank you." He tapped his foot on the floor and glanced at his watch.

"You'll like this one." She continued to hold the offering out.

To avoid being rude to a woman he needed on his side, he took the piece of fruit. He took a bite. Rather than being met with the expected overly sweet and too soft apple, a tangy, crisp tartness ran over his tongue. He crunched away, swallowed and popped the rest in his mouth.

"Yes, I don't think you know your true self." She cut another section and held it out.

Without hesitation he took the treat. "I am very aware of who I am and who I will be." The woman was pulling some power play and before they all lived together for the next year he needed to make sure she knew the hierarchy.

"Which is why you almost lost what you fought for your whole life and are letting an old woman who you don't even know tell you what kind of fruit you like." She hit the table and burst into laughter.

"Nan?" Willow ran down the stairs, her outfit jingling all the way.

At the sight of his bride, he stood. "I see we decided not to change." Before they left he had to make sure of a couple things.

"Come here, Chiquita." Nan held her hand out.

"Are you feeling all right? You seem pale." Without even an acknowledgement his way, Willow put a duffle bag at the foot of the stairs and went straight to the woman, took her hand and knelt down beside her. "I'm sorry I didn't discuss this with you first, but..."

"I'm fine." Nan placed her finger over Willow's lips. "Hold on, Randolph needs to speak."

They both turned to him.

He swallowed.

"What is it?" Willow asked.

"Did you tell Nan everything?"

"I know your mother doesn't know why you got married and I know you signed your life away." Nan cut some more of the apple and gave it to Willow.

Willow took the slice off the knife with her teeth.

The whole action fascinated him.

Nan ate the last slice. "I also know that you are generous as long as you get what you want." She wiped off the knife, put it away and stood with the rest of the apple remnants.

"What if I don't get what I want?" He followed the woman as she waddled over to an oversized bag.

"I have a feeling that hasn't happened to you yet, but I hope you are strong enough to survive it." She walked through the curtains toward the back. "I'll put the peel and the core in the compost pile. Nothing should go to waste."

"Do we need to arrange for someone to pick up your cars?" He lifted Willow's bag."

She shrugged. "No car, I don't drive."

No car? "How did you get around?"

"Two feet and ten toes." She stepped in front of him. "Maybe you should take a walk if it wouldn't be too much of a waste of time."

He followed Willow and peeked up the small stairwell. Her living conditions were not acceptable. No wonder it only took her no time to leave. "How were you living up there?"

"Just fine. Nothing is ever a waste." She echoed Nan's words.

He motioned forward wondering what she would think of the land of waste and excess, or what he called home.

Chapter Four

MANSIONS IN BEVERLY HILLS were normally oversized, ostentatious houses bloated with material possessions. In the city where land was a premium, castles with wings and servants didn't truly exist.

At least those types of homes didn't exist until they drove through the gates to Randolph's residence.

A virtual field of perfect green grass provided the backdrop for planned, pristine flowers, bushes, shrubs and trees, all creating the literal ideal landscape for a mansion. A real mansion. Randolph lived in a mansion.

Willow's breath caught. White columns, a sprawling building, and a fountain in the front. The place had enough wings it could take off and fly anytime, and never worry about losing altitude.

"My great, great, great grandfather bought the land on a lark while on vacation decades ago," as if sensing her need for an explanation, Randolph spoke. "He hated living back east and built the home. Every generation of my family has lived here at one point or another. My grandfather and grandmother lived here, but he loved the east and retired there to be closer to the rest of the family. I have always lived here. Since then, many people have tried to buy it, and though I think my father has been tempted..."

"The house is yours after the year is out." She finished for him. If all Randolph ever did with his life was sell the property, he would be set forever. Still, the thought of having something with such history intrigued her. She didn't know the name of anyone in her family except her mother. Nan's family wasn't large either. Though Nan told her to concentrate on the present, it would be nice to have a past, something to give her a spot in the universe. "If you ever have a child are you going to give it to him or her or are you going to sell it?"

"If I ever give it to a child, it will be exactly that, a gift." His voice seemed far away.

She inhaled and glanced down at her outfit. Maybe with the history and the generations that graced the halls of his home she should have toned it down a bit. No one ever gave her a list of tasks or led her down a path. Nan simply told her to let her heart guide her. In his own way, maybe Randolph tried to guide her, help her. She did have to live with these people for the next year.

"Of course, I doubt I'll ever have any children. I just want my house and my business and then I'm packing up Junior and his trophy." He glided his car to the front of the home, threw it into park and turned to her. "Leave your crystal ball and magic potions in the car. We have staff to help you unpack."

Without another word he got out of the car.

Of course there was always the possibility his history made him narrow minded and a jerk, one who only wanted to conform. Above all else she needed to remember to stay true to her values and not become attached. She reached in her bag, pulled out her sequined headband and put it on as he opened the doors for her and Nan.

"Ladies." He offered Nan his hand first.

Nan took his hand and allowed him to hoist her out of the car. She smiled at him and touched his chin. "How will we all fit in such a tiny place?"

Randolph tilted his head. "It would be much more spacious if we could get rid of my parents."

Nan sighed.

Randolph held out his arm and gave her one of those manufactured smiles. "Mrs. Van Ayers?"

She jutted her jaw out.

"We're married Mrs. Van Ayers. We 're on my turf now and need to enter the home as a couple, as decreed by the paperwork you signed." He took a breath. "Please?"

She agreed to their arrangement, said vows in a chapel and signed a contract she barely skimmed. Rather than argue about being genuine, she hooked her arm in his and let him help her out of the car.

He went to walk forward, but she stopped. She glanced at the huge wood double doors with ornate handles. Her stomach dropped. Something, call it intuition, ESP, or a sixth sense, told her he wanted to lead her into a disaster. She resisted. "Randolph."

"What is it?" He lifted his sunglasses.

The sun twinkled on those green eyes. How on earth could he not find a girl to marry him? Between his money and his looks, many women would forgo the personality to be with him. Hell, even she was taken in, but like the words she said in front of some nondenominational official, she vowed to herself she would keep her guard up. Since their interruption in the hotel, something nagged at her. His whole situation was layered with lies and cover ups, and she added to the whole deception. "Is there anything else I need to know before I walk in? I don't want to be blindsided."

"What do you mean?" He jutted his jaw out. "I've told you everything you need to know."

"Are you sure?" She tried to search his eyes. The sparkle had vanished.

"Shouldn't you be able to tell without me saying a word?" He wiggled his fingers as if casting a spell. "Or is that headgear squeezing too tight?"

"Yes, I suppose I know the answer." She let go of his arm. "I'm ready to go inside."

He motioned forward, and as she walked ahead the door magically opened and he put his hand on the small of her back. The man would make them keep up appearances no matter what it took.

They stepped inside to the most incredible room. She may not have wanted to touch Randolph before, but now she reached for him to keep herself upright. Only in movies did she think such a room existed. Wood paneled gleaming walls were offset by a white marble floor with what she could only assume was an oriental or Persian rug. An antique table in the center held a huge arrangement of fresh flowers. Two matching curving staircases led to the upper floor, and the crown jewel of the entrance was a humongous twinkling crystal chandelier, something one would see in an opera house. "Oh my God."

Nan grabbed her arm and squeezed.

"Sir." A man in a three-piece suit greeted them.

"Willow, Nanette, this is our Head of Staff, Dimitri." He nodded and handed the man his car keys. "This is Willow Van Ayers and Nanette Riviera, their belongings are in the car and need to be brought inside."

"Excuse me?" A woman's voice echoed through the space followed by the click of heels on the stone floor. "Randolph?"

As if made to match the room, a beautiful woman entered. A bit older, the blonde had her hair swept up and wore a pristine pink skirt suit. "Where have you been? Who's this?" She pressed her hand to her throat and her attempt at a smile failed. "We missed your birthday."

"Where's Father? I'll make the introductions all at once." Randolph pulled her over.

Unable to resist, Willow allowed him to put his arm around her.

"Van!" The woman licked her lips and took two steps toward them. "Van? Where are you?"

From yet another entrance to the room, a man joined them. "What's going on?" If she ever wanted to know what Randolph would look like a bit older, all she needed to do was look at the man in navy dress pants and a white button down shirt.

Several other people gathered in the shadows as if peeking to see a show. Willow figured they must be the elusive staff Randolph continued to mention.

"Good, we're all here." Randolph moved them forward. "Willow, Nanette, this is my mother, Lillian Van Ayers and my father, Randolph Van Ayers Jr."

Randolph's mother reached out and took her husband's hand. "Hello."

His father merely nodded.

"Mother, Father, this is Nanette Riviera, and this beautiful woman by my side is my bride, Mrs. Willow Van Ayers." He squeezed her shoulder.

Randolph's father tilted his head. Willow swore she detected something strange behind his green eyes. Amusement? Mischievousness? She couldn't place it.

On the other hand, his mother was an easy read. Her lower lip quivered, her complexion paled and she fanned herself. "Bride? Did you say bride?" Not waiting for her son to answer, she turned to her husband. "Van, did he say bride?"

"Indeed, that is what he said." He shifted his attention to Randolph. "When exactly did this take place?"

Willow held her breath. Anyone else would find the way the man's question was phrased or odd, but she knew the deeper meaning.

Randolph reached into his suit coat pocket and pulled out a paper. "Yesterday, we got married on my birthday. Willow said now I'll never forget our anniversary." He handed their marriage license to his father.

She need not mention they would only celebrate one anniversary. No doubt his father already knew that detail.

With her chest heaving up and down, his mother leaned over. "Married? You got married?"

"Yes mother, Willow and I are married." Randolph's tone was one of boredom as if he had anything better to do.

His mother braced herself against Mr. Van Ayers, well the older Mr. Van Ayers. "He got married? What happened? He got married to a gypsy?" She leaned over.

"Lillian?" Mr. Van Ayers put his hand on her back.

"Van?" She reached up for him, but missed. "I can't breathe."

"Lillian, get control of yourself." He took her hand. "What's done is done. He's married."

"I had plans. Him and Stephanie. He got married." Her breath labored, she lowered herself to her knees.

"Randolph." Willow covered her mouth, keeping her questions inside. Who was Stephanie and why wasn't Randolph doing anything about his mother passing out? She went to step forward.

Randolph pulled her back

"My son is married and we weren't there?" Lillian's words trailed off and she slumped over.

"Someone get me some water!" His father got down on the floor as well.

"I have something for this." Nan went into action. She rushed over to Mrs. Van Ayers and put her tote on the floor.

Her stowaway cargo took his opportunity to free himself, and popped his head out of Nan's bag.

With all the insanity Willow sort of hid the fact she owned a dog. She winced and pushed Randolph aside to lunge for her baby, but before she reached him he jumped out of the bag and ran straight into the scene of the crime. "Jeb!"

"What's that?" Randolph yelled.

"Let me put this under her nose." Nan shoved one of her sachets up to Mrs. Van Ayers' face.

"Jeb, come here!" She tried to catch up to him, but tripped on the long skirt she got with a costume several years ago. Her palms slapped against the unforgiving marble.

"Willow!" Randolph grabbed her around the waist and yanked her upright.

Rather than obey, her dog darted between them, bouncing over to Nan.

"Van?" Mrs. Van Ayers shook her head and opened her eyes.

Jeb barked, hopped up on her and gave the woman a lick.

"Van! There's a rodent attacking me!" She covered her eyes.

"Randolph!" Willow yelled the first name that came to mind before someone exterminated her boy.

"Everyone stop!" Nan swooped up Jeb and stood.

They all froze.

"You must have never seen a rodent." Nan pointed at Mrs. Van Ayers.

The woman peeked through her fingers.

Nan turned to Randolph. "A son who doesn't run to his mother in her time of need." She made a tsking sound and shifted her focus to her.

Willow recognized the glint in Nan's eye and pressed her back against Randolph.

"Chiquita, I told you not to hide yourself, and part of you is the animal you chose to keep." Nan held Jeb out to her.

She stayed silent and took her pup. He licked her and she ground her teeth together at his adorable little face.

At last someone arrived with the glass of water.

"What about me?" Mr. Van Ayers took the water and thrust it toward his wife.

Nan narrowed her eyes. "Maybe you should have got the water for your wife yourself."

"I don't think you should be the one to talk when my son's new wife brought her own maid with her." He crossed his arms.

"We need to get this house in order. Settle my son and his wife in his wing and please help Miss Nanette get acquainted with the rest of the staff."

"Maid?" What kind of people were these? Willow stomped forward and stood in front of Nan. "Nan is not my maid, and she is most definitely not part of your staff."

"Is she your spiritual advisor?" Mrs. Van Ayers held up the sachet, put it to her nose and shuddered.

"Father." Randolph mimicked her actions and stood in front of Nan. "Nanette is part of the family and she will be living upstairs."

Willow stared at the back of Randolph's head. At least the man took charge when needed.

"So in the course of twenty-four hours you took on a wife, her family and a pet?" His father exhaled.

"Yes, and right on time for my birthday." Randolph turned and once more put his hand on the small of her back. "I will show my new wife to our wing now."

"Nan?" In search of anything normal, Willow held her hand out.

"I will make sure Miss Nanette is settled upstairs." His father waved them away. "Right after I fix your mother."

"Go, Chiquita." Nan gave her a wink.

She allowed Randolph to guide her away.

"We have a dog?" Randolph leaned over. "Is that even a dog? It looks more like a cotton ball."

"Yes, he's a dog." She cuddled Jeb to her chest. Everyone said the same thing about Jeb. "He thinks he's big, don't call him a cotton ball."

"He needs to look at the evidence. It's stacked against him." He chuckled.

No truer words were ever spoken. She peeked back at their stunned family. Apparently she wasn't the only person blindsided and something told her there was more to come.

* * * *

Second, third and fourth thoughts went through Randolph's mind after he settled Willow in his wing and asked her to change for dinner. What other costume would his new spouse conjure? What other animals might appear? He walked over to the bar and poured himself a scotch, swigging it down without taking the time to bother with ice or anything else. He welcomed the burn.

"If you're going to do shots, go get your mother's vodka out of the freezer." His father joined him, put ice in both their glasses and poured them each some of the high-priced elixir. He lifted the glass in a mock cheers motion and took a sip. "You pulled it off in the eleventh hour. Kudos, though until you walked in the door I thought you were finally showing your face after you didn't finish your last assignment."

Randolph narrowed his eyes at the glass and gulped it down.

His father chuckled and took a seat. "So, where did you find her? Is she the fun one you kept on the side when Stephanie became too boring?"

"You are a pig." He eyed the decanter once more, but put his glass down. Something told him he needed some of his wits about him to get through the rest of the evening.

"Maybe she is merely a punishment to your mother and me. I mean you practically live in squalor and we never gave you anything." Though the man's words rolled off his tongue as smooth as the scotch, the clink of the ice in the glass betrayed his father's shaking hand.

"I have a task list longer than our staircase that outlines everything you ever gave me." Since his father would never allow him to forget his contract, he would return the favor.

"Without that piece of paper, you wouldn't be half the man you are today."

"How will you ever know what I would have been?" Randolph backed up to glance into the foyer in search of the newest additions to the family.

"I saved you from being a starving artist." His father put the glass down on the side table and ran his finger along the rim. "Art was never your forte."

Heat encompassed him, shooting up from his feet and overtaking the rest of his body. He balled his fist into a hand.

"I need to meet with you after dinner on the Hartford investments."

"Now those are some people who could definitely use some

art in their life." He tilted his head from left to right, the popping of his vertebrate ringing in his ears. His father gave new meaning to the term pain in the neck.

"It's a waste of time."

Maybe he needed to hand the man a shovel to take more digs at him. "Leave it, I am in the home stretch and you can't stand it."

"So, what did happen? Did Stephanie finally come to her senses and walk because you wouldn't give her a real wedding to spite me and your mother?"

"Who said she left me?" He glanced over his shoulder at the man.

"If that weren't the case, I have a feeling you would have flaunted your more interesting selection for us much sooner."

Before countering his father's argument, he turned back to find Nan, the lint ball and Willow coming down the stairs. Gone was the gypsy in a headband with layered skirts and a bejeweled belt, and in her place entered a woman in a short lace peach flowing baby-doll dress, some vintage jewelry and her hair pulled back showing off her features. One thing was certain, no matter the circumstances, his wife was a beauty. "Excuse me."

The legs that were wrapped around him in the hotel were on full display and the heat from his anger morphed into something much more pleasant. Especially once he remembered she wore nothing under the dress. Maybe they could put their miscommunications of the day behind them and have a repeat performance of Las Vegas.

Trying not to smile at the animal trundling down the stairs, he stepped into the foyer and did as he had been taught since he was old enough to stand, offered Willow his arm. "Good evening."

Her focus darted between his face and his arm, but she didn't move.

Fine, they had their fair share of ups and downs today, mostly downs.

Rather than call attention to her non-action he tried a different tactic. "Miss Nanette, may I say you look exceptionally lovely this evening?" He held his hand out to assist her down the last two stairs. Though she never changed from the purple floral dress, she cleaned up and put a flower in her hair. Apparently the woman liked flowers.

Nan took the offering, got to the bottom of the stairs, but stopped short in front of him and shook her head.

"Is something the matter?" He gave her a smile.

She stood on her tiptoes and took his chin in her hand. "You are much deeper than your looks, remember that and be genuine." With her words out, she let go.

"Thank you?" Apparently living with Nan would be like living with a giant, floral fortune cookie.

"Oh, good, there everyone is, even the dog." His mother entered the room in an emerald green cocktail dress and backed up at the sight of the animal. "Does he need anything special?"

"I will make his dinner after we eat." Nan whistled, and the dog ran over to her and sat down.

"Look how he listens." His mother pressed her hand to her chest and forced her lips into a smile. "I set up dinner in the formal dining room and thought we could have a little celebration for Dolph's birthday since we missed it."

"It was also my wedding day, mother." He reminded her.

"Of course, Dolph." Her smile stiffened. "I keep forgetting your wedding was yesterday."

"Not me." Willow came up beside him and at last took his proffered arm. In fact, she absolutely tangled their appendages together. She pressed her body to his side and stared up at him. "We didn't need anyone else to help us celebrate yesterday, or today."

Not sure if he wanted to crack up or sling her over his shoulder and haul her upstairs to a private celebration, he turned to her. Those light blue eyes sparkled with mischief and mayhem. His naughty wife could be bad when she wanted.

"Is your neck hurting you?" Her sparkle subsided.

"A little." How did she know?

She curled her arm around his neck and gave him a few squeezes somehow hitting the exact spot he hurt.

"That's perfect." Her fingers worked wonders and it was all he could do not to close his eyes.

"Oh, you're tight." She continued her massage.

He couldn't help but widen his eyes, at what sounded similar to something he moaned the previous night.

A slow smile took over her face.

Maybe they were done fighting. A jolt went through his body along with a flash of their wedding night.

"Why don't we all go sit down?" His mother let out a shaky laugh.

"Shall we?" With Willow still firmly attached to his side, he took Nan's arm and led them into the dining room.

Willow tightened her grip on him the moment they stepped inside. Done in dark woods to match the majority of the house and with a table that could easily sit twenty, the dining room was impressive indeed.

Apparently, his mother felt the need to put on airs for the two people who wouldn't be easily smitten by their ostentatious display of wares, but instead overwhelmed. She had the staff lay out their best china, linens and crystal.

With his drink still in hand, his father entered from the opposite side of the room and took his position at the head of the table.

His mother took her place beside him, and he guided Willow to their spots. Nan let go of him and took a seat by his mother. The five of them looked ridiculous scrunched together at one end of the table.

"Isn't this room a bit huge for only us?" His father looked around as if he expected a parade of people to join them.

"I wanted to have our dinner in here. Stephanie always loved this room." His mother motioned for the staff to begin serving and sighed. "I thought Willow would like it as well."

The first time his mother mentioned her, the chaos of his mother and the dog blunted any more discussion of the matter. His throat dried out. A staff member came around the table and poured him some water. More than once Willow asked if there was anything she needed to know and told him not to blindside her.

Willow lifted her hand.

He needed a diversion as good as the dog and spied the dish of lemon wedges. Not caring about his next move, he did the unthinkable and leaned way over the table to retrieve it. "Willow."

"Randolph, what are you doing? Sit down." His mother fanned herself.

"I thought Willow might like some lemon with her water." He

practically fell back into his chair.

"Then someone will bring it around."

"I wanted to give it to her." He held out the dish to her and graced her with a smile. "Willow, did I tell you that our grounds have several lemon trees, as well as lime, orange, peach, nectarine, apple and avocado?"

"Since when did you go out on the grounds?" His father grunted.

"Willow loves nature." He kept the dish out. "We also plant herbs, which I will show you after dinner, if you like."

"We do?" His mother shook her head.

He decided not to acknowledge the woman. She might continue speaking, which could mean Stephanie's name would bubble back up to the surface after his successful redirect. "Willow, would you like a wedge of lemon with your water?"

She took the little tongs and selected a slice. "What I would really like to know is who is Stephanie?"

"Someone I used to know." He didn't expect her to be that focused and he answered fast, too fast.

Rather than continuing to deal with him, she looked across the table at his mother, the hub of all gossip and things women wanted to know.

Still, he couldn't give up without trying every last tactic. Once more he stood up. "Mother, would you like a slice of lemon?" He thrust the dish toward her. "It's from our tree."

"Sit down." She furrowed her brow and shooed him away.

He sat. Silence encompassed the room and he drank down his plain water without a lemon wedge.

Luck on his side, the staff entered with the salad and wine. Hopefully the arrival of glazed pecans and blue cheese would get everyone talking about vinaigrette.

"My son is the one who loves the lemon. Will you please bring this to him?" She lifted the dish to hand it to one of the staff. "Stephanie gave this to us that one Christmas we didn't go back east."

He put his arm around the back of Willow's chair. "We will be going back east this holiday."

"Not unless someone tells me who Stephanie is," she growled.

"Stephanie was Dolph's fiancée." His mother spoke as if she

were spewing gossip at one of her lunches. "They had been together off and on since high school. I thought we were going to have a huge wedding, but Dolph would never set a date."

His appetite completely vanished and a glance out of the corner of his eye told him Willow's did as well. Her perfectly pale complexion morphed into something more sallow. The revelation of the identity of Stephanie might qualify as one of those blindsiding items. Willow had asked about the woman he was supposed to marry, but he made it sound as if it were only a passing fling.

"Shame on Dolph. He could have had a wonderful extravaganza." Willow snapped her fingers. The little fur ball ran over to her and she picked him up. She picked a carrot off her plate with her fingers, put it between her teeth, and bent down to the dog. Her pet took the carrot right from her lips and chomped away.

Holy Hell, she fed the dog from her mouth like a baby bird. He wasn't sure if he was disgusted or captivated.

His mother pushed her plate away. One thing was certain. His marriage would be amazing for his mother's diet she always complained about.

"I know. I thought when he didn't' come home last night he would be surprising us with a formal engagement." His mother reached for his father's scotch.

"Well, instead you got the whole thing taken care of at once." Willow picked up a few lettuce leaves, shoved them in her mouth and allowed the dog to lick her fingers. "Well, as you can imagine I am exhausted from getting married and all, so I'm going to head on up to bed and let you celebrate Dolph's birthday. Nan will need the kitchen in a bit."

Without any warning, Willow stood, causing his father and him to stand as well.

"Please stay here with us, I'm sure there's cake." He winced.

"You really have a thing for cake. Maybe you should have had a wedding." She walked around the table, handed the dog to Nan and without another glance at anyone in the room, left.

He caught Nan's gaze from across the table. She lifted her eyebrows and then turned her attention to her salad.

"Well, we do have cake." His mother pressed her palm to her

cheek. "Perhaps we can have one of the staff take your wife up a plate."

"I'll do it." Damn everything. He drank down the rest of his flavorless water. Willow knew what she signed up for. They had a contract and she included a dog. Still, he more than blindsided her, he sort of slapped her in the face.

Chapter Five

THE HOUSE OF VAN AYERS was a lot like living in a fancy hotel. Since walking away from the dinner gone wrong, various members of the staff had knocked. First someone brought her dinner, a scrumptious chicken dish with some sort of rich sauce she wanted to lick off the plate. The second person arrived with her drink, or drinks, including wine, water with the homegrown lemon and a cup of hot tea. Lastly, the famous cake. The dessert with its layers of chocolate and strawberry was amazing. She wanted to shove her face in the plate, but even without Mrs. Van Ayers to watch her manners, she took small bites, wiped her mouth with the linen napkin and sat back politely.

After someone came up and took her dishes, another person arrived and presented her with an extra blanket and towels.

No wonder Randolph nearly melted down over what he called substandard champagne the night before. She was surprised one of their beloved staff didn't pre-chew his food for him.

Finally alone, she took her time to study the suite. Their wing, as Randolph called it, consisted of several rooms including an office for him, a couple of what appeared to be guest rooms, and an extra bathroom. Even with all the space, they still put Nan in her own suite of rooms in a different wing of the house.

Their actual suite consisted of a bedroom area, a sitting area, the largest bathroom she ever saw, and a closet bigger than most people's apartments. In fact, the closet boasted a chair and a couch and a full on changing area. While Randolph's clothes filled racks and racks, her scant few items only took up a few inches. All the furniture appeared to be antique and everything was exceptionally neat, as if no one truly lived here.

However, more than anything, the art stood out. While the

entire mansion contained beautiful works, Randolph's suite boasted incredible masterpieces. His taste skewed more toward modern pop art with vibrant colors, including a set of paintings of suited men and women behind desks in corporate jobs but done up as cartoon characters, and a picture of nothing but multi-colored squares. No wonder he hung around the gallery.

After her explorations, she picked up her contract and attempted to seriously read the pages. A few lines in, she opted to work on crocheting some squares for her next afghan, and lost herself in the repetitive, calming task.

A soft knock interrupted her.

"Come in?" Unsure of the etiquette, she sat back and waited for the next staff member.

Thus far, every knock came with an announcement of what she was about to receive.

Instead, the door opened and Randolph peeked his head inside.

She ground her teeth together. Her alone time was officially over.

"I brought you something." He stepped inside with hand behind his back.

"You're giving me plenty." She put her craft down and lifted the contract.

"Do you have any questions about it?" He closed the door and held out his peace offering in the form of a piece of cake.

"Should I?" She fanned her face with the pages.

He came forward and held the plate out.

"Your staff was much quicker than you, but thanks." It wasn't lost on her that he didn't come running after her after she left. Their marriage was merely a business deal, nothing more. The passion or whatever she felt before was nothing but a much needed a release. She reminded herself to keep her distance and get her job done. It didn't matter if Stephanie was much more than a hired hand.

"Okay, hopefully we can share it later." He put the dish down on the side table, reached behind his back again and offered her a single pink rose. "Maybe you'll accept this little token as my apology."

"What are you apologizing for?" She pressed her back into the overly stuffed chair.

He took a seat on the ottoman in front of her. "I didn't mean to blindside you with Stephanie."

Fine, he used her word, surely the tactic of a businessman. Still, she wanted to see his reasoning. "How so?"

"That is not the way you should have found out about my past relationships. I know it must be hard." He reached forward and put his hand on her knee. "I assure you it's completely over."

She crossed her legs forcing Randolph's hand off her, but stayed silent.

"I don't want you to think I would ever cheat on you." His voice lowered.

"Randolph, I need to ask you something."

"It was over before I ever thought of marrying you." Again, he held the rose out to her.

"Okay, that wasn't my question." She glanced at the flower but didn't accept the token of affection which represented a different kind of relationship.

"Ask me anything." He placed the flower on the arm of the chair, taking a moment to balance the blossom before sitting back.

"Let's say you didn't have to get married and you weren't with anyone, would you have asked me out on a date?" Whether she would have accepted the date was another question, but she needed the answer.

His face went blank. No smile, no frown, nothing. "I don't understand."

"It's simple." She tilted her head. "Would you or would you have not asked me out? Would you have seen me and thought, that is the girl I want to take to dinner, kiss goodnight, make love to?"

A slow smile crept on his face. "I think you are beautiful and we are married and I would love to make love to you again. Last night was nothing short of spectacular. More than I could have ever dreamed of." He extended one finger and traced her kneecap.

At his touch shivers consumed her. Unfortunately, she was privy to what the man could do with those fingers, his tongue, and his body. Deep down she knew if he had ever been nice to her she would have accepted a date with him and kicked herself later. She slapped his hand away like an unwanted fly. "When you dreamed, did you dream of me?"

Once more his face went blank. "We're married."

"I signed a contract as did you," she corrected.

"You were upset, but I want you to know Stephanie is over. My mother made it seem like more than it was."

"Randolph, let me make something perfectly clear."

He continued staring at her.

"I could care less about your past relationships, who you loved, who you didn't."

"I didn't love her." He held up his hand.

"It doesn't matter." She shook her head. "What matters is when you enter into a business agreement with someone there needs to be full disclosure, something you did not give me and therefore you made me look like a fool. That's something I will not tolerate again."

"I don't want to hurt you. I told you, it's over."

"You can't hurt me because we are only connected by a contract." She flicked the papers. "Don't think I don't know it's completely over, and you will stick by your fidelity clause if you end up with red, raw palms before this year is out. For a man to fight as long and hard as you did and almost lose, I have no doubt it's over, and I have no doubt you won't cheat on our fictional relationship."

"Willow." He ran his hand through his hair.

She almost smiled when his curls bounced right back into position as if they were trained. Instead, she handed him back the rose.

"Anyone ever tell you that you would have made a great negotiator?" He took the flower, put it aside and rubbed his neck.

"Maybe." For the most part they called her stubborn, but she would never admit it. "Why don't you go take a hot shower for your neck?"

"Incredible." He tilted his head toward the cake. "Would you like a few bites?"

"No, I think I'm going to go say goodnight to Nan." She got up.

Like every time she stood, he did as well. "Remember, we're still married and we share a bed."

"It's all right here." She pressed the contract into his chest.

"You better hide that before it's discovered." They made a mockery of a sacred pact, turned it into a business deal, but even on the first day emotions came into play. She didn't know how they would fix their mess in a year. Maybe there would be cake.

* * * *

Bed.

Randolph stared at his four-poster mahogany bed.

Up until the moment he brought his new wife to his family home, his bed was his biggest nemesis. He narrowed his eyes at the seemingly benign piece of furniture. Most would call it a place of rest and comfort. He called it a nightmare where the moment he laid down every thought entered his mind, taunting him awake. With Willow's words still fresh in his mind, he didn't see any dreams of her or otherwise happening any time soon. On a night like tonight he wouldn't have even tried, he would have left and let loose some of his pent up energy in a more creative way than having sex.

The bathroom door opened and the jingle bell of one pampered pet's collar and the light humming of his spouse interrupted his glaring.

"It's 11:45, we made it." In a long flowing light blue nightgown Willow seemed to float around the room they would share for the next 364 days. "Are you going to get in bed?"

"Ladies first." He motioned toward the oversized deceptive mound of feathers and stuffing inviting his wife into his bed to sleep.

"Big, beautiful boys first." Willow raised her voice as if she were talking to a baby, bent down and plopped the living powder puff up on his sleeping area.

"The dog can't sleep in the bed." He had never seen a dog that looked like Jeb. Unlike the name which should be given to a big, burly animal, Willow's pet weighed at most four pounds and he was convinced most of the weight was from a copious amount of white fur. If his mother caught the animal on her million thread count sheets, she might faint. Suddenly, he wanted the dog in the bed. "Doesn't he sleep in Nan's room?"

"Jeb and I are a set." She crossed her arms. "We sleep in the same place."

They both stopped and watched as the fluffy thing walked around practically sinking into the comforter. The animal went around in a circle, once, twice, a third and a fourth time and at last, curled up basically blending into the bedding.

He supposed aside from every other item that entered his mind as soon as he entered the bed, he could add fear of killing an almost canine to the list. One wrong turn and they would have a dead dog. "Is he comfortable? Does he need anything else, perhaps a silk pillow?"

"He's low maintenance." She pulled back the blankets and slipped between the sheets.

"I don't know why I don't believe you." He took his side of the bed and stared up at the ceiling.

"Did you ever have a pet?" She leaned over to the nightstand and opened the drawer.

Not sure what she could have put there he glanced over to find her with one of her salve bottles. At least she used her own product. "No, I never had a pet."

"That's really a shame." She opened the bottle, poured some lotion into her hand and rubbed it into her arms.

The scent of roses and lavender filled the air and he caught himself staring at her. "Why is it a shame?"

"A pet is its own kind of love. It is also good for balance and calms the spirit." She moved to her other arm. "If you had a pet what kind of pet would you have wanted?"

Well, at least she was speaking to him, but the conversation had no depth or emotion. He might as well tell her what he did on his summer vacation. "I don't know. I suppose you can't say I don't have a pet anymore." He lifted his head to ensure his pet remained as far away from him as possible.

"Just like the ring and the house, Nan and the pet are only on loan." She laughed and ran her hands down her neck to her chest.

"I need to go to the office tomorrow." It wasn't lost on him that her things were alive. "Should I turn off the light?"

"If you like."

Right as he went to lean over, she snaked her leg out from under the comforter to apply her lotion. Her nightgown rode all the way up to her upper thigh and he knew his wife didn't wear anything else under her pajamas.

He froze and took some time to take in the graceful curves only a woman possessed. Only last night he sampled all the goodness she displayed. Maybe she wasn't his usual type, but she was a beauty. It wasn't that he didn't want to ask her out, he simply never thought about the possibility. Though his mind was spent, his body could use a little relief. "Willow?"

She tended to her other leg. "I thought you were going to turn off the light."

"Do you like the light on or off?" His mouth watering at how her hands ran over skin, he turned on his side toward her. Maybe she said those things before because she wanted him to ask her out. Well, he gave her the whole package. He put a ring on it, literally. The woman might say it was only a contract, but it was what went unsaid that really spoke volumes.

"I can sleep either way." She stretched. Her nipples jutted out from the thin fabric of her blue nightgown.

A twinge of jealousy rang through him at her admission, but he had a surefire way he could make himself tired. In fact, he could downright guarantee he would be able to exhaust both of them. "I wasn't talking about sleeping." He reached forward and touched the lace piping on her sleeve. Maybe with the right persuasion and his spouse at his side, he wouldn't play battle of the bed anymore.

She put the lotion bottle down on the nightstand and turned to him. "Forget it. Didn't you hear what I said before?"

"Yes, earlier today you said you were surprised by my passion." He flashed her a smile topped with a bit of an eyebrow raise for effect. "I've never been told that before."

"I am choosing to file that away as a memory." She pulled the nightgown over her legs and got under the covers once more.

"We can make it the present."

"I think we need to leave the passion out of our business partnership." She adjusted her pillows. "It's better this happened or we may be having too much sex."

"I don't think there's such a thing as too much."

"Well, at least you have the memory as well." She reached over and turned out the lamp.

The room darkened, but the small amount of moonlight

allowed him to make out her form. Not one to lose a deal, he needed to travel a different path to the win. "Willow."

"Yes."

"I know I told you before, but last night was truly spectacular, actually amazing. Maybe I'm only passionate with you." He lowered his tone to ensure the sexy came through. While he wanted to remind her of how he felt how hard her climax hit her, he held back. Maybe rather than sleeping they could try for two. A real wedding souvenir.

"Randolph."

He licked his lips, priming the pump. "Yes."

"We are not having sex." Her voice cut through him.

At least she didn't say ever. He ground his teeth together, but got the next words out. "We're newlyweds." Fine, he would beg.

"Newlyweds don't have contracts specifying when they will get divorced." The bed bounced as she turned over. "This bed is so comfortable."

The woman appreciated beds. She mentioned the same thing at the hotel.

The room became silent. Instinct told him to let the sex go. He stared into the black nothing wanting to head out, but his own contract demanded he stay or take her with him. "Willow?" He never had anyone else sleep in his room before.

"Yes."

"Is it weird to sleep somewhere else like this?" The tree outside flickered a bizarre pattern on the wall, a perfect abstract background for a painting.

"No weirder than marrying you yesterday, wearing a diamond that costs more than most people's homes and living in a real mansion." She yawned, but let out a chuckle. "Who would have thought?"

Once more the bed shook with her movements.

Any other time he shared a bed with a woman it was for the sole purpose of having sex, and it was never his bed, and he never slept.

He inhaled. Willow was in here, even a dog was in here.

Dog.

"Willow?" he whispered.

She answered with a grunt.

"Is Jeb going to be all right?"

Rather than Willow, a jingle answered. The little bells made their way across the bed until the fur ball came over and sniffed him.

"Jeb is here," he informed her.

"You'll live."

Since no one could see him in the dark, he gave in and patted the animal.

The dog rewarded him with a lick on his nose.

"Oh my God." He tensed.

"Go to sleep, Randolph."

"He licked me." He tapped her and wiped his nose. "Jeb licked me."

"That's what dogs do. Why don't you pet him? It will calm you down." Again, she turned over and adjusted the blankets.

"You sure move around a lot." He thought he should tell her. "I have to go into the office tomorrow."

"If you were asleep you wouldn't notice." She huffed. "Maybe you should sleep instead of telling me twice you have to go to your office."

He turned to his back and Jeb climbed up on him. The dog did his turning in a circle extravaganza and curled up on his chest. "I can't sleep."

"Randolph?" Willow sat up.

He decided not to respond.

"Have you ever slept with anyone before?"

"Well, I guess since we're married, we can discuss our pasts." At least with someone in the bed he had a person to talk with. "You already know mine, how about you."

"I meant sleep," she growled.

"No." He sunk his fingers in the dog's fur.

"Do you have issues sleeping?" Her tone was most definitely accusatory.

"What gives you that impression?"

"You are like a little boy." For the millionth time that night the bed shimmied and shook with her various movements.

"You are not much more mature yourself." He set his jaw, but softened when she slid next to him. Maybe she changed her mind about the sleep sex.

"Go to bed, Jeb."

The dog stood, tumbled off him and returned to the foot of the bed.

"He sure obeys." Randolph waved to him.

"Better than you, I'm sure." She lay down next to him. "Give me your hand."

He held his hand out and stayed silent to find out where her actions may lead.

She took his hand in both of hers and proceeded to treat him to a massage.

"Um," he moaned. "That's nice."

"Shh." She paid attention to each of his fingers and squeezed his palm with perfect pressure.

A calm claimed him and he closed his eyes, concentrating only on how she touched him.

Without saying a word she laid his arm out and took her spot next to him.

"Willow, that was exquisite." He turned and wrapped his other arm around her. If her massage was her version of foreplay, it was fantastic. "Do you want to make love?" Though he asked, he could just as easily fall asleep.

"Go to sleep, Randolph." She pulled the blankets up over them.

"Why are you over here? I thought we were only business partners."

She grabbed his hand and massaged again. "The energy in here is all off. No wonder you can't sleep. We may be business partners, but we are married and married people shouldn't sleep at opposite sides of the bed."

Married people also made love, but he swallowed his words, choosing instead to focus on the way Willow's hair brushed his cheek. "You washed your hair." He breathed in more lavender.

"Shh." She settled down.

"One more question."

"Just one."

"May I kiss you goodnight?" He spoke into her ear. "I would kiss a business associate on the cheek. It's for the sake of good energy."

She tensed.

"I'm not making fun. I feel a lot better, please." Okay, maybe his voice carried a little whine.

"All right then."

He moved her hair aside and pressed his lips right behind her ear. "Good night." He closed his eyes and concentrated on Willow's breathing. Maybe he would have asked her out if he hadn't gotten her all screwed up in his life.

Chapter Six

THE BELL AT THE WILLOW'S WONDERS door chimed, indicating a customer. Willow finished measuring out a canister of her herbal tea blend and leaned back. None other than Peter Ward decided to grace her with his presence.

"I'll be right there." She tightened the lid down and carefully applied the label.

By the time she entered the front of the store, Nan had already staked her claim and she hid a laugh.

"You are Randolph's secretary?" Nan crossed her arms.

Peter glanced at her and then back to Nan. "Personal Assistant."

Nan narrowed her eyes. "What's the difference?"

He tilted his head. "I work directly for Randolph, I don't work for the bank."

Nan shrugged and trundled over to the tea bar.

She hadn't seen much of her husband's assistant since the day after their wedding. For almost a week she had been living in marital bliss. Well, not really, but she did start to have a routine.

Normally by the time she woke up, Randolph had already left for work. For all the people living in the mansion it was unusually quiet. To date she never saw anyone except Nan, Jeb and staff members in the morning. With the variety of maids, cooks, butler, assistants scurrying around them, she and Nan would have their breakfast and then the chauffeur would take them to her shop. Actually, she asked the chauffeur to take them a block away from her shop and they walked to the shop. Thus far, though she answered questions from Slate and Jade about her romp with Randolph, she managed to not reveal her secret. The deception ate away at her, but she had her principles.

Like an alarm clock, Randolph called twice a day, once to ensure she arrived at work and once to remind her when he would be home for dinner. Since she didn't make dinner she wasn't quite sure why he told her, but she figured it was his way of reminding of their deal.

After work, the chauffeur picked her up a block away, she cleaned up and she and Randolph had their all-important meal, and then he worked while she studied with Nan or created crafts or strolled through the grounds until it was time to sleep by midnight.

Then they hit repeat, which was why the appearance of Peter seemed a bit unusual.

She patted his shoulder. "What brings you here?"

With his eyes wide, he glanced around her shop. "Randolph would like you to come down to the office, so I came here to pick you up."

She wrinkled her nose at the break in the routine for her husband who seemed to thrive on knowing everything in advance, and without a warning call.

"He wanted to call, but got stuck in a meeting and just told me to come get you and help." As if he sensed her question, he offered her the answer.

"What will I need help with?"

Peter reached into his pocket and took out a piece of paper. "We need to see your check book, both personal and business, business licenses, rental agreement and insurance documents."

She bit the inside of her mouth, staring straight at some of her crystals and watching them catch the last bit of morning sun, trying to visualize where these items could be or if she owned them. Maybe she could buy herself some time. "While I get ready, why don't you have a cup of tea?" She motioned him toward the tea bar.

He shrugged and sat down, strumming his fingers on the counter and nodding to himself as if he were deep in thought.

"You okay?" She went over and heated the water.

He tilted his head.

Before choosing his tea, she reached out and put her hand over his. The man's energy was through the roof, he didn't want to be inside his own skin. "You seem confused." She tried to prod him in a direction to pick his blend.

He squeezed his eyes shut. "I have a lot going on."

"Okay." She chose a tea and prepared a cup of tea for both of them. Once steeped and ready, she put one of Nan's homemade crackers on the saucer and set the cup in front of him. "Try this."

He lifted the cracker, studied it and took a bite. With a tilt of his head he took a sip of the tea and nodded. "Different." He gave the tea another taste, followed by the cracker. "What's in it?"

"It's my Clari-tea." She grinned at the name.

He raised his eyebrows at her.

"It has peppermint, spearmint, ginkgo, rosemary and gotu kola, it should help you bring things into focus, improve mental function and circulation." She took a sip as well, praying her brew would help her remember where she stashed the documents Randolph requested.

"I need this." He gulped it down. "Now if I could just get some direction."

She smiled. The man spoke her language. "How about we do a reading?"

"Of what? I don't think I have any time to read books." He polished off the cracker and glanced at his watch. "We should get going."

"You need direction, sometimes the cards can provide it." She reached over to Nan's deck of tarot cards and held up the purple velvet pouch.

"Like fortune telling?" He wrinkled his nose.

"The tarot only provides insight, but your future is up to you." Nan shimmied by and took Peter's dishes. "Willow is very skilled. She has been studying the tarot since she was young."

"We can do a simple reading." She took the cards out of the pouch and offered them to him. "Give them a shuffle."

"I suppose it couldn't hurt." He took the cards and shuffled them.

She took the cards back and placed the deck in front of them. "Now cut the cards."

He did as she requested and she divided the cards into three piles.

"We will do a simple past, present and future reading." She motioned to the cards, turning over the first card on the first pile.

Peter leaned over and studied the image of a man kneeling over a pool of water with a star in the sky. "The star?"

"Yes, but reversed." She concentrated, focusing on the picture she had seen too many times to count.

"Is that bad?" Concern took over his voice.

"Nothing is bad or good, it's merely a guide." Everyone's first time scared them. Hell, sometimes it still scared her. She shook her head. "The star is opportunity, renewal."

He smiled.

"However, when it is reversed it represents unfulfilled dreams." Every bit of his energy spoke of some sort of disappointment. "Sometimes you need to go after your dreams even if they are in the past."

"Yeah." He shifted in his seat.

She appreciated the way he didn't discount her, but seemed to absorb the words and flipped over the card from the middle pile. "The four of swords."

"That's a dead guy." Peter's color left his face at the picture of the man lying on the coffin, three swords above him one on him.

"No." She held her hand up. "He is resting. This is the card of mediation and reflection. Have you gone through a lot of arguments?"

"I quit med school and I'm a personal assistant to a man younger than me." He touched the card. "I haven't heard from my girlfriend in three days."

He began to fill in for himself. Her job was to guide him. "Maybe you need to ask yourself why you made certain decisions." Without wanting to pry she turned over the top card on the top pile. "Oh, that's interesting."

"The tower is my future?" He lifted the card depicting a tower with lightening striking it and two people falling. "Well, at least it's not like I chose the death card."

"The death card only means transition, an end." She chuckled. Terror struck every newbie at the death card.

"Then why is this interesting?" He returned the card to the pile.

"It represents extreme, unexpected change." She softened her voice.

"Bad change?"

Nan stepped over.

Willow took a breath. No matter what the cards said, she couldn't lie. "Many think it means a catastrophic change." Some felt the card was a bad omen.

"Catastrophe?" He jumped out of the chair and smoothed his suit jacket down. "My future contains a catastrophe?"

"The future is yours to change." She hurried around the bar and took him by the shoulders. His trembling vibrated through her palms. "I think it is a sign to change your outlook or your path?"

He mimicked her actions and grabbed her shoulders. "Do you think so?"

Before she answered, the bell on the door rang out.

"I saw a familiar car outside your store." Jade rushed inside the shop, stopped in the doorway and pointed at them.

As if they were caught in the middle of committing a crime, they jumped away from each other.

"Jade." She breathed her friend's name.

Instead of one of her artistic costumes, Jade wore a normal pair of black pants and a matching shirt. She sauntered over and put her arm around her. "I want to know who you are with."

Peter opened his mouth.

Unsure if he remembered to keep her nuptials under wraps, she stared at Peter trying to send him any psychic message. She held her left hand up to her face showing him her empty ring finger. Every day on their way to work she took her ring off, replacing it on the way back to the mansion.

Peter gave her a slight nod. "It's good to see you again."

"Something is strange." Jade glared at them. "I will get to the bottom of it."

Willow gave her a huge smile. "No art today?"

"Only business, girl." Jade crossed her arms. "We definitely need a girls' night. Yes, I think that is exactly what is in our future."

"I better go collect those items for my meeting with Randolph." A strange vibe went through her at the thought of having to go to her husband's office. Thus far she hadn't gone anywhere as his wife, they only stayed at the mansion.

"Randolph's assistant is picking you up to go to Randolph?"

Jade made a tsking sound. "Yes a girls' night is definitely in order."

"I'll be right back." She walked to the storeroom trying to remember Randolph's list.

"Once the truth is revealed, your friends will not only know why you married Randolph, but they will be upset with you for hiding it." Nan shook her head.

"Nan." She went to an old dresser they found on a curb. They brought it here, repurposed it, painting it with stars and moons and planets, and used it to hold their paperwork. She opened the top drawer to find nothing but labels and recipes. At least they were printed on paper.

"You shouldn't have done anything you needed to hide in the first place."

"We all hide things." She moved to the second drawer. The file folder inside gave her some hope. She peeked inside to find her astrological chart. Thrilled to locate anything in the form of a document, she took it. The rest of the drawer only held wrapping materials, she supposed that was sort of paper. "You told me sometimes it's necessary to hide what people don't understand."

"The older I get the more I find it doesn't work." Nan came over and handed her a frame off the wall.

"Our business license and our first dollar." She ran her fingers over the glass. Their first dollar came from Slate when he bought Jade a candle because she said it smelled like romance.

With only one last place any documents could hide, she bent down and opened the bottom drawer. Once more she found paper but in the form of books. "We don't keep records of anything."

"We have all we need." Nan reached in the drawer and pulled out a book on candle making. "Records mean nothing, what matters is in the heart."

Willow's inner voice told her Randolph wouldn't exactly agree. "I'll be back in a little bit." She headed toward the front of the shop.

"Take your time, it's about time you see your husband in his natural habitat."

She avoided telling Nan to keep her voice down about her spouse, grabbed her bag and shoved her few finds in her purse.

"Are you ready?" Peter asked.

"Did Jade leave?"

"She said she had to run, but would call." He motioned forward. "We better get going. Randolph hates anyone being late."

"Does he hate records and documents?" She clutched her bag to her side.

"He's a businessman, and he loves documents, backup and history." He went to the door.

"I'll be right there." As she grabbed a canister of tea for Randolph, she glanced over at the bar with the tarot cards. What she lacked in documentation she gained in intuition and insight. Too bad she couldn't distract Peter with more readings. She quickly went to the bar, shuffled the cards and concentrated on Randolph as she drew the first card off the deck.

"The Magician." The familiar man holding up his wand with the infinity symbol above his head represented the ability to speak about ideas, being charming and clever. Of course on the other end it told a tale of a con man or a trickster. Something told her that her husband hid something. The cards never lied. Neither did her gut instincts.

* * * *

Van Ayers First Capital Trust. The large gilded letters in the lobby spelled out the name of her husband's bank, but instead of a bank with ATM machines and tellers, she was led into a business building in a skyscraper in Century City. Peter quickly nodded to the receptionist behind a huge gleaming oak desk and led her into the office.

Wood paneling, huge pieces of artwork depicting different historical banks lined the walls. Heavy, dark furniture defined the separate workstations. The office was absolutely quiet except for the subtle clicking of computer keyboards and the employees blended into the stoic background with their neutral business suits. The entire office dripped with authority. Everyone was either here to make money, get money, or keep from losing the precious commodity.

She glanced down at her outfit, a bright orange short hand-dyed halter dress with some jewel embellishments she and Nan added after they found the little frock and a matching sweater at a thrift store.

As she made her way through the office, another noise joined the soft typing, that of hushed tones and whispers. She didn't need to read minds to already know she was the topic of conversation.

Peter opened an imposing dark wood door and motioned for her to go ahead.

She tiptoed inside to find Randolph behind a massive mahogany desk. He didn't as much look up from his computer when she entered.

Peter tapped the top of an oversized hunter green leather chair and joined another older woman at a long table with piles and piles of neatly stacked papers. Yes, the man loved his documentation.

With a smile to no one, she sat. Although her husband was only across the desk from her, he seemed miles away.

Randolph continued to clink away on his computer without glancing her way.

She waited, picked a string off her dress, moved her hair out of her face, swung her leg and tapped her foot.

No one acknowledged her. She took in his office. The shelves of books, the art on the walls, Randolph's framed degrees from college, had all the makings of perfectly planned success.

Once she finished studying the office, she turned her attention back to Randolph. Still, he didn't even bother peeking over at her, give her a friendly wave, or a tilt of the head, nothing. His desk was as neat as everything else about him, no life, no personality, simply the required computer, a clock, a blotter, some pens and stacks and stacks of file folders. He continued to stare at his monitor, his face devoid of any emotion, but the man still had the looks of a gorgeous teen idol, only one who grew up and had to get a real job. Her thought wandered to the tarot card again. What did he hide that he couldn't even take a glance at her?

Lost in watching him, she put her elbow on the arm of the chair and rested her head in her hand.

"I finished the documents for the Hartfords." At last Randolph spoke.

As if he issued a command, Peter and Mrs. No Name stood.

"Get the signatures, and I want no further interruptions while

I meet with my wife." He pushed his chair back from the computer.

With military precision they both walked out of the office, the woman taking a long look at her before leaving.

Only when the door clicked closed did Randolph turn to her. "You really shouldn't slouch like that."

"Hello, how are you? No, I don't mind waiting, thank you." She forced herself to remain in her position.

"As an executive's wife you are going to have to get used to waiting sometimes." He rocked his chair back.

"Did you call me here to teach me that lesson?" Her back ached from her funky angle, but she refused to move.

"No. I called you here to review a few of your responsibilities, starting with some questions on your business."

At the mention of her store, she sat up, her back popping in relief. "What is it?"

"First and foremost," he opened his drawer, pulled out an envelope and pushed it across the desk toward her, "get your rent caught up. Make sure Jade gives you a receipt. I don't like to make it a habit of paying in cash, but until we get your accounts and such straightened out, its necessary since this is so time sensitive."

"Thank you." The man remembered everything. She reached across the desk.

Before she took the envelope he put his hand over hers. "Willow."

"Yes?" She said thank you, was there something else?

"Where's your ring?" He glared down at her empty finger.

"Oh." She slid her hand away from his. "I put it in my bag while I'm at work."

"Our contract clearly states that you are to wear the ring." He strummed his fingers on the desk. "I don't think you should keep something that expensive tumbling around in your purse."

"I didn't leave it tumbling." Even with the room at the ideal temperature, she broke out into a sweat and jammed her hand in her bag in search of the ring. "People from the gallery visit my shop every day."

"And you still have a contract with me. Contracts are binding agreements." He grunted. "The ring needs to be on your person at all times, especially in situations like this where you are at my office, it needs to be on your finger."

"Okay." Her heart sped up and she took a long breath as she continued to search her bag and tried to figure out what he meant by 'on her person.'

"May I ask you to put it on now?" He leaned forward.

"Yes." Her fingers made their way through her yarn, past her wallet, around the papers and frame she brought for him, and hit the leather bottom of the bag where she traced the edges. No ring. An unfamiliar weight settled on her chest. She jumped out the chair, got down on her hands and knees, and dumped the bag on the floor.

"Willow!" In an instant Randolph came around his desk and joined her.

Her stuff scattered over the Persian rug and she clawed through them. "Oh my God!" She tossed Randolph's family heirloom into a bag like a pack of gum for her own strange pride, never mind how much the gem was worth or what it meant.

"Did you lose my ring?" He sifted through her belongings, lifting her ball of yarn.

A flash of yellow caught her eye. "The ring!"

"Stop!" He held up the mess.

She lunged for the yarn, landing with her face basically in his crotch and froze. Actually, she hadn't noticed the slight pinstripe on his navy suit before.

"Willow." His voice tensed with restraint.

She turned away from the pinstripes up to his face and the yarn with the ring dangling from it. "There's the ring."

He plucked the bauble off the yarn and held it out to her. "If you don't mind."

She pushed herself up, returned the jewelry to her finger and glanced down at the disaster. Everything about Randolph seemed orderly and pristine while she came off as a one woman hurricane. "Let me clean up this mess."

Without a word he helped her pile the things back in the bag, lifting the frame.

"I found my business license." She sort of wanted him to say something.

He reached up, put it on his desk and pointed at the file

folder. "May I?"

She nodded, thankful he spoke.

He opened it and with two fingers held up her chart. "Is this your rental agreement, insurance papers or checkbooks?"

The man had amazing memory. "That is my astrological chart. We can do yours if you like."

"I'm good, thank you for the offer." He handed it back to her.

Along with his memory, he also had impeccable manners.

They returned the rest of items to her bag and he held out the little silver canister of her tea. "Calama-tea?"

"I brought that for you." She tried to smile. "It's for stress. I think I'll make some for me and my customers when I get back to work."

He stood and helped her up.

They reclaimed their opposing sides of the desk.

The silence stretched out, the only noise the tapping of his fingers on the tea canister. At last he nodded. "You serve tea at your store?"

"Yes." Though she wanted to slump down again she sat up straight. "We also serve little nutritional crackers and herbal remedies.

He held up the tea. "Where do you make this?"

"Nan and I make it in the small kitchen at the store." She snuck her hand in her purse. "Sometimes she makes candy, in fact, I may have some."

"You serve people food in your store?" He put the jar down.

"Am I on trial?"

"I'm asking a question."

Unsure of the right answer, she nodded. "Just what I told you."

"Do you have a license to be serving food out of your store?" His question came out more as an accusation. "Do you have the proper permits?"

"It's just some tea and baked goods." They needed permits and licenses for a few little snacks?

"You know what that is legally called?" He threw his next question out before she fully understood the one before.

She ground her teeth together.

"That, my dear, is called a restaurant, and if you are caught serving food without the proper licenses you will have some huge issues." He pointed at her. His finger may as well have been a gavel hitting her in the head and giving her a guilty verdict.

Her mouth opened, but no words would form. Restaurant?

"Until we figure this out, no more food service and you are making everything at home." He doled out his ruling. "How did you even get insurance?"

She folded her hands in her lap. "Nan always said we had nothing to lose."

He blinked and stared at her as if she spoke a foreign language. "Did you ever think you might? Did you ever think if something happened you needed to not only protect yourself and Nan, but the person making the claim? What if they were really hurt?"

With no words, she covered her mouth with her hand. She never gave the insurance a second thought, thinking it was there to protect her and Nan, she never realized it protected others.

"I will take care of this. Just don't do anything or kill anyone until I have a chance to decide the best course of action." He hardened his jaw.

Yes, she married him, and yes, she agreed for help, but she didn't agree for him to take over her life or treat her like a toddler. "I can handle my business, thank you."

"Not when what you do can negatively impact me." He stared right at her. "Read your contract."

Her mouth dried out and she licked her lips. "While you are fixing my business, what am I doing?"

"I do have something for you." Once more he opened his desk drawer.

Not wanting any more gifts or help, she pushed her back into the chair.

He revealed a rich brown book with a little brown ribbon to be used as a bookmark, at least his offering held potential. "Here you are."

She took the book. "A calendar?"

"You are in charge of our calendar as a couple."

"What do you mean?" She flipped through the pages and noticed some entries already written inside.

"Part of why my father felt I needed to get married is I need to take over some of the social duties of the bank. My wife handles those arrangements." He picked up one of his pens and twirled it between his fingers. "My secretary will update you on any events that need to be arranged. You will need to become familiar with the restaurants and venues."

"I'm not doing this." She shut the book.

"I beg to differ." For the third time he opened the drawer. He took out some stapled sheets. "According to our contract you will perform all duties of a wife including managing our social calendar and attending all events with yours truly at your side."

"I signed away my social life?" She grabbed the document from him.

"Fourth paragraph down."

She scanned the page, finding the said paragraph. "I thought we were only supposed to get married and sleep together." At her own words, she threw the contract on his desk.

"You put the kibosh on that." A wide know-it-all smile took over his face. "Do you think for all that I'm offering on my end that would be the only things required? Good business is when both parties do well. It can't be all one sided. I would have thought you would want balance."

The man knew how to use her words against her. "For someone who seems to hate his father's plan, you are doing the same thing."

"You may want to look ahead to the next couple of weeks. We have several dinners." His expression remained the same, no doubt the exact one he used when he won a deal.

"What else is in the contract?" The meeting was over for her at least and she stood.

"I thought you read it, but I have an extra copy if you need to review the terms of our agreement."

"I'm fine. I just need to get back to my store." She backed up. Where did her life go? He couldn't take over everything, but he did, right down to her store and her Saturday nights.

"I will take you back. Maybe we can grab some lunch." He seemed to rise from his chair like an otherworldly demon.

Again she opened the book and glanced down at the day. With a breath, she turned it toward him. "Looks like I'm free today."

"Nothing is ever free." He leaned on the desk.

Her breath quickened, she needed some fresh air and turned. "I am learning that."

"Willow." His voice teased her.

"I think I'll pass on lunch." She peeked over her shoulder. "I need to get back to work."

"Don't forget this." He held the envelope with the money out to her. "I'll see you tonight."

The envelope. All she needed to do was walk away, not touch it, pack up her, Nan and Jeb and bolt. As she told him, she had nothing to lose.

She balled her hand in a fist. Of course, if she left she would welch on a contract, her vows, and Jade. The way things were going, she and Nan would never have a home, and they would be on the streets...again. "How could I forget?" She took the money and left.

Chapter Seven

RANDOLPH PRACTICALLY SPRINTED down the hall to his suite with the papers to get Willow her insurance, and a bottle of wine. Maybe he was a bit hard on her, and he needed to make it up. He already made reservations at one of his favorite restaurants. Actually, his secretary made them, and soon Willow would be doing the same.

He opened the door to an empty room, not the kind of empty where someone had been there before him, but a cold empty, devoid of life, or the energy Willow mentioned.

He glanced at his watch and slid his phone out of his pocket and dialed his missing wife. After the fourth ring he hung up, and with his presents still in hand, went to Nan's suite.

Music permeated from inside her room, New Age music, the kind he would hear in a spa with wind chimes and such. Willow must have joined her. He knocked softly on the door.

Right before he went to knock again, Nan opened the door.

"Good evening." He grinned at his sort of mother-in-law dressed in a bright red muumuu with palm trees and little Jeb who trotted up to him. Before the puffball scuffed his shoes, he bent down and scooped him up, wincing when Jeb licked him.

"Same to you." She backed up and motioned for him to join her.

The scent of spicy incense hit him and he entered to find Nan had done a little decorating in the room, complete with some candles, flowers, stones and pieces of fabric draped over the lights to give the room an ethereal dark quality. Willow only put her lotion in the nightstand drawer. "How are you?" In search of his wife, he tried to see into the closet and bath area.

"Is that what you wanted to know?"

"I'm just looking for Willow." He put Jeb down, crossed his arms and waited for her to produce his spouse.

She moved in front of him, blocking his view. "She's not here."

"Didn't she come home with you?" The muscles in his neck tensed.

Nan walked over to her armoire. "No, was it my turn to babysit her?"

"We're supposed to be together in the evenings."

"Did you have a work event tonight?" She returned and held a small brown paper bag out to him.

"No, not tonight." A glance inside the bag revealed little lumpy cubes of something.

She shook the bag. "Eat one."

"We haven't had dinner yet." Still, he reached in took a piece and popped it in his mouth.

Apricot and vanilla filled his mouth, creating a sweet, chewy treat. Really chewy, extremely chewy, he prayed he didn't crack a crown chewy.

Nan gave him a one-sided smile. "Good?"

The confection was worse than a caramel but he managed a nod.

"I make that candy out of dried apricots. Apricots stones are thought by some to be medicinal, but they also contain high levels of cyanide. It used to be thought apricots were an aphrodisiac, but today dried apricots are used mostly to relieve constipation." She narrowed her eyes.

He continued to chew with his mouth closed. At the moment he could only pray she didn't put any of the pits in the candy.

"It is my understanding that she only has to be with you for sleeping unless you have an engagement." She stepped toward him and took his chin in her hand. "Everyone at one time or another needs some time alone to clean out their system."

At last the candy softened, he finished chewing, swallowed and opened his mouth.

"Do you know what I called that candy when Willow was little?" She tightened her grip on him.

He waited, eager to hear a story about when his wife was little. His preliminary searches found nothing after about the age of ten and her mother passing away.

She pulled him down. "I called it 'Be quiet and think.'" She laughed and put the bag in his hand. "Give her some when you run out to find her."

"Who said I was going to run after her?" He didn't need to retrieve her, she would return, her contract specified it. It might be nice to have an evening to decompress alone, though his wife should have informed him of her whereabouts.

She patted his shoulder. "Then give her some when you meet her in bed later."

"I must get going. There's some work I need to attend to." He smiled, but crumpled the bag in his fist.

She waved. "I'm going to go cook with Chef."

"Have a good night." He turned on his heel and left, glancing in the direction of their wing and then toward the stairs. In an attempt to answering questions about Willow's absence to his parents, or sitting alone in his suite, he decided to heed Nan's advice and take some time alone to clean out his system.

He tossed the candy on a side table and raced out of the house, thankful to get his car before one of the staff parked it in the garage and took off.

He continued his drive past the upscale boutiques and bistros. Once the flashing lights of the vintage clubs like the Whiskey A Go Go reflected in his windshield, the vibe of the entire street changed, Hollywood happened. At the edge, between the wealth and the real, stood the gallery.

He made his last couple of turns and pulled into the alley behind the gallery, coasting slowly past Willow's store which appeared without any flicker of light or life inside. Technically she wasn't gone, didn't breach her contract, but he shuddered all the same. He parked outside her shop and walked to the gallery, letting himself inside and allowing the fumes of paint, clay and canvas to overtake him.

"Have you come looking for a job?" Slate came over and shook his hand. "Come to the back, I have a surprise for you."

"Why do you ask that?" Randolph followed, glancing at the blank walls of the gallery, Slate must be preparing for his next show. His mind wandered to Willow. Where the hell did she go? She could have called, texted, left a note, told Nan where she went, anything. Her actions were deliberate.

"The last I saw of you, you were with Willow after you were left at the altar and about to lose all your money."

He opened his mouth to tell Slate he had it all taken care of. At least he thought he did, but his wife was missing and he didn't know her all that well, couldn't even find anything about her online. The woman could have disappeared with a ring worth seven figures and while he was out searching for her, she was picking up Nan and her fur ball and hightailing it out of LA.

"Randolph?" Slate waved his hand in front of him.

Ring. His wedding ring. Damn! He shoved his hand in his pocket, wanting to dig his nails through the fabric at abiding by his wife's wishes to keep his marriage secret when he didn't know her whereabouts. If she decided to disappear, he swore he would use every last dollar at the bank to find her and watch her spend her life making his universe in balance again. "You know, everything in life can be negotiated. Life is nothing but a big business deal."

"Exactly the words I would expect to come from the banker of Beverly Hills."

Worse than nails on a chalkboard or even finding a hair in his food, Randolph shuddered at the all too familiar voice coming from the gallery storeroom. Ignoring the intrusion, he turned to Slate.

"Guess what, Argyle Brink is here and he wants in on the co-op idea." Slate pushed him toward the storeroom.

Sick curiosity and the need for distraction alone made him walk over the threshold.

"Your timing is perfect." With the flourish of a gaudy Las Vegas performer, Argyle bowed, taking much longer than necessary to straighten up. Boasting a large smile, he motioned to some sort of strange playhouse created out of crisscrossing pieces of wood.

"He made this for you." Slate rubbed his hands together. "He is Jade's inspiration and teacher."

Randolph crossed his arms. Years of being around money mongers told him that Jade paid for every lesson. However, unlike Jade who lived the lifestyle only part time, Argyle was a living, breathing art exhibit twenty-four hours a day and had gained some notoriety on a couple reality shows. Randolph had met him several times, and even with his fondness for art, he couldn't appreciate Argyle's exhibits. With dark hair and a tall frame, Argyle had the looks and the attitude of an actor, not an artist.

"Everything worthwhile starts as a mess." Argyle's voice boomed through the space, and he walked around the sticks. "Only when people come together for the greater good, for a unified cause, can an idea be born."

With his mouth open he watched Argyle reach into a tall black cylinder and pull out panels as if he were delivering a baby.

"Every entity must offer something. Creativity." Argyle attached a panel with paints and brushes and other art supplies onto the wood.

Slate elbowed him. "Wait for it."

"Knowledge." The man fit a panel with a three-dimensional brain on the structure.

Randolph leaned back on his heels as the over-the top artist continued building.

"Collaboration." A panel with a bunch of images of people fit in the mix. "And lastly, but most important, funding."

Slate pointed.

Argyle placed a roof tiled with golden coins on top. "When all these facets come together you have a gem." He reached into his pocket and pulled out an oversized diamond shaped stone and fit it into the panel with all the people and opened the makeshift door. A golden light glowed from within. "You have an artistic co-op."

Slate went into a round of applause. "We're going to be exhibiting some of Argyle's pieces including this prosperity structure. He'll also build more during his show."

"Perhaps he needs to get a factory to start making pieces for him." Randolph swallowed down his own laugh. "The real money is selling to the masses."

"No one will ever be able to say you're not always looking out for the bottom line." Argyle joined them.

"What do you think of the co-op idea?" Slate asked.

Randolph looked between the men and then down to his phone. Still nothing from his 'wife.' "Why don't you explain it to me?"

"I am envisioning a place where artists come together, share expenses, ideas, marketing, and pool their knowledge." Argyle continued to use his performance persona.

"There are government grants for such entities. What do you need me for?" Randolph asked the obvious.

"Never trust people who simply give money away." Argyle narrowed his eyes and lowered his voice. "We want our project to be a business, not a charity."

"We really want to meet with you about our financial options," Slate interjected.

"What collateral do you bring to the table?" He went into business mode, the same stance he should have taken with his spouse. At 12:01 he would act.

"I am my own collateral. I know everyone, directors, producers, if they are in the industry they want Argyle."

In truth, Randolph barely paid attention as the men spoke. "I need some time to think about it."

Argyle lifted his chin, but Slate shook his head. "We wouldn't want a finance man who made snap decisions."

"In my business you need to make sure we get a return on investment." He walked away from the other two men and paced around the storage room, stopping in front of what he could consider a bunch of junk including some metal plaques, a pile of some handcrafted nightmare and some large letters off of a sign. Maybe he needed to put Willow's picture on a billboard. "What is this?"

"This is the newest trend." Argyle came up behind him. "Talk about return on investment."

"Vintage architectural reclamations." Slate joined and them patted the letter Z. "It's all the rage."

"It looks like garbage." He tilted his head. "Those rags are part of an architectural restoration?"

"Those rags, my friend, are blankets created by your one night stand." Slate lifted one of the green monstrosities. "Jade thought we could sell them here."

"Willow knitted those?" He longed to tell Slate she didn't need the pittance those would bring in anymore. Inside his pocket he twirled his wedding ring around his finger and ground his teeth together as his mind wandered again to the whereabouts of his wife. He let her walk away from the office when she was obviously upset. She could be doing more than stealing, she could be breaking other parts of the contract, like the fidelity clause. Heat overtook him and he half expected steam to come out of his ears. Maybe she went on a shopping spree with the money he handed her in that envelope. He should have used marked bills.

"Crochet." Slate corrected. "We have one on our bed."

"You spent the night with the wondrous Willow?" Argyle chuckled. "I would have never seen that one."

"By the way, have you heard from Willow?" He blew out his breath slowly, and ignored Argyle, instead choosing to look around and appear nonchalant.

Slate's laughter joined Argyle's. "No wonder you're not all sad about your money, I always had a feeling she would be amazing, take someone to the stars. She must have given you some birthday present."

He stared off into nothing and vowed not to beat Slate for mentioning his wife in such a manner or Argyle for being Argyle. When they stood at that chapel in Vegas, his only concern was to get everything done by the book in the time required. The last few days had been a whirlwind and his work was all encompassing. It took until today for him to even think about what he needed to do for Willow. However, there was something indefinable, about arriving home and finding her and the dog, if one wanted to call it a dog, waiting for him. It was nice to have someone to make a little small talk with before she drifted off to sleep curled up next to him, someone who asked him how his day was without wanting to know about the accounts he worked on. "She made my day."

"Apparently," Argyle muttered.

Slate's cellphone went off and he lifted his phone. "Hey listen guys, Jade wants me home and since this meeting wasn't planned, I better go make her happy."

He wanted to ask Slate if he knew if his wife paid the rent, preferably he wanted his friend to tell him where she was and answer with something other than a sex comment. "Hey..." He tried to be casual and with his hand still in his pocket, leaned back on his heels. "...speaking of Willow, have you seen her tonight?"

Both Slate and Argyle shook their heads.

If he asked again, he would risk sounding like a psychopath.

Though he longed to keep asking, he simply held up his hand. "Well, I'll walk you out and get going."

He and Argyle followed Slate as he walked around the gallery setting locks and alarms. "You never did tell me what you thought about that phantom artist I showed you with the murals."

"The mural man." Argyle clicked his tongue. "He's an interesting man."

"I think it's probably a big publicity stunt by a corporation and a lot of garbage like you showed me in your storeroom." He took a breath and followed the other men out the front. "Let me do some more research on your idea. I need to think about it. We'll set up a meeting soon."

"Sounds good." Slate saluted him. "Later."

Argyle bowed.

He watched the men leave and took a walk down the block and stopped in front of Willow's store. "Willow's Wonders." He read the sign in the window.

Again, every possibility ran through his mind as to where she went. What did he know? He didn't know her. Whenever he asked about her past, she never answered. He couldn't find anything on the Internet about her and he had sources. He slid his phone out of his pocket and dialed the house.

"The Van Ayers residence." Dimitri answered.

"This is Randolph, but don't tell anyone I'm calling. I need you to answer the following questions with a yes or no. Do you understand?" He needed to collect some data.

"Yes." Dimitri's punctuated tone at least told Randolph he attempted to comply.

"Is my wife home yet?" He paced back and forth in front of the store.

"No, sir."

"Don't call me sir." He shut his eyes with his next question. "Is Nanette in the house?"

"No."

He stopped his pacing. Everything he suspected always came true. "Do you know where she is?"

"Yes." Dimitri answered without a pause.

"Where is she?" He squeezed the phone.

Dimitri didn't speak.

He kicked the sidewalk. "You can say more than yes or no. Tell me now."

"She's out on the grounds with the animal."

"Can you see her?"

"Yes."

He breathed. "Call me if either Nanette leaves or my wife comes home, please."

"Yes, sir."

He hung up and walked down to the corner and returned to the back alley, a place much better suited for parking his car, not proposals. While the back passage was familiar and safe, the image of Willow walking through here after dark chilled him. Yet the night he proposed, she showed no fear where most women wouldn't have dared go off alone.

Once again he counted off the possibilities of where she could have gone. With no car, Nan at home and the evening darkening the world, he tensed, adding another entry to his list of horrors. What if she were hurt?

At the back door of her store, he looked up. Yes, the alley was only good for parking his car and maybe one other thing. Maybe he needed to take a lesson from Argyle and create some art. He stepped back, taking in the building, plain beige worn stucco, a perfect blank canvas. For the first time in his life he had nowhere to go.

* * * *

The stars in the sky appeared, little light bulbs turning on one by one, and Randolph stared up in an effort to recreate what he saw. The next time Willow walked down the alley in the daylight he wanted her to feel like the stars were sparkling for her and her alone.

A long time ago, too many years to count, he learned to paint fast, quick brush strokes and splashes of color, realism was not his style. While collecting art was a worthwhile pursuit for a Van Ayers, creating art was most definitely not on his list of goals.

While most children had their art hung on refrigerators, he hid his creations on papers tucked away in hidden spots.

The painting, the risk, the creating all gave him a high unlike any other and his works became bigger, and even though he didn't seek it or claim it, he enjoyed the notoriety his art received.

However, for the first time, he painted for someone. A person who, if she showed before midnight, gave him back his future. For her, he created a star-scape complete with her astrological sign, a couple of mystical planets and a comet for good measure.

He finished putting the final touch on the last star.

"I knew you were hiding something."

At his wayward wife's voice, he turned. For years he hadn't been caught.

"I never would have guessed you were the one making art for nothing but the thrill of making art." Her gauze dress fluttered in the wind and she seemed to float toward him. She looked up at her building. "It's beautiful. Why do you hide?"

He tossed the last of his supplies into his bag. "Where have you been?"

"Walking." She held out her hand, his ring catching the moonlight. "I wish I could have watched you."

With no resistance he took her hand, pulled her closer. "Who were you with?"

She shook her head. "Just my two feet and ten toes."

"Why didn't you call?" The anxiety from her absence and the adrenaline from his painting waned, leaving him exhausted.

"I needed to think."

"Tell me." At her soft demeanor he intertwined their fingers.

She shrugged and continued to gaze up at his creation. "I just had to think."

"I was worried about you." He put his other hand on her hip.

"I would have made it home by midnight." She ran her finger down his tie.

"How?" He focused on his questions rather than the way his body reacted to her. Somehow he needed to get inside her head. They were miles and miles away from Bel Air.

"I would have gotten there."

"You can't walk around at night by yourself, it's not safe." He leaned down to try to catch her gaze.

"I've always taken care of myself." She continued to study his tie.

He hooked his fingers under her chin and tilted her face up to his. "But I'm here now." "Nothing is going to happen."

"How do you know?" Part of him wished he could have the faith she possessed.

She didn't answer.

"Is that why you didn't get insurance?"

She took a step back and shook her head. "It was an error, but it's my life and my business."

"You can't walk through Hollywood at night thinking nothing will happen, you can't not have insurance praying no one slips and falls in your store, you still need permits no matter how badly you don't want the inspectors there." He needed to make her understand.

"Why did you have to break the spell? I don't know what I expected. Can't you be the artist?" She went to her door and opened it without using a key and walked inside.

"You didn't lock the door!" He ran after her. "This whole time your store was completely open!"

She stopped short and spun toward him. At the movement, the chimes throughout the space clinked out their supposedly soothing sounds. "It's my store."

Before colliding with her, he caught her by the shoulders. "Then act like you care about it."

With a huff, she pushed him aside and walked toward the front of her store.

He dragged his supplies inside, shut and locked the back door and sprinted to join her. Exactly like any other deal, once his opponent got riled he would win. "Willow!"

Rather than yelling, she held her palm up, closed her eyes and took a breath. Once she opened her eyes she turned, picked up a candle and with slow steps headed toward the stairs.

"Where are you going? We need to go home." He dashed ahead of her, blocking her way.

"We only need to be together by midnight." She swept her hand around the room. "Well, here we are, and if you want to keep to the contract, here you will remain. You can watch the paint dry."

He refused to allow her to dismiss him like one of their house staff and stared right at her as he put his arm across the passageway, blocking her way.

Her eyes widened and she pressed her lips together. He stood up straighter, tightening his grip on the wood trim.

The color in her perfectly pink lips and her surreal blue eyes stood out against her pale complexion, but she didn't move. In fact, she remained absolutely still.

He ground his teeth together. "I said we can't stay here."

"Why not?" she whispered. "If we couldn't stay in a different place, we would have been in breach of our contract the very first night."

Something had to make her react, break her calm and centered façade. "If you want to go to a hotel, I am more than happy to accommodate." He cleared his throat. "We can't stay here. If the place burns down, we don't have any insurance if we get hurt."

"How is this possible?" She threw the candle down.

At last she cracked and he fought a smile. "How is what possible?"

She hit her fist into her leg. "How is it possible that a man who is as passionate, creative and gorgeous as you, be you!" The second the words left her mouth she turned away.

"I suppose the same way a woman as utterly breathtaking and ethereal as you is you." He closed the distance between them and took her shoulders. "I know what my problem is."

Her muscles tensed against his hold, but she didn't back away. Instead, she glanced at him. "What?"

"I spend the better part of my existence thinking about how bad I want you." He inched their faces close together, slid the strap of her dress down and kissed her on the junction between her neck and shoulder. "The whole time I painted I was thinking about you."

She gasped.

No way would he let up. While his tongue trailed over her skin, lapping up her sweet taste, he pulled the other strap down.

Her breath quickened and she braced herself on the wall.

He nipped at her collarbone and down over her shoulder. With both hands, he kneaded her breasts, her already hard nipples scraping against his palms.

"Damn it!" She twisted her hand in his hair.

He reached behind her and pulled down the zipper to her

dress. With no straps to support the garment, it pooled at her feet between them. The site of his wife's nude body caused his erection to throb. "Something wrong?" In an attempt to show her how everything would go down, he unknotted his tie.

She jutted her jaw out, took hold of his shirt and pulled. The buttons popping off starting from the center and working their way up to his collar and down to his belt. "Is something wrong with you?" She snuck her fingers inside his shirt, scratching her nails across his chest.

"Nothing we can't fix." He pushed her hand down to the front of his pants.

She stared into his eyes and gave him quite a squeeze. "I thought you didn't want to stay here." Keeping her hold she slid her hand down his erection.

Turnabout was fair play. He cupped his hand between her legs. "Yeah, well I thought you said we weren't having sex."

"Who says we're having sex?" She betrayed her own words by bucking her hips.

With no resistance, he slid a finger inside her. "You tell me." He added a second.

"Damn it." She closed her eyes and bit her lip.

The sight of her writhing beneath his touch was all he could stand. "Tell me you love the way I touch you." He continued to dole out his pleasure and using only one hand practically tore himself out of the rest of his clothes.

"Randolph." Once free of his pants, she wrapped her hand around him and returned the favor.

"Tell me." He put his arm around her waist and sped up, wanting to bring her close.

Her body shook. "Oh, God."

"Tell me you want me inside you." He prodded her some more.

She held her breath. Any second he could make her come.

In an abrupt move, he stopped.

"Ah!" Her knees went weak and she held on to him. "Now, Randolph."

At her plea, he held her to him, laid her down on the floor and entered her. Warm and wet, she encompassed him, a metaphor for every second they had been together.

She sucked in her breath, and let out a little whimper.

Though he wanted to continue the torture, tease her to show her what he could do to her, he couldn't resist and instead drove into her. Hard thrusts shooting needed pleasure though him.

An active lover, she kept up with him, her hips meeting his with every stroke, their bodies colliding together. "Like that."

"All week I couldn't stop thinking about you." He hooked his arm around one of her legs, pulling it up and back, giving into his own primal urge to be deep inside her. Damn if he didn't want to ravish her.

"Don't stop." She grasped his shoulders. "Randolph."

"Do you need to come?" His own desire accelerated, he sped up his strokes.

"Randolph!"

He got his answer by how she screamed his name, how her body froze, but her core rippled around him. Never had he felt a woman orgasm like his wife, her pulses around him only served to edge him on. "Like that, baby."

Unable to slow down, he lowered his face to her neck, closed his eyes and relished in the buildup. His breath ragged, he fought to inhale as his body climbed. He was almost there. Almost. "Willow." He broke out into a sweat. "Damn."

She wrapped her arms around him. "Let go."

Her breathy request was the last bit he needed. He propelled into her one last time. "Yes!" Wracked with the first flood of release, his body went rigid.

"Come on." She held him tighter and continued to coax him on.

Another wave hit, and another, ecstasy and satisfaction took over as his climax continued. His tight muscles went weak, his body still resonating with the ultimate pleasure.

"Randolph."

"I need a moment." He didn't want to be apart from her, didn't want to move. All he wanted to do was be right here. Right here on the hard wooden floor of Willow's shop.

"Take your time." She combed her fingers through his hair. "Learn to take your time."

He let out a laugh.

"Tell me something about your art. Something no one knows."

Her whisper sent chills through him.

"You already know more than anyone." He panted. "You tell me something about you."

"I can tell you that you can trust me that I will never say a word. Tell me something that's only mine."

He paused, concentrated on how he felt her heart beat. "One day I was driving and got turned around and I began driving through some poorer neighborhoods and noticed how some tried to make their area nicer with art. Then I saw a school in a rundown area and thought it needed that touch." With a little strength finding him, he lifted his head. "I couldn't get it out of my head and I came back that night and made them a garden to look at instead."

"Thank you for telling me and thank you for my art." She ran her fingers over his chin and shook her head. "Promise that one day you'll let me see you create something."

"Come here." He turned over and put her on top of him.

"Promise." She pushed herself up.

No one ever took an interest in anything about him but his money. "I promise."

Her body melded into his and her hair fell around him. She lowered her head to his chest. He closed his eyes and traced the outline of her ear with his fingertip.

She moaned.

"Willow."

"Yes." She shivered.

He found his suit jacket and draped it over her. "I hated going home and not finding you there."

"Did you miss me or were you scared I would foil your plans?"

"I started out thinking the worst." He shrugged. "Every bad scenario."

She raised her head. "And?"

"I never came home to someone before. I don't know." He looked up at the ceiling, noticing the fluorescent stars she must have stuck on the ceiling. "We can stay here tonight, whatever you want."

She stared down at him. The stars behind her fit her to a tee. Unable to resist, he leaned up and brushed his lips against hers. A soft kiss, the one he should have given her before when she first came walking through the alley instead of talking about insurance. "Don't walk alone again, please. Call me and I'll get you." Nothing he wanted to say would leave his mouth.

"You can't always look out for me." She sat up. "I think we should go back to the house."

He propped himself up on his elbows. "Why?"

"Though I would love to sleep knowing my art is right here, Nan and Jeb are there, we have a shower there, and our bed is really comfortable." She stood and gathered up their clothes.

"That's not what I asked." He joined her and held his hand out stopping her dressing. "Who said I couldn't look out for you?"

She handed him his shirt. "Our contract."

Chapter Eight

WILLOW STARED INTO THE FLAME of the candle trying to clear her mind, to focus on the yellows and oranges, the flickers and the small bit of heat. Somewhere, there had to be answers.

She shut her eyes and swore she saw mountains. "You know, maybe we should go to Sedona early." Every year she and Nan went to the Sedona for the solstice to welcome the light. The trip gave them renewal and a fresh start and was one of the one true traditions she and Nan managed to keep. Only she needed to talk to Randolph about the trip. They couldn't be apart and she wasn't sure how he would take to being out in Arizona without his plentiful comforts of home.

"Maybe someone should learn to sleep in her contracted bed." In the four days since she found Randolph's shirt buttons scattered around the shop Nan hadn't done anything but bark at her.

Willow opened her eyes. Maybe the images she saw behind her lids were only reflections from the light. She snuffed out the candle, got up off the floor and returned to the counter, turning through pages in Randolph's calendar. They had a dinner coming up next week with the Hartfords, marking her debut as Randolph's wife. The name rang familiar. It seemed as if someone from Randolph's work called him at home, he spat the word out, and if Peter happened to be around he would roll his eyes.

"If we go to Sedona I don't have to plan this dinner."

"Promises are sacred no matter how you make them." Nan didn't even bother facing her. The buttons didn't upset Nan, nor did the sex. It was Willow's mixed feelings about what she did with Randolph in her shop. Nan always said sex was fine as long as she didn't regret the act. Willow wasn't sure if it was regret or something else.

She ran her fingers along the cream colored pages, but the chime of a text message jolted her. Unable to look she slid the phone down the counter. Even though she resisted, Randolph took care of her. In record time he got the insurance, he got the licenses, even got Jeb his license. The man, her husband, adored insurance, licenses and paper as much if not more than art. Every night after dinner and after he finished his work he sat with her and studied her business. Only the other day, a shipment of her supplies arrived. Hell, he even insured the shipment. She guessed it didn't need a license.

Without even thinking she returned the favor, or tried to in her own way. She brought him tea, made him snacks, sat with him while he worked at night after he told her it calmed him down, and even blended an aftershave for him that wouldn't sting his skin. Rather than letting him disappear in the morning, she joined him for his coffee and tried to make sure he ate something before he started his day.

Her path led to nowhere, no matter where she turned only disaster stood on the horizon. "We just need to go." With their change in schedule came the texts, little checkpoints throughout the day, a small gesture most spouses made to each other. However, next year they wouldn't be together, and she didn't want to miss the texts, watching him work or waking up with him.

In the middle of the room, Nan plopped a candle and some incense down. The scent of vanilla and roses filled the air, the scents used for love.

"Why are you doing this?"

Before Nan answered, the door to her shop opened and the space filled with late afternoon sunlight, blinding her.

"There she is!" A woman voice called out.

At the sound of her mother-in-law's voice, she straightened up and froze. The woman was invading her safe place and her time of reflection.

The door closed and Willow blinked to adjust her eyes and found another women and an older man.

Lillian put a shiny yellow shopping bag on the counter. No matter what time of day, Randolph's mother always looked exactly the same. A living fashion doll who only changed her clothes. Even living with the woman Willow never spotted her without makeup, impeccably dressed and salon-styled hair. The lavender dress she wore fit her as if someone designed it with her in mind.

"So, this is your little shop?" Lillian clasped her hands.

"Yes, welcome." Her throat dried out. Lillian Van Ayers didn't really speak to her, mostly she spoke around her, but at least after that first night she was never nasty. Randolph's mother seemed mostly interested in keeping her lifestyle and appearances, and they learned to coexist in the mansion. However, having her here was strange and off balance.

"We saw the art." Lillian smiled. "I was hoping there was a way to get it off the building so we could take it home, but all the experts say that's impossible without destroying it."

"Maybe it should just stay where it is, since that's where the artist wanted it." She wasn't sure if her answer made sense, but then again she wasn't sure about the question.

"Do you know the artist?" Lillian pointed to her ear.

"No," she whispered. Her husband's secret was safe with her, she hadn't even told Nan.

"I bet it's good for business."

"It's not hurting."

"She is just as lovely as you said." The other woman, a near carbon copy of Lillian but with brunette hair and a blue colored dress, came forward.

Randolph's mother called her lovely? She didn't think the woman could pick her out of a crowd. "Thank you?"

"Oh dear, where are my manners? Willow, dear, may I present to you Teresa Tuttle and Sam Burns? Together they are T&B Couture, and I brought them here to measure you and Nanette for the dresses you need for your wedding party." Lillian gave her silent clap. "Terry, Sam, this is my daughter-in-law, Willow."

"Nice to meet you." Party. Yes, the party. His mother continued to talk about it every time Willow saw her. Mrs. Van Ayers declared she had to do something to cover up her son's abrupt elopement, and somewhere she vaguely remembered nodding when dresses were mentioned. It may have been around the time she was watching Randolph do whatever Randolph did, which seemed like always. Unsure if parties and dresses were included in her contract, and not wanting to check, she went with the flow.

"And of course, we need something for little Jebby." Lillian picked up the bag.

Jeb let out a bark and trotted out from the back.

"Oh my God!' Teresa squealed.

"Isn't he precious?" Lillian beamed, reached into her bag and pulled out a collar. A bejeweled collar. "May I, Willow?"

Precious? When did this take place? The brand logo dangling from the collar told her the little bauble cost more than her monthly rent.

"Now, we don't put our paws up on Lulu." Lillian bent down and wagged her finger at Jeb.

Lulu? Willow braced herself on the counter, trying to let the situation unfold rather than take control. Maybe if she let the universe take over, everything would even itself out.

Everyone watched while Jeb sat as Lillian adorned him with the collar.

"When you said you needed something for a dog, I had my doubts, but he owns it." Sam knelt down.

Jeb lifted his head, as if showing off his new look.

Everyone clapped.

Everyone but Nan, the woman who taught her to accept it if someone decided to try to make amends.

"This store is incredible. I can already feel the good vibes." Lillian seemed to float around the small shop, flitting from one thing to another. She stopped in front of the skin care, lifted a bottle of lotion and smiled at it. "You make this?"

"Yes." Willow joined her. Maybe they found a bit of a common ground. She took the tester bottle and held it out to Lillian. "All natural ingredients."

Lillian sniffed the bottle. "Oh it's yummy." She poured some on her hand and offered it to the other woman.

They both rubbed the lotion into their arms.

"This would be perfect as favors for my Beverly Hills Women of Action luncheon. I'll take two hundred. I need them by next Friday and I don't want the family discount." Lillian reached in her purse and handed her a black credit card before continuing her self-guided tour of the store. "Make sure you attach your business card to each bottle. Everyone will just die when they find out my daughter-in-law creates lotion, just die."

Two hundred? Was she serious? She needed to call Randolph, she never made two hundred of anything before. Also she didn't have business cards. At her thought she ground her teeth together. Randolph couldn't be the first person she thought to talk to about lotion or cards.

"Hello, Nanette." Lillian stopped at the candles and incense on the floor. "What's all this?"

"I am creating an altar."

"For what?" Lillian asked in a singsong voice.

"Randolph and Willow. They made love on this very spot and I wanted to commemorate the moment." Nan crossed her arms.

Willow took a deep breath, vanilla and roses filling her sinuses. Nan decided to use the location where her passion got the best of her to prove her point. She wondered at what point she should return the credit card and hide.

"Well, at this stage of their marriage there would be something wrong if they didn't make love everywhere they could." She patted Nan's shoulder. "One time Van and I made love at the ninth hole at the country club. To this day he says he always gets a birdie there."

Everyone laughed and Lillian returned to her. "I thought Willow would look gorgeous in that champagne colored dress you showed at my charity fashion show. Who else has worn it?" She took her phone out of her handbag, slid her fingers over the screen and handed Willow her phone.

Willow held back a gasp at the picture of a long, lanky dress, the kind she would see on an award show on television. Dresses like those didn't belong on her.

"It's only been worn at your show." Sam tilted back on his heels. "We had a request for it from Dr. Lawrence's wife."

"Oh my. Willow dear, someone is forgetting who helped Sam with that nasty, unfortunate incident with his credit two years ago." Lillian put her hand to her chest. "I think Van would be very unhappy to not see his brand new daughter-in-law in this dress. It would make such a lovely wedding gift."

"The dress is worth over ten thousand dollars." Teresa

stepped forward.

She didn't own ten thousand dollars worth of anything let alone clothes.

"Oh, it is, I have no doubt. Were you using it to barter for the good doctor's services?" Lillian cupped her hand over her mouth. "Dr. Lawrence is a plastic surgeon."

"I am sure Dr. Lawrence and his wife will enjoy seeing the dress at Willow's party." Teresa reached into her pocket and took out a tape measure. "On Willow."

Willow needed to wonder who the real deal maker was in the family. Damn if she didn't want the dress. Her life was all off kilter.

"Let me get some preliminary measurements and then you can come to the shop for a formal fitting." Teresa approached and wrapped her tape measure around her chest. "Thank God."

"For what?" Lillian glanced down at the number.

"Do you know how many dresses I ruin trying to fit artificially large breasts into my clothes?"

Sam came over with a paper. "Very nice, Willow."

The door to the shop opened. Again the sun streamed in, hitting right in her pupils. She shielded her eyes, but only made out a tall form.

"Well, this is interesting." Randolph's voice rang through. "What going on?"

Her husband's cologne wafted over the incense. Earth and expense mixed with the vanilla and roses made her light headed, but her vision cleared. Randolph came over in his suit, his sky blue tie and his curls.

"Admiring your wife's natural chest." Sam made a note on the paper.

Randolph bent down, lifted his sunglasses and nodded at the number. He then leaned over and gave her a kiss.

"What are you doing here?" There were too many people in the shop. What used to be calm, turned chaotic.

"Didn't you get my text?" He kissed her again. "I said I was picking you up and thought we could go out to dinner."

"Randolph!" His mother came over. "I don't know if you can be here."

Teresa moved the tape measure down to her waist.

"I can say the same to you, mother."

"I don't know if you should see Willow's dress before the party." She shooed him away.

"Why not, he's seen her undressed on the floor of her shop." Sam laughed.

Lillian patted her son. "I am glad you and Willow have a good and active sex life. It's very important. Your father and I never had an issue in that area, still don't. It's very good for the skin."

Teresa moved down to her hips.

"Well, that is information I never needed to hear." Randolph grabbed Willow's hand and interlaced their fingers.

"Maybe there is something about the Van Ayers men." Sam stood and elbowed him. "Whatever you did netted you some altar."

"Mother, isn't it time you get home?" He bent down and picked up Jeb, allowing her dog to lick his face.

"Yes, we must get going. We'll leave and take Nanette home so the two of you can..." She pointed over at the altar and took Jeb. "Well, it's all set up for you."

"Thank you." Randolph squeezed Willow's hand.

Lillian smiled and kissed him and then leaned over and kissed her. "Willow, dear, keep my card and charge what you need for the lotion, you can give it back to me later. Bye."

In a scurry of activity, they all gathered their things and left. Nan didn't even bother with a wave, leaving Willow a bit breathless with the man she married.

"So, how are you?" He took both her hands. "Aside from your natural yet magnificent chest?"

Heat crept into her cheeks. "Your mother bought two hundred bottles of lotion from me for one of her functions."

"Good, charge her double."

She closed her eyes. "I need business cards."

He let go of her hands and took her by the waist. "Give Peter the information. He loves going to the printer."

Her plan of not going to him completely failed. It had to be the sex. Since their altar creating extravaganza, the whole no sex thing sort of didn't exist anymore.

She opened her eyes to find Randolph staring at her. "How was your day?" Without even thinking she reached up and grazed her fingers across his chin. A scant bit of sexy stubble met her fingertips.

"I have something for you." He pulled her closer.

She prayed for a bit of strength. Instead, he leaned down and kissed her. She wasn't even sure who opened their mouth first, not that it mattered, their lips, bodies and hands moved in unison, their days together giving them a bit of familiarity she never had with any other man.

He wrapped his arms around her, leaning her back as if he couldn't get enough.

In turn, she snuck her hands underneath his suit jacket taking in his slender yet muscular form hiding beneath his clothes.

"I knew it!" Like a bomb, Jade boomed into her store with Argyle behind her.

"I told you." Argyle saluted them.

Randolph shot up and away from her, holding his hands out like a shield.

She gasped and, as if on automatic, hid behind her husband. Her mind didn't belong to her anymore. She never even heard the bell on the door.

Randolph cleared his throat. "What is it that you knew?"

Jade glanced behind her.

"Go ahead." Argyle nodded.

Jade narrowed her eyes and stalked forward. She held a piece of what appeared to jail bars in front of her face. "We are all putting up barriers in one way or another." She flipped the prop over to reveal what looked like a white picket fence. "Are they the same? Are they different?"

"An interesting question my little protégé proposes." Argyle sauntered forward.

"Mr. Money, good day."

Randolph didn't respond.

Willow stared at Randolph's back, her hand on his back. Her ring on her hand on his back. No, she never took it off today, or yesterday, maybe the day before and these people were all about truth and creativity. "Jade." She came around Randolph and held out her hand.

Before she got the chance to utter another word, Randolph grabbed her hand and put both their hands in his pocket.

"Yes, we are seeing each other. Is that your big reveal?" Randolph put his other hand in his pocket as well.

"No, I knew it anyway. Argyle told me." She trotted over, gave them both a hug, and handed her an envelope. "I was practicing my art and wanted to give you the receipt for your rent, you forgot it the other day."

"Thank you." She took the envelope and fought the urge to hand it to Randolph.

"Speaking of which I got a chance to study the gift of art you received." Argyle's gaze traveled over her. "You must be a very special woman to be gifted with such an offering."

She let out a little giggle. The man owned every room he walked into. Creative and sure of himself, he possessed a different sort of confidence than Randolph's more subdued elegance. Of course his tall, commanding frame, picture perfect features, clear golden eyes and flowing black hair didn't hurt his cause.

"What did you think of the work?" Argyle tilted his head to Randolph.

Willow forced herself to have no reaction to the question. How would Randolph address his own art?

"It fits the store." Randolph exhaled.

"Critiqued like a true accumulator of art and a jealous beau." Argyle bowed. "We must get going. Jade isn't nearly done with her lesson."

"Yes, sorry, we didn't mean to interrupt any foreplay, so I'll make myself scarce." Jade smiled and looked between them. "Too bad you didn't get together a little earlier. I always knew Willow rocked, and she could have saved you a bundle. Come by the shop later!" With the words out, both she and Argyle left, the bell on the door ringing loud and clear.

Kisses and sex was one thing, but she could never forget why she was here. Even without knowing everything, Jade knew the role of Randolph's wife, which was why she couldn't reveal her true status. "Well, at least I managed to save you a bundle." She returned to the counter to gather her items.

Randolph joined her. "I thought we would go grab something to eat."

"Sure." She picked up her calendar.

"How is the planning going for the dinner?" He moved her

hair off her shoulder. "I need to make a good impression for this client. They are very big for my company."

She shivered at his light touch. "I'll do my job." It was a dinner not a wedding or a party, at least the kind his mother threw.

"Is everything okay? Did my mother upset you? Was it that so-called artist?"

She shook her head. Of everyone at the moment his mother was her favorite person. Lillian thought they were truly married and in her own way tried to accept her. "Your mom was great. Argyle is eccentric."

"Whatever. I said earlier I have something for you." Randolph reached into his magic suit jacket pocket and handed her a thick envelope.

She opened the flap and took out a burgundy leather checkbook from the same designer as Jeb's new collar, a far cry from her cracked blue plastic one. "What's this?"

He opened the checkbook to reveal a deposit slip. "I got your account all set up and deposited your monthly allowance. Since you are a Van Ayers, you don't have to pay any monthly fees."

In her whole life she never saw that sum of money in one spot. Her cheeks heated and she dropped the checkbook on the counter.

"Are you all right?" He put his arm around her.

The numbers stared her down, his arm weighed her down, and the calendar tied her down. "I'm doing my job."

Chapter Nine

"WILLOW." PETER DROVE into the parking lot behind the restaurant and twisted around to face her. "Are you sure this is the right place?"

From the backseat, she nodded. "The Vines of Los Angeles." Except for an occasional treat or sometimes when bartering, Willow rarely frequented restaurants. Instead she chose to eat what she and Nan cooked when they were lucky enough to have a kitchen, or would pick up little items at local farmers markets.

Since her marriage, Randolph had taken her out several times to quiet restaurants where everyone seemed to know him and all were the kind of places where she could taste the money more than the food. Afraid of embarrassing him and with luck on her side, Randolph was the ultimate gentleman and seemed to get a kick when she asked him to pick something for her, and he always seemed to get it right. What made her blush and swoon only accentuated the way she stood out from his world.

The way Peter asked his question put a spotlight on her issues about the responsibility Randolph gave her when he presented the calendar. All the paranoia and planning about exactly the right outfit and food seemed silly when his clients were discussing gaining or losing huge sums of money or other life-altering deal. Her gut told her she didn't belong. She needed to renegotiate her contract, or break it or get thrown in jail for wayward, paid off wives.

"This doesn't look like the kind of place where Randolph would eat." Elizabeth Glick, Peter's apparent girlfriend, also turned to her. "Aren't we supposed to be at The Vines of Beverly Hills?"

Probably. "They didn't have reservations for tonight, but

helped me get a table here." She inhaled. The people at the restaurant in Beverly Hills explained that their Los Angeles location had the same delicious menu in a trendier, up and coming location. It wasn't as if she asked them to meet at the local drive-thru. These people needed a little lesson on perspective. She did her job, made the reservations, got everyone the address to the restaurant, and put on a dress.

"Did whatever plebian you spoke to at the Hills location know who you were?" The woman narrowed her eyes.

Unsure how to answer Elizabeth's question, she shifted her focus to Peter. "The Vines was on the list of restaurants Randolph's secretary gave me." She chewed the inside of her mouth. On the other hand, she didn't want to mess up any business for her husband.

"I bet his secretary would know how to get into the one in Beverly Hills." Elizabeth plopped forward in her seat.

"Do the Hartfords and Randolph know where we're meeting?" Peter smiled at her.

She nodded, but all the questions only amplified her doubts, and magnified what she didn't know about Randolph's world. Was there more to what she needed to do than make a few phone calls and don some lipstick? The Vines in Los Angeles, The Vines in Beverly Hills, couldn't be that different. The two places were only a few miles apart.

"Well, as long as we all end up in the same place, that's half the battle." Peter finished parking the car.

"I don't think Randolph will like coming to a place with no valet parking." Without waiting for anyone, Elizabeth got out of the car.

Peter shook his head and exited as well.

Ivy took a moment and with a frown opened her own door. Since Randolph found her in the alley on his birthday, she hadn't touched a car door. She slid on her coat and watched Peter practically sprint to Elizabeth.

After Randolph's secretary called and told her he was running behind and to meet him at the restaurant, she went to call the house driver. When Randolph texted her and told her to entertain his client in case they arrived before him she admitted she panicked. Not knowing who these people were, and not wanting to be their entertainment committee, she called Peter at the last second and invited him. She never gave a second thought to him bringing his girlfriend. It seemed natural they would be in couples.

Then she met Elizabeth.

When the woman in the black cocktail dress and precision cut shoulder length blonde hair first entered her store, Elizabeth announced how she was shocked that Randolph even liked the store. Peter's girlfriend also imparted her opinion on Willow's chiffon dress and velvet coat. By the time Willow got in the car with them, Elizabeth also announced her stance on Peter's hair, his car, and decided to tell her that Randolph would rather that she carry an evening bag.

Willow hugged her non evening bag to her chest and caught up to them.

They made their way around to the front of the restaurant. Peter opened the door and the three of them were blasted with noise, which might as well have been an alarm bell.

She went toward the bright white light and stepped inside to the crowd surrounding a bar and a dance floor.

Peter guided them through the people to the podium where a woman wearing a short skirt and an attitude stared at them.

"Reservation for six for Van Ayers." Peter glanced around the restaurant. "Maybe there's something in the back a little quieter? We have a business meeting."

Elizabeth crossed her arms and tapped her foot. "Randolph hates crowds."

No matter how or why she and Randolph got married, the man was still her husband and she was getting a bit fatigued with Elizabeth's continued spouting off about her knowledge of Randolph. She squeezed the bridge of her nose. Truth was, Elizabeth knew more about her husband than she did. Maybe Randolph should have married the other woman. At least he would have gotten a wife who knew him, Peter would have his freedom, and she could go to Sedona and no one would care about her bag evening or not, or where she ate.

"We have no Van Ayers reservation." The woman leaned one elbow on the podium.

Elizabeth let out a laugh and leaned over to Peter. "Tell them you're a Ward, unless your mother asked you not to use your name again."

Willow turned from the negative force, stared at the entrance in search of Randolph and tapped Peter. "It would be under Day."

"Well, that answers my earlier question." Elizabeth crossed her arms. "Why wouldn't you use the last name that means something?"

"This is the second time tonight I answered that question." The lady gathered up some menus and pointed over to the bar where an older skeletal woman wearing a grey dress and a scowl sat next to a rounder man with the same expression.

"Peter?" Willow barely whispered his name, wishing somehow Randolph would appear.

"There are the Hartfords. Where is Randolph?" Peter straightened up and pulled his phone out of his pocket.

"Someone better walk over there, Randolph won't like it if he knows they were kept waiting." Elizabeth's voice scratched up her spine.

Honestly, there was no kidney in the cooler awaiting a transplant. They only had a little mix up with names and restaurants. "I'll smooth things over." Nan always said most misunderstandings could be solved with an apology and a smile. In her case, she also added a shot of vodka. Randolph's life of worry over restaurants didn't fit her.

Since neither Peter nor Elizabeth protested, she forced a wide smile across her lips and made her way toward the unhappy couple.

The woman narrowed her eyes as she approached.

Once more she peeked over at the door, praying for Randolph's appearance. "Mr. and Mrs. Hartford?" She raised her voice and practically curtseyed.

"I am Ms. Hartford, this is my brother, Mr. Hartford." Ms. Hartford pursed her lips, the wrinkles around her mouth digging into her face even deeper.

Awkward. Willow swallowed. Her need for a shot of vodka quickly increased to a glass of vodka. "I am Willow Day–" She cleared her throat at the mistake. "I mean, I am Willow Day Van Ayers. I apologize for the mix up with the reservations, but I believe our table is ready and we can go have some appetizers."

"Well, congratulations are in order." The man gave her a hearty handshake.

Already his good vibes reverberated through her. Maybe everything would be all right. She exhaled.

"You are Randolph's wife?" In harsh, precision movements, Ms. Hartford flipped her small evening bag open, took out a pair of glasses, shoved them on her face and stared at her. "You are Randolph's wife?"

Suddenly she couldn't breathe. In less than a second the woman summarized her and Randolph's relationship. After a week spent practically prancing after her husband like a lovesick teenager, she needed to redirect her energy, focus on her life, her reality and her job.

"Are you or are you not Randolph's wife?" Ms. Hartford stood. "Or is this whole thing some sort of a joke?"

"Yes, this is my wife." Like a superhero, Randolph materialized by her side, complete with a long coat swirling around him.

Funny, she wanted to answer she was indeed the joke.

He shook Mr. Hartford's hand and then took Ms. Hartford's hand between both of his. "I apologize for my tardiness, but I was detained at the office."

"I thought we were an important client of yours." Ms. Hartford jutted her jaw out.

"You know that is a fact." He produced one of his magazine worthy smiles.

"Mr. Van Ayers, how can I believe that when you take us to a place more suitable for a drunken brawl than a business meeting and then turn up late?" She snatched her hand away.

Willow glanced down at the floor, willing it to open and swallow her up. While she might not care where or what these people ate, it was part of her agreement, and it was never her intention to cause an issue.

"Then you present us with your so-called wife who doesn't know her last name." The woman pursed her lips, a fitting expression for her sour disposition. "Dare I add we weren't given a proper wedding announcement or invitation?"

No matter how nasty these people were, she would never forgive herself if she ruined the client relationship for Randolph.

Truth be told, he would have the Hartfords longer than he had her.

"Millicent, please." Randolph bowed his head. "Willow and I eloped very quickly. Do you honestly think I would exclude you out of any major event like that? My mother is throwing a huge party to celebrate between Thanksgiving and Christmas and invitations are being hand delivered this week. You are at the top of the list."

The woman continued to glare at him. From behind her, the brother shook his head.

"As far as the restaurant goes, surely you can understand a little mix up? My wife is new at this." Randolph tilted his head and one curl bounced over his eyebrow. "I am more than happy to call any other restaurant myself and get us in. Simply say the word."

Willow held her breath. She went to grab Randolph's hand but stopped.

"This is fine," Mr. Hartford mumbled.

"I *am* starving." Millicent shook her head. "I suppose we can make a concession."

"Let's go sit down, then." Randolph corralled them to the front.

Willow allowed herself the luxury of inhaling.

"Our table is ready." Peter pointed to the back.

"Good to see you, Dolph." Elizabeth gave him a huge smile. "I'm surprised we're staying here. I told your wife you wouldn't care for this place. I remember when we used to meet up at the club and you hated it when your parents made you eat at the snack shack rather than in the restaurant."

Next, maybe Elizabeth would visit the bar and ask for the margarita salt to pour on the wound. The over-sized crystals might dig in a little deeper.

"Who are these people?" Ms. Hartford spun on her heel and faced Randolph.

"What are they doing here?" Randolph growled under his breath, while jerking his chin toward Peter and Elizabeth. The cords on his neck stood out and he swallowed. "This is my personal assistant, Peter Ward, and his girlfriend Elizabeth Glick."

Ms. Hartford shook her head. "Unusual when we are going to discuss sensitive business matters."

"Maybe we should go." Peter took a step back.

"No!" She raised her voice well above the noise in the restaurant. "I invited you."

"Now she remembers etiquette." Ms. Hartford turned away.

Without another word, Randolph motioned for everyone to follow the girl to the table.

Another mistake. At last her heart gave up and simply fell, landing in her empty sick stomach. Willow hung back with her husband. An apology didn't seem appropriate, but she needed to say something. "Randolph."

"Let's just get through this." He spoke through gritted teeth.

She managed to get to the table and took the seat between Randolph and Elizabeth.

At least once everyone took their spot, the mood lightened with small talk. Randolph even ordered for her, and she sat back and sipped her wine, even though she longed to chug from a bottle of vodka. At least Randolph could take over and the disaster seemed diverted. Maybe she didn't need hard liquor after all.

Randolph and the Hartfords discussion morphed into business, and she resolved to remain quiet and allow the evening to play out. They made it through appetizers and salad and at last the main course was served. Her husband ordered her an amazing fish dish and she took a bite allowing the rich cream sauce to coat her palate.

"I suppose once you get married it's fine to eat all the things you wouldn't allow yourself when dating." Elizabeth leaned over and let out a laugh. "I can't remember the last time I had anything as decadent as that."

"I would rather eat a little of what I want than a lot of what I don't want." She took another bite. "More isn't always better."

"Of course more is sometimes nice as well." Mr. Hartford lifted his fork and took another bite of his food.

Peter chuckled.

"So, you never said how you and Randolph met." Elizabeth put her fork down.

"Yes, how did you meet?" Ms. Hartford stared down her long thin nose at her. "What led to your sudden elopement?"

For weeks her husband kept up the ruse in front of their friends and unwilling to make one more error, she put her hand on Randolph's shoulder. "I'll let Randolph tell you."

Randolph took his time wiping his mouth. "Willow owns a little shop."

"What kind of shop do you own?" The scowl took over Ms. Hartford's face again.

"Isn't it like a voodoo shop?" Elizabeth leaned back in her chair as if trying to get Randolph's attention.

"Voodoo?" Again, Ms. Hartford pursed those lips.

Mr. Hartford sat up and grinned.

"It's actually a little metaphysical and holistic shop." She spat out the correct answer.

"What exactly does that mean?" Ms. Hartford asked.

"You know, hocus pocus stuff." Elizabeth wiggled her fingers. "She even gave Peter a tarot card reading and now he's all freaked out."

"Was she accurate?" Mr. Hartford asked.

Ms. Hartford only blinked.

"You know that artist who goes around painting random murals?" Elizabeth leaned over the table. "He or she painted one on Willow's building and now Peter thinks it's a divine sign."

Like a freight train trying to outrun a boulder speeding down hill, there was nothing Willow could do to stop the crash that was Elizabeth. Out of the corner of her eye she glanced at Randolph. His pale complexion said everything.

"Divine sign?" The woman shook her head.

Elizabeth laughed. "I'm as shocked as you. Randolph doesn't seem the type to fall for that kind of stuff, especially after that two-bit elementary school art drawing attention to it."

Call it the pressure, the heat of the moment, instinct to protect her temporary mate, or whatever, she finally snapped. "How much do you actually know about Randolph? I sleep with the man every night and never once has he mentioned your name. No wonder Peter is looking for a divine sign. He's probably looking for a way to exorcise you from his life."

"Willow." Randolph muttered her name under his breath.

"Seems as if your wife needs to learn a little more than simply the right restaurant and her last name." Ms. Hartford reached for her wine glass.

"I pray to any deity out there that this evening is the worst thing that ever happens to you, but from the sound of some of your financial affairs my husband is working on, I am wrong again." She resisted the need to stand and stomp away.

The table took on an eerie, all-encompassing silence.

Elizabeth lifted one side of her mouth in a sneer. "Willow."

"It's time for us to go." Peter stood and put his hand out to Elizabeth. "Thank you for dinner."

Elizabeth followed Peter, leaving the four of them alone and everyone staring at Willow, the outcast. She stood, causing Randolph and Mr. Hartford to stand as well. "If you don't mind excusing me, I need a little air, and I know you have business to discuss."

"Willow." Randolph widened his eyes.

"Please take your time. I just want to take a little walk." Uncertain what to do in such a situation, she bowed, took her bag and her jacket and forced her head up as she walked outside. Throughout her life she had seen real problems, people without homes, money, food but these people acted as if the wrong vintage wine would be the death of them.

Fresh air did nothing to cleanse her. Every error she made replayed in her mind, down to the horrified expression on Randolph's face at her outburst. Maybe she should have taken more than five minutes planning this nightmare. What seemed like a simple dinner was obviously much more.

She turned back toward the restaurant. Something about being human made everyone want to fit in, and for the millionth time the flares went off. She would never be one of them, couldn't even fake it enough to make it, even for the year she had to live Randolph's life. For the life of her, she couldn't go back in there and pretend it mattered. Instead she decided to take a walk around the block and use the fresh air to cleanse her energy.

* * * *

Randolph stared at his secretary. Mrs. Avery had been with the bank since he was a child. She used to work for his father, but in a life made up of contracts, deals and negotiations, Randolph won Mrs. Avery when he finished graduate school, a semester early. Good old Mrs. Avery left her desk in front of his father's office and took her post outside of his on the day Randolph claimed his office.

Over the years Mrs. Avery had been invaluable, doing everything from tending to his social calendar to making sure he had the right paperclips. Hell, if Mrs. Avery wasn't married to Mr. Avery and a decade or three too old for him, he would have asked her to go on his one year marriage extravaganza with him. Yes, the sex would have been non-existent, and she wasn't a gorgeous blonde, but in the end she was a better match for him.

He put his elbow on his desk and his head in his hand and gazed at the woman who was going to play human mop.

She shook her head, reached in her pocket and handed him a mint.

Though he didn't really want it, he took the candy anyway and popped it in his mouth. Lately, he couldn't help himself from being fed things he didn't want from old ladies.

"Yes, thank you, I will get Mr. Van Ayers on the phone." With the expertise only Mrs. Avery possessed, she pressed the buttons on the phone, transferred the call to his desk and stood.

Randolph put his hand on the phone. "Where are you going?"

"Back to my desk." She wagged her finger at him.

"I need you." He swallowed practically choking on the mint, though if he did, Mrs. Avery would save him.

"What you need, I can't give you." With a shake of her head, she walked out. "Your wife will be here soon, ask her."

"Traitor." He didn't remember when Mrs. Avery met Nan, but they needed to stop taking lessons from each other. Rather than wallowing, he lifted the receiver. "Millicent?"

"Randolph, are you coming to me with your tail between your legs?" The battle axe snickered.

"A Van Ayers only whips his tail to cut through the air." He spent the last twenty-four hours making sure he was phone call worthy and the woman would be squealing for him by the time he was done.

"Well, you said the word whipped, not me."

He pounded his fist into the desk. "I called to get your approval to transfer some money between your investment accounts."

"Don't tell me I'm overdrawn."

He leaned back in his chair and chuckled. The family had enough money in their bank to power a small country a couple of times over. "Not quite. I just managed to secure an investment that will net double the yield of the last project, and I thought we may want to add a little more. The funds will remain fluid."

"Is this supposed to make me forget about that travesty you called a dinner?"

"No. It's called doing my job. What *is* supposed to make you forget the dinner are the men entering your office right about now with a gourmet lunch, carrying the invitation to my wedding celebration on a silver platter." The ruckus in the background told him everything arrived on time. He stared up at the ceiling and waited.

A little breathless, she returned to the phone. "Randolph."

"Yes, Millicent?"

"I am sending in my RSVP now, but I want you to remember something."

"I'm listening."

"Remember who your client is," she snapped. "Now transfer that money."

"Yes, ma'am. I will talk to you soon." He hung up the phone and crunched down on his mint. The Hartford Corporation account was saved, but his wife was another story.

As if on cue, a light rapping at the door indicated the arrival of the next situation he needed to handle today. "Come in."

Mrs. Avery opened the door. "Mrs. Van Ayers is here."

He motioned for her to bring it on.

With her huge bag in tow, Willow entered. If she were anyone else he would have sworn she hired people to follow her around with a wind machine to give her that perfect ethereal presence with the way the skirt of her sky blue dress billowed and her hair wafted around her.

Since their unsuccessful meal of the previous night, they hadn't really spoken to one another. He hated the way his heart sped at having to confront her. He confronted confrontation. "Good afternoon."

She took a breath and made her way to the chair in front of

his desk. "Hello."

He strummed his fingers on his leg waiting to give her the opportunity to speak first. Possibly an apology was in order, or at the minimum an explanation.

She settled in the chair and put her bag on her lap.

Once more he found himself with his elbow on the desk and his head in his hand, taking in the woman he married yet didn't know anything other than her occupation and the secret to making her squirm in bed. What motivated her? What did she want?

They stared at each other.

He glanced at the small antique clock on the corner of his desk. The second hand went around once, twice, and then started its third revolution. He tensed.

Once the second hand went for its fourth time around, he hit his desk. "Willow!"

She jumped. "Yes."

"Do you have anything to say to me?" He picked up a rubber band and stretched it between his fingers.

"Yes, I do." She pressed her back to the chair.

He exhaled. "I would love to hear it."

From her bag, she pulled out a little pouch and placed it on the edge of his desk. "I brought this for you."

"What is this?" He didn't touch the gift, if it was a gift.

"It's my Serene-tea." She pressed her back into the chair. "I thought maybe Ms. Hartford could use it to calm down."

Filled with a rush of adrenaline, he shot up out of his chair. "You know what you need?"

She looked up at him with wide eyes.

"Insani-tea!" He turned his back to her and looked out the window overlooking Century City. No one else in any of the tall buildings was having such an inane conversation at this moment. He would bet on it. With a huff, he faced her once more. "Maybe you already drank some while planning that dinner and that's how we ended up at some bar with food rather than a real restaurant."

Willow swiped her hair out of her face. "Did you ever think that your account should have just been happy having a meal out on your bank's dime?"

"Everything..." He swiped his arm around the room.

"Everything that you see, this office, the bank, the house, the cars, everything has been brought to us courtesy of clients like Ms. Hartford."

She opened her mouth, but he held up his hand. Perhaps she would understand his argument in her terms. "Do you know that we have several assistants who only work on that account? Do you know that if we didn't have them I would have to fire those employees? They have wives and children who need their salaries."

She put her hand over her mouth.

He sat at the edge of his desk. "What may not seem like a big deal to you, an account like the Hartfords takes as an insult, a slight. They have trusted me and my bank and my family with their fortune and to show up at an unplanned, inappropriate restaurant with other people who had no business being there, could hurt everyone."

"Randolph." She barely whispered his name. "I didn't know."

"Did you not know or didn't care?"

Her silence answered his question.

He returned to his chair and sat down.

"She was so nasty." She looked down at her lap as she spoke.

"Then it is your job to take the high road and then we gossip and make fun of them on the ride home."

"It all seems so silly."

"It wasn't to me." He lowered his voice.

Once more they stared at each other.

"Well, it doesn't matter cause you won." He leaned over the desk. "I would like the calendar back. Mrs. Avery will resume her duties as social planner. All I ask is that you attend the functions with me."

Her complexion paled yet her cheeks turned red. "Won't that be against my contract?"

He stifled a sad laugh. "I will have my attorneys make a formal amendment to it if you'd like."

"Well, it is a sacred contract." She shrugged. Again, she reached into her bag sliding out the calendar and putting it on his desk. "Here you go."

He took the book and returned it to his desk drawer, wishing she would have fought for it. "I'm sorry it was all silly for you. I know it probably doesn't matter, but after the last few days we had together, I was really looking forward to showing off my new wife." Stupid images of having a partner at one of these meetings, someone to hold his hand while he talked business and someone to take a drive with afterward all but dissipated. Maybe he put too much on her, should have offered help, but since she found the whole thing foolish it was a moot point. He learned time and gain he couldn't change someone's inner makeup, though he thought she was the type to be open minded even about things she didn't understand.

"Then what were you going to tell them next year?"

"What?"

"Were you going to show off your brand new divorce papers?" She looked down.

Her words might as well have slapped him across the face. Was the disaster about something else entirely? During the last days and nights they had become closer and now she tried to put distance between them. "Maybe we shouldn't think about that part." A strange emptiness took residence right in his throat. They had months to go before they needed to address their year anniversary.

"How can we not? We started a relationship knowing the end. Everything is there in black and white." She stood and bolted for the exit. "There's just something wrong with that."

He shot up and managed to beat her to the door. "What do you want Willow?" If she wouldn't offer the information, he would point blank ask.

She wouldn't even look him in the eye.

"Willow, tell me what you want. Everything is negotiable." He tried to push her.

She lifted her face, but stared off in the distance as if she were speaking to someone else. "I want to do the job I promised to do."

"Anything else?" he pressed.

"No." Her word fell like a boulder between them.

"Then I suppose you can be off the clock until tonight." He opened the door and returned to his desk.

Chapter Ten

"WILLOW, LOVE, DON'T MOVE." With a huge smile, Lillian stood back and clasped her hands, admiring her handiwork. "Fix the one curl."

One of the three hairdressers in Lillian Van Ayers' private dressing room suite rushed forward and micro adjusted something on her hair.

Willow learned during hour one of Lillian's preparations to remain absolutely still while other people dressed her, did her hair, and put makeup on her. She wasn't even allowed to buckle her own shoe.

"Oh." Lillian pressed her hand to her chest. "Oh, Willow."

One of the makeup artists ran over and dabbed Lillian's eye with a cotton swab.

"You look..." Lillian fanned her face. "You look..." She shook her head, backed up and motioned toward the mirror. "You look like a Van Ayers."

The crew of people surrounding them clapped.

Willow gasped as she took in her reflection. The woman staring back at her was still her, but changed. While it felt as if the artists painted her face like a canvas, she actually looked quite natural, except perfect. They left her hair down, long and flowing over her back as she preferred, but the strands seemed to gleam, smooth and soft with the curl she always wanted.

Of course there was the dress. They called the color champagne, but it was more a liquid shimmering cream. Smooth and silky, the simple yet elegant floor-length strapless gown hugged every inch of her, made to appear as if it were part of her. She turned to Lillian and then glanced at the team of people who created her. She looked like a Van Ayers.

At the end of the day she needed to remember it was all on the surface. She was created to look like a Van Ayers.

Though part of her wanted to shake her head and wipe the makeup off her face, the other part knew that no matter what, for Randolph, for Lillian and for herself, she would play nice at their party. Next year, when she was nothing but a memory to these people, she didn't want the memory to be of awkward scenes with their coworkers and friends. She wanted them to smile and at least know she gave it everything she had.

"She was already gorgeous." Lillian came over and gave her a silent clap. "But tonight is special and she is most definitely the belle of the ball."

"My Chiquita, you look *muy bonita!*" Nan joined them from the other room with her own team trailing after her.

"You do too." Willow had no choice but to smile at Nan. In a million years she never dreamed she would see the woman in anything but one of her muumuus, but Lillian worked her magic and found a deep purple fitted dress that showed off Nan's attributes.

"That is exactly what I pictured." Lillian was a vision as well in a pink strapless floor length dress. "This is perfect."

"Maybe we should wear these outfits to Sedona." Nan posed for her. "Do you think they would kick us out?"

"They don't allow evening dresses in Sedona?" Lillian looked them all over once more. "What do you do there?"

"We celebrate the winter solstice." Nan nodded. "It is the return of the light after the dark winter days."

Yes, Willow allowed Lillian to primp and prod her, she kept quiet since the disagreement about Randolph's dinner over three weeks ago, and as long as the universe remained on her side she wouldn't cause any issues tonight. For all those good deeds, she would be rewarded with a trip to Sedona, she hoped. Randolph still needed to agree, and she hoped he would, they needed the trip.

She glanced down at the intricate mosaic floor. Randolph asking what she wanted in his office was one of the last things he said to her aside from a grunt here or there or a quick question. Even Thanksgiving came and went without anything to truly be thankful for. Yes, Lillian put out a spread fit for any cookbook cover, but it lacked any meaning. Maybe it was better. They needed to stay separate, but then she was the one hoping he took her to one of her sacred places.

A knock interrupted her thoughts.

"Well, my guess is people are starting to arrive." Lillian smoothed down her dress. "That must be the men."

Willow tensed. The last she'd seen Randolph he was slumped over his home desk working.

One of the staff opened the door and her breath caught.

There was something about a man in a tuxedo. Of course there was something else entirely about Randolph in a tuxedo.

Rather than the typical outfit with a bow tie and cummerbund seen at many high school proms, Randolph wore a three-piece ensemble, black pants, black jacket a cream brocade vest and a regular tie that matched her dress.

He left his curls untamed and they bounced as he walked into the room adding to his sexy swagger and allure. His curls were the tiny drop of mischief in the overall power he possessed. He stopped, almost causing his father to bump into him.

Randolph's gaze traveled over her. "Willow."

A shiver ran through her. His blank stare gave nothing away, no approval, no repulsion. A poker face, the same one he must use in a negotiation for a percentage or two of profit. "Randolph."

"Should we get going to your party?" His tone came out tight and businesslike. At last he crossed the room.

"It's your party too." Her throat dried out.

"Well, then I say we should join our guests at our party." Without a word about her dress or anything else, he held his arm out to her.

Maybe he thought their relationship should remain more business-like as well. More than once she heard Randolph's father say the evening was nothing more than one big meeting in uncomfortable clothes. She put a smile on her face and in keeping with her vow for the evening, laced her arm in his.

"We should make an appearance." The senior Van Ayers nodded at her. Most of the time, he didn't really deal with her at all. Of course he knew she was only a temporary addition. "We put the dog in the locked laundry room so he wouldn't get spooked with the guests."

While Mr. Van Ayers might not care for her, Willow noticed he did have a fondness for Jeb.

"This is perfect, just perfect." Lillian went to her husband and motioned for Nan to join them.

"You all look lovely." Mr. Van Ayers led Nan and Lillian away.

"Let's do this." Randolph guided her out of the room.

Light classical music wafted through the mansion, mixing with Randolph's cologne and causing her head to spin. She barely realized they made it to the staircase until he stopped.

"Oh!" For the girl who never even had as much as a birthday party, the scene below was overwhelming. She tried not to focus on the excess, instead focused on the moment and her job.

The illuminated chandeliers gave the whole downstairs sparkle. Uniformed staff members walked around carrying silver trays of appetizers and champagne. The guests who already arrived appeared as if they were ready to walk a red carpet. Lillian had turned the house into a veritable winter wonderland, a Charles Dickens picture perfect postcard.

Randolph pulled her closer.

She held her breath waiting for him to say something.

"Ready?"

"Yes." She exhaled, blowing away her expectations.

They made their way down the stairs while the whole party seemed to stop and watch them. Throughout her life whenever she had entered situations where she felt on display, Nan always told her to move outside herself, let things happen and watch them roll by. With each step she took, she heeded Nan's advice.

Her strategy worked. Though the guests bombarded her with introductions, questions and well wishes, she stayed close to Randolph's side smiling, nodding and sipping the champagne Randolph handed her.

"I'm so happy for you." One of the guests, an older woman in a light blue beaded gown, leaned in and gave Randolph a kiss on the cheek. "Everything is lovely. I was shocked to hear you eloped."

"Sometimes you have to seize an opportunity when it finds you." He chuckled.

Willow continued to smile. Thus far every conversation seemed to be a carbon copy of the last.

"At least you decided to have a celebration fitting for your family." The woman patted him on the shoulder. "You wouldn't want to look bad. You have a name to uphold."

More than once the guests made similar comments about family, reputation, his name and appearances. Her smile waned and she glanced around the foyer, taking in the people from a different perspective. Rather than becoming blinded with the jewels, the clothes, and the trappings most everyone wished for, she suddenly saw the riches as weights. Each person there was trying desperately to outdo another for position, waiting for the right moment to knock someone off their pedestal. Any small thing could hurt them.

"Please enjoy yourself." Randolph nodded.

The woman walked away to be replaced by a younger couple.

"I never thought I would see the day the bachelor of Bel Air would be married." The woman elbowed him.

"Well the day has come." Randolph produced his poster-worthy smile.

"I see this." The woman held her hand out toward Willow. "Let me see the ring. It's all anyone can talk about."

Why was seeing the ring such a critical point? What about the jewelry made it important? Instead, she held her hand out and gazed down at the stone with the woman. If the marriage had been real, had he gotten down on one knee and proposed to her because he loved her and married her because he couldn't envision his life without her, Randolph could have given her a ring made out of tin foil and she would have loved it.

"I have heard about this diamond for years." The woman sighed. "It's a lot to live up to."

Out of the corner of her eye she noticed Randolph looking at her.

"I love the history." She kept her hand out. Yes, any mistake, no matter how silly or superficial, could harm Randolph, any mistake including choosing the wrong restaurant. She faced him.

The couple went on their way and he wrapped his arm around her waist, the first true attention he showed her since the office when he asked her what she wanted.

"I don't know." She meant to only think the words but realized she said them aloud. How did she end up here? The man had everything and with one slip almost lost it all until he earned his consolation prize. What was it like to live knowing that with one error, everything he worked for could vanish?

"What?" He tilted his head.

"I meant I didn't know." She wanted to explain, dare she say apologize, but she shook her head and put another smile on her face. "Never mind." Randolph and his father were right. The party was more akin to a business function with no time to talk.

"No tell me." He gave their empty glasses to one of the waiters passing by and took both her hands. "But first there is something I need to tell you."

Damn her stomach for fluttering. Those sensations didn't belong to her, not for their sham marriage. She didn't need to talk to him she only made a mistake about the dinner, she didn't commit a crime. No, not true. She took a breath. No mistake on her part, no, she completely disregarded something of importance to the man she married. After always being taught to appreciate the differences, when it came to her husband she only saw one side. "Randolph." Even upset, the man still had her business cards made and sent Peter over to help with the two hundred piece lotion order.

He ignored the next couple of people who came up to them and took her by the waist. "With everything going on, I didn't know how to tell you how absolutely gorgeous you are tonight." He stepped closer and leaned over to her ear. "You did what many couldn't, made me speechless. Honestly, you do that no matter what. I wish we could just go be alone. I hate these kinds of parties."

She closed her eyes and let the shivers he created by whispering in her ear take over. "I'm sorry about the dinner, I didn't understand, but I think I do now." Her chest lightened, letting her heart swell. Part of her wished the organ would set her free, but Randolph seemed to have some bizarre control over her.

"I'm sorry I was so upset. I shouldn't have just expected you to know." He kissed her ear and trailed his lips down to her neck. "I can't tell you how proud I am of how you are acting tonight."

It took her a moment to realize what he said. At first she only heard him apologize. Almost like an after taste of something sour did her mind process the words about him being proud of her.

"Proud of me?" She found the strength to put her hands on his shoulders and push him back.

"Yes, so proud. I didn't know if you would ever understand. I'm glad we got that out of the way." He went to kiss her once more.

If anything, there was a huge obstacle with spikes and a ring of fire looming between them. She leaned back, but swallowed her words. No matter what, she would keep her promise.

"Oh, you are being too good." He raised his eyebrows. "Let's sneak away for a while. We've talked to everyone."

"There's one couple you didn't talk to." A woman's voice interrupted them.

She turned. Slate and Jade entered the foyer.

"Randolph?" She gave into her urge from before and pushed him back. Did he get back at her by inviting them without warning?

"Oh my God." He growled from behind her.

"We wanted to wish you a happy wedding." Jade came forward in a form fitting dress covered in oversized diamonds intertwined with what appeared to be a cord made out of money, her statement more than apparent.

In an old fashioned tuxedo and tails, Slate simply stood there shaking his head.

Her entire body broke out into a sweat. What did she expect from hiding? Again, she tried to step outside herself, but it didn't work. Instead she was acutely aware of the how they simply stood staring at them and could pinpoint the exact moment her two worlds converged. Along with every other horrible thought running through her head, the one that stood out was that her only friends might not know not to say anything about their unique marriage.

Jade handed each of them a box. "I didn't know if we should bring gifts." No hug, no excitement, no laughs.

"It wasn't necessary." Even though her mouth seemed lined with sandpaper, she managed to speak and take the lid off the box to reveal a sugar bowl filled with artificial sweetener packets. The message clear, the present was for her artificial sugar daddy. Her friend nailed everything.

"I guess it wasn't necessary to tell us you were married?" Jade looked between them, her eyes settling on Randolph.

Randolph opened his box. "What's this?"

"A lock. If you want the key, you'll have to buy it." Jade narrowed her eyes and spoke through clenched teeth. "Are you embarrassed of us? Are we only good enough to lend money to, but not good enough to invite to a life changing event? We were always on your side."

"No." She wouldn't allow them to blame her husband and held her hand out. Already people were glancing their way. How many fiascos could she cause? "I asked him not to say anything, so he was just abiding by my wishes."

"What?" Jade shook her head.

"No one is embarrassed of you. I was embarrassed of myself." Unable to look at the faces of the people she lied to, she put the box on a side table, turned and rushed away. In her haste to flee she nearly bumped into two waiters, but even in the blur of her party, she spied her exit route. She turned and collided right into someone, the crash of crystal against marble echoing around her.

"Oh my!" Ms. Hartford gasped.

Three waiters rushed over and cleaned up the broken glass.

"I'm sorry." She backed up. Every guest seemed to stop and stare in her direction. With her promise as broken as the glass, she bolted in the opposite direction. Randolph should have waited before telling her he was proud.

* * * *

Everyone held secrets. Everyone. Randolph learned that fact when he was a young child. No one was immune to hiding information when they felt they had no other alternative. Sometimes the information remained hidden, but many times, probably more often than not, it was uncovered.

When caught in one of these unfortunate situations, the best course of action was to address the situation in a calm, cool manner. Lucky for his wife, she was married to one of the best negotiators around, if he did say so himself.

He corralled Jade and Slate into the library, shut the door and put their gifts on one of the shelves.

"Well, we thought you were just sleeping with her." Slate

laughed.

"I thought she was my friend. We had a connection." Jade hid her face in her hands.

"She is your friend." He lifted his hand and paced back and forth across the floor, buying himself a moment to catch his thoughts. All night Willow tried to be the perfect wife, and he needed to help her. At last he stopped and faced them. "With knowing what you know, she was concerned you would think less of her. Please forgive her."

Slate patted his girl. "We were shocked when the invitation was delivered. Actually it was delivered to me. Jade was my plus one."

"You don't understand." Jade kept her head down.

No, he would never understand women's relationships. He likened it to some sort of mystery like the pyramids. He tried to bend down to look her in the eye. Jade's friendship was exceptionally important to his wife. "For what it's worth, she adores you."

She shrugged. "I don't know. I suppose we have to talk."

Jade went out of her way to help Willow and deserved to hear from her, but he didn't think his wife could handle anything more. "Maybe it can wait until after the holidays?"

She paused, but finally spoke. "It's fine. I just thought we were part of her life. I don't know if it will ever be the same."

Though he wanted to get the situation tied up with a nice bow for Willow, he could only force the issue to a certain degree. "Listen, why don't you go enjoy the party?"

Slate nodded and took Jade's hand. "Come on baby, you wouldn't let me eat anything, and you always said you wanted to see Randolph's home."

"Even dressed like this?" She lifted her head.

"Especially dressed like that," Randolph raised his eyebrows.

His friends made their way toward the door. With the scant bit he knew about fashion, he predicted the women here would be wearing knock offs next week.

"Wait." He hated the next words he had to say.

They turned toward him.

"You know the circumstance with our wedding isn't the usual case." He took a breath. "It goes without saying..." Even though he trusted these people, he needed to remind them of the most important detail.

"I think Jade's dress and our gifts said it all. Give us some credit." Slate held out his hand.

He shook Slate's hand and smiled at Jade. "You're always a plus one."

She let out a lone laugh. "Can I ask you something?"

"Of course."

"Is there more than just your contract thing between you?" Her voice lightened a small amount. All women loved romance wherever they could find it.

He froze, considering her words. Up until her question he didn't consider it and no one asked him. Honestly, he didn't have an answer. "I thought you were going to enjoy the party. I'll be out in a moment."

"When someone doesn't answer a question, the answer is obvious." Jade laughed.

His friends filed out of the library. He closed the door once more and stared up at the ceiling. The night he married Willow he was desperate and she was there. He never gave a second thought to entrenching her in his life. Hell, after all these weeks he didn't really know her, didn't know what she was like as a child, didn't know what her favorite food was, didn't know about her family. He only assumed she would catch on and be thrilled to be thrust into the world of excess without as much as an instruction book. Then, as icing on the cake, he told her he was proud as if she were some dog.

No wonder she didn't want her friends knowing they were married.

He had to find her. They needed to talk.

The thought of returning to the party made his stomach clench. He opened the door and devised another plan.

With metered steps and a smile chiseled on his face, he snuck toward the kitchen. Once through the double doors, he fought the need to wipe his brow. Before locating his spouse, he needed one critical thing. The one item guaranteed to make anyone smile, including him.

He turned toward the staff.

They all straightened.

"It's good. All's good." He pointed in the direction of the locked laundry room. His timing needed to be perfect in order to make a clean getaway before he was intercepted, but he needed the magic elixir to make everything right.

From his pocket he retrieved his keys, unlocked the door and crouched down in anticipation of an attack.

Nothing.

No puffball ran toward him, barked in a mock imitation of a canine, no licks, no pawing his pants or scuffing his shoes. "Jeb?" He shut the door and scanned the room.

"Come here." He got down on his knees and made a kissing sound. "Jebby, come here big boy."

Still nothing.

His heart took residence in his throat. Not caring about the tuxedo, he crawled along the floor, glancing under the washer and dryer for any particularly adorable tuft of lint. "Why is everything so damn clean!" He pounded his fist into the marble floor. There wasn't even an errant towel or piece of clothing for any living creature to hide in. "Clara!" He yelled for the head housekeeper.

"Mr. Randolph, get off the floor!" She scurried toward him.

Rather than allowing her to pull him up, he motioned for her to come down. "Where is he?" With labored breaths, he fought the need to grab the woman and shake the pet out of her.

"Who?" She joined him, and her hand instantly went to his forehead.

"The dog." He swiped her away and cupped his hands indicating the place the animal would fit if he were here where he belonged. "Jeb."

She looked under the washer, then the dryer and back in his empty palms. "Mr. Jeb." Her eyes welled up.

Clara served as the hub of everything in the house. At her reaction, he knew what happened. Someone, some monster, some criminal had taken his one and only pet, the only item that made his wife smile no matter what. Sweat broke out over his body. He clawed his way back into a standing position and pulled out his phone.

"Sir, is everything all right?"

He narrowed his eyes. Junior put the dog down here and like always it he would be the one who paid. "Dimitri, put the house on lockdown, we have a breach."

Before he pressed end, a siren rang, lights flashed, and the staff went into motion. He crossed his arms and waited. His GPS security system would be his rescue. If nothing else bankers were prepared for theft.

"Sir." As if on cue, Dimitri rushed into the laundry room. "What's the trouble?"

"Oh my." Clara hid behind him.

"We have a kidnapping in the form of one canine." He reached into his breast pocket, pulled out his wallet and produced a picture of Jeb. "Nobody comes in or out until the dog is found. I want everyone strip searched." No one would ever say he did not take care of his wife.

"Yes sir." Dimitri dashed away.

"Clara. Go ask every staff member if they have seen him." He put his hand to his forehead. Why would anyone take the dog? Amid all the people, the microscopic animal could be trampled, hurt, or could have slipped away. Maybe Jeb was wandering the mansion looking for him, Willow or Nan, lost, alone and terrified. The room seemed to heat up. "Damn." He bent over and braced himself on his knees. Somehow he would have to tell his wife her beloved animal was missing.

"Randolph! What is the meaning of this?" The click of his mother's heels on the tile barreled toward him. "Dimitri just opened up Mrs. O' Ryan's purse and cards to three different plastic surgeons fell out. I swore I saw him eyeing Mr. Jamison's toupee. He should really get a hair transplant. I should give him one of the cards from Mrs. O' Ryan's purse."

"Mother!" He grabbed the woman by the shoulders. "Someone took Jeb."

"What?" She pressed her hands to her heart. "Jeb? Someone took Jeb?"

He nodded. The woman wasn't good at much except making things pretty, but she would never allow him to be in distress.

"Dimitri!" She let out a screech.

"Sir." Dimitri returned without anything furry.

"I insist we look under Mr. Jamison's toupee." She wagged her finger toward their Head of Staff. "It's a terrible toupee anyway."

"Where's the dog?" Randolph balled his hand into a fist. If he had to beat the dog out of the party he would do it without delay.

"Come with me." Dimitri tilted his head.

The music resumed and the lights returned to normal and the party continued as he, Clara and his mother followed Dimitri through the dining room, the ballroom, and the main foyer.

A rumble of male laughter and cheers reverberated out from the billiard room.

Dimitri pointed inside.

With the same stance he used to tell a client he couldn't finance them, Randolph took soft steps toward the entrance.

All the men huddled around the pool table, blocking his view. The yelling died down. As if they were participating in some strange unknown ritual, they threw some money into the center of the mix.

Slate added his money and waved him over. "You have to see this."

Unable to spy what captivated all the men, Randolph shoved himself into the overcrowded room, joining his friend. "What is it?"

"I have no doubt why you married Willow." He pointed to the table. "It was definitely for her dog."

Randolph pushed aside someone he didn't know to peer down at the table. His knees went weak at the sight of the fluffy, furry cue ball.

"Okay, okay." From across the table his father scooped up the money, patted Jeb and put the eight ball in front of him. "Eight ball in the side pocket."

Damn if the little dog didn't push the ball with his nose. The men called to him and whistled as Jeb made his way around the green felt, a custom artificial yard for one pampered pet. The dog growled and tried to bite the ball, rounding two corners until at last he nudged the ball into one of the side pockets.

Once more the room went wild.

"Good boy!" His father held out his hand.

One of the staff held a silver platter out and Junior chose a little cracker, not one of Nan's handmade biscuits.

"A delicacy for the dog." His father held his finger up. Jeb sat down and the man placed the cracker into his mouth. "A dog with the taste for caviar."

The room broke into applause once Jeb crunched down.

"Caviar!" Randolph maneuvered his way to the edge of the table. "Jeb cannot eat caviar!"

At the sound of his name, Jeb turned and trotted over to him.

He scooped up the animal and cradled him to his chest.

"That is the best caviar." His father stood. "Over two hundred an ounce."

"Jeb is on a special diet." He held the dog up to his face, trying not to melt at the three black dots that created Jeb's two eyes and his nose. Fine, he liked the dog. Maybe a little more than liked.

Jeb licked his nose.

He swore his teeth hurt. There was a reason they called it puppy love.

"Come on, Jeb is cleaning up. We will be able to buy him his own wing soon." His father let out a hearty laugh.

"Well, why don't we give him a little break?" He hated to stop the fun, but he was quite certain his wife wouldn't appreciate her pet being used for monetary bets. "I need to go locate my wife."

"All right, probably a good idea on both counts. The billiard table is still dry." His father waved him away.

Without hesitation, he took advantage of his dismissal. Armed with his bit of adorable ammunition, he went to find Willow.

While he may not know much about his wife's past, he knew at least one item about her present. Once more he made it through the house, out the back door and headed toward the fruit trees. On more than one occasion he came home to find his spouse and Jeb wandering the garden.

He spotted her shoes before he found her, but like a trail of breadcrumbs it led him down one row to find her holding the hem of her dress up and simply studying one of the trees. "I take it back, I'm not proud of you."

She turned.

"I mean I am, but not in the way it came out." He walked down the aisle.

"I don't think I've done anything to make either of us proud." She wrapped her arms around her shoulders.

"It's just one of the many things we can differ on." He joined her and handed her the dog.

"I needed a break. I don't know if I can face them right now." She put Jeb down and allowed him to sniff and explore. "Do they know not to say anything?"

He appreciated her concern. "They do and they understand, don't worry. It's all good." Fine, he sugar coated the situation. He stepped toward the tree, taking his time to examine a leaf. The citrus scent floated around them. Jade's question from earlier echoed in his head. He wanted to reclaim what they had at the party, or those incredible few days before the dinner. "What I don't understand is how my father taught Jeb how to play billiards. I rescued him. He ate some caviar, I hope that's all right."

"He ate caviar?"

He nodded.

"You like Jeb." She let out a chuckle.

"Guilty." He shook his head.

"What's the difference between pool and billiards?"

"Pool is what you play in a bar. Billiards is what you play at my house." He exhaled. "I really have no idea."

"Thank you for whatever you said to Slate and Jade." She stepped closer. "You were right. Hiding didn't work."

At seeing his opportunity, he took her in her arms. First, she tensed but then rested her head against his shoulder. "Funny what comes back to bite us." In a way, his situation was no different. Both he and his father hid the truth from his mother, and except for a select few no one knew he had to get married or lose everything.

She nodded. "Sort of like not having a more refined back-up for your wife?"

"Actually, that worked out in my favor." No, maybe she wasn't his typical choice, but he couldn't picture anyone else in her role. Was that the answer to Jade's question?

She looked up at him.

"What's your favorite food?" He studied her. Though gorgeous all dolled up by the makeup artists, he thought he preferred her as her natural self.

"I can't tell you, it would be bad for my reputation." She gave him a slight smile.

"Come on. Lay it on me."

"Rib eye steak, rare."

"Sounds good." He laughed. A juicy piece of meat. Intriguing. "What were you like as a child?"

The scant bit of humor lighting up her eyes dimmed and she shrugged.

"Where did you live? Where did you grow up? How did you end up with Nan?" He finally dared ask only a few of the questions piling up in his mind.

She turned away.

The more she didn't answer, the more he wanted to know. "Willow."

"Why is it so important?" She refused to look his way.

"I want to understand you." He took her chin in his hand and turned her face toward him.

"Why?" Her eyes searched his.

"Because I want to." He lowered his face to hers. "Because right now I don't care that there are people asking where we are, because I don't care that you're standing barefoot outside at night, because you are here with me and I want to know."

"Do you think we could go to Sedona before we go to Vermont?" She reached up and moved his hair off his forehead. "I think it will put us back on balance."

His only image of Sedona was hippies and red rocks, though her talk of balance sounded promising. "If I say yes, will you let me in?"

"I need you to open your mind and celebrate the return of the light with me."

His wife spoke her own language. "I will head toward the light." The light better be where he found some answers.

Jeb trotted over.

"We should get back to the house." She bent down and picked him up.

"You are right, Mrs. Van Ayers." He picked up her shoes, took her hand and headed toward the house when he heard the sound of a woman's laughter.

They both stopped.

"*Cuidado con las manos*, Vincent."

Willow squeezed his arm. "Randolph, that's Nan."

"What did she say?" He loosened Willow's grip.

"What did you say, Nanette?" The definite sound of kissing made its way to their ears. "My gorgeous, voluptuous Nanette."

"I said watch your hands, Mr. Hartford." Nan giggled some more. "And your tongue."

He and Willow looked at each other.

With wide eyes and a grimace, Willow put her hand to her chest. "Are they having sex?"

Oh Lord he prayed not. "He's using his tongue somewhere."

"I knocked a glass out of Ms. Hartford's hand earlier." Willow handed him Jeb and hid her face in his shoulder.

"Well, it doesn't sound as if her brother is holding it against you." Unwilling to witness his client and his sort of mother-in-law using their tongues or anything else, he guided her the long way back to the house.

"Will you come with me to go freshen up?"

"Yes, I will." He kept his dog and his wife close, snuck into the kitchen and headed right for the laundry room.

"Thank you for taking Jeb out for some air." Still, she didn't move.

"I suppose we all need air, and I suppose they have a lot of it in Sedona." He put Jeb down and gave her a hug, liking a bit too much how she stayed close by his side. Once more, Jade's question echoed in his mind. "Yes, we need air and balance."

He supposed he would get the answers in Sedona.

Chapter Eleven

THE POUNDING OF THE DRUM matched the pounding in Randolph's head, while some squealing flute reverberated through his skull causing him to wince. After a forty-five minute walk through the Arizona wilderness, carrying a backpack of his and Willow's clothing and supplies, he saw nothing but red, literally. Everything around him was red, the rocks, the ground, and the sky. Unless someone produced some nice red lips in a convenient spot, he was completely done with the color.

When he agreed to go to Sedona, he pictured a spa. The type his mother frequented on vacation. She would leave in the morning to be massaged, exfoliated and polished, while his father played golf, went to a casino or did whatever his father did when the man wasn't handing out orders. Several hours later his mother would return rejuvenated and primped so they could go to dinner. Yes, he expected a spa maybe mixed with some incense and granola. He never thought he would be hiking to a clearing in the woods preparing to spend the night in a tent.

Actually, he would have gladly spent the night in a tent, on a dirt floor, or on another planet if he could get his wife to speak to him about anything other than the weather. The Willow who watched him, blushed and blundered, but then made love to him disappeared completely after the party and left in her wake a quiet, distant woman who seemed to avoid him at every turn. After the business dinner gone bad they traveled over rocky terrain, but the night of the party he thought they moved beyond. Apparently, he was mistaken because in the three weeks since the party the woman seemed intent on ignoring him.

Rather than a celebration of the winter solstice, he should have gone on a vision quest. His vision – Willow, his quest –

figure out his wife.

"Welcome Willow, Nanette." A woman in an embroidered orange robe took their hands in hers. "I am so blessed to see you again."

"Suzanne." Willow motioned toward him. "May I present Randolph Van Ayers?"

Along with losing the flushing cheeks and the sex, he lost his title along the way. He flashed the woman a smile and held out his hand. "The husband."

"Oh, I expected big changes for Willow this year." She gave him her hand. "Is this your first experience with welcoming the light?"

"Yes." With night upon them, he flipped up his sunglasses and looked the woman right in the eye.

She smiled. "I will be your Shaman guiding you through this journey."

"Then may I ask you a question?"

"Of course, ask anything." She gave his hand a squeeze.

"Will the light also lead the way to truth? A time for full disclosure to welcome in the New Year?" He needed to plant the seeds.

Willow turned to him. "Randolph."

"Randolph is right. Use this time for reflection of yourself and of your relationship." Shaman Suzanne reclaimed Willow's hand. "Oh, I feel it."

"What?" Willow's voice took on a dreamy tone.

"The energy between you two." The woman closed her eyes. "It's a thunderstorm and when it hits the ground it creates fire. Harness that power and together the two of you will do great things."

Well, they may not create actual fire, but Willow's cheeks went up in flames turning positively red, the color of the hour. Maybe there was one shade he could still tolerate.

"What about Nan? What do you feel with her?" Willow deftly deflected the attention away from her.

The Shaman opened her eyes, put Willow's hand in his and turned to Nan.

Along with him, Nan was also in Willow's doghouse. At least he wasn't alone. Since Mr. Hartford put his hands and his tongue to use, Willow widened her distance. The few conversations he caught between the two only dealt with topics regarding the store or Jeb.

"Nanette." The woman nodded. "A bit of excitement you haven't had in a long time is sizzling through you. Make sure you take advantage and take care of yourself."

Nan simply laughed.

Willow dug her nails into his hand.

He winced, but since she didn't pull away, he didn't move.

"Why don't you join the drum and flute performance and spirit dance? We will then be retiring to our tents to reflect on the solstice and awake for a sunrise stretch. We will take your bags so you can enjoy." Suzanne gave them a smile and two men came over and held their hands out.

Nan surrendered her satchel. Only because he was out of his element did he surrender his backpack. Also, because he hated backpacks.

"Go enjoy the earth and each other." Like a theatrical performer, Shaman Suzanne motioned behind her as if welcoming them on stage.

He let Willow lead the way to a circle marked off by stones. In the center some musicians played and other attendees of the event gathered around.

Willow chose her spot and sat right in the dirt. He took a breath, glanced down at his jeans to bid them adieu and sat next to her. Gravel seemed to cut through the denim, but he swallowed back his complaint, instead remembering that Willow owed him a talk and he wanted her to be comfortable.

He scanned the area. Willow fit right in here with her billowing clothes and hair, her lack of obsession with material goods and the need to connect with her surroundings. Why couldn't he get her to connect with him?

For a moment he simply watched her, took in her profile, with her perfect upturned nose and her pouty lips. Even without makeup her lashes extended long, creating the ideal frame to her eyes. Maybe rather than her connecting with him, he needed to connect with her.

He moved her hair off her shoulder. "Tell me about the music."

"It just speaks about the sacredness of life. It celebrates the return of the light, the New Year." She leaned into him. "Close your eyes and try to feel the music rather than just listen."

Fine, he would try it her way, but before shutting his eyes he took her hand.

The music continued and he tried to experience it in a new way. He concentrated on the throb of the drum, the lightness of the flute and how Willow's hand finally relaxed in his. Her hand fit within his, soft, smooth, small. He brushed his fingers against her wrist and smiled after he found her pulse.

"What is it?"

"Your heartbeat matches the beat of the music." He opened his eyes.

Once more, her cheeks reddened. "Randolph."

"What made you interested in all this?" He pulled her closer and brought her hand to his heart. "Tell me something, anything."

She stared into his face.

"Was it Nan? Did you grow up with her?" He needed some clue as to what made his wife his wife.

She licked her lips. "Nan told me to choose what I believe in."

He waited.

"I believe in a higher power, I just never knew what." She looked beyond him. "I didn't want to exclude any belief, so I tried to be open to all of them. I'm really looking forward to Christmas."

Her words replayed in his mind. At last she gave him something. "You never celebrated Christmas before?"

"You never celebrated a solstice before."

"You never celebrated the more traditional holidays then." He moved over into her line of vision.

As he learned, she answered how she answered any question she wanted to avoid, with silence, or sometimes an added attraction of a shrug. With his question he got the shrug as well.

A weight settled right in the center of his chest. No Christmas? No holiday? Even in his insane asylum of a home, they had all the trappings of the holidays, simple things that served to ground them as a family. He could count on his mother being more excited over the gifts than anyone and his father buying his way out. As a child his grandfather always purchased the gift he wasn't supposed to have and his grandmother allowed the junk food. "Willow."

The music ended.

"We need to go get settled in the tent." She used him for leverage and stood.

Once more she put him off, but they made headway and rather than forcing the situation, he got up and together they found their tent.

Tent.

"This is a tent." Though he spied the little triangles set up around the campsite, he didn't really expect to be staying in a tent. Honestly, he assumed they were only for show and somewhere off in the distance there would be some sort of building or a bus to take them to a proper hotel.

"Right, I told you we would be staying in a tent." She pulled back the flap. "You never went to summer camp or anything?"

"I went to summer camp." He bent down and peered inside neglecting to tell her they stayed in cabins and had a staff that waited on them. In truth, the cabins were more like five-star hotels. Well, four-star, they were roughing it. At least their backpack found its way back to them, and took up a good portion of the space. "Ladies first."

Willow took off her shoes and crawled in.

He followed suit, slipping and landing on an air mattress. "That was unexpected." As unexpected as the skylight in the roof he spotted when he rolled over. At least the place wouldn't be claustrophobic.

"You'll be okay." Willow grabbed their backpack.

"I'm not so sure about that." He watched her dig through their bag.

"I made us some food, are you hungry?"

Not quite sure if there was any such thing as a solstice feast, he nodded. "I don't think you have made me anything to eat yet." Curious, he wanted to discover what she would produce.

"Nan may be allowed in the kitchen, but I think Clara and Chef would rather me stay far away." She giggled and proceeded to take out some containers with fruit, cheese and crackers and some cookies.

"I have no doubt you are welcome to cook or do whatever you

please anywhere in the house." He sat up. "They probably just want to serve you."

"I always feel bad having them do things for me, especially when I can do for myself." She arranged her treats on a plate and put it between them.

"You'll get used to it." He sampled one of the cheese and crackers.

"Is everything tasting good?" She handed him a bottle of water.

She didn't respond to his comment, but he let it slide. Instead, he opened the bottle and tilted it in her direction. "Best I ever had."

She smiled.

They sat in silence and finished their makeshift meal. He reclined on the mattress and stared up at the ceiling. The top of the tent consisted of some plastic and mesh giving him a window to the sky. "I have a confession to make."

"Oh really?" She took a sip of water and adjusted her pillow.

"I've never spent the night in a tent before. I also never spent a day in tent before." He glanced at her out of the corner of his eye.

She gasped, let out a noise and coughs wracked her body.

"Willow?" He shot up and grabbed her, patting her back. "Are you all right?"

She caught her breath and went into a round of laughter.

He put his arms around her and joined her.

With laughter still claiming her, she collapsed against him.

He lay back, taking her with him and for the first time ever, they simply laughed together.

At last the giggles died down. "I never pictured you the type to go camping."

"I never pictured you the type to either, but in a different way."

"I've spent many nights in a tent." She started to push away from him.

Again, she let something out and he held her in place. "Stay here."

"We are supposed to use this time for reflection." She moved until she lay by his side.

"I'm trying to use it for enlightenment." He turned to her. "About you."

"I don't know what you want." Her breath brushed against his lips. "There's nothing to tell."

"I disagree." He reached down and took her hand. "I want to learn about you, why won't you tell me?"

She flipped over to her back. "The stars are amazing."

He ground his teeth together. If they were celebrating the light, her New Year, he needed some answers. "Willow."

"Are you going to be able to sleep here?"

"Why would you ask?" He balled his hand in a fist.

"Last year I spent my time staring at the stars. This year the first thing I noticed was the air mattress."

He willed himself to remain quiet.

"The mattress back in your room is incredible. It's just perfect. I never understood why you have a problem sleeping there. The other day I looked under the sheets and found the label with the manufacturer. I think if I buy nothing else next year, I'm going to buy that brand of mattress."

"What are you talking about?" He pushed himself up and stared down at her. "I ask to know something about my wife and all you talk about is a mattress? What are you hiding?"

Her focus remained on the sky. "You hide every day. You stifle your creativity and deny what you want to do."

"I have too many responsibilities to do what I want to do." Unlike her, he would give his spouse a straight answer.

"No. I think you're ashamed of what you want to be. Maybe ashamed because you don't have the guts to go after it."

Rather than spew the first words to come to his mouth, which most likely involved a profanity, he took a breath. "What are you ashamed of Willow?"

She didn't move.

"What are you so ashamed of that you can't tell me? What have you hidden away so deeply that I can't find any trace of you anywhere except for a birth certificate with only your mother's name?" He kept his tone even, calm.

She continued to gaze into the sky.

"What makes you not spend one penny of the money you get from me except for the bare necessities, but you will spend thousands on a mattress?"

"You might understand if you ever didn't have a mattress to sleep on." She sat up.

"What are you saying?" Again the weight pressed down on his chest, especially as all the clues filled in the picture.

"I am saying it doesn't matter." She spun to face him, her hair whipping around and hitting her in the face. "Why do you have to know? It doesn't matter! You didn't marry a woman with any background and it couldn't make a difference, because in a few months I'll be gone and then you won't have to worry about it!"

He recoiled as if she slapped him in the face. Again she mentioned the end and again Jade's question replayed in his mind. "Willow, I asked you before what you want."

"I can't give you the answer until you know what you want." Tears sparkled in her eyes.

He resisted the urge to reach out to her. "How can I know what I want when I don't even know who I married?"

"You know all you need to know and now you have your answer." She turned her back to him.

"So that's what you want."

Again, silence and a shrug.

Stagnant heat seemed to take over the tent. He had to get out of there and crawled out of the tent. "Am I allowed to go outside? I need some air."

"You are free to do what you want. Maybe you should create something."

"I was trying to." The night air instantly cooled him. A bon fire in center circle lit up the area.

Two tents over, he spotted Nan standing outside staring up at the sky.

He shoved his hands in his pockets and went to her.

"There's a regular bathroom just beyond the trees." With a laugh, Nan pointed. "Unless you want to commune with nature some more."

"When you and Willow didn't have a mattress to sleep on did you have a bathroom?" He rocked from his heels to his toes.

"That is not my story to tell."

"Fair enough." He didn't even know why he asked. "May I ask you something that is your story?"

"Of course."

"Why did you never marry?"

"Does a woman have to marry to be valid?" She hooked her arm in his and led him away.

"No." They walked around the circle. "Neither does a man."

"I was given a blessing when I got Willow, but she began her life on unstable ground and I needed to give her my heart to make her whole. I would give it to her a million times more, but now it's time for her to find her own soil."

"Can you give me anything to go on?" No, he wasn't beyond begging.

"Before you get what you want, you need to think of why you want it." She stopped and stood in front of him. "Do you want to win or do you want something more?"

Before he spoke, he took a moment to think about his answer. If nothing else, he wanted to give her the truth. "All I've done my whole life is try to win, so I don't even know how to answer your question."

Nan pressed her palm to his cheek. "Willow fears anything ending and your life is based on a series of finishes."

He absorbed her words. "I need to think."

"A good revelation for the New Year." She smiled one of those wise smiles that told him she knew more than she ever let on.

Arm in arm they continued their walk. Yes, he needed to think.

Chapter Twelve

"LILLIAN, HOLD IT TIGHT while I secure the ends." Mr. Van Ayers leaned over and tied one side of his tamale.

"Van, don't get my nail stuck in there." Lillian winced, but per her husband's instructions kept her fingers in place.

"I spent a lifetime watching your nails, do you think I would tie one up over three thousand miles away from your nail lady?" He moved to the other side. "Stay still, I know we can beat them."

Willow shook her head at the scene in front of her. Not in a million years did she ever think she would find Mr. Van Ayers making tamales on Christmas with the rest of the Van Ayers clan, but more surprising than anything was watching them work together. They were a true husband and wife team. Even with Mr. Van Ayers' commanding presence and Lillian's unique look on the world, the love between them was evident.

"We are already one up on you son." Randolph Van Ayers the first, otherwise known as Randolph the third's grandfather, otherwise known as Judge for his work in local politics, nodded. "Hurry up Caroline, we can get at least a two-tamale lead on Junior."

The family resemblance among the Randolphs was as incredible as the experience. Randolph I, II and III were like gazing upon a movie where the lead character gradually became older and Judge possessed the appearance of the star that aged but still kept his spark.

"We got this. You need the nimble fingers of a woman to tie the ends. My son's fingers are too large and he's too concerned with his wife's grooming." Caroline, Randolph's grandmother, finished her bow, held her hands up and gave Willow a wink. "Come on old man, get the next one, I want to spend time with my granddaughter-in-law. She promised me a reading before we open the presents. I want to know what I got before I get it."

With the grace and looks of a queen without the attitude to match, Caroline Van Ayers playfully, but dutifully, commanded all she surveyed including a mansion in Vermont that rivaled the one back in Bel Air, a staff and her husband. Willow observed her in awe. All the Van Ayers males practically cowered in her short, but powerful shadow.

"You talk about me father, but you haven't even mentioned your grandson, who walked away to go get something right in the middle of the fight." Mr. Van Ayers cradled his tamale in his palm and held it up. "Nanette, please inspect this one and tell Judge speed does not match perfection."

Nan bent down and gave him a thumbs-up. "You are right on."

Mr. Van Ayers put his in the pile and returned to his wife. "Come on Lillian, we can catch up. We'll leave the seniors and the babies in our wake."

Suddenly, Christmas music filled the air and the kitchen door boomed open. "I have returned." With a large burlap bag in his hands, Randolph entered the kitchen like a makeshift Santa Clause and headed straight for her. "Willow, I brought us something."

Since they arrived in Vermont, Randolph had gone Christmas crazy. Thus far he presented her with candy canes, made sure they strung popcorn and cranberries for the tree, decorated sugar cookies, and they tried to build a gingerbread house. They were never to speak of the collapse of their cookie cottage again. She swore her husband got tears in his eyes at the mention of the demolition.

"Anytime you want to take this playlist off repeat it is fine with me." Mr. Van Ayers shook his head.

"Bah Humbug." Randolph brushed him away.

In Mr. Van Ayers' defense, Randolph had played the same series of about fifteen songs for the last seventy-two hours. Of course, in same amount of time, he also stopped asking about her past. Either the man realized she was right and it didn't matter, he respected her wishes, or he didn't care anymore. She wasn't sure which answer she wanted, but she knew which one she didn't want.

"You better get going on these tamales, or you'll never catch up." Randolph's father held up another finished product. "The winner gets to pick the wine for Christmas dinner."

"Maybe it's not so much about winning, but the process of making the tamale and the spirit of the holiday season." Randolph opened his bag.

Everyone, including her, stopped and stared at youngest of the Randolph Van Ayers in the room. Had he honestly said it wasn't about winning?

Of course, along with not asking about her past was the other side of Randolph. Since Sedona, the man who had contracts down to what brand of sock he would wear, changed. He seemed deeper, he listened to her, and he doted on her. She shook her head. Maybe he did all these things before, and she tried to ignore him. No matter what, keeping her distance wasn't working at all.

"Randolph, baby, did you have too much eggnog?" Lillian twisted around to look at him.

"No, Willow and I already did eggnog yesterday." He reached in the bag and pulled out what appeared to be little brown nuts. "Today is spiced wine, sugar plums and roasted chestnuts."

"Honey, where are you getting these ideas?" Lillian narrowed her eyes.

Willow wanted to ask the same question. In truth, she wanted to ask many questions.

"The Traditional Christmas handbook." Judge let out a laugh and put another tamale in his pile.

She managed to not ask if there was such a handbook, but she caught Randolph reading on the flight to Vermont. The moment he discovered tamales were part of the holiday festivities and Nan knew how to make them, she would have thought he uncovered a Christmas miracle. Upon their arrival to the senior Van Ayers' home, Randolph insisted everyone join in the tamale making and refused the help of the staff.

"I didn't know there was a book." Lillian wrinkled her nose. "I hope we're doing everything right."

"I have it covered, Mother." Randolph returned his attention to Willow and handed her one of the chestnuts. "I talked to the chef and he said he could make these for us, and he said it would be his pleasure. He will even put them in paper bags for us. But first we have something to do."

She held her breath in anticipation of what he would conjure next.

"Like make tamales?" Randolph's father barked.

"We made tamales, and we are going to allow the rest of you to continue with this fine culinary craft while I take my wife into the snow." He took her hand. "I am busy being a husband."

And there was the problem.

He was being a husband.

An amazing one.

One who insisted on throwing her whole world off balance, and she didn't know how to get back on track.

"Keep talking son, you're slowing up your grandparents." His father lifted another cornhusk. "Lillian, I don't think there is the proper amount of meat on this one."

"Come on." Randolph shook his head and led her to the back door. He stopped and helped her put on a puffy white coat, and matching boots, mittens and scarf, items that seemed to materialize for her the other day. "You look like a gorgeous ice princess. It's the eyes."

While her mind begged to remain firmly grounded in reality, her heart fluttered, longing to soar away on the fantasy Randolph created since they left Sedona. He could easily take her heart. Half the time she wanted to give it to him on one of his mother's expensive designer platters and get it over with.

He put on his black cold weather gear. His blond curls and green eyes popped. The man should have forgotten finance altogether and simply sold pin up pictures of himself in various outfits. At the sight of him and the way he spoke, her body and her heart fought her mind. It was an all-out war and she decided to simply try to go with the flow, relax and capture some of the spirit overtaking her husband. "Well, then you look just like a handsome prince." She wrinkled her nose at her words.

"Then let's stroll about the kingdom, shall we?" With a smile that only needed a starburst to be complete, he bowed.

"Are you sure you don't want to return to the war zone and win the tamale trophy?" She couldn't believe he actually walked away from a challenge.

"Don't worry, I'll win." He held out his arm.

Powerless to ward off his overwhelming energy, she took hold of him. If nothing else, she needed the support.

Randolph's grandparents' property was at least as impressive as the California property, but more natural. The house was set against what she would describe as a forest, and even included a small iced over pond. With a dusting of snow on everything, the setting was right out of a catalog for Christmas, or the Christmas handbook.

They walked along the shoveled path over to the trees.

Randolph held up his hand. "I want to show you something. Stay right there." He took several steps into the snow and bent down.

"What is it?" She stood on her tiptoes to try to see.

"Hold on." His voice came out strained. "Close your eyes."

She shut her eyes and waited for yet something else she hadn't known she missed but wanted all the same.

Out of nowhere a ball of cold exploded on her. "Randolph!" She gasped and opened her eyes. Her coat was covered with pieces of snow, blending into her outfit.

Another snowball in hand, he grinned. "I'll give you a moment to catch up, but I warn you. I told you I would win."

Yes, they needed fun. She bit her lip, stomped into the snow and gathered up as much snow as she could into some sort of warped ball.

"I'm waiting." Randolph called out in a sing-song voice.

Without any knowledge of snowballs, she paused, going for a surprise attack. At last she spun around. In preparation of propelling her own projectile, she cocked her arm back, but before she fired off her weapon, another blast hit her right in the face. "Ah!" She jumped and fell back in the snow and dropping her own snow blob on her head.

"Willow!" In an instant Randolph skidded to her side, landing on top of her. "I didn't mean to aim so perfectly."

She opened her mouth and snow dropped onto her tongue.

"Are you all right?" Randolph brushed her off.

She blinked to find him gazing down at her. "You know what?"

"What?"

"The fight isn't over." Using her legs for leverage and the element of surprise, she somehow managed to turn the both of them over and straddled him, pinning him down.

"Is this how we're going to play it?" His eyes sparkled with mischief.

She slid her hand off to his side and scooped up some snow. "You started the game and didn't tell me the rules."

"I think no matter what the rules are you make up your own."

"Yes I do." She threw the snow on him at exactly the same time he returned the favor.

Like two animals set free, they let loose. Snow flew everywhere as they tried to pelt each other with the freezing white flakes. Despite her best efforts to win the cold war, she ended up on her back under Randolph.

"Had enough?" He panted, his breaths coming out as little white puffs.

Her throat dry from the exertion, she managed to gather up one more handful of snow.

He caught her wrist, lifted her arm, and with his free hand gave her a playful poke under her ribcage.

The tickles ran through her. At her laugher, she released her hold on the snow and dropped it on herself.

"You win." Her arm went weak and she blinked away the snow on her lashes.

"See? I told you I would win something today." He leaned down. "Do I get to choose my prize?"

"I don't think I have any choice over you picking the wine for dinner." She shivered from the cold and the way he looked her over.

"I want something much more tasty." He lifted his eyebrows.

"I'll see what I can do. I don't want to be a sore loser." Her heart sped and she willed it to slow, leave her alone and stop begging for something it couldn't have.

"You have what I need right here." He curled his hand around the back of her head, pulled her up and grazed his lips over hers.

His light kiss warmed her in all the right places, but before she had the opportunity to open her mouth, he pushed back and stared into her eyes. "I missed kissing my wife."

His wife. He wanted a wife if only for the year. Still, her

breath caught. She didn't realize she missed him as well and in her attempt to go with the moment, leaned up to connect their mouths once more.

In an instant he gave in and their tongues touched. While her center heated, the combination of lying in a pile of snow and a light breeze caused her to shiver.

Randolph moaned and moved his mouth to her ear. "You're freezing."

Somehow with him there it didn't matter.

"We are going to have to get ready for dinner and presents, but first I must warm you up." He stood and helped her up.

Better than the idea of presents, was the anticipation of how he planned on raising her body temperature. As he guided her inside and up to their suite, the snow clinging to her hair melted chilling her, and her mind yelled out a warning.

He corralled them both into the huge grey marble bathroom, turned on the water in the shower built for multiple people and returned to her. "Let's get out of these wet things."

On automatic she undressed, and dropped her clothes in a pile on the floor. Her mind overruled the rest of her body, and she realized she at least better figure out what she wanted before stepping into the shower with her husband.

Yes, Nan always told her to go with the flow, but she didn't think the woman meant getting washed away. What was it about Randolph the third that made her forget everything?

"The hot water awaits." He took her hand.

She turned and practically fell over. No wonder her mind turned to mush around him.

Yes, she had spied Randolph without his suit of armor many times, but for some reason it was always a flash, or the room was dark, or something prevented her actually being able to take him all in.

In the brightly lit bathroom, she finally got to truly take in the man she married.

His poster perfect looks didn't stop at his face. In fact, the rest of his body would have made the ideal centerfold. Muscles in all the right places encapsulated by smooth skin, everything fit, strong, and tight.

"Come on." He gave her a little tug.

Without a thought or a protest, she stepped inside with him. Several strategically placed showerheads ensured they both remained under the warm water. Once she spotted Randolph with his damp curls, she closed her eyes lest she attack the man. Images of him making love to her in their wet wonderland instantly filled her struggling mind.

"My God, you are beautiful." His voice echoed, bouncing off the marble.

She gained her courage to look at him. No matter the arguments, the miscommunication, the bizarre circumstances where they ended up together in the here and now, they had the same effect on each other. Though privy to the size of his erection, it was truly impressive in the stark bathroom lighting.

"I want you to know that from day one I thought you were beautiful." He took her by the shoulders and turned her back to him. "I want to do something."

Fine, she wanted it as well. Damn, she needed it. She might as well make love to him, he was right at the beginning. They couldn't stay celibate, it wasn't natural, and it made sense. "What do you want to do?" The shower boasted a seat in the corner, but she could easily brace herself on the water spigots.

"Tilt your head back."

Unsure of his plan, but up for anything, she complied.

Rather than answering, he combed his fingers through her hair. The aroma of lavender and lilacs took over the shower as he shampooed her hair.

She already knew what Randolph could do with his fingers, but she wasn't prepared for him to expertly massage her scalp, bring her follicles and the rest of her to life. With the strength leaving her body, she leaned back against him.

After all the back and forth, one part of her finally claimed the winning position. Her body wanted him and for the next several months she wouldn't deny her desires, but would indulge. Hopefully, the man would prove to be like a chocolate sundae and after feasting for months she would be sick of him.

He rinsed the shampoo out of her hair. "Are you enjoying Christmas?"

"I think I'll never be able to thank you enough for such an incredible holiday." With her new resolve set, she spun around and ran her hands over his wet, slick chest.

He tilted her chin up to his face. "I want to tell you something."

Her heart sped and she took a breath. "What?"

"Remember when you asked me if I would have dated you?"

She nodded but wondered how the topic bubbled up again.

"The answer is yes." He stroked his thumb across her lower lip. "I wish I would have asked you out instead of teased you. I wish I'd taken the chance to know you. I wish I would have had the opportunity to wine and dine you and I wish I would have done all of that instead of getting you caught in the middle of my situation."

The water continued to cascade over them. Yes, Randolph had changed and she liked it, liked him. Hell, she liked him before though he made her insane. Even if he was hard on her, he tried to be a husband, while she simply fluttered around him thinking signing her name on a marriage certificate was enough when in her heart she knew she faltered.

Beyond her control, she reached up and wrapped her arms around his neck. Though unsure exactly what he tried to tell her, his words raged havoc on her heart. Did she go with the flow or did she fight her feelings? Did she live each day or plan for the end of the year when they parted? Most importantly did she even out her world and step up and act like a wife? "I need to do a reading." For the first time she wished she really could tell the future.

* * * *

"Well, I did not know there was truly such a thing as Figgy Pudding until we had it tonight." Randolph's grandmother sipped her tea. "I'm not sure what you have done to my grandson, but I like it. Normally, he spends the holiday staring at his phone or computer."

Willow's cheeks heated, a normal occurrence for her these days. Caught in a food hangover from the amazing Christmas Eve meal and a Randolph hangover from his attention, she didn't speak.

"Yes, last Christmas he didn't even want to open presents.

Willow is having quite an effect on him." Lillian tilted her cup toward her. "You said to leave some of the tea in the cup?"

She nodded and distracted herself from Lillian's words by taking in the unique room. While the mansion in Bel Air possessed a million different beautiful rooms, the solarium Caroline took her to was one of the most magnificent places she had ever been.

Round and entirely made out of glass on half the circle, the little spot presented the perfect picture of the outside view. The evening lights sparkled off all the snow with the only break in the perfect covering where she and Randolph raged their mock war. Her heart fluttered. "I've never seen anything like this room."

"When Judge and I took over this home, he added the room for me so I wouldn't miss the California sun." Caroline nodded. "Something told me you might appreciate it as much as I do."

"It's beautiful." Maybe along with her mattress, once the year ended she would find a place with a solarium or sunroom. Nan would love it. She wished Nan would have joined them, but the woman insisted she needed to spend time with Caroline and Lillian alone and told her she needed to nap for a bit. The men of the family retired to the library for brandy and to digest before opening their Christmas Eve presents.

"Well, I am very happy that I could share it with you. Having you here has made the holiday's extra special." Caroline patted her arm.

Her heart both warmed and constricted at the wonderful traditions the Van Ayers allowed her to take part in. Aside from Randolph and Mr. Van Ayers, she was sure no one else knew her time here was only temporary. She swallowed and cleared her throat, wishing she didn't know either. "I'm so happy to be here."

"Are we ready to start?" Caroline set her cup down. "Randolph told me you have amazing talents."

Randolph told her that?

"Oh she does!" Lillian sat up straighter. "She's so smart, and she can make anything. I am having the most fun showing her off, and her store is amazing. She is everything I could have asked for in a daughter."

Daughter? Willow dug her nails into her hand refusing to have any reaction other than a smile. Even Nan didn't give her that title. She gulped her tea down, swallowing a couple of leaves in the process. "Okay, everyone hold the handle toward you and swirl the cup three times." She demonstrated and Caroline and Lillian followed her lead.

"Now what?" Lillian's voice took on a tone of wonder.

"We turn the cup over on the saucer." She showed them and guided them through turning the cup. "Lastly, we tap the cup three times."

"Is there a reason?" Caroline seemed to be spending more time watching her than tending to her tea.

"The gypsies used to say that it called the spirits to the tea leaves."

"May I go first?" Lillian pushed the cup and saucer toward her. "Maybe ask what is the silver box for me under the tree."

"I'm sure it jewelry." Caroline sucked in her cheeks.

"I hope so." Lillian pressed her hand to her chest and took a breath. "I'm ready."

"I'm going to turn the cup over and we will look for the picture." She lifted Lillian's cup.

All three of them gazed inside.

"It looks like a dirty cup." Lillian sighed.

Willow studied the configuration. "To me it looks like a fireplace." She traced the outline for them without disturbing the leaves.

"Well Santa is coming." Lillian practically bounced in her chair.

"A fireplace deals with matters related to your home." Willow returned the cup to her.

Lillian stared inside. "That's because my home expanded with you and Nan and little Jeb." She cradled the dish in her palms. "I have my son back."

"What do you mean, Lillian?" Caroline patted Lillian's arm.

"Before Willow, all he did is work, I never saw him and he didn't talk to me. It was as if he was dragging around a 100 pound bag of worry with him all the time." Lillian put the cup down and fanned her face. "Then he came home with Willow, and he changed. He comes home and he talks and he does things other than stare at that damn phone or computer. She turned him into a husband."

She held her breath. Randolph had changed, turned into a husband while she only signed a paper.

"The Van Ayers wives have a history of turning their boys into men." Caroline took their hands. "Willow fits right in."

Every muscle in her body tensed. With these women's words, she knew what was wrong, why she struggled. "No." She shook her head.

"What's wrong?" Caroline squeezed her hand.

She closed her eyes. No wonder her entire world was off balance. She was the weight. While Randolph moved on, went with the flow, became a husband, she fought her commitment, focused only on the end, what she wouldn't do, struggled at every turn. Her husband even went to Sedona and slept in a tent. He helped with her business and even defended her in front of her friends and she soaked it up like a sponge offering only sex in return when she felt like it and avoiding his questions.

"Willow." Lillian grabbed her free hand. "What is it?"

"I'm not a wife." Her voice cracked. She wasn't even a year-long wife. "I don't fit in. I messed up the dinner and I don't look right. He took my calendar away."

Silence took over the room and she opened her eyes.

Both women stared at her then, as if they were related by more than marriage, broke out into matching smiles.

"Is the calendar brown leather with gold edges on the paper?" Lillian giggled.

"I swear they buy them in bulk." Caroline winked at her. "I think the bank gave them away one year."

Willow looked from one woman to the other.

"When you first fall in love, it's hard to remember that being a wife also comes with responsibilities." Caroline's tone turned maternal, or grand maternal.

She bit the side of her mouth. Yes, she had responsibilities, ones she neglected. She wasn't sure about the love. No. She meant she didn't have the love.

"Men in the position of the Van Ayers men need a strong woman who can take charge. The job you hold with your husband is just as important as his job." Caroline continued.

Lillian nodded.

"You are part of an amazing history with a lot of tradition."

Caroline stared right into her eyes as if trying to relay a message. "Did you know we can trace your husband's ancestors back to before the Mayflower and every wife went through the same set of trials and tribulations?"

Did Caroline know why they got married? She opened her mouth but Caroline's serious expression and intuition told her not to react, give anything away. Wait. The situation made no sense. They were only in the situation for a year, how did that explain the marriages with the women who sat in front of her? She took a breath. They had the love.

"Van gave me the worst time when we got married." Lillian moved her chair closer. "I grew up in the valley, I didn't know how to do anything but go to the mall."

She took in Randolph's mother somehow finding it hard to believe the woman was anything other than the perfect complement to Mr. Van Ayers.

"One time we were at his finance meeting and he told me just to stand next to him and look pretty."

"My son." Caroline growled.

"What did you do?" Not wanting to miss a word, Willow leaned in.

Lillian sat up and smoothed her hair back, though she was perfectly coiffed, and glanced at Caroline.

"We gave her a crash course in banking, event planning and getting to know the right people." Caroline lifted her chin.

"That was after I showed up to one of his events in dirty dungarees and looking a mess, but managed to tell Van everything I knew about how to split up our finances in the event of our divorce." Lillian smiled, but covered her mouth with her hand.

Holy hell, these women were brilliant.

"I have the book upstairs, I'll lend it to you." Caroline patted her shoulder.

"Did you mess up his reservations?" Lillian asked.

"Yes," she whispered as if she wanted to keep the walls from hearing. "I didn't think it was important."

"Why didn't you ask me?"

She shrugged. The solution would have been obvious, should have been, but she ignored it like everything else.

"When we get home I'll get you a list of the six restaurants that not only are acceptable for a Van Ayers dinner, but all you have to do is say your last name and they will seat you at the best table." Lillian gave her a huge smile. "Next week we can go visit them so they know you, is that all right?"

She exhaled. "Thank you."

"You only need to develop your own style." Caroline piped in. "Beverly Hills is a hard town, but you have moxie, and I can help. I have been waiting for an opportunity like this."

Willow wanted to hug these women.

"Are you going to give her the vintage gowns?" Lillian's eyes widened.

"You were always a Rodeo Drive delight, but our Willow has more of an edge. She's Melrose and metaphysical."

"She's going to be even more beautiful and the envy of everyone." Lillian gave Willow a hug.

Caroline winked at her. "I hated seeing the clothes go to waste."

The woman understood. "I can't thank you enough."

"You already did." Caroline pushed her cup toward her.

Willow lifted the cup and showed it to both of them. "There's no surprise with this one. It's a square, a symbol of peace and protection."

The door opened and Randolph entered, staring at his phone. "Did Willow tell you what presents are in your future?"

"What are you doing on Christmas eve with that thing?" Lillian furrowed her brow.

"I'm watching Jeb. Junior rigged it so we can see him at the house in California. The staff is fawning all over him." He smiled and turned the phone around.

Willow's heart filled even further. For two hours she listened to the Van Ayers discuss the logistics of bringing Jeb on the trip. Once Lillian found out she couldn't pretend Jeb was a stuffed animal and bring her on the plane with them, she insisted her husband fix it. Within hours a crew was at the house installing surveillance equipment in what they turned into Jeb's suite. Honestly, Willow never saw a man move quite that fast to please his wife, except maybe Randolph.

"Randolph, look I'm a fireplace." With her cup in hand, Lillian shot up from her chair and showed her son while she watched the live feed of Jeb. "It means family."

"Well, we are all family." He narrowed his eyes at the cup.

Her stomach twisted at the word family.

"How on earth did Willow learn how to do all these things?" Caroline asked.

"She is but a mystery to me. One I had to learn to accept, Gran."

"Maybe some mystery is good." Lillian patted him and headed toward the door.

What kind of wife wouldn't even answer a simple question for her husband? Like it or not he was her husband, and she liked it.

"Come on." Randolph held his hand out to her. "This is the first time I've looked forward to presents since I can remember."

Without hesitation she put her hand in his, but before getting up from the chair, she quickly looked under her cup.

"What did you get?" He leaned over.

"Spider." The scent of his cologne swirled around her. She laced her fingers in his and looked up at him.

"Does that mean your husband will always save you from spiders?" He grinned. "Because I will, you know."

"Oh, I hope there is never a spider in the house." Lillian shuddered.

"In this case it means good fortune." She put the cup down.

"Excellent." He led her out of the solarium.

"It also means your wife would save you from a spider as well." She gave him a playful elbow but hoped he heard her.

"Also excellent." He wrapped his arm around her waist. "One day you need to do a reading on me."

"When you are at your most receptive." She left out the part about the spider meaning secretive and hidden things. Her energy needed a major overhaul. Maybe it was time to let him in, return the favors he had given her and at last be a wife no matter if it was only for the year.

Chapter Thirteen

LAST CHRISTMAS RANDOLPH sat in the main foyer of his grandparents' home and watched everyone open gifts. He received the gratuitous designer ties from his mother, some rare coins or something else of value from his father bought by his mother, and something bizarre from his grandparents, like the ship in the bottle kit that remained in the box.

He glanced around the couch. A box of ties, some collectable stamps, and an antique clock piled up next to him. However he had a couple of wild cards to make his carbon copy Christmas unique.

Wild card number one, Willow, held up the scarf his parents gifted her. Only Lillian Van Ayers could pull off getting one of the collectable scarves from that brand at the holiday season. The damn store didn't want to sell anyone anything. He knew, he tried, and then had to get Mrs. Avery to get his mother's gift. He took the scarf, folded it for her and put it around her neck using the vintage scarf ring his grandparents gave her to secure the thin piece of silk. "Beautiful."

She bit her lip and curled up on his side. Thus far she had given his mother and grandmother custom essential oils she created and named after them, slipped his father a box of his favorite cigars and with a huge smile, handed his grandfather a bottle of cognac. He would have preferred they gave their gifts as a couple, but she never brought the subject up and he didn't want to push her.

"Guapo, here." Wild card number two, Nan, thrust a thin box wrapped in craft paper in front of him.

"Are you feeling better?" He leaned down to the gifts Mrs. Avery wrapped and gave her his offering.

"Don't you worry about me, you have your hands full." Without waiting she ripped the paper off the small box, tore away the lid and revealed a pair of earrings. The multi-colored stones were made to look like flowers.

She smiled and held them up to her ear. "What made you get these?"

Everyone around the room oohed and ahhed.

"I saw them and they looked like you." The woman loved her floral prints and the earrings matched her. He took inventory of the presents he doled out. His mother was the easiest for someone with money and was thrilled with anything with a logo, while his father got whatever Mrs. Avery chose from her list. His grandparents were easy as well, a collectable book for his grandfather and anything classy for his grandmother along with a visit from him did the trick. However, he did struggle with Nan and Willow and Mrs. Avery wouldn't help.

"Then I will always cherish them." She bent down and gave him a kiss on the cheek. "Open mine."

He unwrapped his gift and opened the flat box to find a dream catcher.

"Do you know what that is?" Nan asked.

"It's a dream catcher." He smiled and lifted the intricate piece for the rest of the family to admire.

"Oh, it's so pretty!" His mother stood and touched one of the feathers.

"Maybe it will make you sleep better and expand your mind." Nan raised her eyebrows and resumed her seat.

"Thank you." For his last wild card, he bent down and handed Willow her gift. A larger box with glossy red paper and a big white bow. He had wrapped, unwrapped and wrapped the present multiple times and his chest constricted at the thought of her opening it, wondering if she would understand. Over the years he had given women gifts, and while they usually loved his taste, Willow was a wild card.

Apparently his wife had a case of nerves as well. Her cheeks glowing, she sat up from her relaxed state by his side and lifted a fairly large package wrapped in gold paper and held together with ribbon.

Without a clue of what it could be, be placed the squishy gift on his lap.

"Randolph, open it." His mother came to the rescue.

He glanced at Willow, untied the ribbon and pulled the paper open. Out of the corner of his eye he saw her lean over as he unwrapped one of her hand-crocheted blankets.

"Oh, how gorgeous." His mother ran her hand over the yarn. "Did you make this, Willow?"

She nodded.

Only a few weeks ago he called something similar a rag, now it was a precious keepsake. "I love it." He studied the perfect little stitches. She must have spent hours making the blanket. Done in the muted creams and tans, the colors matched their suite. Between the dream catcher and the blanket, he would have some truly unique pieces made for him not only showpieces. "No one ever made me anything before, thank you."

"Now you." His mother motioned toward the box.

After one more quick glance at him, Willow returned her attention to her own present and tore the paper away.

"Oh Randolph!" His mother screamed, bounced over and put her hand on the box in Willow's lap. "You didn't tape the box, did you? You have to keep the box."

"I even kept the bag from the store. It's at home." He knew the rules. "Let Willow open her gift."

"Let's see which one you got." His mother clapped and reluctantly took her seat.

Willow's hands shook but with great care took the lid off the box, moved away the tissue paper and lifted out his gift.

"Oh my God." His mother fanned herself. "It's gorgeous. The black one in large is always the perfect selection for the first one. It fits everything."

"A new bag?" Willow whispered the question, no smile, no excitement.

"That's not just any bag, that is THE bag, will always be THE bag." His mother took over the explanation. "It's an icon. This bag has history."

"It's incredible." She ran her fingers over the leather, the clasp, and the strap. "I needed a new handbag."

He held his breath waiting for the verdict.

"Thank you." She faced him.

Almost any other woman on the planet would have had his mother's reaction. Two weeks ago if Willow simply looked at him and softly said thank you he admitted to himself they would have gotten in a fight. Not anymore. Luck on his side, he unwrapped the gift one last time after the Sedona trip and his talk with Nan. "You didn't look inside."

"Did you get the wallet?" His mother practically fell over.

He didn't answer and waited for Willow to do as he asked.

With careful movements, she lifted the flap, reached inside and pulled out what he considered her true gift.

"This is rose quartz." She lifted the necklace strung with the pink stones. Her eyes widened as she gazed at the jewelry. "Oh my."

"Isn't that pretty." His mother breathed.

Nan nodded.

"Yes, rose quartz." He slid over and took the necklace. "I found it in Sedona."

She gave him the necklace, turned and lifted her hair.

He fastened the necklace around her neck and leaned into her ear. "The man who sold it to me said it was the perfect gift for a wife." Other than that, he honestly thought the pink semi-precious stones would look nice against her skin tone.

"I love it." She turned back and gave him a kiss, a soft one on the lips.

At the unexpected affection and after their shower earlier, he held her tight fighting the need to take her under the blanket and ask her to change into nothing but the necklace.

The room clapped.

"Randolph." She cupped her hand over her ear.

"Yes, Mrs. Van Ayers." He lowered his voice though his entire family had leaned into hear their conversation.

"I need you to help me change into my new purse."

His father gave him a thumbs-up.

Her whisper made him shudder. "You need help?" His mother screamed anytime his father even glanced in the direction of her handbag let alone touched it.

"Yes." She gave him a light kiss on the ear. "Meet me down here after everyone goes to bed, I need to do a few things." Once more she cuddled up on his side and laced her arm in his.

He unfolded the blanket and got them both underneath.

She reached down and put her hand in his, for the first time seeking him out.

Maybe that was the best present of them all.

* * * *

The flicker of the fire in the fireplace gave the main room of Randolph's grandparents' mansion an ethereal glow. With her new handbag cradled in her arms, her old handbag slung over her shoulder and her amazing necklace around her neck she made her way down the stairs. Her instinct told her Randolph had no idea he gave her the stone representing unconditional love and peace, but no matter what he had been drawn to it and the day she signed her name on the contract their lives were forever intertwined. Maybe it meant more that he didn't know.

In the main room she found Randolph on the rug by the tree staring into the fire and holding a glass and a sketchpad by his side.

"I thought we would have a nightcap on this fine Christmas Eve." He didn't turn to look her way, but he lifted an empty glass. "Come join me."

Something about Randolph Van Ayers the third made her stomach spiral like when she used to like a boy when she was younger. She supposed they called them crushes for a reason.

"What are you drawing?" With a breath and a swallow she joined him and put both bags in front of them.

"I can tell you beyond a shadow of a doubt that I never helped a woman change purses. I thought it was one of those things that would elude me for my entire life." He handed her the pad and reached out for her bag.

"How about we drink first?" Maybe some liquid fortification would help calm her nerves. One thing about Randolph was that once someone put a goal in his path he pursued it, from completing his list to running an empire to changing a handbag. Not ready for her conversation to start quite yet, she took in the picture he drew of the two of them in their snowball fight. "Your talent is incredible."

"It's passable." He poured her some of the amber liquid and

handed her the drink and tapped his glass against hers. "To an amazing holiday."

"Absolutely." The alcohol burned yet warmed her as it made its way down in one smooth stream.

"A woman who can sip a single malt scotch without wincing is very sexy." He downed his drink and put the glass aside.

She stared right at him and took another taste without as much as a flutter.

"Do it again." His tone lowered.

"You don't have any."

"Don't worry about me." He kept his focus on her.

Without breaking eye contact, she put the glass to her lips and tilted it back, polishing off the rest of the liquid.

In an instant he took her into his arms and kissed her. His tongue searched out hers and he bent her back.

Oh, he made it incredibly easy to become lost, forget what she came down here for. Though she made up her mind she wanted to be a wife, she needed to let him choose if he wanted someone more than a person who put her name on a paper.

He moved his lips to her ear. "You are delicious."

She shivered.

"Are you cold?" He chuckled. "Do you need some more Scotch?"

The question handed her the perfect opportunity, the ideal introduction to her story, and she decided for once in her life to take full advantage. She put her palm to his cheek. "What if I told you that since I was ten years old, Nan would give me tastes of alcohol to keep me warm on the coldest of nights? She said it was a natural heater."

The man was smart, probably too smart. He froze, the shine in his eye dulled and he nodded. "I would answer that I have a multitude of questions that go along with your statement."

For only a second, she paused. They couldn't handle any more back and forth, no more fights. If they were married, they were married. "Then I would say go ahead and ask me anything."

He took her hand and helped her sit up. "Why didn't you have heat?"

A long time ago she even forbid Nan from talking about their history. Exactly like she stopped Randolph from mentioning their situation to Jade and Slate. She couldn't hide anymore. "Because not everywhere we stayed had heat."

"What about your parents? Didn't they mind their little girl being without heat?"

"I told you we need to switch bags." She pulled her old bag over and spilled the contents out between them.

"I thought we were talking." He balled his hand in a fist.

No more frustration. She forced herself forward and turned the bag inside out, ripping off the bottom and revealing her history she hid in the one place she knew would be safe. "I'm sure whoever my father is didn't care about my lack of heat, since my mother never bothered to provide a name for him." For a man with history dating back several hundred years, she wondered if he could even process what she told him.

"Willow?"

"My mother died right before I turned ten. It was a car accident. They wouldn't even let me into the hospital room, but Nan held me and said it didn't matter, she wasn't there anymore anyway and couldn't see me." She rifled through the documents and handed him her mother's death certificate and her birth certificate.

He carefully unfolded the papers, running his fingers over the official seals. "How did you end up with her?" His voice lost both its sharp slant and its teasing tone. The game ended.

"Nan promised my mother to take care of me, but it was never in writing. I had nowhere to go and she swore not to leave me, so we sort of disappeared."

"Disappeared?"

For the first time, she rendered the man nearly speechless. "No school, no home, no history. Though Nan tried to make it magical and tell me we lived like spirits flitting from one thing to another, it was more like we didn't exist."

"That's why I couldn't find you." He stared down at the papers.

"When you tiptoe around the edges and never truly settle down in one place it's easy not to be found. If you don't have an address, no one can come take you away. Where would they look?"

He rifled through her items strewn on the floor. "How did you survive like that?"

"Nan taught me. People liked getting tarot readings and such from the young girl with intuition." She watched him put the things into his predetermined groups, makeup, papers, change, a ball of yarn and a crochet hook, and her little treasures, some rocks and a few twigs.

"How did your mother and Nan meet?" He lifted a little photo album. "May I?"

She opened the book for him and showed him the few pictures she had of her past. "They were best friends. I don't really remember a time where Nan wasn't there." She stopped at a picture of her mother and Nan on the beach.

"You look like your mother." He brought the book closer to his face. "Nan is different."

She smiled at the photo of Nan in a bikini. Since she was with the woman every day she didn't see the metamorphosis. One second Nan was teaching a twelve-year-old how to gaze into crystal balls, the next taking naps and complaining of jet lag. "It's strange how time changes things and people."

"It is, sometimes I walk into my office at work and wonder how I got there. I turned into the person I used to watch and say I would never be that person." He opened her new bag and slid the photo album inside. "What did you want to be?"

"I don't know." She faced him, the firelight lit up his already gorgeous features. For the man with the finish line always in sight, not having a goal in mind had to be a foreign concept. "Nan always wanted to own a metaphysical shop, and I swore I would make it happen." If it hadn't been for Jade's kindness she wouldn't have succeeded. Yet another person she needed to come clean with, and be real.

"What did you want?" He put the bag down and turned to her.

"A mattress." She looked down at the rug. No matter where they settled for a time, the beds always seemed wrong, worn and used. Not a serene place for rest, only a place to sleep before moving on. "One area I could return to every night and sink in the sheets and know it was mine." Until Nan taught her to never be afraid of what she couldn't see, she used to stare out the window terrified of every shadow.

"Oh my God."

"You were right when you said ink was sacred and things should be put in writing. I never wanted to believe that until you." Refusing to see his pity or disgust, she was grateful for the tears clouding her eyes. She remembered the day she finally got a bank account and her name was printed on something without the fear she would be swiped away from her only family.

"Willow." Again, he gathered her up in his arms.

She shut her eyes and pressed her face into his shoulder, breathing in the scent that would forever be him. Except for Nan, her Mother, and Jade, he was the longest relationship she ever allowed herself to have.

"Why wouldn't you tell me until now?" He combed his fingers through her hair.

She shrugged.

"That's not an answer."

After taking a minute to breathe, she lifted her face to his. "I didn't want you to know you bought a basically homeless, uneducated woman into your life." Along with not being a wife, it seemed as if she wasn't holding up her end of the deal. Especially for what he paid.

"Correction, I *brought* you into my life." He gazed into her eyes. "Do you hear me? I *brought* Willow into my life."

"Only because I was the last person available."

"Then the fates saved the best for last. You were a limited edition."

She pressed her lips together not wanting to say that if the fates brought them together, maybe they needed more than a year to see what happened once he reached his goal. Her throat dried out at the admission. She wanted to be with her husband, the man who brought Willow into his life, not the wandering weed with no roots. "Randolph?"

"What is it, Mrs. Van Ayers?" He gave her one of those smiles and returned to arranging her handbag. "Tell me what I can do for my wife?"

She lost herself in watching him. How did she tell him what she wanted? "I want my calendar back."

"Look, everything has a place and there is still room for the calendar." He closed the bag and presented her with his handiwork. "We will get through the year and then we won't need it anymore."

Yes, one thing about her husband was when he set his mind to a goal he went after it full force. Everything had a place. She had a place in his life, and even if she wanted it to change, it wouldn't happen until he won. All her life she lived in limbo. She needed to wait until he reached the end, but at least he knew the person he would cross the finish line with.

Chapter Fourteen

RANDOLPH STARED DOWN at his desk and rubbed his tight, aching neck. Actually, he didn't know where his desk disappeared to, but he assumed it had to be somewhere under the stacks of file folders.

While he rang in his second and more traditional New Year resolving to spend more time with his wife, Ms. Hartford must have resolved to invest in any opportunity the new year brought her. At the moment he and his father were playing tug-o-war with their employees, which left him, Peter and Mrs. Avery to pick up the slack.

The Hartfords business would net them an amazing profit.

There was only one major downside.

He was failing miserably keeping his resolution. Since his talk with his wife, things changed and he liked the new Willow. Liked her a lot.

His neck seized once more when he caught sight of yet more emails flooding his inbox. The muscles cried out in protest of him sitting in the same position for hours. For once, he wanted to get home with enough time to take Willow somewhere. Do more than kiss her hello, eat a quick bite, work some more and go to bed.

Wait. The going to bed part was non-negotiable. In fact, it was his favorite part of the day, or night. Since Vermont, going to bed did not mean sleeping right away.

A smile crept over his face at the memory of last night. Willow had been especially happy to have him home. He glanced at his watch. Maybe he could sneak out for a quickie. As Willow would say, he needed the release and she was adamant that making love was therapeutic. No one would deny he needed therapy.

With his resolve set, he no sooner stood than he was

interrupted by a knock at the door. A quick scan around his office told him there was nowhere to hide. "Come in?" He winced.

The door opened and both Peter and Mrs. Avery charged inside carrying papers, more papers.

He tried the assumptive close. "I was just about to go home for lunch."

"There are some more files for you to review." Mrs. Avery shook her head and managed to slide over one stack of files folders to make room for another. "We also need you to draft that proposal."

"I'm hungry." His tactic changed to whining.

Mrs. Avery pointed to his chair. "Do you want me to call you in something before I leave for the day?"

"You can't order what I want." He returned to his seat and put his head in his hand. "Please don't leave."

"I have a doctor appointment, you will live. You have Peter." She patted his head and without even offering him a mint, left.

He watched her go and averted his attention to Peter.

"Guess who called me today?" Peter sat across from him.

The law of deduction would tell him not Elizabeth. His relationship was much stronger than Peter's. Relationship? His mind wandered as he pondered the word. Yes, he and Willow were in a relationship, they were married. Of course everyone had a relationship to one another, but were they *in* a relationship in addition to the way he threw them together? He already established that he would have dated her, he couldn't wait to see her, he thought about her. How did she feel?

"Hello." Peter waved his hand.

Randolph blinked and refocused. Damn, he wished he had the time to go home or by Willow's shop. "Who called you?"

"Slate."

"What?" Peter didn't appreciate art. Willow did. She appreciated everything. Again his thoughts went off in another direction. She kept asking what happened after the year was out, and now he wanted to know as well. Would they date after their marriage ended? His throat constricted and he stood.

"What is wrong with you?"

"Nothing." He pulled out his cell phone, resumed his seat and glanced at his messages. Willow rarely initiated text messaging, she seemed exasperated by the whole idea of her cell phone, but she always replied. "Why did Slate call?"

"He says you've been putting him off about his co-op and thought you had something for him."

Randolph stared straight ahead. The co-op. He froze, his neck muscles stretched to the point of breaking at his recollection. The last he remembered he needed some signatures. "I need you to do something for me."

"That is why I am called your personal assistant."

He opened a drawer and found the co-op file along with a piece of stationery and an envelope. "Please go to the gallery and have Slate sign these documents so I can run some reports." He found a pen and quickly jotted a note to Willow asking her to dinner that evening. Perhaps a more old-fashioned mode of communication was in order and he was on a quest for yet more answers from his wife, but not about her past. He put the note in the envelope and wrote her name on it. "While you are on that block will you please hand deliver this to my wife?"

Peter took the folder and the notes. "Would you like me to spray some cologne on it too?"

"Go." He pointed toward the door, hitting a pile of the folders. The pile gave him a courtesy teeter, enough time for him to react.

Instinct took over and he jumped to save the stack, but only succeeded in knocking it over and ended up showering the room in manila folders and scattered papers.

"Oh holy hell!" Peter got down on his knees, crumpling several of the documents.

"Don't touch it." Randolph pressed his fingers into his temple and took in the disaster. Peter would only make it worse. "Just go and forget the letter to Willow. Just go."

Without saying another word, Peter put the letter on the top of the mess and tiptoed out, shutting the door behind him.

He slumped down in his seat and gazed at the picture of his wife. No dinner, no talking, no bed. Instead, he would be here for the duration. The mishap no doubt added hours to his workload.

A light rap at the door interrupted his self-loathing. All he needed was a visit from his father or the garbage man. "What!"

The door opened.

"Randolph?" A golden glow entered his office in the form of

one Willow Van Ayers holding a basket in one hand and her handbag over her shoulder.

He exhaled, his body weak with relief or some emotion he didn't know quite how to describe. "Willow?" Maybe the power of wishful thinking did work and the energy she always spoke of called her to him. He straightened up.

"Don't move." She walked around the papers.

He remained perfectly still.

"The vibes through here are off the wall." In a figure hugging wrap dress with a geometric pattern and the necklace he bought her, she waded her way through the war zone to him.

"Be careful." He took her hand and pulled her to him.

"What's wrong?"

"Now it's getting better." He put his hand in the curve of her waist, leaned in and kissed her.

"Don't lie to me." The bangles around her wrist made a satisfying click as she lifted her arm and pressed the back of her hand to his cheek.

He swore the woman was psychic. "I'm a little stressed out."

"I can fix it." She pushed him back into his chair and put her basket on the one clean spot of his desk. "First, you need to eat."

"I am starving." He gazed up at her. The sunlight danced over her features. For the first time since he walked into his office, he took a breath.

"Then it's a good thing I brought food." She let out a light chuckle and handed him a bowl and a fork.

The aroma of spice filled the air. Unfamiliar spice. "What did you get?" He took hold of the white china bowl and peered inside. The mish mosh of food seemed mixed up and...he tried to think of the right word. Well, it seemed healthy. Mess of papers or not, maybe he should be a man and treat Willow to lunch at the nice five-star restaurant in the next building over.

"It's mixed vegetables and grilled organic free-range chicken on a bed of kale and quinoa with cumin and turmeric and other Moroccan spices, and I topped it with some currants to give it a little sweetness." She held out a fork.

"You topped it?" If she topped it, she may have done more than pick his meal up at a restaurant.

"Oh there was the most amazing farmer's market and I saw

those vegetables. They looked like they belonged on the cover of a cookbook, so I bought them, and then I did something I never did before." Her voice vibrated with excitement.

"Tell me."

She put a bottle of water down on his desk and walked over to the papers strewn about on the floor. Without even asking she started picking them up. "I went back to the house and Chef and everyone let me have the kitchen so I could cook for you."

Holy Mother of God, she had made a meal for him. He was quite certain his mother never made his father anything beyond an olive for his martini. Hell, he would put money on the fact Elizabeth never made Peter anything. Even if it took his last ounce of strength, he would get down every bite. He stabbed some of the healthy goodness with his fork. "How did you get to the house?"

With grace and smooth movements, she continued with the little task she deemed her. "I took a bus and then walked up the hill."

The vision of Willow taking the bus through Los Angeles made his hunger wane. "Why didn't you call Dimitri?" If he found out their Head of Staff didn't drive her here he swore he would make the man eat all of food in his bowl and any leftovers.

"I didn't want to bother him, but he drove me to your office. Insisted on it. Even made me sit in the back seat." She put the papers and file folders in a neat pile on a chair and returned to him, leaning back on the desk. "You're not eating."

With no choice, he put the fork in his mouth. Rather than the strange textures and weird combinations he anticipated, a flurry of flavor cascaded over his tongue. Spicy sweet and plenty of bite, the dish was refreshing rather than repulsive and he nodded. "This is quite good." He took some more.

"I'm glad you like it." She walked behind him.

To top her treats, she massaged his neck.

Her fingers pressed in all the right places. Tight, sore muscles gave way underneath her touch. He leaned his head forward, basking in the way she tended to him, in the way she sauntered around his office taking over like a...like a wife. "Willow?"

"Shh." She slid her hands to his shoulders. "Try to relax. I've been worried about you."

He put the bowl aside and closed his eyes. How did she know

exactly what he needed? No one ever worried about him. "Why?"

She continued to work over his shoulders, his arms and back up to his neck. "You've been working way too much."

He wanted a real answer, one not recycled about every banker on the planet. If anyone in investments was any good, he or she was also working too much. "How do know how much I'm supposed to work?"

In a surprise move, she bent down to his ear. "I'm your wife, I know."

An amazing shiver ran through him at her voice brushing against his ear. For the first time she actually referred to herself as his wife. He grabbed her hands. "Since you're my wife, what else do you know?"

"That you may need more than food on your lunch break."

His body reacted instantly to her teasing tone. Without waiting one second, he pulled her over onto his lap and chose to sample something even more delectable.

Their mouths melded together, their lips and tongues working in unison to tempt and taunt the other.

A small coo escaped her throat and she wrapped her arms around his neck.

He held her tight and ran one hand down her arm and cupped her breast, his thumb grazed her tight nipple.

She squirmed and deepened the kiss.

After tending to her other breast, he skimmed his hand down her body until he found her bare knee.

His erection swelled and he lifted his hips, grinding into her. "What else do I need?" He spoke into her open mouth.

She connected their lips once more and without a word answered by lifting her knee.

"Oh, God." He toyed with her mouth and inched his hand up her thigh, stopping short.

"Don't stop." She tangled her fingers in the knot of his tie. While she once struggled with unknotting the accessory, now she managed to perform the action with ease.

He pulled back and looked into her eyes, the blue as incredible as the first time he saw her. "Do I turn you on?"

Before reaching his goal, she caught his wrist. Without breaking eye contact, she untied the bow on the front of her dress.

The garment fell open, revealing his gorgeous wife. "I think you know the answer to that."

The lunch hour had to be ending. At any time his office would be deluged with more people, more work, but maybe he had time for a little indulgence. "Let me take care of you and then tonight you can return the favor." Feeling his wife orgasm against his hand would be enough to get him through the rest of the day.

She shook her head. "No, both of us."

He kissed her. "There's no time, no room."

"There's always time." She got up, let her dress drop to the floor

"Willow." He stood and took her all in, his hand automatically going to his belt buckle.

"We can make room." With a slight smile on her face, the same one he used when he knew he made the right financial choice and bested someone else, she moved her basket to the floor, propped herself up on his desk and spread her legs. "It's easy."

At the sight of her practically splayed across his antique desk he ripped his pants open. "I want you."

"Then you better take me." She reached out for him.

Not bothering to think and going simply with his own wants, he let his boxer briefs drop, took hold of her hips and entered her.

Warm and ready, her body accepted him with no resistance.

"Jeez." In an attempt to calm down, he held her tight and took a breath. After spending the afternoon thinking about her and then watching her, he would go over the edge too fast.

She put her hand on the back of his head. "You better hurry."

"Oh, man." With her permission, he let loose and thrust into her.

"Take out your stress on me." She wrapped her legs around his hips.

"Willow." He shut his eyes and drove into her, fast, strong strokes designed to rush him to his own end and it worked. His entire being focused on the pleasure the two of them created together. There was something to be said for making love to the same woman, getting to know her, being able to do anything including a quickie in his office. It was one of the many definitions of a wife, and the thought only served to stoke his arousal. He never wanted a woman as much.

"That's right." Her voice hitched. "Come on."

"I need you to." Though his body tensed preparing for the ultimate release, he snuck his hand between them to give her the extra required to catch up to him. Making love to her wouldn't be the same if they both didn't obtain satisfaction. They had to get there together.

"Ah." She dug her nails into the thin fabric of his dress shirt. "I'm there."

He waited to hear those words, but even more glorious was the way her body undulated around him. The ripples of her orgasm reverberated through him giving him the last push to completely let go. His climax hit him hard, wracking him with multiple surges of unbelievable ecstasy. "Oh, God!" He grabbed her, a needed and welcome support as his knees buckled from exertion and euphoria. "Oh my God." He lowered his face to her shoulder, grazing his lips against the salty sweetness of her bare skin.

"You needed this." She combed her fingers though his hair and chuckled.

"I need you." He closed his eyes and tried to catch his breath. The words left his mouth with barely a thought, but damn if that wasn't exactly how he felt.

"I know you need me." She leaned back.

His strength returning, he caught the meaning of her words. The awkward moment gave him the perfect lead into the question he had before she ever arrived here. "Do you need me?"

She let her hands drop to the desk. "We need each other."

He lifted his head and stared into her face. "More than the obvious?"

"Is it?" Her lips twitched threatening to smile.

The woman was definitely turning into an executive's wife, answering a question with a question was an old trick used by the best. He moved in to kiss her.

A knock at the door interrupted them.

He froze and Willow giggled. What did he do with a wife naked on his desk, him with his pants around his ankles, and both of them in complete disarray?

The door handle jiggled. "Randolph." A familiar female voice called to him.

He turned to her. "That's one of the analysts."

"Answer her." The smile she fought, took over her whole face.

"Don't come in! Give us a minute." He pulled up his pants and attempted to put himself back together.

"Well I suppose this afternoon we won't have time for a second round." Willow got off the desk and slipped back into her dress.

He stopped his unsuccessful attempt to rid his clothes of wrinkles and watched her wrap her body back up.

She glanced over her shoulder at him. "Well at least I found one thing that makes you stop and take a breath."

"It's you."

"Are you working late tonight?" She cleaned up her basket, found his tie and wrapped it around his neck, holding both ends.

He used her tactic and shrugged.

"How about I go back to the house for a bit and then return with dinner and a change of clothes?"

He used the spare suit he once kept in the office the day after they got married and he never replaced it. "That would be amazing." Only a wife could pick up on what he needed.

"Okay, I'll be back." She picked up her handbag and her basket.

"You don't have to rush." He caught her arm and gave her a light kiss. "But hurry."

Her cheeks betrayed her with a blush. She walked across the office and opened the door. The shadow of the analyst darkened the exit.

"Give Mr. Van Ayers a few minutes, will you?" She peeked back inside and winked.

He waved even though she was only a few yards away. She changed, but she was still Willow.

"How's your neck?" She raised her eyebrows.

"Never better." He watched his wife leave and he didn't want to see her go. Yes, things had changed.

* * * *

One thing about the mansion, dare she call it her home, was

that Willow never walked into an empty room. The staff always offered a comforting presence and a smile. However, in the middle of the day with the men working, Lillian off at one of her events and Nan still at the shop, everything seemed unusually quiet and she didn't realize until that moment how vibrant her life had become.

She tiptoed up the stairs, but she may as well have floated. What she wished for at Christmas might turn into reality. The man who tormented her, then married her, seemed to want her. Once she did as she believed, and let it go and opened her mind, he came to her. Yes, maybe they met and married in an unconventional way, but she was never known for following any convention.

Her instinct told her Caroline and Judge and Lillian and Mr. Van Ayers met the same way. Unsure if the strange ritual was some bizarre tradition or something else, the method no doubt worked for at least two generations.

After making her way into their suite, she put her bag down with a pat, and went to the closet. Her side was merely a fraction of Randolph's but she got a nice boost when Caroline gave her the vintage clothing Lillian squealed over. In truth, the pieces were gorgeous and amazing and they fit her. After struggling to merge her style and Randolph's life, she found her answer and loved the new look. Lillian clapped every time someone doled out a compliment on her clothes.

She slipped out of her dress into her robe and turned to her husband's overstuffed side of the closet. Shirts, suits, pants, everything in copious quantities, all perfectly hung and color coordinated. The man even had an entire separate section for ties, little racks that pulled out from the wall revealed multicolored and textured ties, her favorite part of his normal uniform. She ran her hand along the shirts wondering what she should choose.

Until Randolph she dated only briefly, a few men here and there, and she never lived with one. How on earth would she dress him? She sat down on the floor and scanned his shoes sorted by color and type, touched the sneakers she never saw him wear, and smiled at the dozens of dress shoes.

At spying a pair of what she would dub rock star boots, complete with buckles and zippers, a laugh escaped her throat. He practically hid the pair at the end of the row where they were almost camouflaged by some long hanging garments, like robes one would wear for a graduation.

What would Randolph do if she brought these to the office? She leaned way over, practically lying on the floor and picked one boot up. By the wear on the soles he never wore them, but she wondered if he secretly wanted to, maybe like he wanted to create his art. She wished he would take her on one of his secret creations.

A slight blue glow caught her eye when she went to replace the boot. With a shake of her head she scooted over on the thick carpet, moved the clothes aside and unveiled a small, simple safe with the door ajar. The glow she observed came from a light on the combination keypad. Though she never owned anything worth enough to put in a safe, the fact her husband had one didn't alarm her. Everything about him seemed to have a value attached.

Every molecule in her body told her not to peek, but almost beyond her control she inched over, opened the door a bit more and looked inside.

Papers. A few file folders inside, holding more of Randolph's precious papers.

She exhaled and went to leave the safe as she found it, taking one last snoop before returning the door to its almost locked position, but she spotted her name written on one of the tabs.

For at least two minutes she wrestled with the idea of spying. Four times she reached in the safe to touch the folder and four times she recoiled. Her struggle told her the answer, but still, on the fifth time, she reached in and grabbed the stack of papers. "He's my husband." She said her justification aloud to make sure the universe heard her.

Without leaving room for her to turn back, she opened the folder and exhaled. Her birth certificate and mother's death certificate lay on top of the stack. She smiled. Randolph must have put them away for safe keeping along with their marriage contract. She touched the stationery. Their wedding almost seemed to have happened to someone else while their marriage was most definitely grounded in reality. She crossed her legs and took her time turning through the rest of the pages.

Behind her contract were several more stapled documents.

As she read the next paper, her chest tightened. The document was the one outlining Randolph's marriage circumstances. Though a tiny part of her always wondered if everything he said was true, outlined in front of her were his tasks, everything he needed to complete to earn his spot in the family. Everything except marrying her.

No doubt her husband was incredible. Most people couldn't accomplish half of what Randolph had done in thirty-three years in their entire lifetimes. She pressed her palm to the paper, praying his father realized who he had for a son.

She turned to the next page and held her breath. As she suspected the page dealt with his marriage, but was scratched out with a thick black pen and a note to see the revised contract.

Revised?

Her throat dried out, but she continued on and went to the next document, not a contract, but a formal letter from Randolph to his father.

She skimmed past the salutations and other business conventions and focused in on the main paragraph.

> *Regarding the marriage duration, it should be noted that any marriage I undertake will be under duress. While I have no desire to ever be married, I will comply with your demands but only for one year. At the end of said year, the marriage will be dissolved and that will complete our contract in total. I further request it be noted that I find this convention a cross between some medieval torture and an arranged marriage, the practice antiquated and unnecessary even for a Van Ayers. Know that no matter what the circumstance is of my forced nuptials, it will be ended as fast as I can have the papers signed.*

Though her hand shook and her eyes burned from tears she would not allow to fall, she took a quick glance at the last page. Sure enough, the final contract with Randolph's end date was clearly noted and contained the required signatures to make everything legal. While Randolph might be in constant competition with his father, there was no doubt as to the winner. Randolph the third could manipulate everything, including changing one of his sacred contracts to suit his needs. Certainly he made the year easy for himself by manipulating her to fall in love with him.

Her heart stopped at her own admission, and rather than swelling, it shriveled, sank into her non-feeling stomach where the organ could suffer in a pool of acid. With robotic movements, she managed to return the papers to the safe, stood and put on some of her old clothes.

Her instinct betrayed her. Since Christmas she swore he felt something for her, but no matter what, as he eloquently stated in his letter, the marriage would end, which was why every time she mentioned the end he didn't argue. He didn't want a wife, and therefore, he didn't want her.

She spent weeks trying to distance herself, a strategy she should have continued, but she followed yet another dream only to be woken up in a shocking manner. Oh she wished she would have gone to school then maybe she would have been smart enough to see this coming. Unfortunately, the tarot and tealeaves betrayed her.

Nan would simply tell her she asked for a disaster the moment she agreed to marry a man with the end in sight.

The tears dried, she couldn't afford them.

Instead, she left Randolph's closet, walked across Randolph's suite and pulled her wallet and cell phone out of Randolph's purse.

The light on her phone flashed indicating a message, probably her so-called husband needing something else when she had nothing left to hand over. Randolph owned everything.

She exhaled, hit the button and froze.

No, Randolph didn't call, but Jade had as well as Slate multiple times. She hadn't yet spoken to them, apologized for all that happened, and in turn they kept their distance only giving her waves or head nods if they passed each other in the alley.

Before she had the chance to listen to even one message, Jade's name flashed across her screen.

She almost dropped the phone in her attempt to answer. "Jade, I'm sorry."

"Willow!" Jade practically screamed into the phone.

"What's wrong?" She held on to the edge of the dresser and concentrated on hearing her friend over her own heartbeat.

"I went to your shop to talk to you and found Nan passed out on the floor. I called 911 and we are on our way to Cedars Sinai Hospital."

The tears she fought won out and streamed down her cheeks. "What happened?" She only remembered Nan having one cold in all the years they were together. Nan called it a sniffle, took some herbs and the next day she was fine.

"We don't know. Slate and I are on our way, meet us there."

She rushed toward the door. "Is she alive?" Bile stung the back of her throat and her muscles threatened to give out, but she managed to reach the stairs.

"Yes," Jade whispered.

"I'm on my way." She hung up and went to call Randolph. A woman should be able to call her husband in times like these. He would make it better, he should make it better. She wouldn't be alone.

Instead, she dropped the phone and ran down the stairs in search for someone else to help her. He was her husband in name only. She would have been better off as one of his staff members.

Chapter Fifteen

ON CHRISTMAS EVE WILLOW told Randolph how strange it was when time changed things. Equally as strange was how many things remained unchanged. A hospital never changed. Maybe technology changed or staff changed but at its core a hospital was a place where one faced the bare essence of being human, life and death, gain and loss, every emotion here had a corresponding side. A yin and yang.

The last time she entered a hospital she lost. Maybe the universe would balance itself out and give her a gain. Though almost two decades had passed since that day, the passing time didn't change the hurt.

After running through a maze of corridors, she finally caught sight of fluorescent green and ran toward the woman she considered her friend before she lied.

"Willow." Jade held her hand out.

Even with everything, she encompassed her with love and Willow held on and waited for her to deliver her fate.

"Nan is still in the emergency room. They're evaluating her, she's alive." Jade held her tight. "Slate has Jeb at the gallery."

"Thank you for finding her." She hid her face in Jade's shoulder, partly for comfort, partly from shame. Her mind had been cluttered with Randolph, what she thought she had, and while she went off chasing rainbows she never noticed Nan was ill. Yes, she noticed the woman had been tired but she thought it only natural. She didn't look beyond.

"Of course." Jade patted her back.

"I'm sorry about everything, please forgive me." Before she did anything else she needed to cleanse the air. She lifted her head, and at last faced her actions. "I did it all for every reason you thought and I didn't want you to think less of me."

"But not now, right?" Jade asked.

Funny how time changes things. Her little saying rang through her mind. A few hours ago she would have said she got married and then found her partner. Of course, he would have been here and she wouldn't have to answer.

"Is the family of Nanette Riviera here?" A woman in scrubs called from a doorway.

"Here!" Willow held up her hand.

"I'll stay with you." Jade stayed by her side.

"I promise I will tell you everything later if you forgive me." She turned to her friend. "I just need to be alone, if that's all right."

"No forgiveness needed, I just wanted to be there for you." Jade hugged her. "Are you sure?"

"Please." At the end of the day it was always her and Nan. She gave her other friend a hug and went to the nurse. "I'm the family of Nanette Riviera."

"Your name?" The woman opened the chart.

"Willow Day. May I see her? Is she okay? What's wrong?" She wrapped her arms around her shoulders. "Please, she's my only family."

"We have a full house and are swamped, we can't let you back there. Go wait in in the outpatient waiting room. Once I have any news I will come get you." The nurse pointed to a door.

"Please." She only wanted a peek.

"I told you we're very busy." The woman left.

"Please." She spoke to an empty door and turned behind her to find Jade gone. With no other choice, she went to the small hospital waiting room and took a seat in the corner.

If Nan had been sitting next to her she would have told her to use the time to meditate, visualize what she wanted. At the moment she could only think of two things, one was lying in a hospital unconscious, one wanted to get rid of her no matter the circumstances on their one-year anniversary.

After simply staring into space for some undetermined time period, she glanced up at the clock. After she saw Nan she would call Randolph, tell him what happened, and ask for a reprieve on their bizarre curfew. Never would she be the one to welch on their business deal. Until then, she would sit and wait.

Suddenly, the door flew open and two men in green scrubs ran in. "Sir, I think we found her," one man yelled.

Her heart ground to a halt and she tried to stand. "Nan?"

"You are all useless, and don't think I haven't made a note of every error this hospital has made." Out of nowhere, Randolph stomped into the room.

Her breath caught. In a long black overcoat and with blond curls bouncing, he appeared to be more of a superhero than her on-paper husband or a teen model. How did he get here?

"Now if you don't want to end up mentioned by name at the next Board of Directors meeting, I would find Dr. Eli Huntley, give him Nanette Riviera's Chart and get him here STAT!" He tilted his head toward the door.

The men bumped into each other and hurried away.

Once the door closed, Randolph turned. Somehow he appeared by her side, and without saying a word took her into his arms.

His overcoat surrounded her and she became encompassed in the serene scent of Randolph. Beyond her control, she held on, taking hold of him and giving in to her own weakness by pressing her face into his already wrinkled shirt.

He combed his fingers through her hair. "Why didn't you call me?"

She chose to stay silent. The hospital didn't seem the place to discuss his contract or her sneaking around and looking at documents. Nothing was important but Nan.

"Willow." He forced her back and looked into her eyes. "Why didn't you call me? Why did I hear about this from Dimitri and Slate?"

The tears in her eyes blurred her vision giving Randolph a golden aura. "I left my phone at home. I was going to call. I don't know." She shrugged. "I would have called you before midnight." Yet another thing he manipulated to keep her controlled.

"I thought we were beyond that. I want to know why I wasn't the first person you thought to call?" His hands squeezed her shoulders.

Not quite sure how to answer, she swallowed. "Can we not do this now?"

He ground his teeth together, but nodded. "Where's Nan? What's happening?"

Her lip quivered. "They won't tell me anything, the nurse just told me to come here. When I asked again, she walked away."

After watching Randolph for months, she thought she figured out every one his expressions, except the one he wore at the moment.

His eyes darkened and narrowed, his mouth opened as if prone with something to say. The boyish charm that made everyone smile and swoon at the sight of him had vanished. "They wouldn't tell you anything?" His voice came out disjointed and metered, as if he were holding back some great pressure.

"I didn't know what to do, so I sat here."

He let go of her. "Let me get this straight. They wouldn't tell you anything or let you check on her at this hospital where my mother is in charge of the charity events and my business donates money?"

She swore she saw a vein on his neck pop out.

"Why are we even in here?" His face turned red and he glanced around the room as if finally noticing his location. "What room is this?"

"Randolph." She held her hand out.

He pointed to one of the plastic chairs. "Sit there."

Scared to do anything else, she sat.

Right as he spun on his heel and headed toward the door, it opened once more. A man in a doctor's coat entered. Around the same age as Randolph, he seemed to be the anti-Randolph with dark hair and eyes. "Randolph!" All smiles, he extended his hand. "I'm glad you caught me on call. I'm upstairs, handling the VIP's."

Randolph crossed his arms. "Doctor."

"What brings you here? Why are you in here? Who is Nanette Riviera? Everyone okay?" The doctor kept his hand out.

"No everyone is not okay." Randolph leaned forward. "My wife's Nan is here, where they relegated us to no-man's land on this floor and wouldn't tell her anything." He motioned toward her as if showing exhibit A.

"Wife? I must have missed that memo." The doctor glanced at her and hit Randolph on the shoulder. "Congratulations."

"Doctor." Randolph tapped his foot.

The doctor held up one finger, flipped through the chart and took a pen out of his pocket, clicking it several times before turning to her. "What is your relationship to Nanette Riviera?"

"She raised me." All her life she tried to come up with a word to describe their relationship, but none ever fit.

"Mother." Dr. Huntley made some notes on the chart.

"Doctor." In need of nothing but good light around her, she had to tell the truth.

The doctor winked at her. "No one ever checks."

She sat back. "Is she going to be all right?"

Randolph returned to her and held out his hand.

Her resolve completely gone, she reached up and took the gift.

"Let's see. She came out of ER a while ago and was placed in a room on this floor. She was diagnosed with hyperglycemia." He clicked the pen some more and shook his head. "She came in with an astronomical blood sugar. She has diabetes. I'll change some of these test orders, but once we get her sugar stabilized and get her on some meds, she'll be fine with a change in diet and lifestyle. Let's get her upstairs and then you can all crash for the night."

For the first time since she walked into one of her worst nightmares, she exhaled. "She's going to be all right?"

The doctor nodded. "This is all treatable."

"She's been out and then taken to the non-private rooms?" Randolph laced his finger in hers. "What's going on here?"

"Here's the main problem." The doctor tapped his pen on the chart. "Someone forgot her married name."

"What?" Randolph let go of her and stepped forward.

"She put her name as Willow Day. If they heard her name, you know they would have been jumping at your feet." Again, the doctor wrote on the chart. "Let me fix this."

For a brief second Randolph looked down to the floor, a momentary break in his aristocratic façade. "I don't need to tell you that I want Nanette to have the best of care. Money isn't an object, and Nanette is covered under our insurance policy."

Insurance? Randolph got Nan health insurance? A lump formed in her throat. He certainly wasn't acting like the man who wanted out of their marriage come his thirty-fourth birthday. She hoped she was covered as well because she might pass out.

"Let me get this handled. Go upstairs, I'll try to hurry them and we'll all meet you there." The doctor handed Randolph a plastic card, saluted and walked out.

Randolph held the door open. "Come on. I doubt you ate, and we can't have you getting ill as well."

Her cheeks heated. Gone went the protective husband, and in his place the businessman returned. He was as upset as she. Was it Nan or something else? On wobbly legs she stood and followed Randolph out.

Never forgetting his manners, he guided her through the maze of hospital hallways, over to a wall of elevators and pushed the button. Inside, he slipped the card in a slot and pushed the button to the eighth floor.

For the entire ride they didn't speak, but she gasped when the doors opened.

No antiseptic smell, no stark white sterile setting, no oppressive stares. Instead she was met with dark wood paneling, light classical music, fresh flowers and plush furniture. "What is this?" The long corridor looked as if it could be a wing of the mansion rather than a hospital.

"May I help you?" A nurse came around the corner.

"Nanette Riviera is being brought up here," Randolph told her.

"Yes, we're readying her room. Please go make yourself comfortable in the lounge, and we'll let you know when the suite is ready." She smiled. "Will you be staying here the night?"

"Yes." Without any hesitation, Randolph answered.

"Not a problem." The woman's sing-song voice washed over the room matching the music. "Have a bite to eat, and give us just a little time. We also have complimentary Wi-Fi, so make yourselves at home."

Once the nurse left, they made their way to a matching room to the hallway and contained what appeared to be a buffet of food. Everything from fresh fruit and salads and hot steaming silver domed chafing dishes.

Rather than going for the food, she took a seat on one of the overstuffed brown leather couches.

She watched Randolph take off his overcoat and put it on a coat rack. Even with the slight wrinkles, his suit fit him to a tee. The man could have stepped off a runway and right into a boardroom. He went over to the bar, took two mini bottles of wine and two glasses and joined her, but at the far end of the couch.

While he busied himself with his phone and sending out a few text messages and pouring the wine, she continued to stare at him.

He slid one of the glasses down to her. "One of the staff is on the way with some clothes for us. They're also packing a bag for Nan. I hope you don't mind, but Peter will be dropping off some work for me."

"They have free Wi-Fi." She lifted her glass and stared at the dark red liquid. Her chest wanted to collapse under the weight of unsaid words. "Thank you for coming here and helping me and for the insurance. You don't have to stay." She still didn't understand where they ended up. Part of her wanted to rejoice her problems were fixed but another wanted to cry for the people who didn't have her false luxury.

"I know I'm not a stupid man, but right now I care to differ." He shook his head and drank the glass down, wincing at what was no doubt a substandard vintage.

"What makes you say that?"

He let out a lone laugh, but didn't answer.

"Why?" She took a sip of the wine and wrinkled her nose. Something must be wrong with the beverage or with her to notice.

"If it's all the same with you, I'll stay with you and Nan tonight." He loosened his tie. "I want to know why you didn't call me."

The emptiness in her chest turned into a full on ache. She shrugged again.

"Damn it, Willow, then answer me this, why didn't you use your last name?" He pressed his fingers into his temple.

"It won't be mine forever." At her admission her breath caught. She hated her real last name, it wasn't attached to anything or anyone, but with Randolph her last name went back to the pilgrims. Sometimes she wished she could be one of those people who only went by a first name.

"No matter what ever happens between us, you may always have my last name to do with as you please." He shook his head. "You're probably one of the only people who has ever truly earned it."

For hours, maybe for years, she fought the urge to cry. Yes, her eyes filled with tears too many times to count, but she didn't cry, didn't have time, couldn't let go. Randolph's gift meant more than any money, her shop, anything. Maybe at the end of the day it was all he had to give, and the emotion of everything surfaced.

Instinct took over and she slid over to his side, leaned in and hugged him, pressing her face into the crook of his neck and breathing in the scent she would be able to recognize the rest of her life. At last she let the tears out.

"Willow." He took her into his arms, held her tight and ran his hands through her hair. "It's going to be all right. I'm here, I'm not going anywhere."

She tensed and held back telling him he wouldn't always be there.

He took her shoulders and pushed her back. "Look at me."

When her eyes met his, her cheeks heated at his intense focus on her.

"Like my name, I will always be here for you."

She pressed her lips together trying to stop crying. The tears fell anyway. He might say the words, might even mean them, but what happened in a year? Why did she know that document even existed? What was real and what was the man she first met trying to get his way?

He wiped her tears away. "Incredible."

"What is?" Damn her for leaning into his touch.

"The color of your eyes. I've never seen anything like it." His fingertip traveled across her cheek, down her jawline and traced her lower lip.

She shivered.

"Do you think once we get Nan home and she is better we can try to recapture what we had today?" He moved her hair away from her face. "Maybe we can go over to the Marina Del Rey Apartment? Would you like that?"

"I want to watch you create something." Unable to stop herself, she reached over and uncurled one of his curls watching it spring back.

He pulled her close, pressing her head down on his shoulder. "I'm trying my hardest."

Tired of the struggle, she cuddled up to his side. They sat

together in this strange space, and he continued to stroke her hair while she toyed with his dark blue tie with the tiny white dots. She should have never tried to choose clothes for him.

"Mr. and Mrs. Van Ayers?" The happy nurse who greeted them before came into the lounge or waiting room, or whatever.

At the intrusion she jolted up, her body protesting at the sudden movement. All she wanted was to lie back down on Randolph. "Yes."

"That's us." Randolph sat up.

"The patient is in her room, and you're more than welcome to join her now." The nurse smiled.

"How is she?" Randolph asked the question before she could make a coherent sentence.

"She is stabilized and sleeping. We'll set you up in the adjoining room." The woman motioned for them to follow.

Randolph put his arm around her.

As they walked out, she grabbed his overcoat off the hook and hugged it to herself. A silly thing a lovesick pre-teen would do, but she was married to a man who looked like a teen idol no matter what the circumstances.

"Are you cold?" He rubbed her shoulder.

"Not really."

"She called you Mrs. Van Ayers." He chuckled. "You answered to your name."

Her name. He offered to let her keep it, but truth be told she couldn't be a Van Ayers without him.

* * * *

"This is not a hospital." Nan glanced down at the IV in her arm and back to Willow. "Chiquita, what is this place?"

"It's called a V.I.P. suite. Some people pay extra to have certain amenities. That's how Randolph and I got to stay with you last night. There's another room over there." She pointed toward the second bedroom. Their hospital room reminded her more of a fancy hotel on television rather than a hospital.

"Why do we get this and no one else?" Nan shook her head.

"It would be amazing if everyone could have something like this, but it is suites like this one that help generate extra revenue for the hospital, and the money made here, helps fund other programs people need." Fine, she also asked the same question more than once. "Randolph explained it before he left for work."

Nan tilted her head. "I understand."

"I'm just thankful..." Willow took her hand. "I'm just thankful Randolph could do this for you." A little while after Nan was brought to their suite, they met with Dr. Huntley and an endocrinologist. Later, Lillian arrived with Mr. Van Ayers, Dimitri, changes of clothes and a flower arrangement that rivaled a royal wedding. Peter also swung by with work and well wishes, followed by more flowers and phone calls from Jade and Slate. At everyone's concern, her heart filled.

Once alone, she couldn't help herself and curled up with Randolph on the bed in their suite, watching him get some work done and do a little sketching. She must have dozed off because when she woke in the middle of the night to check on Nan he had her in his arms asleep and the picture of Nan and Jeb on her pillow. Where she used to wish for a mattress, nothing would ever compare to him and she couldn't shake the thought he didn't want her past their first anniversary no matter how incredible he acted. Even when he gave her his name, he qualified the gift, said it was hers no matter what happened. His words didn't speak of a man who wanted anything long term, but his actions said different.

"Chiquita, your eyes are dark, full of questions. The doctor told you I am going to be okay." Nan squeezed her hand. "What's the matter?"

"I'm sorry I wasn't there when you got sick." She shut her eyes. Even with Nan there speaking to her, if she envisioned getting Jade's phone call her stomach spiraled as if it were happening in the present. "I should have been with you."

"No, you shouldn't have."

Willow shook her head. "I left for nothing." If she stayed with Nan she wouldn't have gone to the office, wouldn't have found that document. Damn, she needed to find the note, no longer could she hide, and pretend painful items didn't exist if she didn't talk about them. She bit her lip, the guilt returning along with a nice bout of nausea for a side dish. "I'm just a terrible person."

"Look at me." Nan's tone hardened.

She opened her eyes and stared down at the woman who

basically raised her.

"Tell me what you love about him."

"Nan." She tried to pull her hand away. "This isn't about him."

"Your world is about him and there's no reason you shouldn't love him." Nan held tight. "Tell me what you love."

"I saw something." She needed to let the news or the confession out.

"Was it something you were meant to see?" Nan lifted her chin.

She shrugged. Even with Randolph at the office, she glanced over her shoulder and back to Nan.

"Did you search for it or did you stumble into it?"

She lowered her head and studied how Nan held her hand. Not too long ago her hand disappeared inside the protection of the woman lying in the hospital bed. Somewhere along the way her hand caught up.

"When you search you end up with what you deserve good or bad, when you stumble, you can fall."

"I stumbled, then I searched." She got what she deserved and she fell flat on her face.

"I hope no one is stumbling."

What appeared to be an entire Rose Parade float entered the room along with dozens of multi-colored and metallic balloons.

Willow watched while the man put the oversized arrangement down. "Mr. Hartford?" Only the fact the man was Randolph's account stopped her from jumping up and spreading her arms out to protect her Nan.

"Vincent. I must look a sight." Nan's voice lowered.

Willow spun back to Nan, was the woman trying to be sexy in a hospital? Nan never cared what she looked like.

"Nanette." Mr. Hartford let the balloons soar to the ceiling. "You are always gorgeous." Without asking for proper permission he came around the side of the bed, gave Nan two kisses on the cheek, one a bit close to her mouth, took her hand and sat.

Nan giggled. She actually giggled. Her eyes sparkled and she sat up straighter. "What are you doing here?"

Willow wanted to ask the same question but with a less breathy voice. Yes, Nan called him earlier, but a hospital visit took a relationship to the next level. The man could have just sent a tasteful vase, not arrived with a florist's shop.

"How can you ask such a question?" Mr. Hartford reached into his suit jacket pocket and pulled out a little stuffed heart with a happy face. "I knew not to get you candy."

Nan smiled and took the gift. "You got me enough."

"Not nearly." He winked. "But I did take the liberty of hiring a holistic nutritionist for when you are out, and I thought we could both take some cooking classes together."

Willow ground her teeth together.

"You just want me to cook for you again." Nan teased.

"It was delicious." He made a little noise of contentment.

They chuckled that low chuckle shared between two people who knew each other a little too well.

Willow didn't belong here and shot off the bed.

"Chiquita?"

"I'm going to take a quick walk and let the two of you be alone." She wrapped her arms around her shoulders. If she didn't belong with Nan where did she belong?

"Hold on." Nan motioned for her to come back.

She returned to Nan's side.

"Answer my question. Tell me why."

Mr. Hartford did her the favor of glancing at his phone.

"He takes care of me, I feel safe when he's around." She took a breath. "I want to take care of him, but..." But she wanted him to be there after he turned thirty-four, or at least know there was the possibility.

Nan grabbed her hand and pulled her down. "That's how it should be."

"You don't understand."

"Whatever you saw, if it didn't cause you to slap him across the face then let him kiss the scraped knees you got when you stumbled." Nan gave her a smile, the same one she used when she actually fixed scraped knees.

"What if —"

"Don't you tell me he doesn't love you. You just told me he takes care of you, and that is how a real man shows his love."

"I should have been with you." She repeated and peeked over at Mr. Hartford again. "At least I thought so." Of course she didn't hire a nutritionist.

"No, this is how it works." Nan pulled her down for a hug and spoke into her ear. "You and me, we are more than blood. We will always be together, but I did my job and raised a magnificent woman and now we are equals."

She pulled back slightly and took in Nan's profile. Through the tears in her eyes, the woman who raised her appeared out of focus, but Willow could still make her out.

"Go love him and don't be scared. Whatever you saw, let him know. Let him pick you up after your fall. It's not my job anymore." Nan kissed her cheek. "Nothing is ever certain, there are no rules. Maybe you met him this way because it was the only way you would allow yourself to fall in love."

She pressed her lips against Nan's cheek. Necessary or not, her wonderful words still left a hole in her heart. She stood. "I'm going to go take that walk."

Nan nodded.

With a sigh, she backed out of the room taking in Mr. Hartford and Nan together.

"Careful." Randolph came up behind her and caught her. "Don't want you tripping."

She looked backward, up at the man she married. No matter the angle, he was a sight to behold. "What are you doing here?" It seemed the question of the hour.

He bent down and kissed her nose. "I wanted to make sure someone took care of you while you took care of Nan."

"You want to take care of me?" She managed to get herself into his arms.

"It's becoming my favorite past time." He took hold of her waist. "I can do my work here."

"I want to take care of you." She let her admission out.

He kissed her lips. "I think maybe we should just take care of each other and toss away the score sheet. I have enough of those in my life."

At his words, she couldn't help but wrap her arms around his neck and give him a real kiss, soft but lingering. Her husband had the right idea and she needed to take Nan's advice. "That sounds like a plan." Maybe her plan would outweigh his contract.

Chapter Sixteen

"WILLOW." WITH HIS DUFFLE BAG slung over his shoulder, he pushed them both up against a wall near a huge abandoned factory in a questionable area of Long Beach.

"Is this the spot?" She turned toward the dilapidated wall.

"Willow." Breathless, he held his hand out. Armed only with a paintbrush, he purposely brought his wife into an area that might be deemed unsafe. "This is not a good idea."

"I want to watch you paint." She moved in front of him.

"We're going to get arrested." In all the Van Ayers generations of men, he was certain no one took their bride directly to the scene of the crime.

"We aren't doing anything bad. We are turning something ugly into something beautiful." A smile took over her face.

"You're beautiful." He pressed his palm to her face, loving how she looked in her all black attire, pants, sweater and her hair up in a cap. His little gorgeous criminal. "Graffiti is technically illegal."

"Then it's a good thing that you are creating art and not graffiti." She moved back and faced the wall once more. "You've never been caught."

He raised his eyebrows.

"You wanted me to catch you." She rubbed her hands together. "How did you pick this place? When did you find it?"

For the first time in at least two weeks his Willow was back, blushing and sweet and soft with a bit of edge. Ever since Nan returned from the hospital, he watched her run herself ragged trying to take care of everything. If being a workaholic was contagious, he gave his illness to Willow and he needed to find a cure.

It took every one of his persuasion tactics to get her to take a break and let him take her out for their weekend away. The only thing she wanted was to watch him paint, and he planned a weekend at his family's Palos Verdes apartment overlooking the ocean, but gave into a promise he made to her and took her on a secret excursion. Though he tried to convince her otherwise, he could deny her nothing. "Why?"

"Why what?"

"Why would you want to watch me paint out here? We could have purchased some paints and a canvas." He glanced over at her.

She leaned over. "I want to watch you in your element. I want to know a part of you no one else does."

"All right." He scanned the area and put his tools down. "Don't leave my side."

"That's not up to me." Her tone came out low, breathy.

Unsure what she meant and with his heart thumping loud enough to set off an alarm, he shook his head, took out two spray paint cans and assessed his cracked and chipping canvas.

She pressed her hands together and waited.

He gave the can a quick shake, cursing the little ball hitting the metal, but blessing it as well. The moment the distinctive sound echoed off the walls of the can, he knew magic would begin. With a vision coming together, he stepped forward and made the first swipe. A black streak appeared over the grey, dirty wall.

Willow's gasp rang through the air.

"I've never worked with an audience before." He began his outline.

With her eyes wide with excitement, she lifted her chin at him. "Keep going."

For several minutes he painted. Once the image he wanted took shape in his head, he could practically close his eyes and still create it. "I found this wall when I was checking out some property in the Bixby Knolls area around here. I started driving and was taken in by the oil refineries and factories. When I stopped here, I realized that the people living around here could see this old wall and it was a perfect place to put some art."

"You are much deeper than you think, Mr. Van Ayers, with a much bigger heart than I ever imagined." She moved closer to him.

He chose some different paint cans. Though he had been called many things in his life, deep was never one of them. In fact, most would describe him as rather shallow. Somehow Willow saw more in him, but not enough to remember her name the night Nan became ill, not enough to call him first. He wanted to use their time away to show her what they could be together. "I don't know."

"I do," she whispered. "While you're with me I always want you to paint. This is the best night."

In all the insanity, he found the one woman on the planet, quite possibly the universe, who was more than thrilled and appreciative of a drive through the greater Los Angeles area watching her husband basically commit a crime all for the name of art. He wanted to give her everything and more. Above all else, he needed to broach the subject of their contract. Did it even apply anymore? What did she want? He needed to get her to tell him, wanted her to fight for them as well.

Again, silence overtook their little makeshift art studio. The picture began to come together and the release of creating something real took over. He found his rhythm. When he first agreed to their expedition, he didn't know if he would be able to conjure something with her staring at him, but he found her presence, or her energy, enhanced the experience. Though he purposely kept the details sketchy, as he neared the end, he had no choice but to let her in on the reveal.

"Oh." She sucked in her breath.

He glanced back at her. Her tears caught the little bit of light, leaving shining silver strands down her face.

"Come here."

Without hesitating she went to him and he pulled her in front of him and gave her a paint can. "Randolph."

"I thought we would put the final touch on together." He put his hand over hers.

As a couple they added the last little detail to finish the piece.

"We should go." He normally took off the moment he finished, only coming back a few days later to get a picture, but rather than racing away, he wrapped his arm around her waist to give her some time to take it in.

"How do you know what you are going to paint?" She looked up at him.

"It just comes to me. Usually something that I'm thinking about, a flash, something I find inspirational or I just need to express." He shook his head. "It's always been an outlet for me."

"Why here?" She reached back and curled her arm around his neck.

"Why don't you tell me what you think first?" Still, he didn't let go of her. "I painted it just for you."

"I know." She continued to gaze up at him.

They really needed to go, but he needed an answer more. "Willow?"

"Tell me why this is a better canvas than let's say, a canvas."

"You are a tease." He shook his head.

"I don't think so." She smiled.

"You made me wait until our wedding night to make love to you."

The red he coveted took over her cheeks. "Of course that was our first night together."

"I would have made love to you before if you would have given me anything more than a glance." Unable to resist he gave her a little kiss on the tip of her nose.

"Well, at least I waited long enough to get a ring on my finger." She let out a little giggle.

He took her hand and tangled his fingers in hers. "I'm glad you're wearing it and not hiding it anymore."

"No one should ever try to hide what they are." She stared at the mural again. "By the way, I think you have magnificent talent, and I love that the world will be able to see the beauty in the piece, but I will be one of the only ones to know the special meaning behind it."

He turned until they were nose to nose. "Only special because of you."

She took the initiative to connect their mouths.

Even though they should leave, he couldn't help but indulge in her kiss. Though he didn't know how he could want her more, he found he was practically insatiable when it came to Willow. He pulled her tight against him and moaned. "Maybe it's time to go to our next destination."

She put her hand on his chest and pushed back. "Before we leave tell me why you chose to display your art as you do."

"I couldn't show my family, I guess I just wanted someone to see the art." He never told anyone about his thoughts, his doubts. "Maybe I just didn't want me or the art to disappear without notice."

"I don't want you to ever disappear." She traced his lower lip with her finger.

"I don't know about that, I think I added a lot of complications to your life."

"I can't picture being anywhere else."

"At least we have luxury." He tried to lighten the mood. "Luxury we should get to."

"I don't care about that, I have you." She turned away. "Let's just look a moment more."

His breath caught at her words and he had no choice but to stare at his creation, their creation. As always, he painted what was top of his mind, and more and more Willow occupied that spot. He recreated their relationship on a wall in the middle of the industrial section of Long Beach. Though careful not to create too close a likeness to them, he included his rendition of a proposal in the alley, Las Vegas, moving to the mansion, and even silhouettes of Nan and little Jeb. They created the starburst sparkle on an oversized hand with one magnificent yellow diamond on it together. "I'm going to call this piece Our History Part One."

"Part one?" Her voice came out more as a squeak.

"Yes, part one. Maybe we can pick a different spot to put part two, maybe even a different part of the country." He ran his fingers in her hair. "I would like to take you on a real honeymoon while we're still newlyweds."

She shrugged.

Damn, he hated that shrug. "No?"

"We'll only ever be newlyweds." Her whole body tensed.

"I don't understand." How did they go from planning their future to shrugs in less than a second?

"Being newlyweds lasts the first year of marriage."

He nodded. "Right."

"That's all we'll ever be, because deep down that's all you want." Without warning pushed him away. "There will never be a

Part Two."

"Willow." He gathered up his things. At last they would address what she wanted, what he wanted. "About our contract."

"This has nothing to do with our contract." She backed away. "I know what you really want, I saw the proof in writing. You were right about creating a document, signing your name."

"What are you talking about?" In his haste he kicked a paint can, and it rolled down the street. "Where are you going? You said you would stay by my side."

"I need a minute." She walked away.

"Willow!" He ran after her, scooping up his errant paint can in the process. Eventually she would have to face him and her wants, and not hide.

* * * *

"From up here the lights from the boats look like moving stars." Willow stared out over the balcony railing watching the boats in the marina. Randolph's footsteps echoed around her, or maybe she simply had super senses when it came to his whereabouts. What Randolph called an apartment, she called a penthouse sitting on the top floor of a fifteen-story building and allowing her to take in the endless ocean.

"Yes, they do. Funny how during the day, the boats don't look nearly as spectacular." Randolph came up behind her and put a red flannel blanket around her shoulders. "Sometimes the most beautiful things can be hidden by something that shines too bright."

True to Randolph's form, he stuck with their plans and drove them to their little weekend getaway. As if sensing her needs, he remained quiet, only speaking once they arrived and he told her to go enjoy the view while he tended to a few things. While watching him paint, she never felt closer to anyone. Except for when they made love, he never let go in such a way, the emotion in his work evident.

"Maybe the stars are happy hiding until they get their turn." The wind picked up and she offered part of the blanket to Randolph and sighed. The last thing she wanted was to ruin their night. All she truly wanted was to be his real partner, and be truthful with him.

Rather than standing by her side, he took the blanket, draped it over himself and stood behind her wrapping his arms around her and encompassing them both in the warmth. "I may be right about putting things in writing, but I think in our case the papers may have overshadowed something much more important."

"I saw the contract with your father." She shut her eyes and inhaled. "The one saying you didn't want to be married no matter for what or to who."

"Where did you find that?" He moved over to one side. "How do you know about that?"

"I didn't mean to find it, I wish I didn't." She stared beyond the boats and into the blackness of the night ocean. "The original contract you had with your father never had a time limit. You don't want a wife."

"I didn't want a wife."

At least the man wasn't a liar. She closed her eyes.

"You didn't hear me." He took her by the shoulders and turned her toward him. "I said I didn't want a wife."

She opened her eyes and not daring to look at his face, focused on his neck.

"Do you know I finally sleep?" He leaned down. "Do you know that every day when I wake up and you're right there curled up at my side sometimes I lay in bed an extra minute because I don't want the peace to end?"

"You stay in bed?" She searched his face for answers.

"Only because you're there." He dipped his head down and brushed his lips against hers.

She willed the electric shivers he created out of her body.

"You always say I'm right about the documents, but you know what you're always right about?"

"What?" Her voice didn't feel connected to her own body.

"No one should ever start a relationship knowing the end."

She shook her head.

"So I'm going to ask you the question I keep asking you." He took her by the shoulders. "What is it that you want?"

"Randolph."

"That's not an answer. Tell me. Be honest for both of us."

"You tell me." No way could she answer first.

"I'll tell you this, I care what happens to you and I think about you all the time. For the first time in my life, I want to rush home from work just to see you. I want to tell you everything and I trust you more than anyone."

Her eyes filled with tears.

"Somewhere between the alleyway behind an art gallery and standing here on a balcony, I found my wife." He stepped back. "I never want you to forget your name again or think you can't use it. You are Mrs. Van Ayers. Mrs. Randolph Emerson Van Ayers the Third."

"Am I?" The tears escaped.

"God, I want you to be." He opened his arms to her.

Her heart swelled, threatening to burst out of her chest and run to Randolph itself. Instead, her legs did the job for both her tired chest and herself and carried her to her husband. As always, she had to follow where her heart led, but maybe for once it led her to the right place.

The moment she reached him he tossed the blanket aside and took her into his arms. She buried her face in his chest and fingered the soft fabric of his shirt. " I care what happens to you, I think about you all the time, and every day I wait for you to come home. I never had a home or a last name until you, and I trust you with my life."

"Look at me."

She wiped her eyes on his shirt and tilted her head up, staring at him in a whole new way. While he got a wife, she also got a husband, a real husband. "Don't leave me."

"Never." He pushed her hair away from her face.

"I am Mrs. Randolph Van Ayers." For the first time she said her name and meant it.

"For as long as you want to be." He stared into her eyes.

In their own way and their own time, they came up with another new set of vows, unique to them. At last she could give her heart to him completely with no limits. She wrapped her arms around his neck, pulled him down and kissed him.

At last, after all these months, she got the chance to simply kiss her husband. Slow and easy, she took her time tasting each one of his lips. His taste belonged to her and her alone.

He moaned and bent her back, opening his mouth. Their

tongues touched and she leaned against him. Something about Randolph made her week in the knees.

In one fluid motion he picked her up.

"This reminds me of our wedding night," she whispered as she kept hold of him.

"This is our wedding night." With her in his arms, he turned and kissed her as he took her inside.

For someone who tried to spend her whole life going with the flow, bending with the wind, a concrete commitment from Randolph gave her the grounding she always lacked, but secretly craved. Finally free to soar, she pulled off his shirt before he even made it to the bedroom.

She ran her palm across his chest. Even when she spread her fingers, her hand barely covered him. With him she would always be safe.

No alcohol stupor, no anger, no rush, he lowered them both to the bed, and they simply lay among the pillows and blankets kissing and caressing.

Clothing seemed to disappear and they tangled their bodies together. She found a place she fit, and in the most primal and basic way, it was here with Randolph with nothing in between them.

Everywhere his hands touched or fingers roamed came alive. She also took her turn to explore him, trace his muscles on his arms and chest, reach down and stroke the confirmation of his desire, only serving to amplify her own arousal.

"Come closer." He turned to his side and pulled her flush against him and kissed across her jawline to her neck.

"I'm right here." She leaned back to give him access to her chest.

His fingertips grazed her over sensitized nipples.

A jolt of pleasure overtook her body and she squirmed against him in an attempt to satisfy a bit of her need.

"I don't think it will ever be close enough." His tone low. "Look at me."

She did as he asked. Unable to help herself, she combed her fingers through his curls.

He hooked her leg over his hip and slipped inside her.

Her body welcomed the stretch to accommodate him. She

sucked her breath and arched her back.

"You are so gorgeous when I'm making love to you." Once again he found her lips.

They moved together. On their sides facing each other they were on equal footing to move toward their ultimate goal, but for the first time the finish line wasn't the orgasm, the rush. Rather simply being united, acting as one was the endpoint, a metaphor for the rest of their lives.

Still, the desire built. Randolph thrust into her with more power and speed and he panted with the heat they created.

"Randolph." Needing him even deeper, she slid her leg up by his chest. Her climax was there on the horizon. A little move and she would sail away in bliss.

"Yes." His voice came out strained as he held back the inevitable. "Willow."

"I'm there." She buried her face in the crook of his neck breathing in the remnants of his cologne mixed with paint and a bit of the ocean, a heady combination.

"I need you." He lowered his hand to her backside holding her steady as he plunged into her. "Come with me."

She concentrated on the way his body took over for him, his strokes becoming more erratic, his pending orgasm taking over everything. The knowledge she could bring him to here threw her over the edge. While he stiffened with his release, she gave way diving head first into her orgasm, the intense throbs rippling through every inch of her. "Ah!"

"Willow." He called out to her and filled her body with the heat only a man could produce. "God, I love that."

They ground against one another, allowing the last few moments of ecstasy to fade away into the ultimate relaxation.

"What do you love?" She looked up to his face smiling at the smile on his lips.

"I love the way I can feel you orgasm. It's incredible." He gave her a light kiss. "Actually, even more than that, I love you."

Time stopped, the world stopped, her heart stopped. In the universe those were three of the most powerful words one could speak. "Randolph?"

"I do, Willow." His playful smile faded and he stared into her eyes. "I love you."

She studied the man she married in a moment of desperation. Even in the middle of their insane situation, they still found each other. No one had said anything like that since she became an adult. "I love you too." More than any vow, those were the words that would bind them together forever. "I love you, too." She could never lose him and hugged him close.

Chapter Seventeen

RANDOLPH TOOK A BREATH to abate the dread that wanted to take over him before giving a nod to Dimitri.

"Your wife is waiting for you." Their head of staff smiled and opened the door to the car.

He paused for only a moment more, vowing that no matter what the night held for him, he would not get angry, upset or frustrated. Though he didn't want to attempt another dinner with the Hartfords, the plans were put in place before he had the opportunity to intervene. The first dinner ended in a disaster of such epic proportions, then Willow spilled wine on Millicent at the party, as the saying went, bad things happened in threes.

In the week since their getaway he watched, or tried to watch, Willow plan the event, but she wouldn't allow him to touch her calendar or be privy to any of the happenings. Every time he asked, she distracted him with, well, with her. All he knew was the family car would be picking them up at seven to take them to a restaurant. What he really wanted to do is get her back to their apartment at the marina and recreate their weekend.

Their apartment. He smoothed down his suit jacket. Everything that was once his was now theirs. At last he entered the car, slipping across the leather seat to join his wife.

Well, one thing was his and his alone. He took in his gorgeous bride. Dressed in a black strapless gown, with her hair swept up and light makeup, the word gorgeous didn't accurately describe her. He ran his hand through his hair. "Good evening beautiful Mrs. Van Ayers."

"Hello Mr. Van Ayers." She slid over and gave him a kiss.

"Please tell me this is a big surprise and we aren't having a business dinner, but instead we are going to a hotel or somewhere." He kissed her again, a light one to not mess up her makeup. "Alone." Maybe the worst thing that happened could be they stood the Hartfords up, but with his plan he would only have to take the fall and keep Willow out of the line of fire.

She pressed her palm to his cheek. "I am sorry, but we have reservations at The Heights and your big clients are meeting us there."

All right, she got into The Heights on a Friday night. Could be a good sign or a bad one. The proper restaurant only meant the proper restaurant. They were still open to a whole host of variables that could wrong. He tilted his head.

Dimitri drove them through Beverly Hills. Willow took his hand and sat back. "I offered to have a car service pick up the Hartfords, but they are coming separate and Ms. Hartford's secretary said it wasn't necessary." She glanced at him out of the corner of her eye.

"That was very kind of you." He stared at her. Could be her plan was to get the Hartfords drunk and they wouldn't remember the evening, therefore the car service.

She simply smiled and crossed her legs revealing a slit right above her knee, tasteful but tantalizing, and above all else distracting.

"Are you trying to torture me?" He traced his finger along the bit of skin showing.

"It's not torture when you know you will be relieved. Then it's anticipation." She squirmed in the seat, making the dress rise up a bit.

"From where I'm sitting, it's torture."

"Would it make you feel better if I told you I have something for you?" She opened her handbag.

Nothing he wanted would fit in her purse. He used her move and shrugged.

With a shake of her head she pulled a little black box and opened it, revealing two cufflinks with dark brown stones. "You got me some quartz, and when I saw this smoky quartz today I knew you had to have it."

He leaned over to admire them.

"Smoky quartz boosts business creativity." She reached for his wrist, took off his gold cufflink and replaced it with his new one.

"It also opens up your perceptive paths. I know work has been stressful."

"Slate really wants me involved in this co-op, and I want to make sure it's right." He swore Willow was clairvoyant even if she denied it. "I'm unsure about his partner and their collateral. I know what Slate owes on his mortgage for the gallery."

"You are just being more careful because he's your friend, that's good." She lifted his wrist.

"I just don't want him to get clouded by the opportunity if it's not right." The stone didn't match his tie, but Willow gave them to him and they had a story that meant more than coordination. "I need more perceptive paths for sure."

"It's also the stone of endurance." She glanced up to his eyes and leaned forward giving him a quick shot of her cleavage.

Without hesitation he offered her his other wrist. "I want endurance." Especially later in bed.

One side of her mouth lifted in a knowing, naughty grin and she replaced the second cufflink. "You don't have that issue." She put his other cufflinks in the box and pulled a tie with a brown swirl out of her bag. "I also brought this with me. I wouldn't want you not to match."

The strip of silk unrolled like a ribbon from her hand, and he stopped short of taking it.

"What's wrong?"

How did she learn about him down to the tie? "Nothing."

"Do you need help?"

"Yes." Help, and a lot of other things, especially if they were going to make it through dinner and on to endurance activities.

She unknotted his tie with expertise and pulled it out from under his collar.

Once more he stared down at her chest, but rather than taking in her assets, he noticed she wore the necklace he gave her for the holiday. "If the quartz you gave me has a meaning, what does the one I gave you mean?"

Her cheeks flushed as she looped the new tie around his neck.

"Don't hold back now." He took her hands and helped her with the knot.

"It's the love stone, love in marriage."

"Then I picked the right one without even realizing it."

She used the tie to pull him toward her. "I guess the stone worked."

"Indeed." Forgetting the lipstick, he indulged and kissed her, opening his mouth to get a little appetizer before dinner.

The car stopped and Dimitri cleared his throat and coughed.

As she pushed him back, he groaned.

"Everything will be fine." She wiped his lower lip then straightened his tie and collar.

"Of course it will," he said, mainly to convince himself. Thus far, everything was too smooth. Rather than it calming him, his stomach twisted. Millicent could find fault in anything.

"Let's go."

Dimitri opened the door and helped Willow out.

Randolph followed and took her hand, opening the door for them. Unlike the last dinner where loud music bolted through him and he waded through a crowd of people, he was met with soft piano music, a classic dim lit interior and a maître d' in a tuxedo. "Van Ayers."

"We've been expecting you." The maître d' made a note on a piece of paper. "Would you like to wait for the others in your party?"

"Would you mind if I checked the table?" Willow practically whispered.

"Of course. It is the one in the back you requested for your meeting." The man nodded and led them back. "I also have the list of wine we keep for your family."

She remembered the table and the wine. Obviously, his wife put some thought into their evening. He tried to inhale. "I could use some wine." Or preferably a glass of Scotch or four.

Willow tangled her arm in his and assessed the table. "Would you mind giving the list to my husband along with a glass of your..." She paused and took a small slip of paper out of her purse. "...Glenden 27-year-old Single-Malt Scotch."

He glanced over to see the paper. She ordered his Scotch, his favorite Scotch.

"Of course, Mrs. Van Ayers." The man nodded. "I take it the table is to your liking?"

"Perfect." She smiled.

"I will go look for the rest of your party." The maître d' left.

Willow led him to where she wanted him to sit. "Are you all right?"

"You ordered my Scotch." He pulled out the chair next to him and waited for her to sit.

"Yes." She sat and took his hand as he took his place.

At last he managed to pluck the little scrap paper out of her hand. "You took notes." While he expected to find a list of items not to forget for their dinner, he found something quite different. "What is this?"

"Nothing." She held her hand out.

"Loves bacon, hates runny egg yolks, light lunch but wants something sweet in the afternoon, prefers red meat but will eat anything at dinner, likes a before dinner drink, likes his dessert, especially any cake, sneaks a soda when he thinks no one sees him drinking it." He read her note aloud. Underneath she noted some of his favorite brands, including the Scotch and two last lines. "Prefers extra starch on his shirts, make sure to remind Rosa. Ask about the boots in the closet."

"Randolph." She retrieved her cheat sheet on him. "That wasn't for you."

"It's all about me."

Her cheeks reddened. "I just didn't want to forget certain things."

No one ever took the time to know him like his wife. Maybe his worries about the evening were unfounded. "What do you want to know about boots?"

"The ones with the buckles and the zippers."

His mind flashed on the pair in question. "I bought them in graduate school and never wore them."

"But you wanted to." She touched his chin.

"I suppose."

"I want you to go with what you want and wear them for me."

"Just the boots and nothing else." He raised his eyebrows and leaned in to kiss her.

She put her hand up to his lips. "Then later I'll just wear the nothing else, but now you must let me play hostess."

"You're right." He took her hand and kissed the back, wanting the dinner to be a success more for her than him.

They both stood when Millicent came around the corner with

the maître 'd. "My brother is running late." She barked. "I have no idea what he's doing, he's not working."

"Good evening to you, Millicent." He rushed over and led her to the chair on the other side of him. "So glad you could join us." Millicent was already in a mood. His chest constricted. Ever since he knew the Hartfords they traveled as a pair.

She shook her head and plopped into the chair. "Well, well, this is different. Much better than before."

Where was that Scotch? Leave it to his client to state the obvious. He broke out into a sweat and glanced at Willow. His wife seemed stuck. He needed to bail her out and opened his mouth.

"Well, I thought I would go for something a little off the beaten path." Willow spoke at last.

Oh no. He grabbed the edge of the table. When riled up, Willow could whip words with the best of them.

"I tried to get reservations at the local sports bar, because I really thought you may enjoy some fried foods and beer, but they were booked." Willow opened her bag and took something out.

A flash of metal caught his eye. Willow brought a gun. He found the strength to lift his hand. His wife was going to kill Ms. Hartford, and with all the witnesses around even with the best attorneys at his disposal he would never be able to clear her name.

With wide eyes Millicent stared at her.

Willow put her hand behind her back and made her way around the table.

"Why don't we choose a wine?" Maybe a red would mask the blood.

"Instead, I opted for my second choice with my husband's first rate clients, and a little gift I made especially for you." She bent down by Millicent and held out her hand, revealing a little metal tin.

"Heart-tea?" Millicent turned to him and back to the tin.

"Yes, I custom blend teas, and this one is for you." She took Millicent's hand and placed the tin in her palm. "This one contains Rhodiola for strength, athletes even use it."

"Oh. A tea named after me." Millicent held the tin up. "I like it."

Willow gave her a broad smile.

His wife calmed the beast. He exhaled and went to sit when the maître d' appeared again with Vincent and Nan.

Nan? Did Willow invite Nan?

"Hello everyone, Chiquita." Nan waved.

Willow straightened and turned to her.

"I thought this was a business dinner." Millicent put the tea aside and stood, glaring in Willow's direction. "Last time it was assistants. How are we supposed to conduct a meeting? There is a protocol here with invitations."

A quick scan of the table only showed four chairs. Willow checked the table, all the evidence pointed to the fact she only invited four people.

"Calm down Millie, I'm the one who invited the woman I love." Vincent lifted Nan's hand to his chest. "I thought since we would have everyone from both sides here we would make our announcement."

He froze and the color left Willow's face.

"What would that be?" Millicent growled.

Vincent held out Nan's hand with a new diamond rivaling Willow's on her finger. "I thought we would turn tonight into an engagement party."

"What?" Willow reached out.

Instinct took over and Randolph hurried to his wife, but he was too late. In an unprecedented move, Millicent took Willow's arm and pulled her close.

A waiter came over and set the glass of Scotch in on the table.

He pushed the glass of Scotch toward the women. "Will you please bring us the bottle?" As soon as they got home he was throwing the calendar away.

* * * *

"So for two weeks I have been walking around with the ring in my pocket wondering when the right time would be to pop the question." Vincent told the story for the third time and waved his fork around like a flag.

Willow stared down at her steak cooked to perfection. She managed to get a few bites down, but the steak, along with Nan and Vincent's announcement, swirled in her stomach creating a wave of nausea. "Is this over yet?" She leaned into Randolph.

"I suppose you decided right before a business meeting was a good time to make a life-long decision. Poor Willow and I were completely blindsided." Millicent downed her wine.

"Are you all right?" Randolph whispered in her ear.

"As long as I don't have to plan dinner ever again." Heat took over her body and she broke out into a sweat. She tried, really tried, to plan a magnificent dinner. Since they returned from their weekend, she wanted to show Randolph what she could do, especially for the man she loved. She researched and planned and had everything perfect, and he was supposed to be proud of her. Instead, she would be forever known as the woman with the planning disasters. They would have been better off in a sports bar. On the plus side, Millicent seemed to take a liking to her which was a good thing since they were going to be sort of related.

"You really did an incredible job if it wasn't for—" Randolph paused. "for—"

"Just say it." Not caring anymore about appearances, she took her napkin, dipped the corner in her water glass and dabbed it on her neck to alleviate the heat overtaking her.

"It's about time I lived my own life. You've lived it enough for both of us. I am finally in love and when the right moment struck, it struck." Vincent shot his words at his sister.

"Except for this." Randolph mumbled under his breath and pressed the back of his hand to her cheek. "What's wrong?"

"Willow understands that," Nan said.

At the sound of her name, Willow turned to her. "What?"

"You understand that sometimes things happen and you make quick decisions because that's what the universe tells you is right." Nan touched her chin.

Not appreciating the reference to her and Randolph, she pressed her lips together.

"My Chiquita also understands that no matter what, certain souls were meant to be together even if things change, because change is inevitable, not changing is not living." Nan took the wet napkin, pressed it on her wrist and motioned for Randolph. "Your instinct was right, she's clammy. Hold the napkin here, it will cool her down faster."

Randolph took over.

"You understand, right, Chiquita? You're not alone." Nan smiled, the one that told her everything would be all right even if she didn't believe her.

The soothing coolness pulsed through her with her heartbeat. Not alone. No, even with her mother's passing she was never alone. Nan had already passed the torch to Randolph. She looked from Nan to Vincent.

"I wanted to ask your permission." Vincent leaned over. "But I couldn't stop myself from asking when I did."

She needed to pass the torch as well and took a breath. "I make medicinal teas for a living. I don't need to tell you what will happen if you hurt my Nan."

A smile crossed Vincent's face. "I wouldn't have it any other way."

"Chiquita, I love him, I really do." Nan took her hand and Vincent's hand and held both together.

"I will do everything in my power to keep your Nan in the Van Ayers lifestyle." Vincent kissed Nan on the cheek.

"Just keep her happy." Too much of her husband's life had been spent trying to keep in the lifestyle. Though grateful because it brought them together, part of her wondered what would have happened if Randolph didn't continue to search. An overwhelming exhaustion replaced the heat and she rested her head on Randolph's shoulder.

"I will do that, I promise." Vincent lowered his voice. "I think everyone should want their family to be happy."

"I'm perfectly fine, and to ensure I stay that way have no doubt that I will be meeting with my attorney and the man who manages *my* money first thing Monday morning." Millicent stood from the table and faced them. "Willow, I look forward to dining with you again. Randolph, be ready on Monday. I just don't have any appetite tonight and I refuse to talk business until the matter is settled." Without another word, she grabbed her purse, spun on her heel and stomped out.

Willow shut her eyes. She craved their mattress and wanted to sink into the sheets.

"Although I think she saw this coming, I think she chose to remain blind." Nan took a deep breath.

"As usual, my love, you're right." Vincent put his arm around

Nan and kissed her lips.

Willow lurched and dug her nails into Randolph's leg.

"Willow!" Randolph grabbed her shoulders and tried to turn her.

She held up her hand.

"What's wrong?" He tightened his hold.

"I don't feel well." She forced the words out.

"I think this evening may have been a bit too dramatic, we have to remember Willow is a newlywed herself," Vincent said.

"I think Vincent is right, we need to go home." Randolph pulled her over to him.

"I am going to pick up the tab on this meal, and I think Nan and I will stay for a bit and finish off the wine."

The mention of wine made her stomach churn, as did Randolph helping her up.

"Thank you for dinner." Randolph put his arm around her.

"I won't be home tonight, Chiquita." Nan gave her a kiss. "I'll see you tomorrow."

"Feel better." Vincent patted her.

Before she responded, Randolph took charge and led her out of the restaurant.

She exhaled at the sight of Dimitri and the car at the front of the restaurant.

Dimitri opened the car door. "Is Mrs. Van Ayers all right?"

"I think the meal didn't settle well with her." Randolph kept her in his arms as he got them both in the back seat. "Would you mind rolling down the windows for her?"

The windows slid down part way and the car took off. As the cool air wafted her over her and the heat dissipated, the nausea ebbed and she sat up.

"How are you doing?" Randolph combed his fingers through her hair.

"Nan is getting married to Mr. Hartford." The news still seemed unreal.

"It's a bizarre turn of events. I thought they were just sleeping together." He wrinkled his nose.

"Please, I'm starting to feel better." She shuddered. "Is that how you feel when you think about your parents having sex? Your mother told me—"

"Stop!" He put his hand over her mouth. "Yes that's how I feel."

"Oh well." She laid her head on his shoulder. "At least he seems like he wants to take care of her." There was no point fighting change.

"He's a very wealthy man, so she'll never want for anything."

She shrugged. Wealth didn't mean everything. All she wanted was for Nan to be happy. After all she did for her, Nan deserved to have some fun and a life free of worry.

"Speaking of which, in my effort to take care of my own spouse, I will deposit your allowance tomorrow."

Money again? She pushed away from him and stared out the window.

Randolph put his hand on her shoulder. "Willow?"

"Is it still about the money?" The lights flickered by the window of the car in little starbursts.

"What do you mean?"

She turned back to him. "I don't care about the money, I have you."

"How did I get you?" He shook his head.

"Well, you tried to buy me." She couldn't help but laugh.

"But you, Mrs. Van Ayers, are priceless." He leaned down and gave her a light kiss.

Dimitri drove through the gateway to the house, stopped the car and opened the door for her. An unfamiliar blue car was parked ahead of them. "Someone's here." She didn't remember Lillian having guests. Normally, if she entertained the house was abuzz with activity.

Randolph joined her, but didn't speak. Instead, he simply stared at the car and his complexion paled.

"Are you getting sick?" She hoped they hadn't caught some bug.

"I'm not sure." He took a firm hold of her hand and led her into the house.

The moment she entered an awful feeling of dread consumed her. Two staff members stood in the main foyer with wide eyes, and everything stood deathly quiet.

"Where are they?" Randolph's voice came out hard, demanding and angry.

Rosa pointed toward the library.

"Go upstairs to our suite, Willow." He let go of her hand.

"Randolph what is it?" Her heart pounded loud enough that she was sure she would never hear his answer.

Before he got the chance to answer, the door to the library opened.

"I told you I heard someone enter the house." A young brunette woman in a tan skirt suit similar to what Lillian would wear rushed out of the room. She stopped and tilted her head. "Randy, I came to see you."

"Stephanie." Randolph crossed his arms.

Randy? Stephanie? The stomachache returned full force. What was Randolph's ex doing here?

Mr. Van Ayers stormed out of the room, followed by Lillian holding Jeb to her chest.

"I waited for you." Stephanie stepped toward him.

Willow bit the inside of her mouth. She never put a face with the girl Randolph was supposed to marry, but the woman fit the bill as to what she expected him to be with. Beautiful, made up, perfectly coiffed. She bet if Stephanie planned the dinner tonight nothing would have gone wrong.

"Last time I checked, it was you who kept me waiting."

"It looks like everything worked out though." At last the woman dared to glance in her direction. "I heard you got married. Did you make it on time?"

"What does that mean?" Lillian leaned over to her husband.

A lump of anxiety formed in Willow's throat.

"That's none of your business."

"I didn't want to leave you, I was forced to." Stephanie came closer still.

Lillian shook her head.

"I hardly think that anyone could force you to do anything." The anger in Randolph's words came through with every syllable.

"Someone can when he is the one person more powerful than you." She turned toward Mr. Van Ayers.

"What do you mean?" Randolph lowered his arms.

"Stephanie, I told you we would talk privately." Mr. Van Ayers stepped forward.

A spectator in her own life, Willow wrapped her arms around

her shoulders.

"I told you, I was forced to leave in the only way the Van Ayers know how to make everyone do what they want." The woman lifted her chin.

Wanting to run, but needing to stay, Willow put her hand over her mouth.

Randolph's face turned absolutely red. "So Father, how much did you pay her to leave?"

Lillian gasped. "What do you mean?"

"I did you a favor." His father shot back.

"It was the last step, the very last thing on the very last day! What you call a favor I call a conspiracy for me to fail!"

"Is this about Randolph's goals?" Lillian rushed over, her heels clicking on the marble floor. "He finished that."

Rather than addressing Lillian, Stephanie walked over to her. "Right. As long as he got married on or by his thirty-third birthday."

Willow straightened and stared her down.

"That's insane, his marriage had nothing to do with it." Lillian scurried over. "His goals were met when he took the job at the bank. It's a Van Ayers tradition."

"Lillian, why don't you and Willow take Jeb upstairs?" Mr. Van Ayers pointed in the direction of the stairs.

"No, Van, we won't go." Lillian stepped away from her husband.

"Don't try to keep your wife from the truth, Randy." Stephanie looked between them.

"I know the truth." Willow's instinct told her to try to stop the scene before her.

"You knew he had to get married? That his father added that to his strange little contract?" The woman put her hands on her hips. "Did you also know Randy here resisted? I was the fall back plan until I was paid to go away. Did you also know that every Van Ayers for the last four generations did the same thing, and no man wanted to get married?"

"What?" Lillian screamed. "What's she saying? Is this true?"

"Lillian, I said go upstairs," Mr. Van Ayers barked.

"Did you know that Randolph had the contract revised so the marriage only had to last a year?" Not able to stand Stephanie's vile words any further, Willow spoke up. "I can only assume he added that because of someone like you."

In the background Lillian cried, truly cried, real tears that smudged her makeup and she didn't even try to fix the mess.

"So what did he promise you to get you so fast?" Stephanie jutted her jaw out.

She rushed to Lillian, took her hand and glanced at Randolph.

"I paid her, and I made her sign a contract." Randolph swiped his hand over the room. "Look around, everything here is a product of some sort of document, made legal by signatures."

Nothing good came of secrets, nothing. Her knees threatened to give out but she managed to remain standing.

"You obviously came here for more money, but you have nothing to offer in the deal. Everything is already on the table." Randolph walked up to her. "You were right about one thing, though, everything in the house of Van Ayers is fake, everything." Without a glance at anyone else, he walked out of the room.

Except for the sound of Lillian sniffing, silence draped the room once more. For several moments she waited for Randolph to call to her or come back for her, waited for him to return and tell everyone that even with the contracts and the craziness he found his wife and his love. It simply happened backward for them. She waited.

Chapter Eighteen

RANDOLPH GLANCED AROUND the library. Here with the dark paneled walls and shelves and shelves of finance books, he was given his task list once he was old enough to understand. It was right here where he found out his SAT results, and he sat in the chair behind the huge desk when he waited to find out if he got into Stanford.

He walked over to one of the walls and ran his finger along the spines of the books. Lest he forget, he sat on the opposite side of the desk when his father dropped the bomb on him about his final task, the marriage requirement.

"I don't think you ever loved me." His mother continued to cry.

"Lillian, how can you say that?" His father's tone was that of a man lying to get a loan.

"I can say it because it's true."

Randolph turned at his mother's voice, what was the inflection he heard? Was it strength? Suddenly the crying stopped, and the fun, flighty woman he always knew sat up in the chair to stare her opponent down.

"You know I love you, we built a life together." His father leaned back in the chair as if he were chastising his mother about some purchase or trip she wanted.

"Your life was pre-planned, and I simply fit into that one slot you could check off." She shook her head. "What was your end goal?"

"What do you mean?" His father jutted out his jaw, clearly annoyed he couldn't make this go away with money or a contract.

His mother looked up to the ceiling and dabbed her finger in the corner of her eye. She cleared her throat and addressed his father. "When you took me on the beach and asked me to marry you, were you envisioning our life together, our son, being with me? Or were you only concerned that you didn't lose this?" She swiped her arm around the room.

Randolph ran his hand through his hair, thankful Willow wasn't the wife doing the asking. Then again she knew the answer. He married her for the money and never even tried to hide it. Willow didn't get a beach or any semblance of a romance. She got an alleyway.

"Lillian." His father toyed with a paperweight in the shape of a diamond. "You don't understand."

"You didn't love me when you asked me to marry you, did you?"

Randolph crossed his arms. For the first time he watched his mother fight for something, and she chose a big thing, her dignity. He stole Willow's the second he made her sign a contract.

His father remained silent.

"Why would you do this to our son?" She shook her head.

"I tried to save him." His father stared down at the desk.

"Save me?" Randolph spoke his first words since his parents joined him in the library.

"I knew Stephanie wasn't right for you, but I knew you would do what you had to in order to succeed." His father wouldn't look him in the eye.

"You sabotaged me." He came forward and put his hands on the desk, closing in on the enemy.

His father shut his eyes. "I didn't want you to get married. You insisted on that year cap and I knew it wouldn't work as it should."

"You set me up to fail."

"The failure would have made you stronger."

The man in front of him spent years pounding into him how he couldn't fail. Failure was for losers. While his friends in high school played video games, he studied. While others partied in college, he made sure his résumé was as perfect as he could get it for schools and awards. While his colleagues started their lives with choices, he had to bribe a woman to be with him. Instead of displaying his art, he hid it.

He pounded his fist on the desk. "How strong did you want

me to be?"

His father lifted his head and stared at him. "I never knew how strong you were until you came home with Willow. I knew then without a shadow of a doubt what you were made of. Even though no contracts or payments were specifically outlined, in light of the monkey wrench I threw in your plans, you were as magnificent as I always knew you were. I've never been prouder. You earned everything and more."

"Now you're proud!" He ground his teeth together and took a breath. "You allowed me to get an innocent, incredible woman involved in this insanity."

"Oh my God." His mother whispered. "Willow."

"You said yourself she knew about the deal." His father sat back and tented his fingers.

The pressure stacked up on his chest, the weight of every contract he ever signed or penned weighed down on him. He did to her what had been done to him all his life. What he hated, he created.

Randolph stood up straight and took in the scene before him, his mother, his father. After over thirty years of marriage, his mother sat on the opposite side of a desk questioning his father's love. Thirty years from now would Willow be asking the same thing? "It shouldn't be like this."

"What?" His mother reached out to him.

"What is your trouble?" His father rocked his chair back. "She loves you now. It's written all over her face. "You love her. I heard you say the words only the other night." "The Van Ayers men are too busy for such things as dating, so that's why your great, great grandfather started this little tradition for fear his son wouldn't carry on the Van Ayers name."

"What is your definition of love?" He stared his father down. Something major was wrong.

"The same as everyone else's."

His mother made a small noise at his father's answer.

"You don't know. I don't know. I look around and all I see are two men who craved power and a lifestyle above anything or anyone." Randolph hung his head and laughed. "Damn it, even after it's all said and done, I was still relieved when you said I earned everything. It shouldn't matter if I have the woman I love, right?" Willow could be happy with where the wind took her, while he would forever be tethered here, fighting for the one thing that made him miserable, but he couldn't give up.

"Van, you wouldn't give it up for me." His mother announced.

"Lillian." His father's voice came out strained.

Willow would give it up. At least he thought she would. Even at dinner she mentioned the money wasn't important. What would she fight for? She seemed to bend and flex with what happened around her.

"You think I'm stupid, you always thought that. Don't think I don't know." As she stood she pointed at him. "Obviously, I am stupid, I never caught on after all these years."

"You are not stupid." His father decreed as if his words could change his mother's opinion.

"I am. I'm stupid and weak. I let you do this to our son." She crumpled the tissue in her fist. "I let you play your little game with the goals, let you ruin his life and my life. I let this happen."

"Look at him now." His father pointed at him.

"You look at him."

In a move he never thought he would see, his mother threw the tissue on the floor.

"Look at him. He's miserable."

"He has it all." His father held his arms out.

"That's how stupid you think I am. You think you can say the words and I'll believe, and I always did." Her tears started anew. "Just like you made me love you."

Neither he nor his father said a word.

"You made me love you." His mother repeated. "Not because you loved me, but because I was a means to an end."

Randolph's stomach bottomed out. His mother's words said it all. Willow went with the flow, and he made her love him.

"Lillian, you know I love you." His father held his hand out to her.

"I don't know anything." She backed up toward the door. "Everything I thought I knew disappeared tonight and I won't be as stupid to think that I can go to sleep and it will be fixed in the morning. It would have been better if you wrote everything down like our son."

"I started my marriage with the end in sight." Randolph

stared across the room at yet more books. One stood out. A splash of color among the burgundy and hunter green volumes.

"She loves you and at least she knew," his mother said.

"Then where is she?" He walked across the library to the light blue book. "Any other woman would be down here fighting, and she went upstairs."

"What are you saying?" His mother rushed over to him.

He took the book about the healing properties of herbs off the shelf. A bit of his wife had begun to permeate through the house, and yet it didn't fit here. She didn't fight for them because she didn't believe, and she would go with her instinct and follow the universe. In the end, she was the smartest of them all. He loved her and he wouldn't allow himself and his family to destroy her.

The walls of the room seemed to close in on him, the air thickened, and he reached for his cufflink and stopped.

He stared down at the gift his wife gave him only hours before. With a low laugh he shook his head. He couldn't put Willow through a lifetime of waiting for him to let go. She needed to be loved by someone who understood love on every level. After all, he wouldn't go, couldn't go.

"Randolph." His mother took his arm.

"I need to think." He needed to do what his father couldn't, he needed to do the right thing and in the process save his family and Willow. One day she might understand he loved her.

He turned and walked away, glancing at the clock, ten minutes after midnight. Their contract was breached, he knew, he was the expert.

Chapter Nineteen

WILLOW WILLED HERSELF to keep her eyes shut. She slowed her breathing and concentrated on the energy in the room. Without even looking, she knew she lay in bed alone except for one small dog, she knew Randolph never joined her, she knew everything changed.

He broke their contract by never coming to bed. Of all the items in the written document, the rule about being together by midnight was one she always wanted to keep. She thought it would bind them closer or be a sweet tradition, but his absence told her what she didn't need to open her eyes to see.

A shiver ran through her and her stomach dropped into what seemed a bottomless pit. Why was it that one could sense doom? What was it about the human psyche that allowed someone to know their life changed without a word being uttered?

Who was she kidding? When Randolph didn't turn back to her, or even put his arm around her and tell Stephanie nothing mattered because his life worked out even better than his contracts and goals predicted, she knew nothing would ever be the same. Rather than run after him, she escaped to their suite. Never would she force Randolph to do anything. He had enough of that to last a lifetime. If he wanted her, he would have turned back or come after her.

Tears heated her eyes yet she still remained still, taking a moment to visualize her life as Mrs. Randolph Emerson Van Ayers III.

A slight jingle by her feet was followed by a sniffing sound by her face and finally the licks of a much too pampered pet. Normally, Jeb went to Randolph first, then her and then bounced between them, but today he had only her. She managed to wrangle him and give him a kiss.

Nan would tell her to open her eyes, see the reality and change it, most likely things were never as bad as they seemed. She tried to believe her words at the hospital when her mother died, and even listened all those times they had to move on from wherever they ended up, no matter what she couldn't change the reality that lay hidden behind her eyelids.

With no other option, she shrugged and greeted her morning, blinking twice to allow her eyes to adjust.

Their suite appeared exactly the same as always. Many mornings she woke up to find Randolph already went to work, but the sense he had been there always lingered in the room. The vibe was gone, and with her heart pummeling the wall of her chest as if it needed to dig itself an escape hatch, she turned to Randolph's pillow.

Her throat dried out the second she took in the scene before her, but even with her hand shaking she found the strength to pick up the large, thick cream-colored envelope with her name written on it in his perfect handwriting.

She glanced at the door. All she wanted was to go get Nan, hand her the envelope, let her analyze the contents, and make it better.

For the first time Nan wasn't here.

She was alone.

Jeb bounced over and she put him in her lap and grabbed the envelope, ripping it open. A set of keys, a smaller envelope and a thick paper clipped document fell on the bed.

She ignored the keys and the other envelope and picked up the papers, on top, a handwritten letter.

> *Willow,*
>
> *I one time told you I hated contracts, yet every aspect of my life seems to fall back on one. When I told you I loved you, I thought I meant it, but now after watching my parents and you last night, I am not sure I will ever understand the emotion the way you deserve.*
>
> *However, there is one thing you deserve more than anyone that I am more than capable of giving.*

Enclosed is a check that will never truly equal the amount I owe you, but will provide you with the lifestyle that you want. I want you to build your dreams, buy yourself something decadent and maybe one day when you are laying back on a mattress that is truly yours, you can look back at this time and not hate me.

Also, the Marina Del Rey apartment is officially yours. You are the only one who will ever appreciate it, look out at the ocean and see something wonderful rather than simply the best apartment money can buy.

Lastly, attached to this letter are the papers to dissolve our marriage, you only need sign in the spaces indicated.

In the end I carried on my family's tradition and manipulated the situation to get what I wanted. I forced you into loving me, and now I need to set you free. I wish I could face you, but I can't even face myself.

The name will always be yours.

Always –

Randolph

Her tears dropped on the paper but never smeared the ink or his signature. Of course in Randolph's world his signature was sacred, could never be washed away. Something she should have realized the second she signed the first contract.

She sat staring at the page without moving long enough for her body to go numb, for the tears to stop, for the reality to hit her.

Randolph didn't want her.

She forced herself up and out of the bed. Her foot shot pins and needles through her leg, and the nausea she fought the night before surged in full force. Still, she trudged forward.

Without thinking about her actions, she found the bag she packed the day she moved in and packed only her old clothes. As fast as she could, she dressed and gathered her scant few toiletries, shoving them into her bag along with his note, the key, the check and the divorce papers. She chose to take only the purse he gave her for Christmas and her necklace as her only souvenirs of her time here.

"Come on, Jeb." She patted her leg, picked up her pet, and walked out of Randolph's suite.

Sickening silence met her in the hallway, the same as the night before. She made her way down the stairs, stopped in the foyer and took in the space.

"My grandmother always said the front room of a grand home should take your breath away." Mr. Van Ayers joined her.

"Then she must have approved." She tilted her head up at the sparkling chandelier and put her hand to her forehead when the room spun a bit.

"I don't know. She always found fault with something it seemed." He came to her side and looked up with her.

"Maybe everything doesn't have to be perfect, but it can still take your breath away." She cursed the tear that escaped the corner of her eye.

"I think you should stay."

"Well, I never knew my grandmother, but Nan always told me that we would never stay anywhere we weren't wanted." She sighed. "I suppose that's why we moved around so much." Although she thought she had found a home here, she didn't even get to stay the year.

"Willow."

"No." She wouldn't allow him to sway her, she wasn't Stephanie, she wasn't the girl in the alleyway. In fact, she didn't know who she was, but she was going to find out. "No."

They both continued to stare at the crystals.

She lifted her hand to wipe her eye and her ring glittered off the sunlight streaming into the room.

"Is there anything you need?"

"Just one thing." She slid the ring off her finger and held it out to Randolph's father.

"I believe Randolph would want you to have that."

"It's not my history anymore. It belongs with your family." Her voice broke. It seemed forever ago when she thought his family was hers, but it was only a few hours. She pressed the ring to her chest and then placed it in his palm. "It still has good energy."

"Let me get Dimitri, he'll take you wherever you need to go."

"I have my two feet and ten toes." She bent down, picked up Jeb and opened the door to the outside world. For the first time in her life she only had herself. Once more she glanced back. She exited in stark contrast to her eventful entrance with the house full of life and drama. Back then she told herself not to get too involved with Randolph because he could easily break her heart. Mission accomplished.

She shut the door.

* * * *

For the first time since he could remember, Randolph spent a weekend day alone. Since finishing school and taking his job, he either spent his weekends working, entertaining or out with friends.

Of course since he got married, he spent his weekends with his wife. If his world didn't implode yesterday, today he would have taken her out. Willow was happy with simple joys, a drive, a small treat at a bakery, or taking a walk. After leaving the house before Willow woke up, he spent the day chasing his proverbial tail, doing nothing and committing the ultimate sin of wasting time.

He never slept. Instead, he sat in one of the guest suites and figured out a way to try to put Willow's life back together again. The day he saw her in the alley he should have let her be, a wildflower that would only wilt if plucked and brought inside. He met her when he thought he was going to lose everything and as he got out of his car and approached the door of the house, he wondered exactly how much he did indeed lose.

Dimitri opened the door and he stepped inside, the world seemed to have paled, lost all its color, and the room stood dull and lifeless. Willow would say the energy was off, and he would agree.

He took a breath and the knot in his stomach tightened, then he trudged up the stairs and stopped outside their suite.

Did she do as he asked or did she fight and defy him? What would he do if he opened the door and she was there? He pressed his forehead to the door. The decision had been made and without pausing further, he turned the knob.

No one.

He told her to leave, gave her money, a boat and divorce papers.

Still, he entered the room and rushed for the bathroom.

A quick inventory of a couple of drawers told him her items were gone. He ground his teeth together and stomped into the closet to her clothes. Some still hung on the rod and he quickly rifled through them. Only the dresses his grandmother gave her remained, everything she originally brought with her had disappeared.

"Damn it!" He ran back to the main room and turned around. His suite was their suite and now it was nothing but a sterile hotel room with no life, no soul, no fur ball biting at the cuff of his pants, no smell of lavender and roses in the air. No wife.

"Randolph!" His mother scurried into the room. "What's wrong?"

"Maybe you should ask what's right. It'd be a shorter answer."

"You said you had to end it, she did as you asked." She put her hands on his shoulder. "We should go get her."

"She went with the flow, didn't fight for us. I guess I knew that's what she'd do, but I didn't want to believe it. Maybe that's why I loved her, because she didn't fight." He put his hand over his eyes.

"Oh my god, what are we going to do?" She wrapped her arms around him.

Truth be told, he didn't remember the last time his mother truly hugged him. It may have been when he still had to look up to see her, but he gave in and bent down. "I don't know." How did he not have the answer?

He pulled back and studied his mother. The woman was still stunning, no wonder his father wanted her. "I don't know."

"You know what I did today?" She picked a piece of lint off his shirt.

Images of luncheons and shopping entered his mind. "What?"

"I went to the dog rescue and tried to find a pet." Her eyes glossed over with tears. "Willow and I had discussed getting Jeb a brother or sister, and she told me that a pet will choose you."

That sounded like something she would say. "What happened?"

"None of them picked me." She exhaled and wiped a tear off her cheek. "You know, whatever dog would have picked me would have had the best of everything, and none of them wanted me. They are smarter than humans."

"Maybe they knew something would always be missing." A quick glance around the room told him the same thing. Never again would he be able to lie in his bed and not think of her. He could never move her dresses out of his closet. Somewhere along the way while trying to do the right thing, he relegated himself to limbo and he deserved it. "I have to leave." He returned to the closet and found a suitcase.

"Where are you going to go?" His mother joined him.

"It doesn't matter, I just can't stay here." He grabbed some suits. "It's just not worth it." Where did that statement come from? All his life it had been worth it.

Both he and his mother stared at each other.

"I'm going with you." She bent down and opened the suitcase. "At least it didn't take you over thirty years to figure it out."

He grabbed the boots he got in college. "I was still too late."

Chapter Twenty

"STARE AT THE FLAME and write down any images you see." Willow placed the candle on the floor and sat down with Jade, Argyle and Nan.

"What's this called again?" Dressed for their casual time in a simple t-shirt and jeans, Jade leaned forward.

"Fire Scribing." Argyle held his hands up as if framing the scene before him. "I like it."

"Fire scrying." Willow corrected. Rather than staring in the fire, she glanced at her friends and her only family. Jade finally found her after she hid for four days. Her friend caught her sneaking out of the shop and demanded explanation. Though she tried to avoid the conversation, she suddenly found herself crying in Jade's arms, revealing a story she never wanted told. At least she faced her fears and came out clean. True to Jade's character, the woman didn't judge her.

"Scrying means seeing. It's a different way of looking into the future or answering questions," Nan explained and peeked over at her. "Maybe give you some insight."

It took her an extra day to tell Nan all the details, and for the first time in her life the woman was without any words of wisdom. Yes, Nan and Vincent both offered to have her come live with them. Vincent even took her aside separately to ask, but she declined. For the first time ever she was alone, toggling between sleeping at the shop and at the apartment, and she wasn't dying.

After isolating herself for a little longer, she braved the world and at last closed the shop and had Jade over for a little spiritual fun, something she had promised to do before Randolph left her, or she left him.

"This is exceptionally good for my muse." Argyle narrowed his eyes and stared into the flame. "I believe I see a camera, a television camera. Maybe another show is in my future, just the other day I called some people."

Willow wished she only cared about her career or being noticed. "Do you see anything else?" The man never spoke of anything but art and moving ahead. Did he want a partner?

"I have no time for anything but the pursuit of my craft." He gave her a quick wink and nudged Jade. "What does my student see?"

"I can see this becoming an art piece for me. I can be an ever changing flame. I think I see a top hat." Jade tilted her head. "Slate loves his top hat."

"When you're in love you see that person everywhere." At the words leaving her mouth, her chest constricted, but she forced a smile on her face and gazed into the flame. She only saw fire.

"Did I tell you that Willow drove Slate to the art supply store yesterday?" Jade motioned to Nan.

Willow's cheeks heated. Two days ago she asked Jade for help in becoming an adult. Slate stepped in and took over her twice-daily driving lessons. Since he got her fresh, he also decided she would be the one woman who would drive a stick shift and parallel park. No matter, she loved driving even if it was only through the residential streets of Los Angeles.

"What kind of car are you going to get?" Jade asked.

While her two feet and ten toes got her around for years, she needed the freedom only four wheels would provide, something she realized the first night on her own when she wanted to go out for some bicarbonate for her stomach. She shrugged. "I just want something simple."

"Don't get something the world has, or something only for the name, get a vehicle that says 'I am Willow.'" Argyle nodded. "Don't get anything typical."

"Maybe you should splurge." Jade's eyes widened.

Yes, she could choose any car, any home, anything. For the first time in her life she had the money for every material thing she could imagine. She started out wanting the money for Nan, but once Nan married Vincent, her net worth would rival the Van Ayers'. "I think I'll choose something I don't destroy." Two feet and ten toes weren't going to work for a girl out on her own.

"I think that's probably better." Jade sighed. "We should still make some plans about what to do with your financial situation."

"Next week." She didn't want to look at the check again, let alone cash it.

"No problem. When you're ready." Jade grabbed her hand. "Of course we could also have Slate beat the crap out of Randolph and then hide the body in some clay."

"Do I get to throw the monstrosity in the kiln?" Argyle cleared his throat. "Unbelievable."

"Now, now." Nan held her hands out.

Jade straightened up as if caught chewing gum in class.

Willow held her breath waiting for Nan's words about negative energy.

Nan took her time looking at all of them. "Tell Slate he has to get in line behind Vincent. He wanted to hire someone to do it."

At the unexpected remark, they all went into a round of laughter. The giggles took over her body, cleansing her, each jolt shaking off a bit of the dark cloud that seemed to hover around her.

"Actually, now that I look at the flame, I see an anvil I would like to drop on Randolph's head." Jade pointed.

They continued to chuckle.

"Has he been by the gallery?" The question simply happened, and she gasped when she realized she said the words aloud.

The laughter stopped.

"It's okay. Actually, he knew you first. I was just curious." She turned her attention back to the candle and saw nothing. A big void surrounded her.

"The order we met you doesn't matter. We're your friends no matter what." Jade squeezed her hand. "We haven't seen him. Slate and Argyle, are going to his office for a meeting about the co-op."

Argyle looked down at his lap, for the first time since she'd known him, the man had no words.

"It's okay." More than once, actually more than a 100 times or a 1000 times, she wondered if Randolph went to the gallery and if he looked her way. "You know, I think the flame needs some time. I'm going to get the snacks and tea I made." She let go of her friend's hand, and walked to the back.

Before retrieving the tray, she stood on her tiptoes and peeked out the window toward the Gallery where Randolph always parked his car.

"Chiquita, I'm worried about you." Nan joined her.

She turned away. "Don't be, thanks to him I can serve food here, and I'm insured."

"When you don't finish something, the energy stays out there, and then it can inhibit your other goals."

"What are you saying?" She leaned on the small counter.

"Maybe you need to talk to him, at least face him." Nan came up next to her.

"He couldn't face me. I can't face him." She inhaled. Rather than staying to make him say the words directly to her, she walked out on him, on them. Maybe that's what her psyche wanted. "Deep down I knew it wouldn't last."

"Your fear is keeping you from closure. You have left the door open a crack, a small amount so only a thin strip of light shines through, and you don't want him to slam the door in your face." Nan rubbed her back. "I see you look for him."

"We should go back out there. I don't want to be a horrible hostess." One thing she learned was how to plan a get together. A new found skill.

"Do you want me to stay here with you?" Nan took the tray of vegetables, fruit and finger sandwiches.

"No, I want you to be with Vincent. This is my time to be alone, and I think I need it." She faced the woman who sacrificed everything for her. "I made a special tea for today." I'm calling it feminini-tea. I'm celebrating being a woman out on her own."

"Chiquita..."

"I'll be right there." She tried to give Nan the hint to give her a moment.

Perceptive as always, Nan left.

She tended to the tea, but before returning to her guests, she stretched over the counter to gaze out the window once more. Her heart seized at the sight of an all too familiar luxury sedan in its rightful spot. For several seconds she stared outside, then backed away. No way would she hold out hope for the door to be opened, no way would she face him only to have the door slammed.

With her heartbeat still speeding, she lifted the pitcher of iced tea. Maybe she should have named it emp-tea instead.

Chapter Twenty-one

"EVEN THOUGH I'VE BEEN here before, I still find it hard to believe you are heir to all this." Slate spread his arms out and turned around the conference room of Van Ayers First Capital Trust.

Randolph put his hand over his eyes. Part of him prayed the meeting about the co-op sped by, while the other part hoped it never ended. He didn't know if he wanted to wallow in work or spend his time sitting and staring at nothing in the hotel suite he rented with his mother. Either way, the gnawing hole in his chest wouldn't ache any less. Willow walked out. She really walked out. No tears, no fanfare, no fighting for the man she said she loved. Nothing.

"So you will run this one day?" Slate asked.

However, he did tell her to leave. He basically kicked her out of the only home she ever knew. "This is a disaster."

"No, it looks like an interior designer did it, you're good." Slate hit him on the arm. "You need more art."

He groaned. Everything about his life was designed, down to the paper that lined his bathroom drawers. Then Willow entered his life and added her flair to things, something unexpected, her hairbrush in his drawer, her hand cream on his desk in his home office, her book in the library. She left many things, including her book. He had it in his suitcase.

"Randy!" Slate snapped his fingers.

"Please don't call me Randy." No one called him Randy except Stephanie, and if there were any lawsuits he could file against the woman, he would drag her to court. Not that it mattered. Stephanie merely facilitated the inevitable. A couple in love should be able to survive the revelations, but he was the first one to throw in the white flag, and Willow never argued. He slid his hand down his face and opened his eyes. "Why don't you sit down?

"This place always reminds me of being sent to the principal's office. It's creepy." Slate took his seat. "Men in suits always think they can take command of everyone's future."

He had been waiting for Slate to address the elephant in the room, and that was what he was, a creepy elephant without a mate. They said elephants could die of a broken heart and he understood. The pain was overwhelming. "Remember, I'm the one who is going to make your vision happen." He needed to save face somewhere.

"Yeah, well you are the king of contracts." Slate strummed his fingers on the table. "So get your act together."

"I'm sure my crown doesn't fit anymore." He didn't want a crown, he wanted her. In the end she would be better without him.

"Jade wanted me to tell you that she saw your car in the alley and then saw you drive away. She said if you wanted to be part of her next exhibit as the wilting wimpy banker, she has a spot for you."

Unsure if wimp was an upgrade from creepy elephant, he nodded at the truth. Yes, he was a wimp. The kind of guy who drove down the alley behind the gallery, not to get art, but to get a glimpse of Willow. He also drove by the marina and anywhere else that he thought she might be at or reminded him of her. Maybe he needed to add stalker to his list of attributes. Creepy, wimpy elephant stalker, though an elephant would make a terrible stalker.

"Is she all right?" he asked, not sure if he wanted the answer.

"She's better than you." Slate leaned back. "Never seen you look worse."

Willow went with the flow, their situation merely a ripple in her pond where everything was Zen-like. He had no doubt Slate's words were the gospel. Sleep was but a faint memory to be replaced by sort of passing out in front of a desk at the hotel suite with his mother trying to tuck him in. Creepy, wimpy, elephant stalker with insomnia only his missing mate would cure. He couldn't even create any art, the one thing he used to turn to when times got rough. His muse left with her. "Thank you."

"Anytime."

Too exhausted for comebacks, he welcomed the light knock at the door. "Well, let's see if we can hammer this out today." He needed to put on his game face. "Come in."

The door opened and Argyle entered wearing a set of black wings made from currencies of the world and holding a globe.

Randolph wished he had as much guts to display his artwork. Yes, wimp fit him to a tee. "Nice entrance."

After the requisite hand shaking between everyone, he guided the man to the table.

"I made these wings to illustrate that while money may not make the world go around, it certainly allows you to soar when you need it most." Argyle turned the chair and sat to not destroy his wings then put his globe aside.

"Well, yes money helps, especially in an endeavor such as this, but we need to clarify some points." Randolph passed out the preliminary documents.

Before they even read a paragraph, the door opened and his mother entered. "Randolph, I heard your friends were here and I wanted to come in and say hello."

Slate and Argyle both turned.

"Mother, that is very kind, but what're you doing here?" He grabbed the edge of the table.

"I thought you may want refreshments for your meeting and our hotel makes the most magnificent cookies, so I bought some for you." She waved and came forward with a pink pastry box.

At the moment he would rather have Willow's quinoa concoction. In fact, he was sure his health had deteriorated since he wasn't eating her food. "Again thank you."

"You do your thing." At the foot of the table, she fiddled with the string on the box. "I've always wanted to see Randolph work. You don't mind, do you?"

"I would say it would be both an honor and a privilege to have you observe what could be one of the greatest artistic endeavors of this decade." Argyle motioned toward the chair.

Randolph gave it to his mother for not exactly asking him to get her invitation to the meeting. She would have made a brilliant negotiator.

"Why don't we get started?" Randolph watched his mother and the battle of the string on the box.

She continued her battle, but smiled in his direction. "Ignore me."

"That's nearly impossible." Argyle stood, and with a lot of flourish held up what appeared to be a bejeweled fingernail and cut the string.

"Oh." His mother giggled. "Thank you..." She let her voice draw out, waiting for an introduction.

"Argyle Brink." He nodded and sat back down. "At your service, if you need anyone or if you need to fly."

"Thank you again kind sir, I'm Lilly." She reached into the box and offered him an oversized monstrosity of a cookie.

"I think I would rather have a flower, but this will have to do." Argyle put the cookie to the side.

"Are you sure you don't mind if I stay?" She walked around the table doling out her cookies but kept her eyes on Argyle.

"I would only mind if you left." Argyle pulled out her chair, got her comfortable and returned to his seat. "Well, let's do this."

"Please." The only positive point of having his mother here was she provided an amazing distraction to Argyle and he could catch the artist off guard. There he was again, no wonder Willow walked away without looking back, he would use his own mother to win. "Why don't we get to the subject of collateral?"

Argyle took a breath. "I am bringing my name to this endeavor. My collateral is my art, my trade, my knowledge. We will make this into an artistic co-op where the creative types can commune together as a collective mind."

Slate nodded. "You know Argyle gets a lot of media attention, so artists will flock to us."

"I am talking about true collateral." Randolph leaned back in his chair.

"I just gave you several examples." Argyle spread his arms, or in his case, his wings.

"Here's what the deal looks like using some property for collateral." Randolph shook his head and distributed more papers.

Both men glanced at the paper and back to him, not even taking the time to read the words. A flash of the night in Vegas when Willow signed her contract went through his mind. He knew then she didn't read it and yet he moved forward anyway. What kind of husband would allow his wife to do that?

"I am looking into having some of my contacts do some filming at the co-op for television." Argyle leaned forward.

"Oh, that sounds exciting," his mother whispered.

"Everyone in Los Angeles has media contacts, and while valuable, they cannot be used as collateral," Randolph countered. As usual, the groove found him, but without Willow it meant nothing.

Argyle pursed his lips, turned to Randolph, his mother and back to Slate. "If we had collateral we wouldn't need a loan."

"I have made a list of acceptable collateral. Slate said you'll be using the upstairs of his building for the headquarters, but you're asking for a loan for other expenses." He picked up his pen and twirled it between his fingers.

"As I explained, I bring myself to the deal. My connections and my art is my collateral." With his feathers apparently ruffled, Argyle shifted in his seat.

"Aside from these nebulous television people, who do you know?" He decided to play the game.

Argyle pushed the paper aside. "Do you understand what an opportunity this is for Slate and his gallery?"

"Just give me one name." He continued his challenge.

Argyle cleared his throat. "What if I told you I know the Mural Man?"

His heart sped at the mention of, well, himself. "Excuse me?"

"You know the man who does the random murals around Los Angeles. Another was just discovered in Long Beach." The man lifted his chin.

"He did a piece outside my daughter-in-law's store." His mother looked down.

Randolph ground his teeth together and inhaled before asking the next question. "What's his name?"

"Is that considered enough collateral?" Argyle asked.

He fought to keep his breath even. "What's his name?"

"Listen here, Mr. *Van Ayers*," Argyle said his last name as if he were trying to spit it out. "I see whose name is on the wall. You have no idea what these artists go through. We need support.

You're nothing but a poser with your silver spoon and fancy works on your walls. I'm sure the most creative thing you've ever done is sign a check."

A poser, another word to add to his ever-growing description. Maybe he had been these things all along. Willow wanted him to create. For her he would claim his art. He stood and walked over to one of the traditional paintings on the wall, taking it off the hook. Without second-guessing his next action, he turned the painting around, revealing paintings and sketches he created in his signature style and hid behind the more acceptable pieces. He propped it up against the wall and went to the next one and did the same as he made his way around the room. "While it's true I may have a silver spoon, I can assure you that I'm not a poser. The reason you don't know the name of the Mural Man is because you don't know him. I am that man."

"Randolph!" His mother shot up out of the chair.

"I can't believe it!" Slate stood.

He and Argyle stared each other down.

"Oh my God!" His mother put her hand to her forehead and swayed on her feet. "Oh God."

In a flash everyone, including himself, charged for his mother, but Argyle caught her.

Her eyelids fluttered, but then she pressed her hand to her chest and looked at all of them. "I daresay that most women would love to be in my position."

"Are you all right, Mother?" He held out his hand.

"Your art." She looked around the room. ""It's beautiful."

Everyone remained perfectly silent as she continued to gaze around the space.

"I'm so glad you didn't give it up." She pulled him down and gave him a kiss on the cheek. "I'm sorry if your father and I forced you to hide it."

With his mouth open, but no words, Randolph shook his head. She was glad he didn't give it up?

"You are quite the woman, Lilly." Argyle pulled her closer.

In order to stop himself from yanking the man off his mother he crossed his arms.

The door slammed open.

"Lillian!" His father burst into the room flailing an envelope in his hand. "I heard you were here."

In his entire life he'd never seen his father in such a state of disarray. His suit was wrinkled, his hair a mess, he even had razor stubble and Randolph swore he had on two different shoes.

"Van?" His mother lifted her head.

Junior went to her and Argyle. "Get your hands off my wife."

In an amazing act of defiance, she wrapped her arms around Argyle's neck. "No. You're nothing but a hater of the arts. I have found a unique man who doesn't want me to gain a fortune. He thinks I'm beautiful."

"You are very beautiful," Argyle mumbled.

"Thank you." She patted his shoulder.

Then in a more incredible move, his father got down on his knees in front of her. "Lillian, I think you're beautiful. I've always thought you were the most magnificent woman I ever laid eyes on." He took her hand and pressed it to his heart. "For these past days I've tried to figure out what to buy you for you to take me back and prove my love for you. But then I realized nothing I purchased would do the trick, but instead I had to give something up and in the process do right by my son."

"What do you mean?" Tears glossed her eyes.

His father held the envelope out to him, but spoke to his mother. "I love you, and I love our son." He looked up to Randolph. "I've made many mistakes, but as of this moment I'm turning the bank over to him. He'll be one of the youngest men in the country with his position."

Randolph scanned the papers. His original contract had Junior heading the firm until he retired, but with the new one, the bank would be his once he placed his signature on the dotted line.

"Hopefully, one day he'll learn to forgive me and realize I thought I was doing the right thing." His father took a breath. "I was wrong and I ruined everything. These weeks without you and your mother were the worst of my life. If that doesn't define love, I don't know what does."

"Van, do you mean that?" Tears streamed out of his mother's eyes.

"I love you, Lillian. I don't remember ever not loving you."

"I believe this belongs to you." Argyle relinquished his hold on his mother

"Oh, Van." She flung her arms around his father's neck. "I love you too."

With his mother in his arms, his father stood and held his hand out to him. "Hopefully, I still have a job working for you."

He never remembered his father saying he loved him or his mother, or the man ever admitting he was wrong. As if in a trance, Randolph shook his father's hand. "Of course."

"Let's go home, Van. You look just awful." His mother attempted to straighten his father's jacket. "Did you see the art our son made? He's the one doing the murals that appear all over."

He stiffened, waiting for the backlash, talk of risks and wasting time.

"We'll discuss everything back at the house, Randolph." His father's voice possessed power once more. "Including where to hang your work. For the record, I don't hate art."

"Mr. Angel Man, don't worry about the art thing. My woman's club would be more than happy to finance it, and we don't need collateral, we just want first dibs on the art. We love to be on trend." She held her hand out.

Argyle took her hand, bent down and kissed the back. "You will have first choice."

"Goodbye now." She giggled. "See Van? I do know about good investments."

"Yes, dear." Junior kissed her once more.

Everyone watched his parents leave.

"What happened to no grants?" Randolph glanced around the shambles of the room.

"Your mother is not the government." Argyle turned away.

"When do we get to do a showing?" Slate lifted one of Randolph's pictures.

"Please forgive me. I think at the end of the day I need to remember to be true to the art and live my vision. We all want to make a name, be someone." Argyle walked the perimeter of the room. "These are really incredible, I never would've guessed."

Maybe in a way he envied Argyle and his freedom of expression. Yes, everyone wanted to be someone, have a name. He gave Willow her name, wanted her to keep it. Randolph let the men examine the art and went to his desk, glancing at his cell phone in hopes of any message, even from Peter. Yes, he stalked Willow and he also had his personal assistant keeping an eye out for her. Though he couldn't think of the exact word to add on to his already illustrious titles he bestowed upon himself, he wished he still possessed the one title he had...husband. He put the new contract aside. Strange how life-changing a piece of paper could be.

Chapter Twenty-two

"I'M DONE ENTERING all the ingredients." Willow turned her new laptop in Peter's direction.

"Great." Peter pushed himself back from the railing around the apartment's balcony and returned to her. "Now, once you enter the quantity you're making, the spreadsheet will calculate your cost per unit. You can take that number and enter it over here, and then this column will calculate your markup and then you will know how much to charge for each SKU."

She processed his words, or tried to. Along with learning to drive, she was determined to get her business under control and not undo anything Randolph created. A few days ago Peter walked into the shop asking for more tea. They chatted a bit, and when she expressed concern about an upcoming order for one of Randolph's mother's friends, he offered to help. She invited him to the apartment for lunch. It was good to have someone around even for a few hours. "What does SKU mean?"

"It means stock keeping unit. It's just a number or code we assign to each product." He leaned in toward the screen. "You did really good."

"How did you learn all this?" She furrowed her brow at the screen.

"Baptism by fire with Randolph." He typed away on the keyboard.

"When you decided you didn't want to be a doctor, what did you want to be?" She leaned back and watched him.

"I never wanted to be a doctor." Peter stopped, looked up at the sky and inhaled. "I think I just wanted to be successful."

"How do you measure that?"

"I thought by money, but now I don't think so." He shook his head. "It's that whole unfulfilled dreams thing. You were right about that."

"The tarot cards?" She got up and poured him a glass of lemonade hoping he would fill in on his own without her prodding though she always loved to hear what people thought about the results of any reading. Since she walked out of Randolph's life, she avoided looking for answers when the answers were right in front of her.

"Yeah, I don't know what my dreams are anymore, but I do feel unfulfilled. I keep searching but I always miss something."

She put the glass next to him and sat back down. "Maybe the dreams are missing." Or maybe dreams were overrated. Maybe they were unattainable, and therefore destined to remain dreams. It seemed every night she dreamed of Randolph in some way. She wanted her slumber time messages to be a sign, and each morning she awakened with the sense something would happen, but nothing ever changed.

He gulped down the drink and nodded. "You were also right about the arguments."

She winced, hoping he didn't take her reading as some self-fulfilling prophesy.

"Elizabeth and I finally decided to end the misery." He turned to her.

"Sometimes when there's so much misery, when it ends it's almost a relief." It would have been much easier if she didn't love Randolph and was relieved when they split. Of course, it would be much easier if she didn't love Randolph now. While she tried to go about her life, even move forward, she seemed stuck. She needed to let go and couldn't and therefore landed in limbo. All her life she had been taught to go with the flow, but she struggled when it came to Randolph. Her husband, or ex-husband, battled the flow every chance he could. He might be at war with himself, but he moved forward.

"I agree. I actually feel a little lighter." He gave her a huge smile and leaned toward her as if to tell her a secret. "Do you want to know what the unexpected change was?"

"Did you memorize every word I said?" She couldn't stop her smiling.

"The whole thing sort of freaked me out. I relived it a few

times." He chuckled.

"Tell me." In Peter's case the change seemed positive.

"I was the one who did the leaving and for the first time I meant it." He shook his head.

"That's so good. I know it's still hard, but when you know it's right it's liberating." She looked down. The problem with her and Randolph was that it didn't seem right that they weren't together. There was no sense of freedom as she imagined when they first got married. Instead, their separation seemed more like a fracture with no brace. They were broken and couldn't heal.

"As you said, I needed to change my path and I did." He stood and stretched. "You even predicted a catastrophe."

She got up as well. "I don't think I'm that good."

They went to the balcony railing and looked out over the boats in the marina. If Randolph were here they could simply look out at forever together.

"I think you were right about it being a sign. I think the catastrophe happened with my family when I quit. Everything else has been the residual from that fall out." Once more he looked out. "I think something is telling me to deal with my family before there's another catastrophe. I didn't fight hard enough for them. I didn't face them. I didn't say all the things I wanted to. I just walked away."

At his words, her chest constricted and the sick nausea that had come and gone for weeks, reappeared. It was almost as if Peter relayed to her the last few weeks of her life. "Peter?" Out of nowhere tears sprang to her eyes, blurring her vision but at the same time clearing things up.

"What's wrong?" He took her by the shoulders. "Are you okay?"

"Randolph." She squeezed her eyes shut, but the tears fell anyway.

He gave her a hug. "Let it out."

"I did all that. I didn't fight, didn't face him, didn't say what I wanted." She cried into his shirt, but managed to look up at him. "In the end, I walked away."

"What are you going to do about that?"

"He told me to leave. Paid me off." She shrugged, wishing she had one tiny hint Randolph wanted her, still cared, something beyond the intuition, something concrete, maybe even signed in ink. "But it always feels like he's around."

"That's because in a way he is." Peter stared into her eyes.

"Not that way." When at last she got everyone to understand her metaphysical world, she needed reality.

"No, seriously. Why do you think I showed up at your shop?" One side of his mouth curled up in a smile.

"I don't understand." She searched his face for answers.

"I wasn't supposed to tell you, but he has been following you or had you followed since the day you left. The other day he called himself some animal wimpy stalker or something like that, and when I asked if he wanted me to stop, he just threw more money at me and told me to continue."

"That's real. It's real." Her stomach lurched. She pushed him away and leaned way over the railing. "I think I'm going to be sick."

"I shouldn't have said anything." He held her hair out of her face and rubbed her back.

The sea air washed over her. She waited until the wave passed and she lifted her head. "No, I needed to hear it. I wanted to hear it." No doubt Peter handed her the proof she wanted, or did he? Was Randolph only checking on her out of some obligation?

"You okay?" He brushed her hair away from her face.

"Actually, for the first time since I left, I think I am." Randolph always fought for them and she just went with everything. If she wanted him, she needed to show him she loved him. "I need to act."

"What are you going to do?"

"I don't know yet. He always used to ask me what I wanted, and it's about time I answered." Her mind went off in a million different directions, but she had what she needed to go after her dream. Maybe they weren't only dreams after all.

"What do you want?" Peter guided her back to the table.

"I don't want to be afraid." She already lost him and survived. "I don't want to always wonder." Going with the flow had its place, but for the first time she realized she might have to walk against the tide to get what she wanted, even if it ended in catastrophe.

Chapter Twenty-three

"DON'T GET MARRIED." Randolph shut his eyes as Slate hung one of his paintings in the gallery.

"Yeah well, after watching you all these months, Jade and I decided to go for it." Slate chuckled. "Take a look."

He opened his eyes and glanced at the artwork of a weeping willow tree.

"We both love women whose names can be depicted by pictures." His father walked over to the picture of the lily, took it off the wall and handed Slate a roll of cash.

"And now you can say you are a professional artist." Slate counted off some bills, and handed Randolph his percentage.

He shook his head. Once his mother declared *avant-garde* art sexy, his father joined him in investing and appreciating. Willow always told him to look for signals and messages from the universe, but unfortunately the universe put him on hold and the flow he was supposed to go with went stagnant. "I'm going to have to do something." He groaned.

"Yes you are," his father and Slate said in unison.

"No, I need to find out why she didn't even fight for us. Was everything just a means to an end?" These questions repeated themselves over and over in his mind. No wonder he couldn't sleep. He handed Slate the money. "I can't part with the willow tree."

"I had a feeling." Slate took it down. "Cool boots by the way."

Yes, he finally wore the boots. He took in the image of the willow tree. He literally made the tree weep, dripping with tears. For the first time, he signed his name to a piece, making it sacred. "I have to do something."

"Yes you do." Slate repeated.

"You don't understand. She never signed the divorce papers. Technically she is still my wife. If she's my wife, I demand to know what is happening!" He slammed his fist into his leg.

"I say you go grab her by the hair and drag her back to that mean old mansion of yours." Slate patted him on the back.

"Or maybe I just need to let her be and stop ruining her life." Randolph raised his arms toward the ceiling. "The universe needs to tell me what to do."

As if on cue, the gallery door opened, and he turned to find Peter walking toward them.

"I normally wouldn't interrupt, but this came for you." Peter held out a manila envelope. "It's from Willow."

The size of the envelope was perfect to hold a signed contract or signed divorce papers. If the way his stomach bottomed out was any indication of how Willow felt when he presented her with a similar envelope, no wonder she simply left. "Well, I asked for a sign." He took the envelope from Peter and glanced around the gallery. At least he had his friends and family here. His actions hadn't allowed for her to have similar comfort.

For a moment he stared at the envelope, relishing in the last few seconds he would be a married man. He created the situation and he would pay for it, maybe her lack of fight said everything at the end.

"Son." His father came over.

"It's fine. It's better this way." Without further hesitation, he tore the envelope open and took out the contents. He squeezed the bridge of his nose at the sight of the divorce papers. "It's over."

"There's more in here." His father took the envelope and turned it over. Some small, ripped up pieces of paper spilled out on the table followed by one intact smaller envelope. "These are pieces of a check."

Her final act to him was not cashing the check, which meant he left her with nothing except an apartment. "Damn it." He snatched up the second envelope, tore it open, and pulled out what appeared to be an invitation.

Mrs. Willow Van Ayers
requests the honor of your presence
to her wedding vow renewal with

Mr. Randolph Emerson Van Ayers III
If accepted, the ceremony will take place as soon as this
invitation is read
at the location you first proposed to me.

His heart sped and he flipped through the divorce papers, the unsigned divorce papers. "Vow renewal?"

"I think that's your sign." Slate laughed.

"I manipulated her." He shook his head.

"Do you love her?" his father asked.

"Yes." Once more he read the invitation.

"Then let's go to your wedding."

Not wanting one more second apart from her, he dropped the card and rushed out the back of gallery, skidding to a stop at the scene in front of him.

Practically everyone he knew, or at least everyone who mattered, had gathered in the alley, including his mother, his grandfather and grandmother, Nan and Vincent, and even Millicent and Jeb, but most importantly Willow. Dressed in a simple white dress with flowers in her hair, she would always be the most gorgeous woman in the world, or the universe.

Somehow in record time, they decorated the alleyway with an aisle and flowers, blowups of his murals, and everything.

Randolph kept his focus on his bride and walked to her, the energy seeming to change with each step he took. Willow would call it a connection, and he would as well. "You used your name on my invitation." He took her hand.

"You said I could have it, but I can only have it with you." She laced her fingers in his.

"Are you sure?" He shook his head. "I made you love me."

"That's what you're supposed to do." She stepped closer. "And I was supposed to fight for us."

"You did. Look at all this," he whispered. Her actions in

planning another wedding told him everything about her and about them.

"I planned everything. We even have cake." She let out a light chuckle. "I wanted to show you how much I love you, and I wanted to start fresh."

Unable to stop himself, he wrapped his arms around her waist. "Will you marry me?"

"First I have a question." A smile took over her face. "If we ever have a baby and if it's a girl can still name her after you? Can she still be the fourth? I don't want to buck tradition and I know it wasn't part of the deal."

"Willow?" He pulled her closer. "Are you trying to tell me something?"

"I don't know. We'll have to find out together." She wrapped her arms around his neck. "I suppose we do get a Part Two."

"We have as many parts as we can fit into our life." When everything started, all he wanted was what he felt was his due, but it all seemed worthless compared to what he had ahead. "Now we're ready."

"Wait, one more thing." She shook her head.

"Why do you always make me wait to get married?" He laughed.

"This will be the last time." She reached out and his grandfather handed her a paper. "You have to sign something."

"No more contracts. We don't need them."

"No, it's time for your reading, you're receptive now." She held the paper and a pen out to him. "You always said your signature was sacred."

Without even looking, he signed the paper.

"Oh, look here, large signature, initials larger than the other letters." She studied the paper. "You have pride and self-confidence, and you're very goal oriented."

"Strange, I think it says, I love you and want to spend the rest of my life with you." He turned them both toward his grandfather. "After all, I signed on the dotted line."

About the Author
Kim Carmichael

Kim Carmichael began writing nine years ago when her love of happy endings inspired her to create her own.

A Southern California native, Kim's contemporary romance combines Hollywood magic with pop culture to create quirky characters set against some of most unique and colorful settings in the world.

With a weakness for designer purses, bad boys and techno geeks, Kim married her own computer whiz after he proved he could keep her all her gadgets running and finally admitted handbags were an investment.

Kim is a PAN member of the Romance Writers of America, as well as some small specialty chapters. A multi-published author, Kim's books can be found on Amazon as well as Barnes & Noble.

When not writing, she can usually be found slathered in sunscreen trolling Los Angeles and helping top doctors build their practices.

To find out more about Kim Carmichael visit:
Website: www.kimcarmichaelnovels.com
Facebook: http://www.facebook.com/kimcarmichaelnovels
Twitter: @kimcarmichael4

www.ingramcontent.com/pod-product-compliance
Lightning Source LLC
Chambersburg PA
CBHW071301170626
46809CB00001B/312